A Stranger's Gift

—— The ——
Women of Pinecraft

ANNA SCHMIDT

PUBLISHING

© 2011 by Anna Schmidt

ISBN 978-1-61626-234-1

All scripture quotations are taken from the King James Version of the Bible.

For more information about Anna Schmidt, please access the author's website at the following Internet address: www.booksbyanna.com

4750 7800 11/11

Cover design: Kirk DouPonce, DogEared Design

Published by Barbour Publishing, Inc., P.O. Box 719, Uhrichsville, OH 44683, www.barbourbooks.com

Our mission is to publish and distribute inspirational products offering exceptional value and biblical encouragement to the masses.

 Member of the
Evangelical Christian
Publishers Association

Printed in the United States of America

Dedication/Acknowledgment

Part One

Hurricane Hester
Headed for Sarasota

Monster hurricane expected to smash Gulf Coast Florida within forty-eight hours.

Hurricane Hester is expected to make landfall by late Friday afternoon. The dangerous storm is predicted to bring potentially devastating storm surges and dangerous high winds well in excess of one hundred miles per hour. Home and business owners are urged to secure all property and prepare to move inland as soon as possible. Once the hurricane makes landfall, the storm is expected to weaken, but there remains the strong potential for heavy flooding and tornadoes. As a precaution, those residents living inland near any body of water including creeks and canals are advised to be prepared to evacuate and stay alert.

Chapter 1

Wisps of Hester Detlef's ebony hair escaped her stiff mesh prayer covering, tickling her face as she unloaded boxes of canned goods from the back of a van. In the Mennonite and Amish community of Pinecraft, within the greater borders of Sarasota, several women had formed a kind of bucket line to pass the boxes to other women waiting at a line of tables set end to end along the protected walkway of the shopping mall. The increasingly strong wind whipped at the ankle-length skirts the women wore, reminding them that in spite of the blue skies, a hurricane lurked just a few miles offshore. Hester had just received news that the entire Gulf Coast, from Fort Myers north to Tampa–St. Petersburg, was under a hurricane watch—meaning that within the next thirty-six hours, it was entirely possible that the storm could move into their area. But with the predicted storm stalled several miles offshore, things could go either way. The hurricane might simply have paused to gather strength before moving east. Or it could weaken to a tropical storm that would bring heavy rains and some wind but nothing like the devastation that a category three or four hurricane might deliver.

"Hester? Shouldn't you let someone else handle this and see to more pressing matters?" Olive Crowder was a large-boned woman of indeterminate age with a permanent expression of disapproval etched into her face. She had never married, and her constant companion was her younger sister, Agnes, a gentle soul who seemed immune to Olive's generally sour demeanor. The sisters were dedicated members of the conservative Mennonite congregation where Hester's father, Arlen, served as senior minister. While women did not usually assume roles of appointed or elected leadership in their church, Olive came as close as any woman ever could to having declared herself an elder of the congregation—the gatekeeper for all things traditional.

Often when Hester was in grade school and other girls were busy learning homemaking skills, she had tested her teachers with her questions about why certain things happened the way they did.

"But why?" she would ask when the answer she got was dismissive or unsatisfactory.

It was that insatiable curiosity coupled with her stubborn determination to explore as much of God's world as possible that made her stand out in a community where sameness was not only preferred but also expected. It was that same insatiable curiosity that had brought her under the microscope of Olive Crowder's concern.

"Getting these food goods sorted and packed is a priority right now, Olive," Hester said, forcing herself to smile.

"Well, you know best, I suppose. After all, you are the lead volunteer for MCC in this area."

The Mennonite Central Committee—or MCC—was a national organization dedicated to offering disaster relief, community development, and international aid with no concern for whether or not those who received that aid were Mennonite. The mission of the organization was to build a worldwide community of people connected by their love and respect for God, each other, and all of God's creation. Following her mother's death, Hester had put her career as a registered nurse on hold indefinitely and volunteered to manage the agency's work in and around Pinecraft.

"After all," Olive continued, "Emma has gone straight to the shelters to oversee the work there."

Emma Keller had once been Hester's closest friend, but the two of them had grown apart after Hester decided to attend nursing school in Illinois. Emma now held the position of local leader of the more conservative Christian Aid Ministries. CAM was the agency that Olive—not to mention several other members of Arlen Detlef's congregation—had suggested might be a more appropriate venue from which a conservative minister's daughter might pursue her desire to serve.

"I understand your concern, Olive, and believe me, I would really love to be able to be in more than one place at the same time. So I am truly grateful that Emma and others have taken on other projects like preparing the shelters." Hester turned back to her work. "With everyone doing their part, we should have things pretty well covered."

Olive stood rooted to her spot in the line of volunteers scowling down at Hester until Hester noticed that others were beginning to wonder what was going on. "Besides, Emma and I will both be attending the volunteer organizational meeting at command central later this morning, so I'll be sure to check in with her then. In the meantime, if you wouldn't mind. . ." She handed a box of canned goods to Olive and nodded toward the woman waiting to receive them and pass them on. Olive's lips thinned into a sharp straight line. "Just because you see this as your little hurricane, Hester, it would behoove—"

"My little hurricane?"

"*Ja.* Hurricane Hester," Olive replied and then turned back to her work.

Certainly Hester could see the irony of a hurricane with her name. Even before she'd learned that this season's eighth hurricane was to bear her name, others had compared her can-do personality to the massive fury of a hurricane. She certainly did not aspire to be linked to something so destructive, but she had to admit that once she latched on to a cause that she believed in, there was no stopping her.

As soon as the van was unloaded and the women began filling smaller cartons with a selection of canned goods, Hester retrieved her bicycle from behind the distribution center. Promising to return as soon as possible, she pedaled off toward downtown Sarasota. At the corner of Highway 41 and Bahia Vista, she waited for the light to change, tapping one foot on the ground as she balanced her bike. Her foot tapping was not an indication of impatience. She was simply filled with energy, ready to face whatever Mother Nature might bring in the hours and days ahead. Hester Detlef was like a warrior prepared to go into combat.

She couldn't help but smile at that thought. Her Mennonite faith had taught her to be peace loving and to avoid conflict, but there was indeed a battle coming in the form of a hurricane that bore her name. The only question was where the storm would focus the brunt of its attack.

Hester had lived her entire life in this area, and she knew that the city of Sarasota with Pinecraft in its midst was an unlikely target. Protected by a line of barrier islands, the mainland rarely suffered a direct hit. Most hurricanes weakened over land so that by the time the storm passed over the islands and reached the mainland, it would likely be demoted to a tropical storm. And because the Amish/Mennonite community lay another five miles inland, it was even less likely that her friends and neighbors would suffer direct damage. But Pinecraft's position on Philippi Creek always carried the threat of flooding. If the hurricane hit shore from a certain direction, it could push waters inland, and she and her neighbors living along the creek would be forced to move to shelters. Whatever the storm's path, it was due to make its move within the next thirty-six hours.

The light changed, and she pedaled on. Down Bahia Vista to Orange Avenue, past the beautiful Selby Botanical Gardens and around the curve where the road ran parallel to the bay. How she loved this part of the city. As a girl, when her friends were busy tending kitchen gardens or joining their mothers for quilting bees, Hester would slip away to wade in the calm clear waters of the bay.

She never tired of observing the wonders of sea life she saw there—jellyfish and sea anemones that looked like transparent floating flowers and the occasional and rare live horse conch, its outer shell black and almost indistinguishable from the beds of oyster shells that at low tide clacked like castanets. Sometimes as she waded through ankle-deep clear water, she would spot a flash of orange as vivid as the skin of a tangerine and would carefully turn the blackened conch shell over to reveal the strikingly colorful animal coiled inside. To this day, seeing a seashell that still housed a crab or sea animal made her smile and, as the old adage stated, was all the assurance she needed that God was in His heaven and all was right with the world. But she had no time for wading this day. She was already late for her meeting.

⇒

John Steiner leaned in closer to the battery-powered radio on the kitchen counter as it crackled and wheezed out the latest weather update. ". . .Hurricane watch. . . Prepare for evacuation of barrier islands and bay-front homes and businesses. . . ."

Reports from early that morning had the hurricane stalled offshore and unlikely to make landfall for another day or so. He had time. Time to board up the last of the windows. Time to double-check his emergency supplies. Time to cage the chickens and get them to safety. He would ride out the storm right here on the property into which he had sunk two years of his life and most of his money renovating.

He ignored the warnings to move to higher ground. He wasn't going anywhere. Since he'd moved to Florida, there had been other orders to evacuate, and they had all come to nothing. On one such occasion shortly after he'd moved in, John had complied only to find himself crowded into some shelter with hundreds of others. For his trouble, he had spent a miserable night among crying babies, unruly children allowed to roam free, and

13

adults who did nothing but complain. He would not leave again.

After nailing a piece of plywood over the last of the windows, he walked down to his pier and closed his eyes as the hot August wind buffeted his shirt and ruffled the red-blond hair on his forearms. It might have been any Florida summer day—hot, gusty winds from the west, humidity so thick it was like being draped in a towel soaked in hot bathwater, and a blinding sun set high in a relentlessly blue sky. It was hard to believe that in just a matter of hours this could all change to blackness and pounding waves and water walls that could topple trees and power lines, rip off roofs, and set mobile homes as well as cars and trucks afloat or flying through the air.

John was surprised that what he was feeling wasn't apprehension but rather anticipation. He was excited. He opened his eyes and saw his neighbor Margery Barker puttering his way in her small fishing boat.

"Came to see if you're ready," she called, throwing him the rope to tie her boat up at his pier.

The woman had a voice like a foghorn and the leathered skin of a native Floridian. She ran a fishing charter business about a quarter mile up Philippi Creek around the point from John's place on Little Sarasota Bay. She'd taken it over from her husband after his death thirteen years earlier, and she'd been the first person John had met when he came to Florida. Without the slightest encouragement from John, she had designated herself his surrogate mother from that day to this. She meant well, but like him, she could be stubborn and refused to back down from her zealous campaign to get him involved in "community," as she liked to call it.

"All secured," John replied, catching his end of the rope and looping it around a post. He jerked his head toward the house, its windows now shuttered with plywood.

Margery had scrambled out of the boat and was standing on the pier surveying his house and the old packinghouse, her hands on her hips. "Looks good," she said. "Where you gonna ride this thing out?"

Her question annoyed John. The two of them had discussed this when the hurricane had first started to form. "Here," he replied with a wave toward the house.

Margery hooted. "Are you nuts or just plain naive?"

Neither, John wanted to snap, but instead he bit his lip and glanced out across the bay to the inland shore of Siesta Key. He had learned quickly enough that it did no good to argue with Margery.

"I guess that it's unlikely you'll take a direct hit," she reasoned, more to herself than to him. "And I suppose if you've never been in one of these things, you can't help but wonder what it'll be like."

"I've been here through two hurricane seasons, Margery. That first year I even left for the shelter. I am not leaving again."

She frowned and then turned back to her boat and knelt down to retrieve two large containers of water. "I figured as much, so I brought you some extra supplies."

"I've got five jugs of drinking water," John protested.

"Well, you might just want to wash up a bit." She sniffed the air around him. "Truth be told, you could do with a shower *now.*"

"I've been working," he protested, resisting the urge to tell her she didn't smell like lavender water herself.

Margery sighed. "You are a serious one, aren't you, Johnny? After this storm blows through, we are going to have to find some way to get you to loosen up, son." She shook her head as if he were a lost cause and climbed back into her boat and unleashed it from the post. "I baked you some of those chocolate chip cookies you seem to like." She tossed him a cookie tin and eased her boat away from his pier. "Stay high and dry," she called as she rounded the point.

John used the stubs of his fingernails to pry open the tin box and took out one cookie. He bit into it, savoring the taste—and with it the childhood memory of his mother's baking. He hadn't thought to ask where Margery planned to stay during the hurricane. The houseboat where she lived would not be much protection against the winds, and her bait shack was no sturdier than a beach shack. She'd probably head for one of the shelters. He suddenly felt guilty that she had wasted precious time coming to check on him. He stepped farther out onto the pier and shouted her name. "Be safe," he yelled.

Margery just waved and kept going.

~~~

Hester arrived fifteen minutes late for the meeting. This was the county's effort to coordinate response activities for all emergency response volunteer leaders from across the entire Sarasota County area. She was there to represent the two largest Mennonite organizations—the Mennonite Central Committee or MCC, for which she was the local representative, and the Mennonite Disaster Service, better known in the community as MDS. Her father was the local director of that agency, and with the hurricane predicted to scythe a wide swath across the Gulf Coast of Florida, both agencies would have their work cut out for them in the days following the storm. Emma would represent CAM, the third arm of a trio of Mennonite agencies.

She parked her bike in a rack and mentally rehearsed the report she was prepared to give. MCC was ready to supply food, water, and shelter for those hundreds of volunteers sure to come once the storm passed over, not to mention those poor souls who might be directly affected by the storm. She had a mobile clinic ready to go into action as a backup to the one the Red Cross was already setting up. There were three large shelters in and around Pinecraft outfitted with cots and generators and other necessities to care for those who had no place to go. Along with MDS teams, her volunteers were fully prepared to go into action helping victims of the storm recover and rebuild in the weeks and months ahead should the storm be as disastrous as was predicted. She stepped into the small foyer of the county's administrative building and took a moment to allow her eyes to adjust to the change from the blistering late-August sun to the cooler shadows inside, then followed the sound of voices down the hall.

But when she opened the door, prepared to make her

apologies as she took her place at the long table at the front of the room, she stopped. Emma Keller stood at the lectern delivering the report for all three Mennonite agencies. Hester squeezed her eyes closed and silently prayed for God to take away the pang of jealousy she felt toward the woman. After all, she and Emma were working toward the same goal. What was the matter with her? Emma was not her competition. There had been a time when they had been the best of friends. But God must have been busy elsewhere, for when she opened her eyes, she still felt a prickle of rivalry as she listened to Emma deliver her report. Hester slipped into a vacant seat at the back of the room and waited her turn to fill in anything Emma might have left out—a scenario so unlikely as to be laughable, knowing how thorough Emma was in tackling any project.

Reports from other local volunteer groups followed, and then the professional hurricane experts and meteorologists got up to give their reports. Hester shook off her jealousy and focused on taking notes to share with her father and other volunteers. Emma slid into the seat next to her.

"*Es tut mir leid,*" she apologized, her voice a whisper. "They called for the report from Pinecraft first thing."

"*Ich verstehe,*" Hester murmured and glanced at Emma, who was looking at her with genuine concern. "Really, it's fine," Hester assured her and grasped Emma's hand.

Emma's smile was radiant with relief. Hester had to ask herself if she had become so territorial when it came to where her volunteer efforts and Emma's overlapped that her good friend felt she had to tiptoe around Hester's feelings.

"*Kaffee?*" Hester whispered conspiratorially in an attempt to break the tension that stretched between them.

As teenagers, the two of them had often saved their money and slipped away to share a cup of cappuccino at one of the sidewalk cafés that dotted Main Street in downtown Sarasota. There they would sit for hours, gossiping and giggling and dreaming about their futures as they ignored the gawkers who stopped to stare at their prayer coverings and distinctive Mennonite style of dressing. It had been far too long since they had shared such a moment—years had gone by. Emma had married Lars, her childhood sweetheart, and they had two wonderful children. Hester had gone to nursing school and then come home to find her mother dying the slow, horrible death that followed a diagnosis of Lou Gehrig's disease.

To Hester's surprise, Emma's large blue eyes filled with tears. She smiled and nodded. "Ja, once this storm passes, coffee would be *wunderbar*," she replied, her voice breaking.

Hester couldn't help wondering if perhaps she'd become so wrapped up in herself that she had failed to appreciate that her friend might miss her as much as she had been missing Emma. "Hey," she whispered, gripping Emma's hand tighter. "It's okay. We're okay." To her relief, Emma smiled.

A lively discussion followed the reports, and the room was electric with anticipation and not a little fear for what the hurricane might leave in its wake. The news was not good. All the experts agreed that the watch status would change to a warning before the day was out. A warning meant the hurricane would be expected to hit within twenty-four hours. According to their best indicators, the only good news was that the storm might yet continue to stall offshore, buying them more time. One meteorologist had confirmed that once the storm came across the islands, it could weaken significantly before it hit Sarasota, but those barrier islands—Siesta, Lido, and Longboat Key— were in the storm's direct path.

Following the meeting, as members of the group broke out into clusters to compare notes, Emma went to the side table where coffee and tea had been set up and got Hester a paper cup filled with two-thirds coffee and one-third cream, just the way she liked it.

"Thanks." Hester took a sip and grinned. "This will do for now, but once this is all over, I'm going to hold you to the promise of a latte on Main Street."

"Just name the time and place," Emma said, sipping her own black coffee. "I've missed you, my friend."

"Ja. Me, too."

The two of them sat knee to knee on the hard metal folding chairs of the county meeting room as they made lists of what each agency would be responsible for so there would be no duplication of services and everything could be covered. They had to prepare for the worst. If necessary, Emma's group would take charge at the three shelters, while Hester's volunteers would feed the army of volunteers from Mennonite churches in surrounding states and as far away as the upper Midwest. Once the initial needs were met, everyone would pitch in to manage the long-term work of cleaning up and rebuilding.

"Sounds like a plan," Emma said as she put away her notebook and finished her coffee.

"How are the kids?" Hester asked.

"They are growing up so fast. Matt is completely wrapped up in soccer. Can you believe that Sadie is going to be sixteen years old? She and her cousin, Tessa, are as inseparable as Jeannie and I were at that age," she said, referring to her younger sister.

"Okay, now you're making me feel ancient. I mean, it seems like just yesterday they were babies."

Emma crumpled her empty cup and nodded. "I know. Can you believe it? Jeannie says that her Tessa is sweet and so reliable just like me, and I tell her just wait. Sadie was a sweetheart at that age as well."

"They'll be fine," Hester said. "Look at who they got for mothers."

"And what about you?" Emma asked as the two of them headed down the corridor.

Hester shrugged. "Not much to tell."

"Really?" Emma's eyebrows arched.

"Oh, you mean Samuel Brubaker?" It was like old times the way she had read Emma's question without her friend needing to explain.

"Oh, you mean Samuel Brubaker," Emma said, mimicking her too-casual tone. Samuel was a young carpenter who had come to Florida for a visit and been recruited by Hester's father to stay and work with him in his carpentry business. And there wasn't a person in Pinecraft who didn't think that Arlen's real motive in hiring the Pennsylvania carpenter was to promote a potential romance with Hester.

"Come on. Tell me the truth. Do you like him?"

"He's nice," Hester said as she drained the last of her coffee and let it burn its way down her throat.

"I see. Well, take some advice from an old friend and don't settle, Hester. He might be a fine man, a good provider and all, but if you don't feel. . ."

"Oh, Emma, I don't know what I feel. It's all come about so suddenly, and I know Papa has the best of intentions and only wants my happiness, but. . ."

"And are you happy as you are?"

Hester shrugged. "I love my work. . . ." She sighed as a realization dawned on her. "So much so that when I saw you up there giving our report today, I felt threatened, like something could be taken away from me. It was the strangest feeling."

"You have no reason to feel that way, Hester. You're one of those people who truly cares for others, who thinks nothing of putting her own life on hold to help someone in trouble or pain. You have a rare gift, my friend."

Embarrassed yet touched by Emma's praise, Hester held the door for her friend as they stepped out into weather that had already begun to change. The traffic was bumper to bumper, and all headed east away from the shore and the sky that was beginning to change from brilliant blue to ominous gray.

"I have the car," Emma said. "We could put your bike in the trunk."

"*Nein, danke.* I'll be fine. I want to go by the bay once more, you know, in case things change." As she pedaled off, she silently thanked God that she and Emma had found their way back to the friendship they had treasured for so many years.

Chapter 2

I f Hester thought traffic had been bad on her way to the meeting, it was nothing compared to the jammed streets and impatient drivers she saw on her way back to Pinecraft. Clearly people had taken the evacuation order to heart in spite of the fact that in the past such evacuations had often been an exercise in futility when the hurricanes missed them completely. As a light changed and Hester eased her bike into the crosswalk, a pickup truck hurtled within inches of her as the driver rushed to make an illegal left turn. Car horns blared a belated warning, and she hesitated. Hester could see panic eroding what she could only assume were the normally pleasant features of the driver.

"Move it or lose it, honey," another driver yelled from the open window of her car as she edged forward to make a right turn. The woman glanced up at the sky, her eyes wide as if she thought the hurricane might well appear full-blown at any second and wash them all out to sea.

The crossing lights were with Hester the rest of the way, although the parade of traffic headed east did not slacken in the least. She was faster on her bicycle than any of the motorized vehicles she passed. Just as she slid her bike to a stop at the small prefabricated building that served as the local MCC headquarters for collecting donations and distributing supplies, she heard a car horn and someone calling her name.

"Hey, Hester, your hurricane looks like it might be pretty impressive!" She turned to see Grady Forrest, the director of the county's disaster-relief program, leaning out the window of his Jeep and grinning. He pulled into the gas station lot across the street from the center and got out. It had been Grady who'd suggested that she volunteer to serve as the area representative to MCC.

"Guess I'll have to treat you with a little more respect," he added as he dodged traffic and jaywalked across the busy street. "I wanted to touch base with you at the meeting, but you were out of there before I could break away. How are things coming here?" He nodded toward the open door of the MCC building.

"I expect we'll see the first volunteer teams from up north start to arrive within hours after the storm hits," Hester said. "We got word that there are groups on their way from Ohio, Indiana, and—"

"That's great, Hester." Grady glanced at his shoes and then up at the sky, clearly gathering his thoughts—or was it his nerve? "Actually, I have a request. . . ." He paused. "There's this. . .thing. After I missed you at the meeting, I drove over here to ask you to help me with what could be a delicate situation."

"How can I help?" The volunteers from all three Mennonite groups would be expected to focus first on the elderly, the infirm, and the underinsured—regardless of their faith or politics. For the county's coordinator of disaster relief to ask for their help was evidence that their agencies were every bit as well regarded as the Red Cross or other more well-known relief agencies. She looked at him curiously. "Our volunteer cup runneth over," she teased, but Grady did not smile at the pun. "Hey, just tell us what we can do."

"Not 'we'—you. I want to do this quietly if possible."

Hester felt a tingle of alarm. "I don't understand."

"There's this one guy out on the point just down from the mouth of the creek where it empties into Little Sarasota Bay."

The creek was Philippi Creek, the meandering stream that wound its way from the intercoastal waters that separated the mainland from Siesta Key eastward through the very heart of Pinecraft and beyond. It was that very creek that posed the greatest threat to the residents of Pinecraft. If it flooded, dozens of people right in her own community could be displaced. "You mean Tucker's Point?"

Grady nodded. "His name's John Steiner. Came here a couple of years ago from the Midwest, as I understand it, and bought the old Tucker place. He's been renovating the property. Word has it that he plans to revive the old packinghouse."

"Okay," Hester said, wondering where this conversation was going and wishing Grady would come to the point.

"Apparently he's also done a fair amount of planting—fruit trees, veggies, and the like. Somebody mentioned that he'd just started keeping chickens." He shook his head. "You'd think the man was living out in the country miles from any neighbor instead of just across the creek from a large condominium complex."

Hester studied her friend for a long moment. "Who is this man, Grady?"

"Well, now there's the interesting part. Seems that he's the grandson of the late Thomas E. Carter. Remember? He was the speaker of the house, and this guy's aunt took the old man's seat in Congress after he retired. She just happens to serve on the House Subcommittee on Homeland Security and is a close friend of my boss, who is planning a run for Congress himself, which is why this landed on my plate."

Hester nodded, although the convoluted government bureaucracy of the outside world remained a mystery to her. "So this congresswoman called you?"

"Worse. She called my boss and his boss, and, well, the message is pretty clear that we need to make sure this guy Steiner knows what he's in for if he stays. Ideally we need to persuade him to head for the nearest shelter."

"That's not our mission," she reminded Grady.

"I know. That's why I'm asking for a special favor. If he

decides to stay and then gets hit, I really can't put everything on hold to rescue him, or we'll be labeled another Katrina by the media. Could you just go out there and quietly check it out?"

"I guess. . ." she said reluctantly. "Why me?"

Grady ducked his head. "Steiner is Amish—or was. I didn't get the whole story yet." He grinned. "So, a woman's touch?"

"I'm Mennonite, not Amish."

"Close enough."

She fingered one of the ties of her prayer covering. Perhaps doing this for Grady was one way of atoning for her bout of green-eyed envy at the meeting earlier. "All right."

Obviously relieved, Grady took out a map of the area where Philippi Creek flowed into Little Sarasota Bay. He tapped the point that jutted out into the bay across from Siesta Key. "Word has it that he's left the road in pretty overgrown, so it might be best to go down the creek from here. Margery Barker can help with that. She's already tried to get the guy to leave but to no avail."

So much for a woman's touch.

As a prelude to the storm, the rain had started to fall in a steady downpour while John was having his supper. He was just finishing when there was a loud pounding on his front door. He knew what this was. No doubt the authorities had come to order him to evacuate. According to the latest data, the beast that had been lurking offshore for days had awakened and was stretching its tentacles toward the west coast of Florida. Throughout the day he'd been aware of the ceaseless stream of traffic crossing over the Stickney Point Bridge as the residents of Siesta Key fled to safety. It was past time to go if he was going, which he wasn't.

Fueled by his determination to stand his ground, John pulled open the door, prepared to state his case, but found himself speechless. Instead of the uniformed muscleman he'd been expecting, there was a young Mennonite woman clinging to her skirt and trying without much success to hold the hood of her raincoat over her stiff white *kapp*. "John Steiner?" she shouted above the wind.

Dumbly he nodded, and the woman strode right past him into his house.

"I'm Hester Detlef with the Mennonite Central Committee," she said as the wind slammed the door. With most of the remaining daylight blocked out by the plywood covering the windows and only the battery-powered lamp on the kitchen table for illumination, it was hard to gauge her expression, but certainly her posture even in silhouette as well as that bossy tone spoke volumes. The irony that a woman named Hester had appeared on his doorstep at the same time that a hurricane by the same name was headed his way had not escaped him. "You really need to leave now," she added.

"No, ma'am. *You* need to leave now," John replied, forcing his voice to remain calm as he retraced his steps and prepared to open the door for her.

"Apparently your aunt is worried about you," she continued. "So worried that she has contacted the local head of county government, who in turn has directed the director of the county's emergency management program to make sure that you get to safety."

John made a show of glancing around. "Well, I don't see anybody from the county or my aunt, and I am not leaving."

To his surprise, she began rummaging through the pockets of her rain jacket until she unearthed a notepad and pencil. "That's your decision?"

"It is, and. . ."

She thrust the paper and pencil at him. "Then please write that down and date and sign it."

She was giving up? Just like that? What had happened to the do-gooder Mennonites he'd known back in Indiana? The ones who quietly went about the work of helping others and did not leave until the work was finished? This woman had been sent to get him to evacuate, and yet. . .

She pushed the paper and pencil toward him again. "Either

write the statement or come with me right now," she said. "Those are your choices, and I don't have time to debate the merits of one over the other."

He grabbed the paper from her and scrawled out a one-sentence message. *I'm staying on my property.* Then he signed it with a flourish and handed it back to her.

"Date it," she said. Only after he complied did she accept the paper. She folded it carefully and headed for the door. "Last chance," she said quietly, her hand on the doorknob.

He reached around her to open the door, bracing it with his shoulder against the force of the wind, taking note that the rain had stopped and there was some light in the western sky. The storm might well swing to the north or south and miss them entirely. "Good day, Hester."

She glanced up at him, and in the fading but yet stronger daylight after the dark of the barricaded house, he was stunned to see genuine concern in her expression. "You really should leave," she said. "This is the real thing."

In the bay behind her, John saw Margery idling her boat near his pier. Irritated that his neighbor had interfered in his life once more, he stepped back inside his house and closed the door. Then he stood next to the door, listening. A moment later he heard the throttle of Margery's boat, and then he was alone. He went back to his radio and, despite the static, received the news that the watch had changed to a warning.

In all the time that John had occupied the point of land that jutted out from the mainland into the mouth of Little Sarasota Bay, there had been only two other times when a hurricane watch had turned to a warning. Both storms had missed Sarasota and its protective barrier islands, but neither had come close to the power that this one was predicted to be. John felt a surge of adrenaline as he digested the storm's change in status and mentally went over his checklist. Every window was securely covered. He'd gathered ample supplies—drinking water, first-aid kit, a change of clothes, and nonperishable food. He had enough to cover his needs even if he got stuck here for several days.

That was a distinct possibility. His property had stood abandoned for years before he'd bought it and started renovating the main house, the packinghouse, and a variety of other outbuildings. The work had gone slowly because he was determined to do it all himself. He had deliberately ignored the overgrown lane that led to the house from the road, preferring to access his land by kayak so as to discourage visitors until he had the place ready for business. But getting in or out by water might prove impossible depending on the path of the storm.

Still, John had come to this place to prove to himself—and to others—that it was possible to live a strict Amish life in the midst of the outside world. Even the battery-powered radio was stretching the boundaries, but it was the one concession he had made to Margery after the last hurricane. He picked up his Bible and his dog-eared copy of Henry David Thoreau's *Walden: Life in the Woods*. The book had been a favorite of his mother's, and other than his Bible, it was the only book he had brought with him to Florida. It had also been at the root of his break with his Amish community—or theirs with him.

After his father died, John's interest in Thoreau's ideas of living a completely self-sustaining and separate life had increased. Thoreau's experiment seemed to John to go beyond even the strict traditions of separateness practiced by those of his faith. His zeal for Thoreau's idea had been his undoing in the tightly knit Amish community where he had grown up. Stubborn like his mother, John had stood his ground, and she alone had stood with him. And then his mother had died, and he found himself standing utterly alone.

He washed his supper dishes. Then he made a final survey of his emergency supplies. Satisfied that he had everything within his reach that he might need to ride out the storm, he picked up his Bible and let it fall open one last time. He closed his eyes, praying for guidance, and let his finger run down the page to whatever passage of scripture God might choose for him.

"And seek the peace of the city whither I have caused you to be carried away captives, and pray unto the Lord for it: for in the peace

thereof shall ye have peace. "

His Bible had fallen open to the book of Jeremiah, the twenty-ninth chapter. His finger had stopped on verse 7. It seemed an odd message—in some ways appropriate yet in others a mystery. He was hardly a captive. John considered finding another random passage, but that would be like saying God had not guided him to this one. He marked the page with the red ribbon bookmark, and then placed his Bible and Thoreau's book into a plastic bag that had once held nuts delivered by Margery the previous spring and zipped it shut. Whatever the meaning of the verse, he was prepared to face whatever came.

He checked the clock and saw that he had a couple of hours yet before dark. Outside, he stood on his porch and let the wind and rain take their licks at him. He surveyed his property—perhaps some of it for the last time, depending on which way the storm hit. In between remodeling the house and cleaning up what remained of the abandoned orange groves, he'd started planting what he would need to sustain himself. Near the house he'd put in a large garden of herbs and vegetables in the Japanese raised-bed style that he'd read about. He'd also added to Tucker's groves, planting a variety of kiwi, orange, lemon, lime, and mango trees, carefully orchestrated to give him a harvest during most of the year. More recently he'd bought a couple of laying hens to supplement the steady diet of fish he'd been living on since arriving in Florida.

The chickens! He'd forgotten all about them. The rain had let up some, but the sky had a sickly yellowish-green cast to it, and the air was heavy with moisture. The winds were already gathering strength. *It's coming too fast,* John thought as he took precious seconds to pause and consider the rapidly rising level of the intercoastal waterway and creek. This storm was definitely on the move.

Oversized raindrops plopped onto his head and shoulders, and within seconds the intermittent drops turned once again into an opaque curtain of pelting rain that had accompanied the Mennonite woman's arrival earlier. Visibility beyond his hand in front of him was nearly impossible. Too late he covered his head with the hood of his slicker and stumbled on toward the chicken coop. In spite of his muscular six-foot frame, he had to fight to maintain his balance in the wind that had every tree on the property swaying in a ghoulish dance.

On the far side of the house he spotted one piece of plywood that had come loose from a window. Grabbing a large rock, he tried without success to hammer it back into place. Repeatedly the weight of the wood in tandem with the power of the wind threw him against the house, and when he heard the glass shatter, he dropped the board and focused on making it across the yard to the chicken coop.

The chickens were in full panic as John tried to corral them into a wire cage. They squawked in protest and pecked at his hands. He'd been stupid to wait so long to take them to shelter, but he'd gotten caught up in trying to protect the house and dealing with Margery and the Mennonite woman. He'd been sure that he had time, that he would know when the storm was about to hit.

"Come on, ladies," he muttered as he tried in vain to catch the hens. Just then he heard the ear-splitting shriek of metal torn from the roof of the coop. John heard more glass shatter as the metallic missile apparently found its target. He looked up in time to see a giant royal palm sway drunkenly for a moment. "Tucker's folly," the realtor had called this place, noting that this specific breed of palm was not made to withstand the winds of a strong tropical storm, much less a hurricane, but Tucker had planted them anyway, wanting to mark the location of his citrus business with something uniquely tropical. Now, decades later, a double row of the giant palms lined each side of the lane that ran from the house out to the main road.

As John watched, the tree seemed to find its balance, and then, as if in slow motion, it started to fall right toward the open roof of the coop.

"You're on your own," he shouted at the squawking hens as he raced out of the coop and tripped over his kayak. The vessel had apparently come loose from its bonds and flown halfway across the yard. So much for properly securing everything. He stumbled for several feet and then fell. And as he covered his head with both hands, the falling tree missed him by inches. Entreating God to keep him safe, John scrambled the rest of the way back to the main house, half crawling and half running for what he hoped would be safety.

It took him what seemed an hour but was probably no more than a couple of minutes to force the door closed and block it with the vintage desk he'd inherited with the house. Breathless and battered, soaked through with perspiration and rain, he sank to the floor, hugging his knees to his chest like he had as a boy whenever he was frightened. From outside he could hear the wail of the wind. The thunder rumbled an apocalyptic chorus in concert with the rain, which seemed to offer its own brand of percussionist accompaniment. It felt as if the house were shifting on its foundation as the walls groaned in protest. Florida homes did not have basements, and John had foolishly thought the heavy oak table would be enough to protect him. As he huddled against the wall, John had to admit that his decision to stay had been born of sheer stubbornness. Perhaps Margery and the Mennonite woman had been messengers, messengers he had ignored. He took out his Bible from its protective plastic and clutched it to his chest as he awaited his fate.

Hour after hour on through the night, the wind howled like a banshee, and the rain stoned the house relentlessly. And just when John would doze off from sheer exhaustion or when he thought he would go mad from the ceaseless pounding, he would hear the sound of another tree ripped from its roots and crashing against an outbuilding, followed by a swell of water breaking over the land. There were times when he imagined that he could hear the sea itself—that it had already wiped out Siesta Key. If that were the case, what chance did the rookeries—the small islands of mangroves that provided roosting and nesting havens for the flocks of pelicans, ibis, and egrets that inhabited the area—have of standing between him and the full fury of Hurricane Hester?

The house continued to sway and moan under the beating it was taking, but it held. After what seemed like forever, John stopped trying to figure out the source of the various convulsions and quakes that threatened to tear the place apart. His mind raced with the need to do something, anything to stop the chaos.

Then he saw water creeping across the floor toward him and knew he had to get to higher ground. He grabbed what supplies he could carry and ran for the stairway, hoping the surge of water would recede before it could reach the second floor. But just as he reached the landing, he realized that the winds had in fact abated significantly, and the rain was no more than a steady late-summer shower. Through the small round window at the top of the stairs, which he had decided to sacrifice rather than climb up and cover, he saw the black sky lighten slightly. He stood frozen for one long moment until the only other sound he was hearing was that of his own ragged breathing. And then he started to laugh.

It was over and he had survived.

He sat down on the step, his feet on the landing where he had stacked his supplies and his elbows resting on his knees. His breathing came in heaves as if he had just run a marathon, but he was smiling. He had made it through his first real hurricane. He threw back his head and let the release of laughter and relief roll through him. He had done it and his house had held. For the first time in hours, his breathing became normal, and as he savored the blessed calm, he felt the tension that had hog-tied his entire body for hours drain away. He opened a jug of water and drank a long swig, then pried the cover off Margery's tin of cookies and pulled one out.

But after he'd given himself permission to celebrate by devouring two more cookies, he heard the wind start to build again. His body and mind went on immediate alert as he listened. He was confused by the exact replay of the ominous sounds he had spent the last several hours enduring. Only now they seemed to come from the opposite direction. Once again the house sang out in protest as rain and wind blasted away at the stucco of the outer walls until it succeeded in working its way in around the plywood window coverings and moldings.

John stood up, unsure of his next move. The calm had been the eye of the storm. How could he not have known that? He berated himself for his stupidity, his arrogance in thinking that he had won. Then he saw the water rising rapidly on the main floor. It was pouring in now, inching its way up the sturdy legs of his kitchen table. He turned to complete his journey to the second story, praying as he went that it would be high enough.

But just as he turned to clamor his way up the last of the stairs, the ceiling above him collapsed, and the stairs dropped away beneath him as the house surrendered to the storm.

Chapter 3

On the night the hurricane was predicted to strike, Hester prepared supper for her grandmother and her father. The three of them held hands as Arlen asked God to bless the food and keep them safe through the night.

"Amen," Hester's grandmother, Nelly, pronounced as she passed the plate of sliced rye bread to her son. Arlen took two slices and slathered each with the dark spicy mustard he liked before stacking on slices of ham and cheese.

"*Und das Gemuse,* Arlen," Nelly instructed, handing him the bowl of green beans. "I never could get you to eat your vegetables. It's a wonder Hester and the boys are as healthy as they are, given the way you eat."

"Sarah made sure they ate right," Hester's father replied as he bit into his sandwich. "That was her department."

Nelly rolled her eyes and looked at Hester's plate. "This one eats like *der Vogel*—reminds me of one of those little birds on the beach as well. All nervous energy, always ready to just fly off somewhere."

"I'm home tonight, Gramma," Hester assured her. "We've done everything we can to make sure as many people as possible are secure, and Grady tells us there's plenty of time to get you and the others to shelters if the creek floods after the hurricane passes."

"We'll be fine," Nelly assured her. "*Gott ist gut*. Now eat. Wherever that hurricane lands, I know you and your father are going to be out there in the thick of things trying to help folks recover and rebuild. You need your strength."

Hester smiled and heaped another spoonful of Nelly's famous potato salad onto her plate.

"There's a good girl."

Shortly after they had finished supper and washed and dried the last of the dishes, her grandmother yawned and announced her intention to get into bed and read her Bible for a bit before going to sleep. Arlen had insisted that his mother spend the night with them. Hester kissed Nelly's cheek, knowing that she would need to gently remove the Bible from her grandmother's hands before getting into bed and turning out the light.

All through the night she and her father sat together inside their secure house miles from the Gulf or even the bay. Unless the creek flooded, they would suffer little damage so far inland. Some trees down and roof tiles blown off but generally no real damage. They listened as the edge of the storm passed over them on its way inland. Her father read aloud from his much-worn Bible as the winds weakened and her grandmother slept through it all.

Before going to bed, she told her father about going to see John Steiner the day before. "I abandoned him, Dad. I let my irritation at being asked to go there get the better of me."

Her father handed her his Bible. "Seek guidance, *liebchen*, and remember, God forgives us. You pray on the matter and I'm sure you will find your answer."

As always she found comfort in her father's lack of censure when it came to her actions. But then her father placed his arm around her shoulder as they walked down the hall together. "You know, Hester, sometimes even I lose sight of my role as pastor to others. Being someone others look up to can be heady stuff." He did not have to remind her that in their faith, such pride was unacceptable. "Your post with MCC is not unlike mine as pastor—we have both been chosen to show others the way, but we are no different than those who follow our leadership."

"I can't help it if I've been given a good deal of responsibility," she replied defensively.

"And if God saw fit to relieve you of that leadership role, to have you simply follow, do you believe in your heart that you could do that?"

"Of course," she replied. But as she drifted off to sleep, she had to admit that a good part of her annoyance with John Steiner had been that he was keeping her from her responsibilities as director of MCC's efforts back in Pinecraft. "I'll work on that," she promised herself—and God.

⋙

"How soon can we get started?" Hester asked Grady early the following morning as she dashed across a parking lot, dodging puddles and hoping the light drizzle falling was the last of the rain. Grady was making his rounds, checking in person with the various relief groups around the county, all of them anxious to get to work.

"We've got some serious damage," Grady told her. "Turtle Beach is basically gone, and the entire coastline of Siesta has been devastated. There's probably not a home or business over there that hasn't suffered irreparable damage at least in the short term."

Hester knew what this meant. People were going to need food, water, shelter, and a comforting presence to assure them that everything was going to be all right. This time of year most of the condominiums and homes on Siesta were vacant. A big part of Grady's job would be to work with owners to get the properties repaired in time for the onslaught of snowbirds—the part-time winter residents. Those folks would begin arriving around Thanksgiving, and that meant there was less than three months to get ready. The annual return of the snowbirds was a mainstay of the economy in the area. If they decided to go elsewhere, that

35

could be catastrophic on a whole different level.

"Unfortunately, Siesta Key is not the entire story, although they certainly took the hardest hit."

Hester thought of the sugar-white beaches that were Siesta Key's trademark and wondered what they might look like now. News reports she'd heard left no doubt, though, that all up and down the Gulf Coast, scores of homes and businesses had been totally wiped out by the storm. Those who had waited too long to leave and couldn't make it to a hotel or friend's safe haven were now crowded into shelters, including the ones set up in two schools and a large church just on the outskirts of Pinecraft. She tried not to think about what might have happened to John Steiner's place, or the man himself. "So, back to my question—when can we get started?"

"I should be hearing from the local search-and-rescue teams soon," Grady said, shielding her from the drizzle with a large golf umbrella decorated with comic strip characters. "Crews from gas and power have been out since before dawn. But there is some positive news—a few minor injuries, but no fatalities that we know of."

Hester nodded. "That's better than we might have expected given the power of the storm." She knew the drill. The representatives from the Federal Emergency Management Agency, or FEMA, had arrived on the scene, but they would wait for the local authorities to take the lead. County and state rescue teams would be the first out checking those places that they knew had not been evacuated. Soon the gas and power crews would be roaming the barrier islands as well as the mainland looking for downed wires and other telltale signs of problems, repairing them so that the real process of cleaning up and securing property affected by the storm could begin in earnest.

Grady removed a battered, sweat-streaked baseball cap and mopped his forehead with his forearm. He was wearing a worn T-shirt that looked as if it had seen dozens of trips to the washing machine, faded jeans, and running shoes. The thing Hester liked most about Grady was that he was not the typical government employee. He dressed in shorts or jeans instead of the more formal business attire that FEMA contacts arriving from Washington seemed to prefer. And he always looked like he was ready to get his hands dirty and get the work done. Those qualities above anything he might say gave people confidence. Since Katrina and the oil spill, folks in the Gulf area had had their fill of politicians flying down from Washington, looking around and shaking their heads, and then heading back to their plush homes and offices, leaving people like Grady to take the brunt of people's frustrations and anger.

"Still, this is a biggie, Hester." Grady shook his head. "It's beyond bad. We've got power outages from Fort Myers all the way to Tampa and no word on when power—not to mention water—might be restored. With this heat. . ." He swiped his forearm over his brow.

"Well, we're ready with meals and water for the workers, and we've got generators at the shelters and in other strategic locations to keep the air-conditioning and refrigeration up and running."

Pinecraft had suffered only minor wind and water damage. The streets were a mess, but already volunteers were out, moving branches and cutting downed trees so that the main roads were open. That morning a truck loaded with clothing, food, and other supplies had arrived from MCC's national headquarters in Pennsylvania. In calmer times most donations that Hester received in Pinecraft were shipped north, where there were warehouses set up to sort, store, and distribute the goods wherever they might be needed around the world. This time the donations would be distributed right here in Sarasota—not just to the residents of Pinecraft, but to anyone who might need their help. Hester already had a team of women working to sort through the goods and get them distributed to the shelters.

In fact, the entire Mennonite and Amish communities of Pinecraft had come out to offer their help. She glanced across the street to the assembly line of women in plain cotton dresses and head coverings that ranged from pioneer sunbonnets to small black lace headpieces to the starched mesh caps so familiar to outsiders. They stood shoulder to shoulder filling empty produce boxes with canned goods and other nonperishables, while men in their brown, navy, or black trousers, collarless shirts, and trademark straw hats were handling the work of clearing the debris. Of course, it wasn't just the residents of Pinecraft who had stepped up to meet the challenge. Hester knew that a similar scene was being repeated at churches all over the city.

She also knew that her father had called out the community's full complement of MDS team leaders, who in turn each had six to twelve volunteers they could call upon when needed. Every available crew had gotten the word, and now they were just waiting for the signal that they could get to work. They would begin the weeks of cleanup and ultimately months of rebuilding homes and businesses for those without insurance who had been hardest hit by the hurricane.

"I did a fly-by this morning, past Tucker's Point," Grady said quietly.

Hester knew that Grady had been disappointed when she handed him the signed note and told him that John Steiner had refused to evacuate.

"And?" she asked, curious in spite of her annoyance at the man for wasting time and valuable resources by his stubborn refusal to follow protocol.

Grady shook his head. "I saw no signs of anyone, and the road into the place is even more blocked with downed trees and power lines. The only way in is by boat, and that's tricky as well."

Hester was still wondering how anyone could be so arrogant as to believe that a mere mortal could withstand nature's fury and simply walk away unscathed. "Do you think he survived?"

Grady actually shuddered in spite of the oppressive August heat. "From what I could see on the fly-over, everything on his place is pretty much kindling except for the packinghouse—one wall down and the roof gone but otherwise standing. The main house might be okay, hard to say. The upper branches of a large banyan tree had fallen onto it and hidden most of it from view."

Hester bowed her head. She hadn't done enough. She had

allowed her irritation at John Steiner's arrogance to color her actions. She should have insisted, but the more Margery had talked about the man on the quick bumpy boat ride from her marina to Tucker's Point, the more upset Hester had become. By the time she had knocked on the man's front door, she had been seething with righteous indignation.

Now John Steiner might be dead. A casualty of the hurricane that carried her name.

"I am so sorry," she murmured and swallowed back tears of shame and regret. "I should have. . ."

"Hey, easy there," Grady said, patting her shoulder. "We don't know what happened. Maybe the guy thought better of his decision and moved out. Maybe he was able to ride out the storm—like I said, the house didn't seem to be a total loss. A good part of it was still standing."

"You said 'kindling,' " Hester reminded him.

"I embellish. You know that."

"Well, I hope you're right and he made it."

Grady tapped his pen on the clipboard in a drumbeat. "One way to find out," he muttered, not looking at her.

"You can't seriously be thinking of going out there with everything else you have to do," Hester said.

"Not me. I asked your father if he might go. Maybe take Samuel Brubaker along in case there's any heavy lifting to be done."

Her father had been up and out before Hester was dressed that morning. "And he said?"

"He'd go as long as you came along as front porch sitter."

"You want me to. . ." Hester could barely get the words out. A "front porch sitter" was usually one of her Dad's volunteers who was designated to sit with the home owner in those first moments after the crew arrived. That was the time when the home owner was likely to be most emotional and not thinking clearly. The sitter would listen and offer comfort until the home owner calmed down enough to give written permission for the MDS team to start clearing away the worst of the debris.

Presumably in this case, her job was to get the guy to let them escort him off the property, assuming he was alive.

"You're joking, right?"

"Not so much," Grady replied. "Look, his aunt doesn't want any publicity about this. She's called in some favors, I take it. Arlen's agreed to go, but he says he'll make the time only if you agree to take the hand-holding part of this."

Hester saw the situation for what it was. This was exactly what she and her father had been talking about the night before. This was what she had prayed about.

"If the guy's alive but injured," Grady pressed, "we need to get him out of there, Hester. You're a trained nurse." He waited a beat. "Please?"

Hester closed her eyes, reminding herself that God had given her the mission to serve Him by helping others. Whether she was leading or following was hardly the issue. And even though this man had defied logic to ride out a hurricane, he was a human being in need. It wasn't the first time she'd heard of such stubbornness. Plus, if she helped Grady with this, then Grady would be free to help those who had played by the rules and still lost everything. "I'll take care of it." She took the map from him and folded it up. "How's Amy doing?"

Grady grinned. His wife was eight months pregnant with their first child, and he was already a very proud father. "She's ticked off because this hurricane wasn't a male name. She was all set to name the baby after the storm. I do not even begin to understand why we would wish that on a kid."

"It's a boy, then?"

"Yep. You know what she told me this morning? She said there's still a month before the baby is supposed to come, and even if the little guy is late, hurricane season goes through October." He shook his head, but his smile told the real story of his abiding love for his wife. Hester couldn't help feeling a twinge of envy. Over the years she'd pretty much given up on the idea that she would ever know the kind of deep commitment and love that bound Grady to Amy. The two had so much in common, and in many ways it was hard to imagine one without the other.

Hester had always thought that she had more in common with males like her brothers and the boys she'd gone to school with than she did with the girls she'd known. Guys all seemed to like her, like having her around. But when it came to one of them considering her as spouse material, things changed—fast. She was thirty-three years old now, well past the age when most women of her faith had settled down to the business of making a home and raising a family. Many people thought she had missed her chance at marital happiness when she had insisted on going to college and getting her nursing degree. Others thought that it was her devotion to caring for her sick mother that had made her miss out on the opportunity to meet a suitable young man.

There had been one young man, a farmer from Indiana she'd met after she'd completed her nurse's training and had returned to Pinecraft. He had even proposed. But just a week before their wedding, he had made it clear that while he had found her unorthodox behavior appealing when they first met, it simply would not do to continue along that path once she became his wife and the mother of his children. Hester had called off the wedding, once again setting tongues to wagging throughout the little community. But shortly after that, her mother's battle with Lou Gehrig's disease had begun its downward spiral, and the tide of sympathy had turned in Hester's favor. Many had seen it as part of God's plan that Hester should be free to care for her beloved mother.

"I'd go myself," Grady was saying. "But there are still dozens of people unaccounted for, and. . ."

"It's your job to account for them."

Grady puffed out his cheeks and then blew out a breath of frustration. "Yeah. I have to admit that at times like these I sometimes question my career choice, but this is the path I chose."

And I chose my path, Hester reminded herself sternly. *Just as staying put in a hurricane was the choice of John Steiner. Judge not, Hester Detlef.*

"Okay. Tell Dad I'll meet him at the shop. I need to let Emma know she needs to take full charge of things here for a while."

"Be careful out there, okay?" Grady said. "The area is still unstable with all those downed trees, and, of course, there's no power or water. Don't go poking around. Just see if you see any sign of Steiner. If you find him, do what you can to get him stabilized, and then call in the evacuation chopper."

"Unless he's okay," Hester corrected.

"Either way," Grady said, "call the chopper and get him to a hospital. I'm not taking any chances."

"Got it," she said. "Do you have any further information about him? Anything else that might help in case he's—you know—confused or delirious?"

"Not really. Word has it that his mother—the congresswoman's sister—was some sort of hippie who abandoned the high-society life for a simpler style. She married this Amish farmer and moved out to his place in Indiana."

"So John Steiner's father is Amish?"

"And so was Steiner until a few years ago. I think he was shunned or whatever they call it when he's gotten himself kicked out of the community."

"Banned," Hester corrected quietly. "If he cannot go back, then he has been banned or ex-communicated."

"Whatever. He left, came here, and bought the old Tucker place." Grady let out a sigh. Both of them knew that he might very well be the first fatality of the storm. "Do your best, okay. Just be careful. I warn you, Hester, from the air the place looked pretty unstable."

"We've probably seen worse," Hester assured him.

But an hour later as she and her father and her father's newly hired cabinetmaker, Samuel Brubaker, beached the sturdy fishing boat they'd borrowed from Margery and worked their way over uprooted trees and dunes of wet sand that had not existed the day before, Hester was not so sure.

"How could anyone survive this?" she murmured. In spite of her annoyance that John Steiner was somehow entitled to special attention, her heart went out to the guy. If he was still alive, he had lost everything.

Chapter 4

It had taken John most of the morning to claw his way out from under the rubble that had once been his bedroom above the kitchen and the heavy cypress beam that had proved his salvation. Oblivious to the pain that racked his body, he'd just broken through the last barrier into the gray and ominous aftermath of the hurricane when he got his first look at the fury and devastation the storm had wrought. It looked like Hurricane Hester had roared straight through his property on her way to who-knew-where. His once-pristine cluster of faded candy-colored outbuildings that tourists liked to associate with "old" Florida looked more like an oversized game of pick-up sticks.

The chicken coop was flattened. He hated to think of what he might find beneath the rubble. The cage he'd left behind when the roof blew off the coop was now embedded in the trunk of a palm tree like a spike. The concrete walls of his toolshed had collapsed in on each other, and the corrugated metal roof was missing. He turned toward the old packinghouse and saw that one section of its tin roof now balanced precariously in the branches of the large banyan tree that dominated the yard; one half of that tree was leaning against the house. The second floor of the main house was gone with the exception of the door frame that once had led to his bedroom. On the first floor all of the doors and windows were missing, and one of the four walls had fallen as well. The only recognizable furnishings were the kitchen table, mired in at least a foot of sludge, the stove, and half of the fireplace chimney. He was able to identify his kitchen cabinets and countertops only by the splintered pieces of wood that littered the landscape.

His life had been spared when he was able to crawl onto a fallen ceiling beam and cling to it until the storm finally abated sometime just before dawn. The angle of the beam had protected him as the second floor of the house collapsed and had kept him from drowning in the waters that filled the first floor as he lapsed in and out of consciousness. He tightened his grip on the Bible he'd managed to rescue from the rubble and thanked God for saving his life. He turned to the old citrus groves and to where he had planted his kitchen garden and additional fruit trees.

Muck and sand covered the entire property where just the morning before he had walked through the rows of evenly spaced trees. Over there was where he'd planned to add green beans, and over there, pea pods. This larger bed was to house large heads of cabbage and lettuce in alternate rows alongside tomato plants. But now what little he could see of the remains of the carefully plotted garden was buried under several inches of muck and water. He set his Bible on a window ledge, and then walked farther into the orchard, where he bent to scoop wet silt and sand from the ground. He could find nothing that was salvageable of the work he had poured his heart and soul into for the last two years. Here and there the recycled cypress boards he had used to build the planters stuck up from the sand like grave markers. The branches on the fruit trees that had managed to survive the storm's rage were gray with sea salt. Other trees had been snapped off at the base.

Slowly he took stock of his losses, trying without success to comprehend the fury of a storm that had robbed him of everything he'd worked so hard to build. When he'd settled on the Tucker property in spite of the naysayers who had thought him mad, he had seen not an abandoned homestead and business but a place where at last he could pursue his Walden experiment unencumbered by the disapproval of others. Here he could prove to those who had banned him that he was a man of faith and tradition—perhaps far more so than the neighbors he'd left behind had been. Here he could honor the memory of his mother and the way that she had encouraged him even with her dying breath.

Still stunned by the extent of the storm's damage, he finally registered the steady throttle of a fishing boat puttering close to what had once been his pier. It was now no more than a twisted aluminum sculpture sticking up from the muddy water. "What now?" John muttered as he watched a trio of Mennonites—conservative judging by their dress—beach the boat on a nearby sandbar and wade through the uncommonly high waters of the bay to shore. John bit his lip hard and silently prayed for strength and patience. Like he didn't have enough to deal with.

"Plain people" as the various sects of Anabaptists were often called. Amish, Mennonite, Hutterites—all linked under the yoke of plain dress and a simple separatist lifestyle despite their differences. In particular, the Mennonites seemed to have this thing about needing to help people—whether anyone asked for their help or not.

So here they came—two men and that woman—the one who'd demanded he leave the night before. The men could have been father and son. The elder sported a full white beard, while the younger was clean-shaven, indicating that he was single. Both wore the somber uniform of their faith. Dark loose trousers with suspenders, solid blue cotton shirts with no collar, and the telltale stiff-brimmed straw hat. John had abandoned the dress code when he came to Florida because he believed it would be easier to maintain his anonymity if he did not call attention to himself.

He turned his attention to the woman. She was wearing sneakers that were stained with the brown muck of the creek. Her dress was a pale blue floral print covered with a black apron.

She carried a cloth satchel. Her skirt was wet and muddy for a good foot above her ankle where she'd waded in to shore. Her hair was parted in the middle, then pinned up and back and crowned by the traditional starched white mesh prayer *kapp*. And while the men were both fair, the woman was not. Her hair was as black as the night that had engulfed his property just before the storm struck.

In no mood for company and especially not for the woman's right to gloat, John glanced around, seeking escape. But other than the boat they'd arrived in, he had no other options. Where once there had been a winding lane out to the main road in the days when Tucker had owned the property, there was now a jungle of downed palm trees and uprooted shrubs to add to the maze that had been the overgrown path he'd so carefully avoided clearing. On top of that he sported a long bloody gash on one arm along with a variety of throbbing bruises and possibly a broken wrist given the pulsating pain he was feeling there. His shorts and shirt were both ripped, and his signature planter's straw hat was probably halfway to New York by now—along with most of his other possessions that had not been nailed down against winds that must have topped well over a hundred miles an hour. Three uprooted Norfolk pines that the nursery owner had advised him not to plant now formed a kind of bizarre natural obstacle course for the trio of do-gooders to navigate.

Seeing that there was no way to avoid them, he waited with arms folded across his chest and his feet planted firmly in the soft sandy soil. "Can I help you?" he called out when they were less than ten feet away. Where had they come from? It was as if the storm had dropped them off on its way inland.

"Ah, *mein bruder*, it is we who should be asking that of you," the older man replied with a sympathetic nod toward the chaos that lay all around John. He pulled a brochure from the pocket of his trousers and tapped it lightly against his thigh as he made the introductions. "I am Arlen Detlef. This is my friend Samuel Brubaker and my daughter, Hester."

"Hester." John was unaware he had spoken aloud until he

46

saw the widening of her eyes at the sound of her name. "Like the storm," he added. He had failed to fully appreciate the significance of the connection the night before, but now it made sense, for certainly she had roared in and out like the hurricane itself.

The older man chuckled. "In many ways, yes, my friend."

"Dad," the woman said. Her tone held the rebuke that her smile disarmed. John studied that smile, but she had offered it to only her father—not to him. She had barely glanced at him. The woman clearly did not like him. So much for Christian charity.

She doesn't even know me, he thought. Not that it mattered whether the woman liked him or not. It just irritated him that she had apparently decided to disapprove of him on sight.

"May we know your name, sir?" Arlen asked, and John saw Hester nod at her father.

"John Steiner." The innate good manners of his upbringing clicked in, and he thrust out his hand for a handshake. The male Mennonites seemed inordinately relieved to accept it. The old man gave him the traditional single pump as if priming a well, while the younger man wrapped both his hands around John's and murmured, "We are so thankful that you are safe."

"But apparently not without a cost. We have come to offer help," the ever-cheerful Arlen assured John, handing him the pamphlet. "I have the honor of serving as the local director of this relief agency. My daughter here holds a similar position with the Mennonite Central Committee, and the two agencies work together in times like these to bring assistance to people like you who have suffered loss."

Mennonite Disaster Service was imprinted in blue on a circular emblem that featured two people shaking hands and—of course—a cross. *Staying Safe after a Natural Disaster: Hints* was the title of the piece.

"Thanks, but I've been through stuff like this before. Not a hurricane of this magnitude, but smaller ones down here and tornadoes back. . ." He'd almost said *back home.* "A few years back," he amended and handed the pamphlet back to Arlen.

"Understood," Arlen replied. Undaunted, he folded the pamphlet in thirds and placed it in the ripped breast pocket of John's shirt. "You'll find this useful later, then. For now let's concentrate on your physical well-being. My daughter is a nurse. Why don't you sit a moment while she tends your wounds and Samuel and I have a look around?"

John wiped sweat from his forehead with the back of one hand and almost cried out at the shot of pain he felt with that simple motion. "Look, folks," he gasped. "It's really decent of you to want to help, but. . ." He looked up at the sky, gathering his thoughts, then felt the extraordinary heat and overwhelming humidity more oppressive than ever press in on him until it was difficult to breathe. He realized that he was on the verge of passing out. His wrist and bloodied arm were both throbbing. It was as if having finally accepted that he'd survived, he had no strength left with which to go on.

"You should sit," the woman said as she wrapped her fingers around his good arm and guided him to a spot shaded by a cypress that had survived the storm unscathed. She spoke to him as a nurse instructing a patient, and so he followed her direction. The younger man—Samuel, was it?—fanned John with his hat.

"Drink this." Hester-like-the-hurricane handed him a pint of bottled water after removing the bottle cap and tucking it in the pocket of her dress. "Slowly," she coached when he would have chugged it. While he drank, her father picked up John's Bible and handed it to Hester. She tucked it into her satchel. "I'll make sure you have it once we get you to safety," she assured him.

The older man had removed a two-way radio from his pocket. John could only hope that he was calling for backup in the form of a medical helicopter to get him to a doctor. He truly did not think he could make it to the boat they'd brought. Meanwhile, the younger man kept fanning, all the while looking around as if sizing up the ways he might be able to contribute to their mission. "Do you have battery-powered communication equipment, John?"

"I did," John replied as he drained the last of the water. He tossed the empty bottle onto a pile of rubble. After removing a first-aid kit from the cloth bag she wore bandoleer style across her chest, Hester retrieved the bottle, recapped it, and slid it into the bag. "It's all pretty much garbage," he said, glancing around at the devastation surrounding them.

"And yet there is no point in adding to it," she replied as she splashed alcohol over her hands before pulling on a pair of latex gloves and preparing to treat the open cut on his forearm.

John couldn't help it. He laughed. The Mennonites no doubt took his laughter for hysteria, but he really didn't care. "Have you folks taken a good hard look at this place? There is nothing left."

The two Mennonite men made a visual inspection of their surroundings. John had pretty much seen all he needed to in order to know he was done for, at least financially. "Look, folks, I appreciate your concern, but the Red Cross and FEMA will be getting here before too long. As you can see, there's not much you can do for me now." He waited for Hester to finish bandaging his arm and then stood up, forcing a steadiness he didn't feel into his legs as he stepped forward to extend a handshake of dismissal. "I'm fine. Really."

"Sit," Hester ordered. John was beginning to think that barking out orders was one of the woman's finer skills. "MDS works with FEMA as well as all the other agencies involved in cleaning up the mess that comes after a storm. Furthermore, my father has called for evacuation," she continued. "You need to see a doctor and get that wrist set. In the meantime. . ." She took out a length of cloth and tied it into a makeshift sling. "Let's keep this arm elevated."

John looked past her to what was left of his house and released a long, shuddering sigh.

"It looks dire, but sometimes it may not be as bad as it seems," Hester said, following his gaze. "Of course you'll need to wait for the assessment of the engineers, but overall, I would say you were blessed, John Steiner."

She had to be kidding, right? As of an hour ago, every element of his life boiled down to two eras—before the storm and after the storm. Before the storm there had been a house, a packinghouse, and half a dozen other outbuildings. The remains of most of the outbuildings now lay scattered across the property in no particular order. The interior of the main house that he had worked so hard to renovate before the storm had now collapsed in on itself like a house of cards. The packinghouse was missing an entire wall, not to mention its roof. And that didn't begin to address the devastation his garden and the citrus grove had suffered. Before the storm, those plantings had been the very foundation of his dream of living a self-sustaining life without the need to rely on the outside world. Before the storm, the citrus from his restored groves had been the root of his plan to raise extra funds when needed by reestablishing Tucker's original business. Before the storm, his life had been on track, and now it was a train wreck of disastrous proportions.

"I'm blessed? Do you. . ." he began, then closed his mouth. *I don't know where to begin to tell you the magnitude of stupidity contained in that statement,* he thought, gritting his teeth. These people were just trying to help, he reminded himself.

"Johnny Steiner!"

He was rarely happy to see Margery Barker. But at the moment anything that might interrupt the missionary zeal of these do-gooders was more than welcome. Besides, her chocolate chip cookies had given him unexpected comfort when the tin had floated by his position on the beam and he'd snagged it.

"We tried to warn you, but no," she bellowed, "stubborn as the day is long. That's you, mister." She expertly guided her boat through the murky but mostly calm waters of the bay.

She anchored the boat, then splashed her way ashore through knee-deep water before turning her attention to the Mennonite trio. "I see you found him, Arlen." She grinned at the older man.

"We did and God has blessed us all to have found him little the worse for wear," Arlen replied.

John rolled his eyes heavenward. He was lost. Of course, Margery had been with Hester the evening before. She was in cahoots with them. In fact, she'd probably sent them.

"Well, I see little Hester here has managed to tend your wounds, John," she commented as she wrapped one arm around Hester's waist.

John did not see the need to comment that *little* Hester was actually a good six inches taller than Margery was. Still, he could not help taking note of the change in the Mennonite woman when the older woman embraced her. She actually smiled. A smile that stretched all the way to her eyes. It was the most positive expression she'd managed since arriving on his property.

"Sarah would be so proud of you, sweetie." Margery turned to include John and both of the Mennonite men in her monologue. "Oh, many's the time that dear woman was the first person to come calling when help was needed." Then in a voice so soft that John thought someone new had joined the group, Margery murmured, "We grieved with you over her loss. No finer woman than your Sarah, Arlen."

"Thank you for that," Arlen replied.

"You know that I would have been at the funeral," Margery continued, "but I had charters, and it was the height of the season, and after last year's hard times. . ."

Arlen covered her weathered hand with his. "You were with us in spirit. We felt that."

Absolved of her guilt, Margery turned her attention back to John. "Hopefully you have learned your lesson and will pay attention to these people. They know what they're doing, and trust me, they're a sight more qualified to help you get back to renovating this place if that's still your mind-set than those dandies from DC are. By the time they tie you up in all that red tape they're so fond of, you won't know if you're coming or going."

John cast about for any possible way to turn her focus away from him. "How did you come out?"

She shrugged. "Four or five seriously damaged boats, but they're insured. Blew the roof off the bait shop." She shrugged. "Nothing that time and the right materials can't fix. Who are you again?" she asked, turning her attention to Samuel.

"Samuel Brubaker. I've just moved here from Pennsylvania."

"And what do you do, Samuel?"

"I make furniture with Pastor Detlef."

Margery glanced from Hester to Samuel and then back to Arlen. "Is he son-in-law material?" She winked, and Arlen laughed.

"Now, Margery, don't make trouble where there's none."

But John found himself considering the couple in this new light. Samuel was tall with large strong hands, and his short-sleeved shirt revealed the roped forearm muscles of a man used to hard work. He also sported the pasty skin of someone who had not been in Florida that long. Hester was not tanned exactly, but her cheeks were sprinkled with freckles, and she had the look of a woman who enjoyed the out-of-doors. She was also well past the age when most conservative Mennonite girls married and started families of their own. He found himself intrigued. She certainly had yet to demur to her father—or to young Samuel Brubaker, as most women of her faith would.

Actually, he couldn't help but feel a little sorry for both men. One thing about being of the Anabaptist faith that had always made a lot of sense to John was the idea that there was a clear division between women's work and men's work. He had thought the same was true among these Florida Mennonites, especially the more conservative ones. A woman's place was at home, not out running around taking charge of things as Hester Detlef seemed prone to do.

"Have you got someplace to stay tonight, Johnny?" Margery asked. "I'd have you stay on the houseboat with me, but it's listing badly, and. . ."

"You can both stay with us," Arlen interrupted. "It would be our honor."

Put that way it was going to be hard to refuse, but John was sure going to give it his best shot. "I appreciate that, but I'll just get a hotel room—"

Margery let out her characteristic howl of a laugh. "Did you get conked on the head while you were riding out this monster storm? There isn't a hotel or inn within miles that's got a room to spare—that's if they've got any rooms at all." She turned her attention to the older man. "Johnny is stubborn as they come, Arlen. He's got this bug about going through life alone—no help, no dependence on anyone but himself." She wheeled around to face John again. "Stop being so blasted mulish. Take the man up on his offer. You look like you've been run over by a truck, and that wrist is not going to set itself."

"I've called for medical evacuation," Arlen said.

John had trouble concealing his relief. A muttered "Thank you" was all he could manage.

Margery scanned the sky, and the others followed her lead. "There's the chopper," she shouted, waving wildly as she marched out into calf-deep water with Arlen following.

"Somebody please just shoot me now," John muttered.

"That would be against our traditions and yours," Hester said as she and Samuel helped him to his feet. "You are Amish, are you not?"

"How do you know I'm. . ."

She handed him his Bible, which he tucked into the sleeve of his sling. "Perhaps later you would like to speak with my father about the events that brought you here to Florida," she said, her expression one of pity. It made his stomach roil.

"I came here to live, to make a life for *myself,*" he replied tersely. "Now if you and your father. . ."

She scowled up at him. "You know something? Margery is right. It's time for you to stop giving orders and pay attention to those who only want to help you. In short, please do not cause any further trouble than you already have."

Chapter 5

When John stumbled and nearly fell on his way to the shore, Hester and Samuel were there, prepared to assist him into the helicopter's rescue basket once it was dropped. But he shrugged them off and stood his ground. Given his apparently minor injuries, Hester thought that he probably could have made the trip with them in the boat, but Grady had made it clear that they were to airlift him to the hospital. He had come very close to passing out, and if—as she suspected—he was dehydrated, the team on the helicopter would be better equipped to treat him.

As for him staying with her and her father, she was quite certain that John could not possibly be any more reluctant to return to Pinecraft with them than she was to have to cater to him while the real work of disaster relief was being handled by others. She knew these thoughts were unworthy of her. Why should it bother her one way or the other where he stayed? He was simply one more human being in need. Yet there was something about him that she found unsettling.

"I can walk," he growled when Samuel reached once again for his arm.

He shot her a warning look to keep her distance as well, and she realized that it was those eyes that unnerved her. Their sea-green depths seemed to question everyone and everything. No, he was not a man who would go along with them willingly. She sighed and indicated the route her father and Margery had already taken to the shore, knowing that the chopper could not land amid all the debris and John would need to be airlifted from the open water. Well, let him protest and find his way around her father. That would be quite something to see.

"Look, Pastor. . ." John had to shout to be heard above the beating of the chopper's blades.

"Arlen."

"Okay, here's the thing, Arlen. I'm not about to leave my property to looters and vandals."

Arlen surveyed the wreckage behind them. "I see your point," he said. Hester saw John's eyes widen in surprise and then narrow with suspicion.

"You do?"

"Ja," her father continued. "You are not a trusting man, are you, John? And without trust—whether in the Lord or our fellow man—we cannot see the full range of possibilities."

"I see them quite well," John protested. "I see the possibility that those clouds there on the horizon could develop into another storm or a tornado, and I have at best a few hours to secure whatever might be left of my property. I also see that even if there aren't more storms, there's open water leading straight to my property that could be most tempting to my fellow man living not half a mile away who may have lost everything and decided to rummage through this rubble to find. . ."

The chopper pilot had headed off to make another circle over the property, and in the sudden silence that followed, Arlen's question filled the void. "Do you not see the good, John?"

"The good?" John's mouth worked, but no other sound came out. Finally he shook his head and released a bark that might have been a laugh. "I'm afraid you've got me there, sir."

"Could this not be God's way of suggesting a change for you—a change in the way you live your life, the things you hold in esteem, the lives you touch?"

"Seems to me if God wanted to get my attention, He didn't need to send a hurricane to do it."

Hester heard Samuel suck in a shocked breath at such blasphemy, but her father only smiled.

"Perhaps the Lord has made many attempts, John. Could it be you weren't listening? It's a common fault among young people." He glanced at Hester, and she knew he was thinking of their conversation of the night before.

"I'm thirty-six years old, Arlen, hardly a teenager out to test my wings before I decide to join up."

Again Arlen smiled. "Ja, I had forgotten. You are one of us after all." Hester saw her father glance at John's bright yellow shirt smudged with filth and his cargo shorts ripped in several places. "Perhaps *die Kleidung*," he mused more to himself than to John. "You choose not to dress in the plain fashion of your ancestors?"

"I choose not to draw attention to myself. Look, Arlen, the point is. . ." John prepared to state his case as the chopper moved closer.

"The point is, John Steiner, you cannot stay here. At least not for tonight." Arlen removed his straw hat and fanned himself as he watched the helicopter make its final approach just as it started to rain again. "In a few days the Lord may see fit to bless us with a steady sun that will start to dry things out," he shouted. "In the meantime those clouds out there promise a full day of rain, and we must go and offer our help to others who are as devastated as you."

The chopper hovered, its blades whipping what trees were left in a weak imitation of the hurricane's gale-force winds, as the rescue basket emerged from its belly. Arlen strode back down the path they had taken over fallen trees and smashed shrubbery, waving to the pilot. Samuel fell into step behind him, but Hester waited to see what the Amish man would choose.

"Stubborn old. . ." John muttered under his breath as he watched her father navigate the debris as nimbly as someone half his age.

"He is a respected man of God," Hester said. "And whether you like it or not, John Steiner, he is right."

His answer was a feral growl as he gave up the fight. And when he headed for the beach—albeit by a different route—Hester found that she could not suppress her smile. She watched as Samuel and her father assisted him into the basket. Once he was safely on board the chopper, the pilot dropped the basket again.

"Go with him, Hester," her father shouted above the din. "Samuel and I will meet you at the hospital after we return the boat."

"Why me?" Hester shouted, but her father and Samuel were already on their way out to where Margery had climbed into her boat and pulled it closer to theirs.

<hr />

"How is he?" Grady asked later as he and Hester stood several yards away from where a Red Cross medic was applying a splint to John's wrist and forearm. He was being treated at the temporary quarters the agency had set up in back of her father's church. The doctor they'd seen at the hospital had sent them away, citing the need to attend to a host of people with far greater needs than a broken wrist.

Stubborn. Rude. Arrogant. Hester rejected the litany of adjectives that sprang to mind as she recalled the short flight to the hospital, where they had landed on the roof and been met by a harried-looking team of medics. "I believe he will survive," she said.

"He looks like he could spit nails," Grady observed.

"Like many *English*, he's taking the storm personally." Hester deliberately used the term commonly applied to those from outside the Amish or Mennonite community.

"But he's Amish."

Hester shrugged. "And yet he shows none of the acceptance of God's will that would be common to his faith. So what's in a name? You can contact your boss and let him know that Mr.

Steiner is fine. His property is probably a total loss, although I didn't tell him that, but he's alive." She gestured to the man now sporting a more traditional and substantial sling on his left arm as he stood and looked around. "He's all yours, Grady."

"I don't have time. . ." Grady sputtered.

Hester narrowed her eyes as she studied her friend. "And I do? We're swamped now, and Dad tells me there are at least three more church teams on their way here from surrounding areas. They'll be here by suppertime. I need to make sure they're fed and have a place to stay. There are the food boxes that must be delivered, Grady, and John Steiner—"

Grady grimaced. "Remains a priority."

"Why?" Hester could not disguise the childish petulance that flavored her response.

"It's politics," Grady replied with a long-suffering sigh. Hester knew that Grady was familiar with her lack of patience when it came to the political gamesmanship so common in his world. "Come on, Hester, help me out here. Put the guy to work on one of your teams just until I can get things fully organized at my end."

"He only has one good arm," Hester pointed out.

"So let him serve meals or hand out bottled water. That only takes one good arm."

As if he would agree to such menial labor, Hester thought. He was clearly a man used to being in charge, although she doubted very much that he inspired others to work for him. But then suddenly she thought of something Arlen had said to John: *"Perhaps you weren't listening."*

Was it possible that God had deliberately set this cantankerous man squarely in her path to test her while obstructing her ability to relieve the suffering of more deserving souls? Was it possible that John Steiner was some sort of challenge the Lord had placed before her? Perhaps to show her that He was in charge, not her? To test her willingness to take direction—God's direction—rather than go her own way as her father had noted earlier?

Certainly in all the time she had been volunteering with

MCC, this wasn't the first time she'd seen a person respond with anger and affront at loss or tragedy. Instead of accepting the outstretched hands of those who wanted to help, such people would push past their rescuers determined to go it alone. More often than not they would fail and only add to their loss and misery. With God's help they would sometimes return, emotional hat in hand so to speak, and ask for the help they had rejected in the first place. Hester studied John as he stood outside the Red Cross tent now with his legs widespread as if balancing on a ship's deck. He appeared to be surveying the activity around him. Everything about his posture commanded others to stay out of his way. But when she looked at his face, she saw uncertainty and just the slightest touch of defeat.

All right, Lord, I will see him through this, for now. I don't understand why You have chosen this path for me to follow, but follow it I will.

"Lend me your cell phone," she said, holding her hand out to Grady.

"Not great service," he warned. "Who are you calling?"

"Not me," Hester said as she started across the parking lot. "He should call his aunt and let her know he's alive."

⁓⁓≤

John felt disoriented. It wasn't just the pain medication the Red Cross medic had given him. It was as if he had stepped into a nightmare. The wreckage of his property haunted him, coming back to him in such vivid detail that it took his breath away. As the helicopter had turned north toward the hospital farther up the coast, John had sat speechless staring down at the surreal scene below. He'd spotted bits and pieces of his life cast away among the downed trees and crushed shrubs. In one stripped tree hung a shirt of his, whipped by the breeze until it resembled a flag. And was that his red metal toolbox half buried in the muck of the bay? The packinghouse was useless until he could get the wall and roof repaired, and his own home was equally uninhabitable.

The evacuation chopper had airlifted him to the hospital, where Hester had filled the emergency room personnel in on the situation. Arlen and Samuel had met them there after returning the boat to Margery's marina. But after examining him for injuries beyond a broken wrist and a variety of abrasions and bruises, the resident told Hester that with the more seriously injured people waiting to be treated—three who had suffered possible heart attacks—it would be hours before they could treat John. The doctor suggested that she would be better off to take him with her back to Pinecraft. The first-aid station there could splint his wrist and tend his other wounds. It did not escape his notice that the doctor spoke to Hester and her father, rather than to him.

By that point he'd been overcome by a wave of pure exhaustion, feeling every inch the refugee he'd become so that when his rescuers had led him from the ER to Arlen's car, he had not questioned their destination. He'd heard of Pinecraft, hard not to know something about the Amish/Mennonite haven that attracted tourists in droves in high season. But he had no interest in sightseeing. Instead, he slumped down in the backseat and stared out the window, vaguely aware of palm trees with their crown of fanlike foliage sheared off by the raging winds and water-covered streets through which Arlen navigated his thirty-year-old car. While they were in the emergency room, it had continued to rain, as Arlen had predicted. The usually jammed Highway 41 that cut right through downtown Sarasota was eerily deserted. Only a few cars and the occasional ambulance or patrol vehicle roamed the four-lane road.

Businesses were boarded up and closed. Parking lots were empty of cars and covered in water. Once they turned onto Bahia Vista, the surroundings changed from commercial to more residential, but the homes and condominium complexes were also shuttered and deserted. It was like driving through an abandoned city littered with huge palm fronds and downed power lines tangled in uprooted trees that had been partially pushed to the side of the road. Bits of broken asphalt tiles from roofs and other debris floated on the water that had overflowed from the clogged drains and gullies so that in places the streets were more like canals than roadways.

Then almost as soon as they crossed a main thoroughfare and entered the Pinecraft area, it was as if they had left the worst of the storm behind. The east/west street that bisected the community was filled with people and activity, while side streets bustled with bicycle and foot traffic. The scene had all the attributes of a church meeting, but John was well aware that it wasn't celebration that had brought these people out in force. It was the need to help and to care for others.

In the faces of those he passed, he saw worry and anxiety and concern for a neighbor who might have suffered. Through the rolled-down windows of Arlen's car, John heard a man call out to a neighbor inquiring about damage the second man had suffered from the gale force winds. At long tables on the covered walkway of a shopping mall, women in traditional Mennonite garb worked in unison filling heavy cardboard boxes with clothing, canned goods, and bottled water. As soon as a box was filled, a boy would load it onto a three-wheeled bicycle, and when the bike's rear basket was filled, the youth would pedal away toward another area where a fleet of small trucks and vans waited. At the same time another boy would pedal forward and hop off to help. Their industry was impressive. Their cheerfulness to be doing God's work and helping others was merely annoying.

Arlen had pulled his sedan into a parking lot near a building marked PALM BAY MENNONITE CHURCH, and Samuel escorted John to the first-aid tent set up by the Red Cross at one end of the lot. There he had turned him over to a jovial young medic who had cracked stupid jokes with a nearby nurse while attending to John's wrist. They'd given him some pain medication to get him through the next twenty-four hours plus a regulation sling to replace Hester's temporary fix. "You want to keep it elevated," the medic had instructed. Then he'd patted John on the shoulder and turned to address the next problem.

"Now what?" John said aloud to himself as he looked around

for some idea of how he might get back to his place.

"How are you feeling, *Herr* Steiner?"

John turned to find Hester standing next to him. She shielded herself from the steady drizzle with an umbrella, so it was hard to see her features. Still, he could not help but take note of the fact that she was tall enough to meet him nearly eye-to-eye. Memory told him those eyes were blue, although he had no idea why that detail had registered with him. Certainly with everything else he'd had to deal with, the color of a plain woman's eyes should be the least of his concerns. "I'll be fine," he muttered and turned his attention back to his surroundings as he tried to figure out his next move.

"I thought you might want to call your aunt in Washington." Hester lifted the umbrella higher to cover both of them and handed him a cell phone. "Or I could do it for you if you like. I mean, I appreciate that your people. . ."

"Look, let's get one thing straight. I am no longer Amish, okay?"

"You may have chosen to leave the community, Herr Steiner, but. . ."

"I did not *choose* anything, starting with being born into an Amish community. That was my mother's choice."

"And your father's," she said, clearly unruffled by his attitude. "I'll leave you to make your call, then." She crossed the street and slipped under the canopy that protected the tables where the other women were working.

"Hold on a minute." John hated asking anyone for anything, especially a woman, especially *this* woman.

She tilted the umbrella to one side and waited for him to catch up to her. But just before he reached her, he faltered and for one awful moment feared once again that he might pass out. "Let me get you something to drink," she said, steadying him by placing her arm around his shoulders and shielding him with the umbrella. "When was the last time you ate an actual meal?"

"Yesterday sometime. Maybe the day before," he admitted, trying to remember the meal. Supper, he thought. He recalled a plate of cheese and fruit. Last night. It seemed like forever ago.

"Come with me," Hester said and steered him across the shopping center's parking lot. A few yards away she pointed to an empty rocking chair in a row of similar Amish-made bentwood rockers that lined the porch of a restaurant touting HOMEMADE PIE on the large sign that was now listing to one side. "Sit. I'll be right back."

She handed him a bottle of water and went inside the restaurant. John guzzled and once it was gone wished he had more. His hand started to shake uncontrollably, and he felt suddenly light-headed.

"Here."

She was back and handing him a paper plate stacked with bread, slices of sandwich meat, cheese, a banana, and chips. "Start with the banana," she urged, even as John crammed chips into his mouth. She pulled a bottled sports drink from the ever-present cloth satchel. "Drink this. You need the potassium, and I expect your system needs some electrolytes as well."

"Arlen mentioned that you're a nurse. What kind?"

"A trained one," she snapped, then seemed to mentally count to ten, softened her voice, and added, "Although there are some things you just pick up along the way." She handed him the sports drink, then sank down in the chair next to him. "As soon as you've eaten, if you could make that call. . . I need to return the phone."

"To?"

She nodded toward a man in a T-shirt and jeans and a battered Boston Red Sox baseball cap. "That's Grady Forrest. He's with the county and pretty much the main man throughout the entire region when stuff like this happens."

"Stuff like this being a mere category-four hurricane?"

"Amazingly, it didn't quite hit a four—made a good effort though." She pushed the rocker into motion with one foot.

"Felt like it when I was clinging to that cypress beam." He took a swallow of the sports drink. He couldn't help noticing that her canvas shoes were still soaked and caked with mud.

"Which allows me to politely raise the obvious question," she said softly.

He arched an eyebrow and waited.

"Why were you clinging to a beam that might just as easily have crushed you as saved your life? Why didn't you leave when you were warned—repeatedly, from what Margery told me—to do so?"

John shrugged. "I don't like other people deciding what I should and should not do." He noticed that she had stopped rocking and was gripping the arms of the chair.

"You know something?" She got to her feet and glared down at him.

"What?"

She bit her lower lip and shook her head as if shaking off whatever it was that she'd been about to say. "I'd appreciate it if you could return the phone to Grady as soon as possible. I have to go." She looked both ways, checking for traffic on the street, which was congested with people and bicycles, and then headed left.

"Hey," he called.

She stopped walking but did not come back. He wondered if she had any idea what it was costing him to be dependent on her, a woman.

"When can I go back to my place?"

"Check with Grady," she called, and then she was gone, lost among the hordes of women similarly dressed in plain cotton dresses, their heads now covered by umbrellas or hoods extinguishing the telltale prayer coverings.

~~≷~~

Hester knew the answer to John's question. It would likely be days, if not weeks, before he could return to his property for good. For certain that first look-and-leave visit would be in the company of some trained disaster volunteers who would help him retrieve whatever could be safely taken before bringing him back into town. Although her father had invited John to stay with them, she couldn't help hoping that Grady would find him a place at one of the three shelters that had been set up in the area.

"Surely Dad will understand that we have a lot of work to do and a lot of volunteers depending on us for guidance," she muttered aloud as she made her way toward the church. "John Steiner will be perfectly fine at the shelter. In fact, a night spent sleeping on an old cot might be just what he needs."

"Are you talking to yourself or to God, Hester?" Samuel asked as he fell into step beside her and offered her the shared shelter of a rain slicker he'd picked up somewhere. She'd left John her umbrella, surely a sign that she made no distinction between caring for him and caring for anyone else who might need protection from the elements.

"Myself," she admitted. She was glad of Samuel's company. He was a gifted craftsman and certainly a nice-looking and gentle man. Hester had little doubt that he would make a fine partner to spend the rest of her life with. He was mild-mannered enough that he might not even insist that she abandon her volunteer work in order to devote herself exclusively to keeping house and raising a family. But Hester wanted more from a marriage than a fine partnership. She had always fought against wanting more. It was her greatest failing, that longing for something beyond the norm. She loved her work with MCC, and it was that very idea of being expected to focus on her own household and raising a family to the exclusion of anything else that terrified her. Hester was well aware that her father had been pleased by her agreement to volunteer rather than seek a paid position in a hospital. But he'd made no bones about his preference that after her mother died, Hester should transfer her loyalties to the more conservative Christian Aid Ministries where Emma was the local leader. But neither Hester nor her mother believed that God distinguished between the work she did with MCC and the work that Emma did with CAM. Her mother had not only supported her decision to work with MCC but also encouraged it.

Then Sarah's illness had worsened. The end had not come quickly, and the suffering her mother had bravely endured had inspired Hester as she sat with her day after week after month. Hester's guilt that perhaps her mother's suffering was somehow her punishment for not more closely following the traditions of her faith had been staggering. And even in her pain, Sarah Detlef had seen that. In spite of her loss of physical capacity, Sarah had found a way to communicate to her daughter that she had made the right choice in going for her degree and that she was very proud of her for her decision to come home to Pinecraft to serve others.

After Sarah died, Hester had convinced herself that her volunteer work with MCC was her way of honoring her mother's memory and Sarah's own deep dedication to service. The greater truth was that she enjoyed the diversity and demands of the work involved in the variety of projects for which she could volunteer within the committee. Already she had traveled to Central America to help rebuild communities that had suffered the effects of a rebel uprising that had left thousands huddled in makeshift camps. She looked forward to more opportunities to serve overseas. Yes, this was her calling, and John Steiner was only an obstacle, testing her determination to stay on course and help those truly in need.

"Hester?"

She had been so lost in thought and there were such crowds of people about that she had nearly forgotten Samuel was walking alongside her.

"Yes, Samuel?" She did not miss the way he glanced at her and then immediately looked down at his work boots, soaked now and heavy with mud. There had been many times since his arrival that Samuel had made awkward attempts at engaging her in conversation that she assumed was his way of trying to bring them closer.

"I was thinking about John Steiner's place."

Oh, the sin of pride, Hester Detlef. She had expected Samuel's comment to be something more personal. Perhaps an expression of his concern for her working so hard and not eating properly. He was that kind of man, always thinking of others—in this case a complete stranger. "What about it?" she asked.

"Perhaps it's not nearly as bad as it appeared at first glance," he said, his words coming in a rush. "If we could salvage the first level of the house, then Herr Steiner could move back there in a matter of days."

"And just how would you accomplish that?"

"Arlen mentioned a volunteer crew that is expected to arrive later today from Georgia, experienced builders and even a plumber and electrician. If Grady agrees, I could go with that crew and an engineer from the county to assess Herr Steiner's property."

"And you would do this because. . . ?"

Samuel smiled. "Because I overheard you and Grady talking, and, well, if helping him helps you and Grady attend to those who may be in more dire straits, then why not?"

Hester stared at him as if truly seeing him for the first time. "You are a gut man, Samuel."

"Ja, I am," he replied without the slightest trace of arrogance.

"I appreciate your thoughtfulness, but as each volunteer crew arrives, they must first go where the need is greatest. It's only fair. Herr Steiner will be fine."

Samuel's smile widened. "Nein. Herr Steiner would disagree." He pointed to where the man himself was berating poor Grady.

Hester couldn't help it. In spite of the chaos all around her, she started to laugh. "I would say in addition to being a good man, Samuel Brubaker, you are an excellent judge of character."

"Ja, Ich *bin*," Samuel replied, and he looked at her so intently that Hester stopped in her tracks and gave him her full attention. "I am also well aware that others have their ideas of why your father brought me into his business, Hester, and I know that those are not necessarily ideas that you agree with. But perhaps in time. . ."

He smiled at her, then left the thought hanging as he walked away. Hester watched him go, wondering if she had misjudged him. It had never occurred to her that Samuel might have his own doubts about a future for the two of them. The thought gave her an unexpected sense of relief.

"You should perhaps go," Samuel called out over his shoulder. "Your friend Grady might need your help."

But Arlen was already there ahead of her. Seemingly from out of nowhere he appeared, stepped between Grady and John, and murmured a few quiet words that had the potential combatants eyeing each other warily and then shaking hands. Hester saw her father beam with his usual delight; then he took hold of John's good arm and started across the parking lot, taking shelter under Hester's umbrella. Little good it did either of them as the wind had started to pick up again and the rain seemed to come at them sideways.

"Ah, Hester," Arlen called out when he spotted his daughter. His hand remained on John's elbow. "Our friend here has had quite an ordeal. Show him the way to our house so that he may shower and rest."

"I really need to. . ."

Her father's impressive white eyebrows shot up, and his blue eyes narrowed as he handed her the umbrella. Hester knew that look, and she knew it was useless to defy it. "But that can wait," she amended. Her father's gaze softened with approval. "Come along, Herr Steiner. It isn't far."

Chapter 6

In spite of her polite smile, everything about Hester Detlef told John that she would prefer to be anywhere other than escorting him down the lane bordered on either side by what just a day earlier had to have been pristine white cottages set in well-maintained yards. Now the streets and yards were pocked with pools of muddy water and littered with debris. Every house had some degree of damage from the storm.

She stepped around a neatly stacked pile of flattened picket fencing and into a yard that held the remnants of what must have been a lush tropical garden. She bent and rescued an orchid plant and carefully hung it back in the sheltering branches of a tree.

"I thought I had gotten them all," she murmured more to herself than to him, and seeing that Hester and her father had suffered their own losses, John turned his attention to her.

"It was obviously a lovely garden," he said as he followed her, taking care not to step on any other plant that might have survived.

"Danke." She led the way up a shell-lined path through an obstacle course of puddles to a front porch that stretched across the width of the cottage. "Normally when a storm's on the way, we move the orchids inside. I must have missed that one."

"Are you the gardener?" He was determined to somehow make a dent in that prim facade that she wore like armor.

"My father and I take our turn," she replied.

He couldn't help but notice that she simply turned the knob of the front door. The house was not locked. If they were on a farm in Indiana, he might not think anything of it. But Pinecraft was located right on the borders of Sarasota, a growing and changing city with its fair share of petty crime. More than once he'd had to chase would-be vandals from his property.

She slipped off her shoes and stood aside to allow him to enter. The foyer, if one could call it that, was made darker by the absence of sunlight from outside. He took a minute to get his bearings. A cozy living room to his left furnished with a plain but comfortable-looking sofa and two upholstered chairs. Rag rugs brightened the polished hardwood floors. Next to one chair—hers he assumed—was a basket of sewing. A side table next to the other chair was loaded with books and papers. Both chairs faced the fireplace.

Across the hall was a small room that must be Arlen's study. An old-fashioned wooden desk took up most of the space. John caught a glimpse of a small television set and a telephone on a side table next to a leather recliner. He noticed a hallway that he assumed led to the bedrooms and a shorter hallway leading straight back from the front door, where he was certain that he would find the kitchen. He turned his attention back to the living room, where one wall was lined with bookcases, every shelf crammed with volumes of every size and description. He felt immediately at home. His mother had loved books.

"If you'll wait here," Hester said, starting down the hall toward the bedrooms, "I'll make up your bed and put out fresh towels for you. You can use my brothers' room, and Margery will stay with me."

"You have a brother?"

"Four of them. All married with families of their own and living in Ohio now. We see them often; they come here or we go there. They have a better opportunity to build a good life for their families there. Work is limited here. Of course it's not the same as being all together, but we make it work." She paused briefly to deliver this bit of information.

"Let me help you," he said, starting down the hall after her.

She stopped so suddenly that he almost ran into her. When she turned, her cheeks were flushed, and she seemed to focus on some point just past his left shoulder.

"Or not," he said, retreating back toward the foyer. "I'll just. . ." He glanced around for a place to sit. "I'll just wait here," he said, indicating the living room.

She nodded once and continued on her way.

As John scanned the titles that lined the bookshelves, he could hear her moving around, making the necessary preparations for hosting overnight guests. A dresser drawer was opened and then closed. He heard the snap of fresh sheets as she made up the bed. He heard her move across the hall, where she opened a closet or cabinet for some new purpose. She poured water from one container to another. His mind followed the sounds of her actions as surely as if he had followed her all the way down that hall.

He'd been in the *English* world for far too long, he realized. He should have known that even for a woman who seemed as sophisticated and streetwise as Hester Detlef, she was clearly dedicated to the conservative ways of her faith. The idea that she might find herself alone in any bedroom with a man she barely knew was unthinkable. He pulled a thin volume from a shelf and absently read the title without really seeing it, all the while wondering if he should apologize or just let the matter drop.

"My mother wrote poetry." She pointed to the book he was holding.

As attuned as he'd been to her movements, he had failed to notice that she had finished her work and come back to the living room. He ran his fingers over the cloth cover of the book, trying to decide if opening it would be an invasion of privacy.

"The garden was hers," she added, inclining her head toward the front door. "My father and I try to keep it in order to honor her memory."

He recalled Margery offering her sympathies to Arlen earlier and nodded. "May I?" John asked, indicating the book of poetry.

"Yes." She waited while he opened the book to a page about a third of the way through. He scanned the contents and could not disguise his surprise. "She was quite. . ."

"She was a plain woman," Hester interrupted, and he knew that she was reminding him that in her world as in his, compliments were unnecessary and unwanted. "She recorded her observations of God's handiwork as a way of showing her appreciation and gratitude."

John nodded and replaced the book on the shelf. "She died recently?"

"Yes."

"I'm sorry for your loss."

She accepted his condolences without comment and turned her attention back to the business at hand. "I left towels for you in the bathroom. Your room is the second one to your left. There are dry clothes in the closet and bureau. You're thinner and taller than my brothers, but the clothing there should do for now." She delivered these bits of information as if she were reading from a prepared list as she edged toward the open front door. "I should go and find Margery and see that she gets some rest as well. My father would want you to make yourself at home, so please refresh yourself, and, of course, if you are hungry or thirsty. . ." She waved her hand in the general direction of the kitchen.

She was halfway out the door and clearly anxious to be rid of him when he called out to her. "I still need to know when I might be able to return home."

She stood on the path and made no move to return to the shelter of the porch away from the steady drizzle. "That depends."

"On?"

She let out a soft sigh that he surmised was about as close to an expression of exasperation as she was likely to display. "Many things, Herr Steiner. Surely you're aware. . ."

He felt more certain than ever that it was important to get on this woman's good side. He gave her his most engaging smile.

"Could we make that *John*? Calling me Herr Steiner makes me want to turn around and look for my late father."

"Your father died?"

"When I was thirteen, farming accident."

"And your mother?"

"Couple of years ago." He took a step closer. "It seems we have that in common, the loss of our mothers."

"Yes. Please accept my condolences. Both parents gone." She shook her head. "That must be especially difficult."

"Thank you, Hester—like the hurricane."

She stared at him for a long moment. "I don't mean to be rude, Herr. . .*John*, but I have responsibilities that go beyond. . ." He guessed that she had come very close to saying something like *babysitting you*. But she caught herself, took a deep breath, and said, "The short answer to your question about returning to your home is that it will surely not be today."

She was backing her way toward the missing picket fence, but he was determined to make his point. "I am going back, Hester. I'll stay the night here, but. . ."

"I understand that you are anxious to return to your property, John. What you need to understand is that going back is not the same as going home to stay. Once you accept that, then the day you can return may come sooner than you think."

"Meaning?"

"It's possible that Samuel Brubaker along with an engineer from the county and a crew of MDS volunteers could make a visit to your property as soon as tomorrow to assess the damage and give you a better idea of when you might—"

"MDS?"

"Mennonite Disaster Service." She pointed toward his shirt pocket, where the pamphlet her father had given him lay damp and limp.

"Yeah, well, understand this—nobody's going to my place without me, Hester."

She had taken two determined steps back toward him when a red-haired woman about Hester's age but not in plain dress came rushing down the street. "Hester! Zeke's gone missing."

~⁓≋

Jeannie Messner was Emma Keller's younger sister. Hester had known her since the three of them had played hopscotch and jacks together in Pinecraft Park as kids. Emma and Hester were the same age, but Jeannine—better known as Jeannie—had always tagged along. Emma and her family still lived in the same house where the sisters had grown up just across from the park. But Jeannie, ever the rebel, had left the Palm Bay church that her family preferred after marrying a man from the more liberal congregation. Her husband, Geoff, worked as the athletic director at the Christian school, and Jeannie had taken a job as the activities director at a local senior center. Generally she was a happy-go-lucky sprite with her curly red hair that framed a heart-shaped face featuring an impish smile. But Jeannie was not smiling now. Her brow was deeply furrowed with worry, and her lips were pencil thin and pale.

"Jeannie, calm down and tell me what's happened." Hester led her friend to the shelter of the porch, her heart hammering with this fresh evidence that while she had been tending to John Steiner, people with real problems were being neglected.

"It's Zeke. He's missing."

"Who's Zeke?" John asked with a hint of irritation.

"Zeke Shepherd. He lives on the beach down near the bridge," Jeannie explained. It was a clear measure of her distress that she showed not the slightest curiosity about who John was or why he was standing on Hester's front porch.

John's eyebrows lifted slightly as he focused his attention on Hester, waiting, she assumed, for her to dispense with this interruption and get back to the subject of his property.

"He's homeless," Hester added, hoping to elicit a drop of sympathy from the man. "He camps on a seawall concealed by several mangrove and sea grape trees along the bay downtown." She motioned toward the porch swing, but Jeannie shook her head and kept pacing. "Surely when the storm hit. . ."

"He left," Jeannie finished her sentence. "But he went back. He'd left his guitar there, and. . ." Her huge hazel eyes filled with tears. "No one has seen him since," she whispered.

Hester wrapped her arm around the smaller woman. "Now you know Zeke. He probably found some place to ride out the storm."

"Geoff and I have already checked every place he usually hangs out," Jeannie protested. "What if he got washed away? The surge that came with the back side of the storm was enormous, and the wind. . ." She shuddered. "I just. . .I pray he's all right, and I know you can't spare anyone to join a search party. But could you make sure all the volunteers know to keep an eye out for him?"

"I. . ." Hester understood that for Jeannie, Zeke would always be the brother she never had. *We made special arrangements for John Steiner,* she thought and smiled at Jeannie. "Sure. I'll tell them to be on the lookout. And you should talk to Grady so he can spread the word, okay?"

"Thank you." Jeannie sucked in air and glanced at John as if seeing him for the first time. "Hello," she said, her usual smile restored. She thrust out her hand. "I'm Jeannie Messner, and you are?"

"John Steiner," he replied, accepting her handshake.

"Herr Steiner has suffered the loss of his home. His property was destroyed—with him inside—and as you can see, Jeannie, he's fine. Well, not fine but certainly well enough," she stammered as she considered John's arm and the many cuts and bruises evident on his face and hands.

"Your friend probably just found higher ground until the hurricane passed," John said. "He'll turn up eventually." Hester couldn't help noticing that his words seemed to carry more weight in consoling Jeannie than hers had.

"You're staying with Hester?" Jeannie gave Hester a curious look.

"He's staying with my father, as is Margery Barker. I'll be working, and by tomorrow morning we'll all be packing up to

75

move to a shelter in case the creek floods," Hester said firmly. She stopped short of physically steering her friend down the lane.

"Nice meeting you," Jeannie called as she waved at John.

"Well," Hester said, turning her attention back to John, "do you have everything you need, John? If so, I'll just. . ."

"What's the connection?" he asked, returning Jeannie's wave halfheartedly.

"Jeannie and her sister and I have been friends since childhood, and—"

"I mean with the homeless guy."

"Zeke? He and Jeannie have been friends for years. Zeke introduced her to her husband, Geoff. Then Zeke enlisted, and, well, after he returned from overseas, things weren't the same for him. He fell on hard times and started living on the beach. Jeannie is a social worker at heart. She and Geoff have tried everything to get Zeke to accept help from his family, but he refuses."

"Zeke's not Amish or Mennonite, then?"

"No."

"Maybe she ought to leave him alone," John muttered.

"That's not in our nature," Hester replied. "Now, then, I really must be going. My father should be back in an hour or so."

"And my place?"

The man was like a dog with a bone.

She surveyed her mother's destroyed garden, giving herself a moment to gather strength. Then she took a long, steadying breath and raised her face to look directly at him. "Your property is not in imminent danger. Likewise, you are safe. You have shelter, food, and water. You even have dry clothing available. Do I really need to remind you that there are hundreds—perhaps thousands—of others who are not nearly so blessed?" She closed her eyes again and murmured, "Sorry." Whether John heard this last as directed at him or some higher being she could not have said. She really didn't care. She knew that it was a prayer, not an apology.

"And what I need for you to understand is this. That property is my life. If I lose it, then I have lost everything."

"And still God saw fit to let you walk away from the devastation of your property," she reminded him softly. "Perhaps my father was right. Perhaps you are supposed to start over, take a different path."

"I don't need sermons, Miss Detlef," he growled. It started to rain harder, and the heat and humidity seemed as tangible as the rain.

"Look," she said, forcing a bedside manner that she didn't feel.

"You look," he snapped. "Just don't even think of going out there without me."

"Believe me, *John*, nothing would make me happier than to get you back to tending your business so that I can tend to mine. I suggest you take advantage of the blessings before you," she continued. "The water is still off, but I left you fresh water in the basin so you can wash yourself, put on dry clothing, and get some rest." And with that she walked away from him, her spine rigid, her shoulders back, and her stride determined.

Chapter 7

Hester could practically feel John glaring at her retreating back. Well, they were even, because he definitely tried her patience, too. Still, she was not going to give in to the temptation to tell him what she really thought of his selfishness and arrogance. Let her father deal with him. There were people who needed her far more than John did, people who might actually appreciate what she could offer them in the way of comfort and assistance without asking for, no, without demanding more.

She spotted Jeannie pouring out her tale of Zeke's disappearance to Grady when she returned to the center. He listened intently and then patted Jeannie's shoulder, obviously assuring her that since Zeke was well known and liked, everyone would be looking for him. Hester knew that all Jeannie really needed was some guarantee that Zeke would be on their radar screen as they carried out the rescue efforts. Jeannie gave Grady a brilliant smile and then hurried off, calling out to Emma and then no doubt repeating her story to her sister. Hester couldn't help wondering if Jeannie's charm could soothe the ruffled feathers of John Steiner.

John Steiner is well taken care of, she silently reminded herself. *Surely now I can concentrate on the work I have been led to do.*

"Grady," she called out as he climbed into his Jeep and prepared to drive away.

Perhaps if she got Grady thinking about sending the team where they could do the most good, then by the time Samuel spoke to him, it would be too late to reassign them to the old Tucker place. *Now that just seems vindictive,* she chided herself. What was it about this man that brought out the worst in her?

Besides, if John's place hadn't even been cleared by search and rescue yet or by the gas and power crews and there were all those downed power lines on the main road leading past his place, an MDS crew could hardly go there. "Samuel tells me we can expect a crew from Georgia by suppertime."

"I know. I'm asking them to go check out Tucker Point." Grady drummed his fingertips on the steering wheel. Hester's heart sank.

"Surely. . ." she began, but Grady just shook his head and turned the key to start the engine. "Look, Hester, I have to go. Believe me, I know there are more urgent needs, and I have tried hard to make that clear, but you know how this works."

Actually, she didn't, because in her world attending to those most in need took precedence over political considerations. On the one hand she felt sorry for Grady, because he was a good man and he truly wanted to do the right thing. But on the other, it made her so angry that some bureaucrat in Washington who had no idea of the situation could make decisions for them. She forced a smile. "Politics," she murmured.

"You got that right," Grady replied, and he finally looked directly at her. "I'm really sorry, Hester. But if we get the Steiner thing assessed once and for all, then we can focus on the real need."

"All right, I see your point. And you're only talking about a small crew, right? Just to assess the damage and report back?"

"That's the plan."

"Well then, I suppose there are enough volunteers to focus on the real need *and* address Mr. Steiner's problems."

"That's my girl," Grady said. "Thanks."

"For?"

Grady grinned. "Relieving me of my guilt." Then he sobered. "We've got a long road ahead of us, Hester."

Hester nodded. They both knew that making it through a hurricane without massive physical injuries or deaths was only the first tiny step in the process of truly surviving such a disaster. At the moment everyone was driven by adrenaline and the sheer will to be sure people were accounted for, fed, and had shelter. The news would bring enough shock and awe with it that the media and help from around the country would arrive in droves, at least during those first couple of weeks. After that the residents would face the true test of survival—finding ways to keep going weeks and months from now after the media had turned their cameras to some other story and the relief money had dried up to a mere trickle. By then most of the volunteers would have gone home because they had families and jobs that needed their attention, leaving half-rebuilt homes and businesses under a sea of blue plastic tarps and the residents of the area to make it on their own.

She scanned the sky. The rain had fallen steadily all night and through the morning. Was it her imagination that it was getting worse?

"Wind's picking up," she noted. "Maybe we need to step up the timeline for getting folks moved away from the creek here." The weather reports had predicted steady rain for the foreseeable future, but there had been no mention of the rising winds. Anyone who had lived on the coast for any length of time knew that rain accompanied by high winds would push the already-deluged Philippi Creek over its banks even this far inland.

Grady nodded. "My best info tells me that we've still got at least until noon tomorrow. In the meantime there are other more pressing needs. For starters, we're going to need more cots, blankets, and food at all three shelters. They're already nearly full, and we need to stretch their capacity to handle the overflow." He must have taken note of Hester's expression of doubt. "Hey, if you and Emma can have your people alert everyone to get ready to move tomorrow, that should be time enough to get everyone to a shelter."

"Got it covered." Hester paused as she and Grady watched a large eighteen-wheeler navigate the turn on its way to the donation center run by MCC. "That'll be another load of supplies from national," Hester said. "See you later?"

"I'll be back tomorrow, got to check on some reports of tornado damage further east." Grady shifted the vehicle into reverse and let it roll backward before making the turn out of the parking space. "With any luck at all I'll be able to sleep in my own bed tonight."

"Give my best to Amy," Hester called.

It was after midnight before Hester could be convinced to go home and get some rest. Throughout the long day and well into the night she had been on her feet, sorting through the massive volume of canned goods, bedding, clothing, and other supplies sent from national MCC headquarters in Pennsylvania as she organized everything for distribution to the shelters. She took a break around supper time to meet with her father and Emma and other volunteer leaders in Pinecraft. After that she had insisted that her father go home and get some rest. Once he agreed, she had put in another six hours working in the kitchen of one of the local restaurants that had offered their facility for volunteers to cook and box up meals. She was bone-weary, but her spirits were high. They always were after such a day, a day when people came together to do God's work.

As she walked down the lane, a light glowed in the front window of the small white house where Hester had lived all her life. She smiled. Her father always left a light on for her. He would have retired hours ago—both her parents had always been of the "early to bed and early to rise" persuasion. She opened the front door and was momentarily confused when she heard the low murmur of voices. Then she saw her father sitting at the kitchen table.

"Ah, here she is now," he said, pushing himself away from the table and coming to the doorway.

"Dad? It's so late."

"Is it? We got talking and I suppose we lost track of the hour. Did you eat?"

She nodded just as Margery Barker eased past Arlen and yawned audibly. "Way past my bedtime," she said as she started down the hall toward the room she and Hester would share. "Don't worry about disturbing me when you come to bed, Hester. I'll be asleep before my head touches the pillow. I expect nothing will wake me for the next eight hours."

Hester saw John rinsing out his cup at the kitchen sink before coming to stand next to her father. He was dressed in one of the outfits that her brothers kept in the house for their annual visits, his straight red-gold hair freshly washed. "You look plain," she blurted without thinking.

Margery laughed. "I told him the same thing. But why shouldn't he? After all, our friend here was raised Amish."

"Ja. So he was." Hester half expected John to protest the label, but he said nothing.

"John is most anxious to return to his place," Arlen reported as if this were news to any of them. "Margery told him that it would be unwise to return so soon. I agreed, but he's determined. Maybe you can talk some sense into him."

"Actually, Grady is planning to send a crew there tomorrow." Still addressing her comments to her father and avoiding any eye contact with John, she delivered the news of the volunteer team from Georgia that had gotten delayed and had finally arrived just before she'd left for home. "He'll take care of it, assuming there are no other more pressing emergencies."

"Really? One of our RV teams."

Hester nodded. She was glad to see doubt cloud her father's eyes. Apparently she wasn't the only one troubled by this preferential treatment.

"What exactly is this RV team?" John asked.

This time she met his gaze directly. "In circumstances like these where there has been devastation following a hurricane or tornado, or other natural disasters, members of our fellow churches throughout the region and up into the Midwest mobilize teams of volunteers to come and help. They drive their recreational vehicles—RVs—to the site so there's no need for

MCC or MDS to lose valuable time seeking appropriate housing for them. They bring their own tools and supply of food so that they can go right where there's the most need, park their vehicles, and get to work."

"Sounds like a barn-raising," John murmured.

"Yes. I suppose that would be an appropriate analogy."

"And Grady has assigned this first team to John's place?" Arlen asked.

"To assess the damage," she stressed. "Apparently John has friends in the government who are determined to look out for him."

"I didn't ask them to," John protested.

"Still, Grady's under a lot of pressure, and even though most would agree that our mission is to serve where the demand is greatest, apparently he who makes the most fuss. . ." Her father placed his hand on her arm, a warning to calm herself. In the silence that followed, she covered her embarrassment by setting the cloth satchel down near the front door. It would be the last thing she grabbed as she headed out at dawn.

"Well, good night, all," Margery said quietly, breaking the uncomfortable silence as she stepped into the bathroom and closed the door.

"You look exhausted, Hester." Her father stroked her cheek. "Come have a glass of milk."

"It's been a long day," she admitted. "I'll just have a little something to eat and then get some sleep." They could all hear Margery moving into the bedroom and settling in for the night.

"How about you, John? Will you join us for a late snack?"

"Thank you, no. I'll say good night as well." He took two steps toward his room and paused. "I do appreciate everything you've both done for me today."

"It's our pleasure to be of service," Arlen assured him, but Hester seemed incapable of finding a single shred of graciousness to offer the man. She bowed her head, entreating God to give her more patience.

"Sleep well," she finally managed as she squeezed past her father and headed for the kitchen.

"And you," she heard John murmur, but neither of them looked at the other.

~⟫⟫⟫⟫

When John woke the following morning, sunlight streamed through the open window. The rain had stopped for the time being, but it was going to be another steamy day. He reached for the sling he'd abandoned during the night and nearly cried out with the pain that shot through his body from head to foot. Overnight his muscles had stiffened significantly, and minor movements that most people took for granted were suddenly monumental. Slowly he lifted the covers and stretched out his legs, then swung them over the side of the bed, resting his bare feet on a small cotton rug on the wooden floor between the two sets of bunk beds.

He sat for a minute, sorting out the hum of activity. It didn't take long to grasp the fact that all sounds came from outside the window. The rooms next to and across the hall from his were silent. Cradling his broken wrist, he pushed himself off the bed and padded barefoot to the window. In the yard that backed up to Arlen's property, a woman was clearing away fallen palm fronds and other debris while several small children played nearby. He couldn't help but notice that the cleanup had already been taken care of in the Detlefs' yard. Hester? Arlen? They must have been up well before dawn to accomplish that particular chore. When he'd looked out the kitchen window the evening before, the yard had been littered with debris, except for the front garden. He recalled the neatly stacked sections of picket fence and the way the space had been raked and set to rights in spite of the obvious loss of most of the plantings.

John checked the old-fashioned wind-up clock on the dresser. *Seven thirty.* A jolt of panic rushed through him. He knew the routine. Amish or Mennonite—they were up with first light and by seven thirty had already put in what for some people would be considered a full day's work. So the others had left without him. He headed for the bathroom and awkwardly splashed water onto his face with his one good hand. He didn't miss the fact that the washbasin had been filled with fresh water or that the towels he'd used the day before had been replaced with clean ones. *If she thinks she's going to get around me by letting me sleep in while she and the county guy decide the fate of my place,* he thought, *she doesn't know John Steiner.*

On the bathroom counter he noticed an unopened toothbrush and a partially used tube of toothpaste. He scrubbed his teeth with all the vigor of his irritation at the woman and then limped back to the bedroom to dress.

His regular clothes were missing from the hook where he'd hung them to dry the day before. Meanwhile, neatly folded over the back of the room's single chair were the clothes he'd left when he went to bed—Hester's brother's plain clothes. He dressed quickly as his mind raced with alternatives he might put into action to get him out to Tucker's Point. There was always Margery, though there was no sign of her. When he started down the hallway, he noticed that the doors to both Hester's room as well as Arlen's were open and the beds were made.

"Hello?" he called out as he rounded the corner and headed for the kitchen. A single place was set with a foil-covered plate at the small table, and near the stove sat a thermos that, when he opened it, released the aroma of hot coffee. On the counter next to the cookstove were half a dozen shoofly pies still warm from the oven, their crumb crusts glistening with sugar. And spread over a clothes rack were his still-damp but freshly washed shirt and shorts.

There was also a note taped to the kitchen table. He ripped it free and moved to the open back door for better light.

We hope you rested well. Please enjoy your breakfast. The juice and milk are in the refrigerator. Blessedly the generator continues to function. I will be at the church, and my daughter is helping her grandmother and others move to a shelter before the creek overflows. To reach my mother's house, go to the end of the lane, then left and three lanes over. I'm sure they would be happy to have your help.

Blessings on you, John Steiner, and may you have a good day.

P.S. Please close the doors as you leave; no need to lock up.

John's instinct was to find Hester as quickly as possible. He didn't want to take a chance on missing her, but the smell of the coffee combined with something cinnamon hiding beneath that foil-covered plate made his stomach growl. He supposed he should eat. After all, who knew when he might have his next meal? Surely he would be able to catch up with her at her grandmother's house.

He poured himself a cup of coffee and took his first bite of the cinnamon concoction that clung to his fingers. The woman was multitalented—John would give her that. The minute he uncovered the pan and released the aroma of the cinnamon roll plus eggs scrambled with fried potatoes, onions, and sausages, he knew that Hester Detlef was a first-class cook. He imagined the pies cooling on the counter would be equally impressive and had to stop himself from cutting into one even after he had downed the feast she'd left for him.

Hester was a conundrum all right. It was barely eight o'clock, and she had already cleared the yard of debris, washed the filth from his clothes, made breakfast, baked pies, and who knew what else. And she wasn't that bad looking either. So the question was why weren't Mennonite bachelors lined up around the block to take her out walking or to a church function or out for dinner in one of Sarasota's many restaurants? Why had Arlen thought it necessary to bring in a suitor from the outside?

John was pretty sure he knew the answer to that one. The woman did not know her place—had never accepted her role in either the community or a relationship. She had a college education, still quite rare among the conservative Mennonite population, and she had taken on a job, albeit an unpaid one, that put her in a position of authority. Being the daughter of the senior minister would only buy her so much in the realm of amnesty and respect. He had the feeling that she just kept pushing the boundaries, and he felt sorry for poor Samuel Brubaker. From the way Brubaker looked at Hester and followed her around like a lost puppy, the guy was probably doomed to. . .

"Johnny? Come quick!"

There was no arguing with the alarm in Margery Barker's voice. She rushed up to the screened door, banged on it, and bellowed at him. Then she turned and took off at a run. By the time John gathered his wits enough to follow, she was already several yards from the house. "Well, come on," she yelled. "You didn't break your legs, did you?" She didn't wait for an answer as she turned the corner at the end of the lane. John had been so engrossed in his thoughts that he'd failed to notice that the sun had disappeared behind a solid cover of gray clouds. *So much for a break in the weather,* he thought as he felt the first drops of rain and followed Margery down the lane.

Chapter 8

Hester dragged another sandbag into place and then stared at the floor of her grandmother's carport. In addition to several puddles that were spreading across the concrete slab, water was shooting like a small geyser out of the drain that normally handled any runoff.

"It'll settle down in a bit," her grandmother assured her as she sipped her second cup of morning tea. "It always does."

But Hester had her doubts. Those other times Grandma Nelly was remembering followed a heavy rain when the water had gurgled up through the drain like a bubbling fountain. This was something far more dramatic. This was a really good imitation of Old Faithful. According to revised weather reports Hester had heard that morning, the creek was rising faster than anyone had predicted. There was no way they had until noon to get Nelly and her neighbors out of here. They had to go now.

We should have gone yesterday, she thought. *I should have insisted.*

"Where's Samuel?" she asked, noticing that his small camper was gone from its usual place in Nelly's driveway. He'd been staying with Nelly since arriving in Pinecraft. Nelly clearly thought the sun rose and set in the young carpenter. Hester had hoped to herd the less agile residents living along the creek into Samuel's camper and have him drive them to the nearest shelter and then come back for another group until everyone was safe.

"He left before dawn." Nelly took another swallow of her tea. "Did I tell you that Lizzie Gingrich's generator went out last night? Samuel went over there to check on it and get it going again, and—"

"Margery went to get help," Hester interrupted as she dropped the last of the sandbags into place. "We need to get going here, Gramma. Are you all packed?" She didn't mention what her father had told her that morning—that another tropical storm was forming over the Gulf, a storm that had the potential to blossom into another hurricane. "Come on. We need to hurry."

As if a switch had been turned on, it seemed that Nelly finally recognized the need for panic. "And who's going to help Ivan and Jane next door? And what about Lizzie? She's alone, you know, and just had surgery on her hip. What's she supposed to do?" Nelly pointed to houses in every direction as she continued her roll call of neighbors who were going to need extra help. "At least I can walk and carry my load," she muttered as she headed back inside the house. "*Gott in Himmel,* Hester, come now! The sink's about to explode."

Sure enough. Water was gurgling up through the enamel basin in the kitchen. If it was coming up there, then. . .

Hester raced down the hall to the bathroom, where the toilet bowl was rapidly filling with water and sewage.

"Gram, get your pocketbook and get in the car," she ordered as she ran into her grandmother's bedroom and started grabbing precious items that Nelly had laid out on her bed. The photo of Hester's grandfather, the Bible Nelly had received when she was baptized and still read several times a day, the basket of quilt squares and the quilt of scraps from family members' cast-off clothing that had covered Nelly's bed for decades. On her way out, she grabbed the small suitcase filled with clothing and toiletries that Nelly kept packed and ready for just such emergencies.

In the hallway, water was already spreading across the planked floor. As she passed the kitchen, she set Nelly's suitcase on the counter and scooped the bottles of medications her grandmother took into her cloth satchel and then ran outside, where her worst fears were realized.

Up and down the street people were racing around, their arms filled with whatever they thought they might most need. These goods they deposited in the baskets of three-wheeled bicycles or the backseats of cars as they urged family members to hurry, then sent someone back for something they had forgotten. Next door Ivan Miller assisted his wife to their car as if the two of them were going out for a Sunday picnic; then slowly he walked back up the front sidewalk to lock the door to his house.

"Head straight to Lakeview Elementary, Herr Miller," Hester called. "It's the shelter where we reserved spaces for everyone." Hester shoved the last of Nelly's things into the car and got behind the wheel. "We'll be there. We're going to pick up Lizzie first," she added.

"We'll do all right," Ivan assured her with a wave. But his voice quavered with uncertainty, and she saw him look around as if he couldn't quite believe what was happening.

"Follow me," she called.

Ivan Miller hesitated briefly, and Hester could see his wife pleading with him from inside the car. Just then Margery Barker came running down the lane, and not three steps behind her was John Steiner.

"Where do you need us?" Margery huffed, leaning against the car as she tried to catch her breath.

"Here," Hester instructed as she got out of the car and held the door open for Margery. "Take our car and go get Lizzie and then drive her and Gramma to the Lakeview School while I make sure the others follow. You'll also want to pick up anyone trying to go on foot."

Margery had the motor running and the car backed out of the driveway before Hester got the car door closed. When she took a step back to avoid getting run over by Ivan Miller, who was driving inches away from Margery's rear bumper, she nearly tripped over John.

"I can't take you to your place today," she said, her defenses on instant alert and her mind already assuming the reason he'd come. "Not now. The creek is overflowing its banks. . . ."

"I can see that, Hester," he said irritably. He stood watching as she directed the line of cars and bicycles that formed a surreal parade headed away from the creek for a moment, then muttered, "How can I help?"

It annoyed her that he made it sound like something he was loath to do. She had to bite her lip to refrain from telling him he should go back to her father's house and try getting up on the sunnier side of the bed. Of course their house would also soon be flooded, although it was farther from the creek. And then it started to rain in earnest. Not a drizzle or a gentle summer shower. This time they were deluged as if the clouds had grown weary of their burden and simply burst open.

Anxiously Hester looked down the road and saw Lizzie Gingrich climb into Nelly's car. A moment later the red rear lights of the caravan of cars inched forward. But to reach the school, they would have turned the other way. Margery must have decided that the water was rising too fast to head in that direction and decided on an alternate route. "I should go," she said, but as she looked around for some vehicle to speed her on her way, she understood that with the water already creeping across the road, obliterating its boundaries, the only conveyance that could help was a boat or canoe.

"Come on," John shouted over the lashing rain as he took hold of her arm and started slogging through the mounting water. "Now," he commanded when she hesitated.

Together they splashed their way toward the main road, dodging floating debris and trying hard to maintain their balance as they moved with the swift current. By the time they crossed Bahia Vista, the water was ankle-deep and rising fast. All Hester could think about was that drowning because of inland flooding was the primary cause of death after a hurricane. How could she not have made sure everyone was moved last night? If it hadn't been for John Steiner's stubborn refusal to move to a shelter. . .

"The church?" John shouted, pointing to a large modern structure as the rain formed rivulets down his hair and face.

"Yes," Hester called back as she realized that Margery must have turned in this direction so that she could lead everyone to the church rather than try to make the longer trek to the school. She squeezed her eyes closed against the sting of the downpour as they made their way to the impressive campus of the community's more liberal Mennonite church. It sat on higher ground and had been built with a specially designed drainage system to handle just such emergencies as these. Hester could only hope it would be enough to hold back the floodwaters.

The downpour in combination with the wind made visibility impossible, and Hester had almost bumped into one of the cars from Margery's procession before she grasped the fact that they had stalled out less than fifty feet from the church parking lot after trying to drive through deeper water. Most of the people were still sitting in their cars looking frightened and bewildered. Margery was up ahead, trying to force the door of Nelly's car open against the water that was swirling around her feet and legs.

Before Hester could form the words, John yelled for her to stay put, and then on his way to Nelly's car, he pulled open the doors of the four other cars stalled behind. "Give us a hand here," he shouted to some unseen person he'd spotted. Seconds later Hester had to smile as Zeke Shepherd emerged from behind one of the cars carrying Lizzie Gingrich, with Ivan and Jane Miller on either side of him. They hung on to each other and the dangling ends of Zeke's rope belt. She had never been so glad to see him.

"This way," she shouted and motioned toward the church. Her voice sounded like a whisper thrown against the pounding of the rain. Zeke staggered past her while volunteers from the church ran toward them. They took Lizzie and assisted the Millers, freeing Zeke to go back to help Olive and Agnes Crowder. Hester was relieved to see that with each step Zeke took closer to the church, the water was shallower. "John!" she shouted when she had assured herself that everyone was accounted for except her grandmother and Margery.

"Right here," he huffed from no more than a foot away. He was carrying Nelly, his sling dangling uselessly from his neck.

"Where's Margery?" She tried not to let her panic seep through.

John jerked his head in the direction of the car. "She went back for your grandmother's stuff."

"Go," Hester ordered even as she fought her way against the rushing current to where she could just make out the flashing hazard lights of her grandmother's car. Margery was on her knees in the backseat, bundling Nelly's things into the already-soaked quilt. "Leave those and come on," Hester shouted as Margery emerged from the car and was almost swept away by the rushing water.

"Got everything," the fisherwoman shouted back with a smile of triumph lighting her face as she clung to the open car door. Finally she regained her footing, but then the car started to float and drift.

"The car! Let go, Margery," Hester shouted, swiping at her hair that had come free and was covering her eyes. She wrapped one arm around a lamppost and reached out toward Margery, catching one end of the quilt. Slowly she pulled the fisherwoman toward her until she was able to grab the lamppost as well.

"We can make it," Margery yelled. "Come on." Swinging the quilt and its cargo like a cradle between them, the two women struck out through murky water, carefully measuring the depth before taking each step until the water became shallower.

"Will you look at that?" Margery shouted, her tone filled with surprise as water ran off the pavement of the parking lot back toward the street-turned-canal that they'd just escaped. "Never would have imagined it could drain like that. Just wait 'til those government engineers have a look at this! Might teach them a thing or two." She was out of breath and clearly exhausted, but Hester knew that Margery's running commentary on the world around her was what got her through the day.

"You okay?" Hester asked as she relieved Margery of her half of their burden and slung the sodden quilt with its precious contents over her shoulder. The older woman was out of breath and holding her side.

"I'm fine," Margery protested, but she sat down on the first of several concrete benches lining the covered courtyard of the church and fanned herself with her hat. "You go on and check on Nelly and the others. I'll be okay. Just need a minute to catch my breath."

Hester signaled to a teenage girl who was passing out oversized beach towels that had been among the donated goods to bring one to Margery. "I'll be back soon," she promised as she scanned the throngs of refugees for any sign of her grandmother. When she heard her father's distinct full-throttle laughter, she followed the sound, knowing he would be attending his beloved mother. She took a quick tally to make sure everyone was accounted for and thanked God that they were all safe, soaked to the bone but safe.

⁓⁓⁓

For a man who prized his solitude, the mass of people huddled under the eaves and cypress arbor that covered the church courtyard was John Steiner's worst nightmare. He'd spent so much of the last two years living alone that finding himself in the midst of so many people who were all talking excitedly made him feel as if he might be physically ill if he could not find a way out. There was a lot of milling about as plans for making it the rest of the way to the shelter were suggested and rejected. Everyone was trying to come up with the best alternative for getting people settled until it was safe to move on to a shelter. Chaos reigned in a world where John craved only peace and quiet and order. "At least the rain's let up," he muttered to himself.

"Not for long," a male voice to his left replied.

He glanced over to see the man he'd called to for help in rescuing the stranded senior citizens from their cars. He had straight black shoulder-length hair that hung in wet clumps, and he was dressed in a long-sleeved cotton shirt and cotton work pants—both a couple of sizes too small for his lanky frame. He was sitting with his back against a wall of the courtyard, his knees bent and his chin resting on his crossed hands as he watched the crowd.

"Still, the letup is a relief after what we went through back there," John replied. He was in no mood to be debating the matter or to hear more bad news.

The man shrugged. "God just must have decided to press the PAUSE button. Give us time to get those old folks to a safer place."

Whatever, John thought and turned his attention to his arm, throbbing now from having cast off his sling in order to transport Hester's grandmother to higher ground.

"You get that broke in the hurricane?" the man next to him asked, nodding toward the cast.

"Yeah." John didn't want to be rude, but he couldn't help glancing around, searching for any means of escape.

"Wanna get outta here?" the man asked as if reading John's mind.

"Yeah," John admitted.

"Follow me." And the man stood and moved like a cat along the fringes of the crowd until he reached a small opening between two steel columns that supported the covering of the church atrium. "This way," he instructed as he sloshed through water that covered his shoes and started out toward an overgrown vacant lot. "Get us some water," he added with a nod toward a box loaded with bottles of water.

John hesitated. But then he spotted Hester. She was headed his way. He grabbed two bottles and took off after the stranger before she could spot him.

"Name's Zeke," the long-haired man said after they had plodded their way across a field and finally climbed onto a loading dock at an abandoned warehouse. Zeke settled in with his back against the concrete wall under a torn awning that would protect them if the rain started up again. After he'd screwed the top off his water, he drank half of it in one gulp and then wiped his mouth with the back of one hand. "And you are?"

"John Steiner."

To his astonishment Zeke grinned. "And a legend in your own time, my friend." He patted the place beside him. "No joke. Among folks like me you are the man. Setting yourself up in the old Tucker place with nobody bothering you or telling you where to be and when to be there." He shook his head in amazement. "How'd you manage it?"

"I bought the property," John said.

"Well, I *know* that," Zeke replied, clearly offended.

Something clicked with John. "Zeke? You're a friend of Jeannie Messner's?"

"Ah, little Jeannie with the flaming red hair," Zeke said, and the softening of his features said more than words about the special place the young woman held in his life. "Like my little sister," he added.

"She was worried about you," John told him.

Zeke grinned. "Jeannie's a people person. Doesn't understand folks like you and me."

John was more than a little uncomfortable with the assumption of some kind of bond. He wasn't homeless after all. Well, he was for the time being, but that would change for him once he got back to his place. The night before at the Detlef house, he'd fallen asleep planning what he would do first, where he could stay while he rebuilt, how he would revive the citrus groves and garden.

"I could help you get back there if you like," Zeke said. "You wait around for permission, and you'll be sitting here for a couple of weeks."

John was tempted to laugh. Surely the man was joking. Zeke didn't appear to have any means of transportation beyond his two feet, which at the moment were clad in combat boots with soles that needed replacing. Still, the man deserved some respect.

"How would you do that?"

Zeke shrugged. "There's always a boat around, down at the bay."

"Look, I think you've got the wrong idea about me. I mean, I appreciate your interest and the offer to help, but. . ."

"Relax, dude. We're not talking about stealing a boat. Sarasota's a friendly town. I know people who know people, and, well, from time to time we do favors for each other. You know Margery Barker?"

"We've met," John replied cautiously.

"Thought so. Margie knows everything there is to know about anyone and anything having to do with the bay." He polished off the rest of his water and then stuck the bottle out into the rain to let it refill with the runoff from the awning. "She'd help us with getting a boat."

"Thanks. I'll think about it." John found the entire discussion uncomfortable and decided to change the subject. "Are you Mennonite or Amish, Zeke?"

To his surprise, Zeke seemed to accept the abrupt shift in topics as normal. "Neither," he replied. "Used to be Catholic." He laughed at some private joke and then added, "Can you see me as an altar boy?"

John could not help smiling. "Not really," he admitted.

The two men sat together in the silence of comrades for several minutes. They watched the rain dripping off the awning and studied the restless sky.

"Looks like Ma Nature's not done with us yet," Zeke commented with a nod toward the west.

"Maybe we should get back," John suggested. "There are people who worry about you."

Zeke turned his gaze to John. "And you?"

John shrugged and got to his feet. "You coming?" He jumped down from the loading dock and started back across the vacant lot.

Zeke drained his water bottle, then once again refilled it under a rivulet of rain running off the awning before heading in the opposite direction. "Got to go get my guitar—music soothes the restless and the terrified," he said with a wink. "You let me know if you change your mind about that boat."

John nodded. "Thanks," he called out as the homeless man

headed around the side of the deserted warehouse. "How will I contact you?" he added, realizing that Zeke hardly seemed the sort to carry around a cell phone.

"I'll find you and check in." He slid past a barricade intended to keep people from trespassing inside the deserted building and disappeared into the shadows. "No worries," he called out, the words echoing in the empty structure.

John wished he could agree with that statement.

Chapter 9

Samuel Brubaker liked Hester well enough. She was a hardworking woman who clearly took to heart her devotion to serving others. She was also a good homemaker. The house she shared with her father was spotless. She was an excellent cook. She certainly was an attractive woman. And yet the truth of the matter was that she made him uneasy. She had a gravity about her that should have impressed him, he supposed, and he respected that side of her. But what seemed to him to be missing was some semblance of softness, of lightheartedness. Some evidence that she found joy in her life.

He was younger than she was by two years, and somehow he always felt as if he should defer to her greater wisdom and maturity. She seemed more like a teacher he'd had in elementary school than a woman he might consider a friend, or a wife. He'd tried to convince himself that it was because she was the daughter of a minister, but back home in Pennsylvania, he'd been friends with the daughters of his minister, and they had been nothing like Hester.

On the other hand, she would make an excellent mother for his children. She would know exactly how to instill the respect for others and the love of God that he had always hoped to find in a mate. Samuel himself tended toward softheartedness when it came to children. His nieces and nephews adored him because—to the consternation of his sisters and brothers—he almost always sided with the youngsters. That would not do when he had children of his own. Discipline was key to living the plain life.

He watched Hester as she moved among the crowds of people driven from their homes by the flooding creek, now waiting for permission to take one of the cots that had been brought to the church in case of an overflow at the shelters. She offered them a kind of quiet comfort that she rarely displayed when she was handing out assignments in her volunteer role. She cradled a baby and placed a caressing palm on the tangled hair of a toddler crying over some missing toy. And all the while she knelt next to a woman who looked ready to pass out from fear and exhaustion.

"She's a wonder—our Hester," a woman's voice commented from behind him. When he turned, the young woman he'd seen in church and around Pinecraft was passing out bottles of drinking water. She thrust a bottle of water into his hand. "Here, you look like you could use some." She wore a captivating smile, a white prayer covering gone limp in the rain and humidity, and the unmistakable scars of having been badly burned in a fire.

She pulled an overturned milk crate next to him and plopped down as she opened a second bottle of water and took a long drink. "Hester was the first person I saw after the fire," she continued as if she and Samuel had been engaged in conversation for hours. She absently fingered the purplish stains on her neck. He saw that they also covered her forearms, the backs of her hands, and what he could see of her ankles. "She was the one who had to tell me my parents and siblings had all died, and that I was the only survivor."

It occurred to him that she had simply assumed, perhaps from long experience, that his first questions would be about the burns. "I'm sorry for your loss," he murmured, then quickly corrected himself, "Losses."

The young woman glanced down. "God's will. Hester says

there's a lesson to be learned from whatever happens, and just because we can't figure it out right away doesn't mean there's no good reason."

She turned to face him squarely and smiled. That smile in combination with the deep violet of her eyes took his breath away. "I'm Rosalyn, by the way. Can I get you something to eat?"

Samuel shook his head, still dumbfounded by the unexpected beauty of her smile. "Samuel Brubaker," he said, "from Pennsylvania."

She laughed and the sound was like music. "Well, Samuel Brubaker from Pennsylvania, glad to make your acquaintance." She pushed herself to her feet. "How about giving me a hand over here? We've got about a bazillion cans of tuna we need to open and pass out to people—before they pass out from hunger," she added and laughed again. "Get it? Pass out before they pass out?"

<hr />

Hester heard Rosalyn's laughter and glanced up. Her friend was talking to Samuel, and he was grinning down at her, his eyes fairly dancing with interest, even attraction. Hester wondered at her own lack of jealousy. After all, in the weeks since Samuel's decision to stay on in Pinecraft, they had spent many evenings together in the company of her father or her grandmother. The four of them had played board games and worked in her mother's garden. And more often than not, Samuel came by to share breakfast with Hester and Arlen each morning before the two men headed off to Arlen's furniture store and workshop. Yes, over the short time he'd been in Pinecraft, Samuel had become like a member of the family, and yet. . .

He was handsome in a perennially boyish way, and he was kind and had a wonderful sense of humor. He complimented her cooking and admired her needlework even though Hester was well aware that in that arena she was not as gifted as most despite her mother's and grandmother's efforts to teach her. Surely when she saw him talking to another woman—flirting with her even— Hester should feel some twinge of alarm. Wasn't it normal to become somewhat territorial under such circumstances? So how come all she felt when she glanced up at the sound of Rosalyn's merry laughter was pleasure at seeing her friend so obviously enjoying herself?

"It's too soon," she muttered. "Feelings will grow. . .in time."

"I need to talk to you."

Hester turned to find John Steiner standing across the table that was loaded with cases of canned tuna. He was scowling at her, which seemed to be his usual demeanor. She couldn't help but pity the poor woman who would one day end up married to this cantankerous, not to mention irritating, man.

"Herr Steiner," she began.

"John," he corrected automatically. "Look, what do you know about this Zeke character?"

Okay, she hadn't seen that coming. "Zeke? He's. . ." She narrowed her eyes and studied John. "Why?"

"Why what?"

"Why do you want to know my opinion of Zeke Shepherd?"

"All I want to know is whether or not I can trust the guy or if he's all talk."

"Why?" she repeated, refusing to back down.

John let out a sigh of frustration. "It's a simple question, Hester. Can I trust the guy or not?"

Hester looked over to where Zeke had just made his way through the throngs of people and was now sitting cross-legged on the ground strumming his guitar and singing to a group of toddlers. "You tell me," she said, nodding toward the scene.

She didn't miss the surprise in John's expression. "I thought he was still. . ." he muttered, then shook his head and turned his attention back to Hester. "Looks can be deceiving. Anyone can pull off an act when they've got kids around."

"Even you, John Steiner?" She couldn't help it. There was something about the man that brought out a disturbing streak of impishness in her.

He frowned down at her. "Okay, so he's one of the good guys. Thanks." He started toward Zeke, then turned back to her.

"When do you think this rain might let up?"

"It's not raining at the moment," Hester said.

"You know what I mean—clear skies?"

She shrugged. "Only God can answer that."

"Best guess?"

Hester stepped out from under the arbor that protected a portion of the courtyard and scanned the sky. "There's some clearing there to the west. That's a good sign. Probably by morning we'll start to see the waters recede and the skies clear." She let him take two steps before adding, "Why?"

"Just curious," he said, his voice far too casual. After all, in the short time she'd known the man, he'd done little other than bark out demands or object to the instructions of others. This was not a man who casually asked about anything. He had a plan, and Hester was going to figure it out before he placed himself—and possibly Zeke—in more danger.

"We could use a hand passing out this food," she called as he walked quickly away.

"Can't," was his curt reply.

"Can't or won't?" Hester seethed through gritted teeth as she watched him disappear into the crowd.

By late the following day, the rain had stopped, and the skies had indeed started to clear. True to his word, Zeke managed to get a small fishing boat and meet John at the city's main marina. He fired up the motor, and the two men headed south through the mostly deserted waters of Sarasota Bay.

"I bunked on that boat for a while before I got set up in my place near the bridge," Zeke said, nodding toward a battered old sailboat that was listing badly and had been marked with a neon orange tag warning the owners to move it or lose it. "Does no good to tag these things," Zeke added. "They've been abandoned. Folks think having a boat is romantic. It's work is what it is, a lot of work."

John let the man continue his monologue without comment.

He was thinking about his property, about the last view he'd had of it from the air. Was it really as bad as it had seemed? Maybe not, given the scenery they were passing. The botanical gardens, for example, seemed to be in pretty good shape. Some wind damage to the structures and greenhouses plus flooding near the bay, but overall, the gardens looked to be reasonably intact. He allowed himself to hope.

Zeke guided the boat around a rookery where pelicans roosted by the dozen as if trying—like John—to decide their next move. Zeke steered on past the mouth of Philippi Creek. "Tricky here," he muttered as he maneuvered the boat carefully around trees that had fallen into the water where the rush of water had eroded the shoreline. "You got a pier?"

"I had one, until a couple days ago," John replied, remembering now how Hester and the others had had to wade in to shore that first day after the hurricane hit.

"No worries." Zeke guided the boat toward a fallen tree and expertly looped the rope around a branch stripped bare of its foliage.

Awkwardly John climbed out using his good arm for leverage and reminding himself that his ability to do anything useful in the next six weeks was limited. Not only had an X-ray taken at the hospital that morning confirmed that his wrist was broken, but it was his left wrist, and he was left-handed. Daily activities he had taken for granted had become all-consuming. Already he'd had to teach himself the rudiments of eating and brushing his teeth again. Wielding a hammer, never mind a saw or screwdriver, would be monumental.

"Geezle Pete," Zeke said. The expression came out like a long-drawn-out whisper. He had made it up the bank and over the fallen pine trees and was staring at his surroundings.

John picked his way carefully over the rubble of the trees until he was standing next to Zeke. Speechless, he forced himself to scan the land. His memory of how it had looked when he'd left didn't do the scene justice. He jumped slightly when Zeke clutched his shoulder and squeezed it. Anything Zeke might have said was expressed in that single gesture of sympathy. Grateful for the man's instinct to stay silent, John did not shrug away from the contact. Instead, he drew strength from this stranger's gift of understanding. He was very glad that he had not come here alone.

"Thanks for bringing me here," he muttered and reached down to unearth a dented teakettle that had found its resting place some fifty yards from the main house.

Zeke took a couple of tentative steps toward the house and almost tripped over a kitchen chair buried under a pile of broken palm fronds. He dug it out and examined its metal legs and vinyl seat before setting it next to the kettle that John had carefully placed on a patch of reasonably dry ground.

John watched as Zeke tested the chair for sturdiness, and again he felt a surge of gratitude toward the man. Zeke continued to prowl through the debris for other salvageable pieces to add to the chair and teakettle. "What's your plan?" Zeke asked.

"Not sure," John replied.

That was the last the two men spoke for the next hour as they wandered the property. Collecting the bits and pieces that had once been the makings of John's life seemed as good a first step as any.

Only when they heard the rumble of heavy equipment and the whine of gas-powered saws in the distance did the two men look up from their scavenging. The noise was coming toward them from the overgrown and now completely impassable lane that led from John's house out to the main road.

"Company," Zeke shouted above the din and added a plastic dish rack filled with a couple of unbroken glasses and cups and one plate to the growing pile of goods.

John finished digging out a No Trespassing sign, grasped it with his good arm, and stood at the end of the lane waiting. He couldn't help noticing that Zeke took this opportunity to roost on top of what was left of one wall of the packinghouse as if settling in to watch a baseball game.

The din of the heavy road equipment roared ever closer, although the foliage was so thick that John could not yet see the actual vehicles. He heard the whine of the saw and then the crackle of breaking wood, punctuated by a heavy thud as a large tree branch hit the ground. John tightened his grip on the sign and waited. Zeke leaned back on one elbow and watched.

When the bulldozer broke through the last tangle of pepper vines, scrub oak, and royal palms that had fallen like dominoes during the hurricane, the driver set the engine on idle and stared at John through mirrored sunglasses. Then he glanced back as if looking for reinforcements.

"You're on private property," John yelled.

The bulldozer driver held up one finger and continued to look behind him.

A battered four-wheel-drive open-air Jeep rumbled over broken branches and sand dunes until it came to a stop next to the bulldozer. A man John recognized as Grady Forrest emerged from the passenger side, and then Arlen Detlef and Samuel Brubaker climbed out of the backseat. The Jeep's driver cut the engine and waited.

While Grady consulted with the bulldozer driver, Arlen and Samuel started toward John. Arlen was smiling broadly as if he had simply stopped by for a visit.

"John! *Wie geht's?*" he shouted above the low sustained drumbeat of the motorized vehicles lining the lane now.

"Pastor Detlef," John replied respectfully, but he did not lower the sign. "Samuel."

Undaunted, the two men continued walking toward him. "I see Zeke was able to borrow a boat so you could get here," Arlen continued, glancing at Zeke, who raised two fingers in the peace sign but made no move to leave his position. "We looked for you at the church, but. . ."

John ignored this observation. "What do you want?" he asked. "More to the point, what do they want?" He jerked his arm toward the entourage of men wearing bright yellow hard hats now gathering around the bulldozer.

"Now, John, I explained all this. Samuel and I are with the Mennonite Disaster Service. Those men are with the local utility company, and Grady there is with the county. It is our job to—"

"I know who everybody is. I don't want you here."

"We only wish to help," Samuel said. His voice was soft, conciliatory, but his stance was every bit as unyielding as John's.

"I see you have been able to rescue several items from your home," Arlen observed, moving closer to the pile that Zeke and John had created over the last hour. He held up a ceramic mug. "Not so much as a chip," he observed. "And yet it flew from all the way over there."

"Mr. Steiner?" Grady and the man who'd been driving the Jeep were picking their way across the rubble. "Do you have a few minutes?"

Perhaps because he had been expecting the county's man to dish out orders instead of asking permission, John nodded and relaxed his grip on the sign slightly.

"Great." Grady waved a clipboard in the air. "This is Dennis Jenkins. He's an engineer with the county. I thought maybe we could make a survey of your property and see what might be the best plan for going forward."

"*What's your plan?*" Zeke had asked, and after over an hour of digging through rubble to salvage bits and pieces of his life, John had to admit to himself that he didn't have one. Surveying the damage made sense. Grady was now close enough that John could see that the paper on the clipboard was a sort of checklist. It couldn't hurt to let the engineer have a look around.

"I thought you were bringing in a team of volunteers, an RV team," John said to Arlen.

"Ja, well, we could hardly drive RVs in here with the lane impassable," Arlen reasoned. "Let the engineer do his job, John."

"Very well," John said, "but those guys stay put. And cut off those motors," he added, glaring at the cluster of workers in hard hats.

"Done." Grady gave a signal, and the rumble of machinery wheezed to silence.

As he walked the property with Grady and the engineer, John noticed that Arlen and Samuel followed along. Every once in a while Arlen would murmur something to Samuel, and the younger man would nod and make a notation on a folded sheet of paper with a stub of a pencil. In spite of his fluency in the German dialect common to both the Amish and Mennonite faiths, John could not decipher these exchanges, but he could certainly appreciate that it was far more important to give his full attention to Grady and the engineer. For in the midst of what appeared to be casual and sympathetic comments about the outbuildings, the house and the plantings, Grady was eliciting other information.

"Do you have insurance?" he asked.

The question stopped John cold in his tracks. Of course he didn't have insurance. In his world, neighbors took care of neighbors. There was a fund within the church congregation for helping people in his situation. But he was no longer part of that community, the one that had rebuilt his neighbor's house after a fire. The one that had provided a young mother and her seven children with the funds to keep going after her husband was badly injured in a farming accident.

"I have money," he growled even as he mentally calculated just how little money was left from the sale of his farm after he had paid for the property, the renovations, and the plants he'd had to buy here in Florida. Even before the hurricane, he'd been grudgingly considering the prospect that he would need to find ways to supplement his meager funds by fall. "I have tools," he added. "I can rebuild."

"In time perhaps," Grady said with a barely concealed glance at John's injured arm. "Why don't you wait here while we poke around the foundation of the house?"

The suggestion didn't deserve an answer, and John doggedly followed Grady and the engineer over a mound of wet sand and rubble to what had been the front door of his house.

"Arlen?" Grady shouted, and the minister turned away from the chicken coop that he and Samuel had been inspecting. "Wanna come have a look at this?" John waited while the three men slowly worked their way to the interior of the house. He was aware that Zeke had come to stand with him. The two of them watched as Samuel scrambled up a pile of broken bricks and chunks of concrete to get a closer look at the chimney. He turned to Arlen and shook his head, and Grady made a note on his clipboard. This pantomime was repeated at least three other times before Grady came back to where John waited.

"The good news is that there's no reason you can't rebuild," Grady said slowly, not meeting John's eyes.

"And the bad news?"

"You'll have to start from scratch. This stuff—" Grady waved a hand over the remains of the packinghouse and outbuildings and shook his head. "You'll need permits. I can help you get the survey and flood certification documents, but you're going to need permits for the building, plumbing, electrical—if you decide to put that in—and when it's all up again, you'll need a final inspection and occupancy permit before you can move in."

"It's my land," John argued. "I don't need anyone's permission to live on my own land."

"You're right," Grady agreed. "But unless you plan to live in a tent here, you're going to need those permits."

"And if I refuse?"

"There will be fines, hefty fines that will make the cost of the permit look like peanuts. And you could go to jail."

John felt a sense of overwhelming grief rise up into his throat. He had worked so very hard, and he had come so close. Why would God test him in such a way?

"I'll start over," he said and only realized he had spoken aloud when Zeke grinned.

"That's the spirit," the homeless man said as he clapped John on the back.

John couldn't help noticing that neither Grady, Arlen, nor Samuel seemed to share Zeke's enthusiasm. And their obvious doubt only strengthened John's will to succeed.

"You'll still need those permits," Grady warned.

John did not acknowledge this comment. Instead, he held out his right hand to Grady. "Thanks for coming," he said as in turn he shook hands with Grady, Arlen, and Samuel. He even shook hands with the engineer. "Now, if you don't mind, I've got work to do."

"As long as they're here," Arlen said with a nod toward the men in hard hats and the bulldozer, "why don't we clear away those fallen trees by your beach?"

John weighed his answer against what was most likely to get these people to leave as soon as possible and decided that since the bulldozer and other equipment had to turn around, they might as well move the fallen trees. "I'd appreciate that," he told Arlen and could not deny that it felt good to see the older man's smile. It was not a smile of victory. Rather, it was one of appreciation. Arlen was grateful for John's willingness to allow him to do at least a part of the work he no doubt believed that he had been sent by God to accomplish.

True to their word, Grady, Arlen, and Samuel climbed back into the Jeep driven by the engineer and followed the heavy machinery back down the lane as soon as the trees were moved out of the way and the path from the house to where the pier had once stood had been cleared.

"You're going to need some help," Zeke commented as he watched them go. "Those MDS crews can get a lot done in a short time if you give them half a chance."

"I expect you're right," John replied, "but I just need time to think it all through. Can you understand that?"

"Yep." Zeke headed back to where he'd left the boat. "You ready?"

It was just past noon, and there was so much to do. Surely Zeke wasn't planning to—

"I gotta get the boat back," Zeke called as he unleashed the boat from the tree and waited. "You coming?"

John wasn't ready to go. Not yet. But then, the boat was the only way in or out. He let out a sigh. "Be right there," he called and turned to take one more look around, memorizing every detail. And that was when he remembered that the lane was open. He could stay and walk out to the road.

"You go on," he shouted. "I'm going to stay awhile longer."

"No worries," Zeke replied as he pulled the starter rope and eased the boat back out into the calm waters of the bay.

Part Two

O thou afflicted, tossed with tempest, and not comforted,
behold, I will lay thy stones with fair colours,
and lay thy foundations with sapphires.
ISAIAH 54:11

A single gentle rain makes the grass many shades greener.
HENRY DAVID THOREAU, *Walden: Life in the Woods*

Chapter 10

Hester and her family had spent over a week at the church shelter before Jeannie Messner insisted they come and stay with her. By that time, power and water had been restored to Jeannie's neighborhood as well as much of Pinecraft, although there were still outages in the homes along the creek.

Jeannie and her husband, Geoff, lived with their daughter, Tessa, in a large house on Slipper Street just outside the Pinecraft area. Given that there was no word when they might be able to move back to the houses ruined by the flooding, Hester and her father gratefully accepted Jeannie's invitation.

"Emma and her brood are in here," Jeannie told Hester as she led her down an upstairs hallway past three inviting-looking bedrooms. "My sister insisted on taking only one room for her entire family." She rolled her eyes. "Do not ask me to understand the sense of that when Sadie and Tessa could easily share. They've always been more like sisters than cousins, and we could put a cot in my sewing room for Matt."

"Gramma and I can share a room," Hester suggested.

"Actually, I thought Nelly could stay in Geoff's study on the ground floor. It's close to the powder room and no stairs for her to manage," Jeannie continued. "And the hide-a-bed is fairly comfortable, short-term."

"This is very kind of you, Jeannie. I mean, after all, with school about to start, you and Geoff must have your hands full."

The perky red-haired woman's large eyes sparkled. "Hey, I didn't completely lose my way when I came over to the 'dark' side." She laughed at her own joke about making the leap from the conservative to the more liberal branch of the faith. "I thought you and Margery could share this room, and then your dad and. . .what's his name? The guy from Tucker's Point?"

"John?" Hester's step slowed. Surely Jeannie wasn't thinking of inviting John Steiner to stay with her as well.

"John Steiner," Jeannie repeated, committing the name to memory. "He can bunk in with Zeke and your dad—if I can get Zeke to come in out of the rain."

"Unlikely," Hester said, although her mind was still on the idea of John Steiner in this bustling house.

Jeannie laughed. "Yeah, I know, but I do keep trying. The man is a gifted musician. One of these days he's going to be discovered, and, well, I want to be sure he doesn't forget me when he's rich and famous."

Hester smiled. "You are such a good person, Jeannie."

"Aw shucks, ma'am," Jeannie replied, mimicking a shy cowboy digging the toe of a boot into the carpet. "Just like this friend of mine who will hopefully be getting married to a certain young carpenter from Pennsylvania soon, I just can't stand seeing folks in need."

But Jeannie's brand of service was different. While Hester and Emma were constrained by the rules and protocol set forth by their respective agencies, Jeannie simply went out and did good in the world. She walked down a street, saw someone in need, and took action. No questions asked about should I or could I— just action. Once, when Hester had mentioned Jeannie's gift for helping others, Jeannie had grinned. "Like the ad on TV says, 'Just do it.' Works for me."

This certainly wasn't the first time that Hester had felt confused by Jeannie's references to popular media. Hester and her father owned a small television, but it was used for information like weather updates, not entertainment. But she understood that like any Mennonite woman would, Jeannie was simply deflecting the compliment she'd been given.

"And speaking of good-looking carpenters from Pennsylvania, I forgot about a place for Samuel," Jeannie said, frowning. "Well, Geoff can just bring in another rollaway. How about some lemonade?"

"Samuel has his camper. He had taken it to pick up more cots for the church the morning the creek flooded, so it was unharmed," Hester reminded her.

Jeannie grinned and clapped her hands. "Perfect. We can park it on the drive, and Matt can bunk out there with him." She started down the curved stairway with Hester following. "I mean, my sister is pure salt of the earth when it comes to being good people, but can you imagine expecting two teenagers to bunk in with their parents even for a couple of nights, and this will be a lot longer than a couple nights." She shook her curly hair. "She has got to loosen those apron strings."

Jeannie filled tall slender glasses with ice and then covered the cubes with lemonade. "Tessa cannot wait to have what she likes to call 'our' lemonade," she said, nodding toward a tree that was heavy with fruit not yet ready for picking outside the kitchen window. "And how blessed are we Floridians to be able to walk outside our back door and right there hanging from branches are lemons and limes and oranges and grapefruit? I've lived here my whole life, but I still can't get over how fortunate we are to be living in such beauty." She seemed not to notice the destruction the winds and rain had caused to the variety of fruit trees in her yard. Instead, she boosted herself onto one of the high stools that lined the serving counter separating her kitchen from a large family room and took a long swallow of her store-bought lemonade.

"Speaking of Samuel," she said as she set the glass on the counter and gave Hester her full attention. "What's the deal?"

Hester felt the familiar prickle of irritation that had lately begun to accompany anyone's question regarding Samuel's place in her life. *I don't know,* she sometimes wanted to scream. *And besides, it's none of your business.*

But there was something about Jeannie that invited sharing, and before she could censor herself, Hester was telling Jeannie all about her exasperation with her father's clumsy attempt at matchmaking. "He means well," she said, trying hard to walk the fine line between criticizing her father and expressing her own frustration. "He just wants me to be happy."

"Aren't you?"

The question stunned Hester. For so long she had been going about her life, her daily routine, under the assumption that she was doing what she needed to do to care for others and at the same time find some personal happiness for herself.

"Of course," she replied too quickly.

Jeannie lifted an eyebrow and got up to refill their glasses. "I mean 'happy' as in over the moon, can't wait to get up in the morning to see what the new day might bring," she said. "I mean having someone or something in your life that just thinking about it, or him, makes you glow." She set the glasses down and looked at Hester. "Samuel," she whispered and leaned forward to study Hester more closely. "Nope. Not even a twinkle, much less a glow."

"It doesn't always happen that way. I barely know the man," Hester protested.

Jeannie shrugged. "I met Geoff on a Friday morning down at the bay. He was fishing and I was looking for conch shells. He asked me out. I said yes and three days later he proposed, and I said yes." She glanced around. "And fifteen years later, here we are. . .happy as clams."

"But everyone knows that both you and Geoff are incurable romantics," Hester reminded her. "Some of us are more—"

"Take the word of a romantic, then. Samuel is not for you, and, for that matter, you aren't for him. The two of you might make a go of it, but for all the wrong reasons. Life on this planet is way too short to settle." It was the same advice that Emma had offered her.

Hester took a moment to drink her lemonade and let Jeannie's advice sink in. Emma's sister had always had a reputation for being spontaneous and even a little capricious at times, but she was making perfect sense now, and that alone made Hester uneasy. A clock chimed in the family room. "I have to get back," she said. "Thanks so much for taking us in. We've got crews ready to start scrubbing down the homes that got flooded as soon as MDS gets the go-ahead to go in and take care of the major stuff. I expect we'll be able to move everyone back in by mid-September—that's only a week and a half away, but if having us here becomes too much. . ."

"Hey, stay as long as you need to. We thrive on the ruckus," Jeannie assured her as the two of them walked to the front door. She stood on tiptoe and kissed Hester's cheek. "I'll take care of getting Nelly from the shelter. She'll be all settled in by the time you and Arlen get here later tonight."

"Thanks. We really appreciate it."

Hester was already on her bike when Jeannie crossed the yard to stand next to her. "And don't forget to let John know he's welcome."

Hester felt her cheeks grow pink, and she missed her footing on the bike's pedal and almost fell.

Jeannie laughed. "Hey, is that a twinkle I see?" she called as she headed back to the house.

"Twinkle, my foot," Hester muttered as she pedaled hard down the street. The man had been nothing but trouble from the moment she'd met him.

When Hester got back to Pinecraft, she saw Samuel loading his camper with a variety of tools, gallon jugs of bleach, and boxes of rubber gloves, along with dust masks and protective goggles. Assuming that he was preparing to muck out the houses in the neighborhood by the creek, she pulled her bike up next to him.

"Hi," she said, slightly winded from having ridden away from Jeannie's so fast.

"I was just thinking about you," Samuel said. "Do you have some spare clothes and canned goods I could have? Maybe a sleeping bag or some blankets?"

Hester couldn't help smiling. "Oh, Samuel, you aren't going to have to work all night. The ladies from MCC and CAM will make sure you and your crew have plenty to eat and drink. Just be careful that you—"

"It isn't for me. I mean, it's not meant for cleaning up the houses." He nodded toward the deserted lane where the floodwaters had finally receded and after days of waiting the men could finally start their work. "Arlen's got that covered. I'm taking this stuff out to the Tucker place."

"Why?"

It occurred to Hester that she had seen John Steiner only twice in all the time since he'd helped rescue her grandmother and the others. The first time had been that same day after he and Zeke had taken off together. The second had been earlier that very morning when she was on her way to Jeannie's and she had seen John arguing with Grady. More than a week had passed in between. Where had he been all that time?

"John Steiner has moved back out to his place, and he's refusing to leave," Samuel explained. "I'd really like to help him."

"I saw him in town this morning. He'd traded the splint for a cast and certainly seemed fine."

"Well, yeah, he comes and goes, but he's staying out there and I don't know. There's just something about the guy, Hester. He seems so determined and at the same time so lost."

"What's he doing out there?" Hester had a sudden image of the wreckage of the place the day they had gone to rescue him. It couldn't be much better now. "And how in the world is he managing a boat with one arm in a sling?"

Samuel shrugged. "The utility company cleared the lane to his place, so he gets back and forth by foot, or he hitches a ride. And Zeke and Margery help him out some when he lets them."

"Dad told me that he and Grady surveyed the place and it's pretty much a total loss."

Samuel nodded and continued loading the supplies. "He's got his work cut out for him, that's for sure. So I thought maybe he'd accept the loan of my camper. I mean, he needs a place to sleep and get out of the sun."

"But where will you stay? We're all moving in with Jeannie Messner and her husband, and she's counting on you bringing your camper for extra sleeping space for you and her nephew." She couldn't believe what she was saying. Here was Samuel making a real sacrifice to help a fellow man, and all she could think of was how it was going to be an inconvenience for Jeannie. What was it about John Steiner that made her go against the very mission she had set for her life? Helping others was her calling. She had never questioned the worthiness of a person's cry for help before.

But John wasn't asking for help. In fact, he was doing everything he could to go it alone. And maybe that was her problem. She rarely had faced someone so desperately in need who had neither wanted nor asked for her help.

Samuel pushed back his wide-brimmed straw hat so that he could look at her more directly. "Look, Hester," Samuel said. "I can't explain why I want to help this guy, and I do understand that this may be a fool's errand, but I feel like it's the right thing to do. Spending a night or two in the shelter isn't going to be a hardship for me, but spending another night or two out in the elements with mosquitoes and no-see-ums feasting on his unprotected skin could be a real hardship for John, not to mention a health hazard."

Hester couldn't argue the point. "Stop by the center and tell Rosalyn what you need." She got off her bicycle and leaned it against the back of the RV. "And take this with you so you don't have to walk back to town," she said. "Don't even think of going back to the shelter. Jeannie would never forgive me if I let you do that. There's plenty of room at her house."

Samuel lifted the bike into the camper, then climbed into the driver's seat and smiled down at her. "I won't be gone long, and when I get back I'll get to work helping Arlen and the others get those houses fit for living in again."

John had run out of food. The canned goods he'd put into his emergency kit and unearthed the first day he and Zeke had returned to his property had lasted only a couple of days. The food Margery had dropped off had taken him through the rest of the week. He still had water because he'd rationed that by using water from the creek and boiling it to clean himself up and wash out his clothes and dishes. The first-aid kit had come in handy, especially the sunscreen and bug spray, but both were almost gone. He was well aware that sleeping outside without any protection other than the makeshift lean-to that Zeke had helped him build was just asking for trouble.

On top of everything else, he'd overdone it trying to use his left hand and probably cracked his wrist again. Then he had stepped in a sinkhole while trying to net fish in the bay and sunk in up to his knee, wrenching it badly as he struggled to get out. In short, he was a mess. He knew he should give up, but then what?

He ran his fingers through his hair and swallowed back a lump of sheer panic and frustration. He had put everything he had into this place, and now it was in shambles. He was close to running out of money, and it went against everything he believed to accept any of the help Grady had suggested was available from the government. Back on the farm he would have turned to his neighbors for help. Check that. He wouldn't have had to turn for help because they would have just been there.

Here, by his own stubborn choice, he had deliberately estranged himself from any semblance of community. And although he had out of sheer necessity allowed himself to be helped by Samuel and Zeke, his suspicions had been on high alert whenever anyone representing any official agency—including those run by the Mennonites—offered help. What was in it for them? How much of their concern came from the fact that his aunt held a position of power in the outside world? Hadn't Hester made it clear that there were others who were more in need and more grateful than he was?

He heard the muffled sound of an engine coming down his lane. He waited, knowing he was out of sight on the banks of the bay, well hidden by a cluster of mangroves. Zeke had talked about how he often used the shelter of the mangroves that surrounded his hiding place on the bay as a way of observing without being observed. Stealthily John crawled to a position that would allow him to identify his visitor without being seen.

Samuel Brubaker pulled his camper to a stop under the shade of the split banyan tree closest to what was left of the house. He cut the engine and got out.

"John?"

He glanced around and called out twice more. He walked around the property, picked up a couple of odds and ends, and added them to the pile that Zeke and John had started days earlier. Then on his way back to his vehicle, he paused and studied the ground. After a moment, he bent down, dug into the mud with a stick, and unearthed something that John couldn't quite make out. Instead of adding it to the pile of retrieved objects, he cleaned it off with his handkerchief before carrying it back to the camper. Opening the back hatch, he laid the object inside, removed a bike, and then closed the hatch before taking one last look around.

He balanced the bike against the wall of the toolshed and leaned in through the driver side window of the camper to get pencil and paper. After some thought, he scrawled a note and placed it under the windshield wiper. Then he mounted the bicycle and rode off back toward town, leaving the camper parked there in the shade.

John stayed put for several minutes, making sure that the cabinetmaker was truly gone; then he limped back across the yard and retrieved the note.

John,
Please make use of my camper while you work on your property. I have stocked it as best I could, but if I've forgotten anything, let me know, and I'll see that you get it.

Arlen wants you to know that our offer to send a crew from MDS to help you stands. He's staying at Jeannie Messner's house with Hester and her grandmother if you need to reach him. By tomorrow we should be able to get started shoveling mud from the houses that got flooded there in Pinecraft so hopefully everybody can be back home soon. Power and water are still off by the creek, but in the meantime generators are working. Know that you are welcome anytime to come into town for a meal or a place to rest and refresh yourself. You are in our prayers.

Samuel

John folded the note and placed it back under the windshield wiper. He opened the driver-side door and looked around the cab. Up close he saw that Samuel had basically taken an old pickup truck and mounted the camper top over the bed. The thing looked as if it had seen better days. But John couldn't help but be impressed with how organized and clean everything was inside the cab. Samuel had left the keys in the ignition, and John was unexpectedly touched by that. Samuel had to know that John, being Amish, didn't drive—wouldn't drive. He also had to know that even if he were willing to drive, it was unlikely that he had ever driven a motorized vehicle, at least not in real traffic. The keys were a message of trust. This small camper was probably all that Samuel Brubaker owned other than the clothes he wore. And yet he had entrusted it to John. He considered for a moment whether or not he would have been as charitable had the shoe been on the other foot.

Unlikely, he thought as he walked around to the back of the camper and opened the entrance to the sleeping and storage space. Again, everything was organized and pristine. The area was loaded with supplies. In addition to the cleaning supplies that John would need to get started with reclaiming what he could of the buildings, there were canned goods, bottled drinking water, sunscreen, insect repellant, a battery-powered lantern, and mosquito netting. And lying there in plain sight was his copy of

Walden, still in the plastic bag he had packed it in the night of the hurricane.

John had been looking for this precious book without even being conscious that finding it had driven his search. And here Samuel Brubaker had plucked it from the muck as if it had been right there in plain sight the whole time. John removed the book from the bag. The pages were waterlogged and flattened together, but it was intact. He cautiously turned to the first page. For perhaps the hundredth time he read the words that had started him on this path. Words that had helped him through numerous times when he had grieved for his mother and for all that he had left behind in Indiana, words that led him to this moment.

"When I wrote the following pages, or rather the bulk of them," Thoreau had written, *"I lived alone, in the woods, a mile from any neighbor, in a house which I had built myself, on the shore of Walden Pond, in Concord, Massachusetts, and earned my living by the labor of my hands only."*

Always he had stopped there, skimming over Thoreau's next words, but now that last sentence of the opening paragraph that he had ignored for so long seemed to be the one that resonated. *"I lived there two years and two months. At present I am a sojourner in civilized life again."*

"As am I," John whispered, his voice cracking with emotion.

Chapter 11

In spite of the cooler nights that came with the turning of the calendar from August to September, the days could still heat up to a high in the low nineties. So the volunteers from MDS and MCC took full advantage of the cooler early-morning hours to work inside the small houses along the creek.

The men worked tirelessly from dawn until well after dark to clear out any standing water from the Pinecraft dwellings, using portable generators to power the equipment necessary to get the job done. The neighborhood that had been silent and deserted for days vibrated with the sound of power washers, pumps, dehumidifiers, and fans. Every window and door that could be opened was. Some members of the work crews spent their time outside, making sure that drains and gutters were properly attached so that any additional rain would be directed away from houses.

Once the MDS crews had done their work on a cottage, it was time for Hester's volunteers to do their part. Arlen's crews had taken care of removing larger items such as soaked drywall, as well as mattresses, large furniture, and carpeting that were sure to be fertile ground for mold. Hester's volunteers would take the next step, scrubbing down undamaged walls and floors and washing smaller items that could be salvaged.

Olive Crowder was the first person to show up for work on the morning Hester finally got the green light to begin cleaning the cottages along the creek. She acknowledged Hester with her usual scowl of suspicion as if she were already anticipating a problem. Vivid memories of times when Hester had faced Olive's censure were never far from the surface whenever she had to deal with the woman.

In her youth, if Hester ran up the aisle of her father's church to deliver a message from home, Olive would abandon her work stuffing envelopes in the church office or cleaning the sanctuary to glare at Hester. If Hester failed to take note of this condemnation, then Olive would clear her throat loudly, sounding for all the world like a foghorn warning an errant ship.

Later when Hester was in her teens, she had developed a habit of constantly questioning the ways of her faith. "Why?" she would ask, and her parents would patiently explain the tradition and the history. But Olive Crowder saw her curiosity as doubt, and she would warn Hester's parents that the child was becoming far too interested in the *English* lifestyle or ways of outsiders. When Olive heard the news that Hester was headed off to nursing school, she had been—for once—speechless. Not that it was so unusual for Mennonites to seek higher education. The problem for Olive, and others, was that Hester had insisted on pursuing her nursing degree at an institution that had no ties to the church.

The day Hester boarded the bus for college, there in the midst of her family, friends, and neighbors stood Olive. Her arms had been folded around her chest like a straitjacket, and she had stared at Hester through the wide window of the bus as Hester leaned out to touch her family's hands and shout her good-byes. No, Olive Crowder did not approve of the way her pastor's only daughter had turned out one little bit. But Hester knew that out of respect for her parents, the woman would do her part even if that meant taking direction from Hester.

"Thank you for coming," Hester said as other women arrived.

They all donned galoshes and brought rubber gloves, goggles, and masks in preparation for the work. "Due to the power outage and limited availability of generators, it has taken the men longer than we expected to get the standing water cleaned up in these houses, but finally it's our turn to get to work. And look how the Lord has blessed us with the perfect September day to begin."

She had turned to lead them inside when she heard the unmistakable clearing of Olive's throat. "Yes, Olive," she said, turning to smile at her nemesis.

"You know best, of course, but it seems important to me to review the procedure. . .in case there are those among us who have not done this work before."

"Of course," Hester agreed, deciding in an instant that acquiescence was going to get them to work a lot faster than pointing out that every woman there was experienced in cleanup. "First we need to go room by room, removing any wet materials and personal belongings. . ."

"Wet or damp," Olive corrected.

"This includes any throw rugs, bedding, clothing, stuffed toys, books, and the like," she continued. "If you uncover significant mold or mildew on a wall or other surface that you cannot easily remove, please mark it and call it to my attention. A crew will come back and address those larger projects that may have escaped their notice earlier."

"Ja, leave that to the men and the professionals," Olive chimed in.

Hester bit her lower lip hard and continued, "Once we have everything cleared out, then we can start the process of scrubbing down walls and other surfaces such as countertops, cabinets, and floors. Questions?" She looked directly at Olive, who said nothing. "Excellent. Let's get to work."

She had reached the doorway of the Millers' house when she heard Olive mutter. "A prayer would be nice."

Hester stopped in her tracks. "Ja," she said, "it would." She bowed her head and the others followed her lead. She didn't know what the others were praying for, but in her case it was, as always, patience. "Amen," she murmured after a moment of silence.

Once inside the first of a dozen homes that would need their services, the women paired off and went their separate ways—one pair to tackle the kitchen while another headed down the hall toward the bedrooms. Hester smiled when she saw Olive's sister, Agnes, scurry off to join another woman in the kitchen, leaving Hester and Olive standing in the living room.

"Well," Hester said, "those books and boxes of papers are soaked through." She quickly loaded a box, determined it was too heavy to lift, and started to slide it toward the open front door.

"You'll scar the floor," Olive huffed as she lifted one side of the box and waited for Hester to take hold of the other.

Hester stared at the water-stained floor—a floor that would have to be replaced—and then back at Olive. "I've got this."

"Suit yourself," Olive said and dropped her end of the box. "You always do," she added as she turned her attention to removing books from the shelves and stacking them in piles on the floor.

Hester had had enough. She was past thirty years old and a trained nurse, not to mention an experienced community organizer. She pushed the box out onto the front porch and then returned to face Olive.

"Olive, I am doing the best I can in a situation that is beyond what anyone might have imagined. And yet I sense that you don't agree with my approach to this project." *Or any project I am involved with.*

Olive continued removing books one by one, flipping through the pages of each before setting it in one of the piles. "If you must know, Hester, there are several people who don't think that you are doing your best."

Hester took a moment to listen to the sounds coming from other areas of the house. The rest of her crew was occupied. She and Olive were alone and unlikely to be overheard or disturbed. The time had come. "Please explain that statement," she said quietly.

Olive turned and looked at her. Hester met her gaze directly and lifted one eyebrow to emphasize her determination to get their differences out in the open once and for all.

"Very well. You have an unfortunate tendency to give your attention to outsiders when many in your own community are suffering."

Hester opened her mouth to respond, but Olive held up a restraining finger. "For example, it has been noticed and commented upon that you put the welfare of that man, John Steiner, before the welfare of your own grandmother, never mind others in this neighborhood who should have been evacuated hours before it flooded—"

"The county command center gave specific instructions about—"

"And since when do we take our direction from some outside government agency?" Olive demanded. "That is your problem, Hester Detlef. You have always put far too much stock in what outsiders want."

Hester waited a beat, fighting to quell the tide of her own anger and resentment toward this woman's constant judging of her. "That's really what this is about, isn't it?"

Olive sucked in her cheeks. "I don't know what you mean. You asked—"

"Oh, Olive, I truly believe that you have my best interests at heart. Your respect for my father and the years of friendship you shared with my mother make that clear. But just because I have friends in the outside world and I sometimes—"

"Sometimes? Do you not see the sin that is your ego and pride, Hester? I know you think you are merely following in your dear mother's path, but you are not. And I must warn you. . ." Olive raised one gloved hand, stained now with the ink from the wet newsprint she'd begun collecting once she'd gone through the books. She shook her finger in Hester's face. "I feel compelled to warn you that neither your father's position in the community nor the memory of your dear mother can protect you should you continue down this path of pride and conceit."

In the silence that followed this announcement, Hester was aware of a light tapping on the open door, and then Rosalyn stepped inside. "Sorry I'm late," she said, glancing from Hester to Olive and back again. "I—is everything all right?"

"Fine," Hester said. "I'm just going to check on the others." She brushed past Olive, who had returned to her work as soon as Rosalyn entered the room.

But she stopped halfway to the bedrooms and forced herself to take several deep breaths to regain her composure. Olive's words had struck closer to home than Hester was willing to admit aloud. She had chosen to help Grady with the situation at Tucker's Point when she should have focused on getting her grandmother and the others packed up and moved to shelters. Due to her negligence, they had barely avoided disaster. She twisted the tie of her prayer covering around her finger. Pinecraft was her community, not the world beyond that and certainly not Tucker's Point.

Olive had hit another nerve, too. Ever since her mother's death, Hester had felt this urgency to fill her days with work. It was almost as if by running from one task to the next she might be able to suppress the discontent and restlessness that dogged her even when she tried to sleep.

Hester retraced her steps down the hall. "Olive, do you have a minute?" she asked.

The older woman eyed her suspiciously but put down the cloth soaked in beach solution that she was using to wipe down a painted built-in bookcase and waited.

Rosalyn looked from one woman to the other. "I'll just go see if I can be of help in the kitchen," she murmured as she hurried off.

"I'd like to apologize," Hester said. "Both for my behavior earlier and for my actions over the last days and weeks. You were right."

Olive released a self-righteous huff but said nothing.

"Actually, you have done me a great favor," Hester continued, picking up the cleaning rag that Rosalyn had left behind and starting to wash the wall next to where Olive returned to her scrubbing. "I was feeling such guilt about how long I waited before helping my grandmother and others get moved to the shelters. I am so thankful that nothing happened to any of you. If someone had been injured or suffered a heart attack from the stress. . ."

"Fortunately for you, God was with us that day. Perhaps He was using the situation to teach you a valuable lesson—one you have refused to heed despite numerous warnings from others."

Hester did not like thinking of God placing others in harm's way simply to teach her a lesson, but she held her tongue. This was no time for a theological debate. She had come back to apologize and confess that there was an element of truth in Olive's concern.

"Yes, well, I wanted you to know that my rudeness before was born of that sense of guilt."

Olive sloshed her rag in the bucket of sudsy water and twisted it into a skein to squeeze out every extra drop before she returned to wiping down the top of the bookcase and then started on the wall above it. The two of them worked in silence for several minutes until every inch of the wall had been scrubbed clean. All the while Hester was aware that Olive's lips were pressed into that thin line that was a sure sign that she was about to make a pronouncement.

"Am I to understand that you are telling me that you have seen the error of your ways at long last and that you will be resigning your position with MCC?"

Hester could not have been more shocked if the woman had asked if she planned to cut off her right arm as retribution for her transgressions. "I. . . Why would. . . ?"

Olive ignored her sputtering. "Because if you are truly sorry for what you admit is a fault brought on by your decision to volunteer for that agency, then perhaps. . ."

"MCC is a Mennonite agency," Hester reminded her.

"Do not lecture me, *bitte*. I am well aware of who and what they are. I am also well aware that over time the people who have been given responsibility for running that agency have fallen prey to the ways of outsiders. MCC is barely distinguishable from—"

"They do good work—*we* do good work," Hester said quietly as she tried in vain to stem the anger rising inside her.

"That may be, but as the daughter of a minister, you would do well to reconsider your allegiance to that group. CAM is a far more appropriate group, as your friend Emma Keller has been quick to appreciate."

"Appropriate?"

"For us. For you, the only daughter of our pastor."

Hester bit her lower lip and closed her eyes, silently praying for God's guidance. Aware that Rosalyn had returned and was standing in the doorway, Hester forced herself to remain calm. "My work—"

"*Your* work? What about God's work? Oh, Hester, sometimes I despair for you," Olive moaned. "Against all tradition you decided to pursue a career, and, unpaid though it may be, you clearly see yourself as a working woman."

Hester had opened her mouth to deliver a retort that she was sure to regret when Rosalyn stepped the rest of the way into the room and saved her. "Seems to me, ma'am, that we are all working women, at least until we get these houses cleaned up and folks moved back in."

She did not give Olive a chance to respond, but turned instead to Hester. "Kitchen's almost done, so I thought I'd get started on Lizzie's house. If you'll come show me what you want done over there, Hester, I'll round up some warm bodies and get to work."

Gratefully, Hester dropped her rag back into the bucket and followed Rosalyn outside.

John was having trouble focusing, literally. His eyes constantly clouded over from the sweat that dripped off his face like raindrops, making it next to impossible to see what he was doing. Between his broken wrist and the ankle he'd twisted, he was already severely limited in what he could accomplish on any given day.

Still, he had made some progress. With Zeke's help he'd

managed to get a tarp over the exposed rafters of the house where the roof had blown off. He'd also scrubbed down the kitchen walls and removed anything that had already produced mold or that might if left untended. It would be some time before he could afford the repairs that would be necessary to restore the second story of the main house, so he had decided to focus his energy on the packinghouse and smaller outbuildings instead. To that end his plan was to make use of the plywood sheets that he'd nailed over the windows before the hurricane came ashore to put down a base for the roof of the packinghouse and work from there.

He had leaned the boards against the walls of the packinghouse that had remained standing after the storm and turned them daily to allow them to dry. Of course they had warped, but not so much that they wouldn't do until he could afford something better. With his one good arm, turning the boards took several hours all by itself, and there was no way that he alone could wrangle them up and into place on the rafters without help. So he would wait until Zeke decided to stop by and they could do it together. He had learned that Zeke's schedule was unpredictable to say the least.

Samuel was more reliable. He had biked out to John's property several times in the days that had passed since leaving the camper with him. He always came alone and after dark when his work in town was finished for the day. John understood that his impromptu visits were the young carpenter's way of building trust. And it was working. He never stayed long, just walked around looking at what John had been able to accomplish since his last visit. Every once in a while he would comment on the progress in Pinecraft.

"MDS has cleared out all of the houses along the creek," he'd told John on his latest visit. "The women from MCC and CAM are scrubbing everything down, and Pastor Detlef expects some folks will be able to start moving back in as early as next week."

"That's good." It occurred to John that Samuel never mentioned Hester. Not that he had any reason to talk about her to John. Besides, why should he care?

"Everybody doing okay otherwise?"

"*Sehr* gut. Jeannie Messner and her husband took in a bunch of people, and others did the same. The shelters aren't nearly so filled as they were right after the storm."

John waited for more explanation of Samuel's definition of *very good* as applied to the situation at hand, but apparently Samuel had nothing more to report. "Well, I'll go back now." He paused and studied John for a long moment. "You look thinner, John. Are you eating?"

"I am. Margery shows up regularly to check on that, and to just in general be sure I'm still breathing."

Samuel nodded. "That's good. She's a good person, perhaps too concerned at times about the welfare of others. She probably told you that she suffered some real damage during the storm, but far more afterward when the floods came. Now that we've cleared out the houses in Pinecraft, Pastor Detlef plans to take a team over to help her get her repairs done so that her business can open again." He mounted the bicycle and began pedaling slowly toward the lane out to the main road. "God bless you, John," he called.

As John watched him go, he had the sudden urge to call him back, to suggest a cup of coffee or a game of checkers—not that he owned a checker set. But he wanted to know more about Margery. He'd been so wrapped up in his own problems that he'd failed to consider that Margery had to have suffered such serious losses as well. It struck him that watching Samuel pedal into the darkness and not knowing for sure when he might see him—or anyone—again, he felt something he hadn't felt in a very long time. John felt loneliness.

That night he had trouble sleeping. Usually at the end of the day he was so thoroughly exhausted that he had barely closed his Bible from his nightly reading before he was asleep. But on this night that wasn't the case. Long after the white noise of the traffic that ran along Highway 41 in the distance had subsided, John lay on his sleeping bag in the back of the camper, his eyes wide open as he stared up through the mosquito netting and listened to an owl calling to its mate.

Margery had said nothing about further damage to her place from the floods. He'd asked her how she was recovering after the storm, and she'd brushed him off as she always did.

"You just get yourself back in shape," she'd barked. "I'll be just fine."

And why would she confide in you? he thought. She could hardly count on him to offer any real help or, for that matter, common sympathy for her plight. Margery knew very well that he cringed every time she showed up and that everything he said or did was with one intention—to get her to leave as soon as possible.

He hadn't always been like this. Back in Indiana he had been known as a man who could be counted on to help a neighbor, help a total stranger for that matter. But he had changed. Instead of his move to Florida being the start of a new life healing the wounds he'd suffered, it seemed those wounds had festered. His anger at the unfairness of life had infected his ability to trust. His ability to care.

True, back home, people he had thought he could count on had turned away from him. People who had expressed love for him had sided with those who accused him of becoming too prideful. John closed his eyes and allowed himself to think about Alice Yoder for the first time in two long years. Just as he had been banned by the church, he had banned the woman he'd been ready to marry from his thoughts, refusing to allow anything about her to color his mind. And in time he had succeeded. Once he'd gotten settled in Florida, the work to get the garden planted, the groves back to producing, and the house habitable had exhausted him to the point where at night it was all he could do to prepare a simple supper, read his Bible, and fall into bed.

Every morning seemed to bring with it some fresh challenge that had to be faced and dealt with, and in time, the image of Alice had faded. But it came to him now that in banning her from his thoughts, he had banned anyone who showed the slightest interest in him, regardless of their age or gender. He had trusted Alice because he'd had no reason not to believe that she would stand with him no matter what. But at the first sign of conflict she had chosen the safety of the community over him. That had been the final straw.

Then when he'd moved into the old farmhouse that had sat unoccupied and abandoned for over a decade, Margery had shown up offering him food and friendship, but he had sent her away. His distrust of others and their hidden motives had been too fresh, too painful, and he had quickly decided that what Thoreau had gotten right was the idea of depending solely on one's self. And over the two years that followed, he had thought the plan was working. He kept so busy that his need for human companionship became secondary to his need to prove himself.

But now he found himself wondering if he had ever intended that his self-imposed isolation would go on indefinitely. It had begun for him as it had for Thoreau, as an experiment. Nothing more. But with each passing day, each challenge met and conquered, the idea that it was possible to live a life of near-self-sufficiency had become the ultimate challenge.

The truth was that he had not allowed himself to think beyond getting through each day. Every victory was something he celebrated alone. No, not alone. With God. For when he'd seen the first vegetables thriving in the raised planter boxes or the blossoms on the trees in Tucker's abandoned grove, he had raised his eyes to the heavens, thanking God. He had needed nothing more than that as evidence that he had made the right choice in coming to Florida.

Back then he had told himself that his community had deserted him, resulting in the loss of his farm, his future wife, and the life they would share. But it was long past time for him to admit that he and he alone had made the decision to leave. He had come to Florida to prove a point. Now he had to wonder if he had really intended to stay forever.

He opened the door to the camper and stepped outside. Above him a full moon sat low in the western sky, casting a beam like a path straight onto the waters of the bay. It would be light soon. Tied up at the pier—one of the first things he and Zeke had restored on the property—was a small boat. Margery had towed it over one day, insisting she had no place for it until her pier could be repaired.

"You'd be doing me a favor keeping it here, Johnny. Not that you're inclined to handing out favors, but I'd appreciate it."

"Fine," he'd told her and gone back to working on clearing out the remains of the chicken coop.

"I'll leave the keys in the ON position–that way you just need to pull the cord to get her started. You know, in case you want to use it or have to move it or something."

"Fine," he'd repeated. He had waited for the sound of her boat fading before going down to the pier and having a look at the craft.

Now with his one good arm, he released the rope from the post and climbed in. Awkwardly he managed to get the boat started, back it away from his pier, and turn it toward the mouth of the creek. By the time he was on his way, he was drenched in sweat. The sky had started to lighten. He headed up Philippi Creek, and just ahead he could see what was left of Margery's marina.

Margery Barker had watched over him for two long years. She had never asked for or seemed to expect anything in return. Indeed, she had endured his barely concealed annoyance at her visits with humor and grace. And his bad temper had not deterred her from coming back again and again. How many times had he shown genuine interest in her business, her health, her happiness? What did he really know of her? That she was a widow and that she ran a fishing charter business. That was pretty much it.

Something his aunt Liz had said the last time they spoke by phone—a phone call that had ended with John hanging up on her—came back to him now.

"You were never a selfish man, John. In fact, you have always been one of the most giving people I have ever known. Rachel was always so proud of the way you turned out."

His aunt had been taking a risk. She knew that any mention

of his mother opened floodgates of remorse and guilt for John.

"Sorry," Liz had murmured, realizing too late her mistake. "But really, John, I am worried about you. You've changed so much."

"I'm fine," he'd managed before hanging up the pay phone. And as he'd stood there in the middle of a nearly deserted bus station where he had gone to use the phone, he had felt a lump of grief fill the cavity of his chest like unset concrete until he'd been forced to sit down to catch his breath.

That conversation had taken place six months ago. Since then Liz had contacted him by mail as often as not delivered by Margery without comment.

His aunt was right. He had changed, and not for the better. He had allowed his bitterness to color everything he did, every interaction with others. He looked into every face these days with distrust, expecting the person to have some agenda other than simple kindness. Margery had proved him wrong, and she deserved more from him than the disdain he'd dished out for two years. For that matter, so did his aunt Liz, but one step at a time.

Chapter 12

As the sun painted the sky in streaks of vermilion and orange, John idled the boat, taking stock of Margery Barker's marina. In spite of catastrophic damage to the bait shop and pier, John could see that a lot of work had already been done. Of course Margery would have gratefully accepted the help of neighbors and friends. She was well known and deeply respected, at least among those who lived and worked along the bay.

Margery's houseboat was tied up at one end of the pier, a pier that he was surprised to see had been fully rebuilt. To either side, small boats in various stages of repair bobbed in the calm water of the creek, the pulleys used to raise their sails clanking against metal poles as if someone were picking out a tune on a row of glass bottles. A tarp covered what had been the roof of the bait shop, but the place appeared deserted, abandoned even. The creek waters smelled faintly of dead fish and the fuel that had obviously leaked out of the damaged boats. In addition to the bait shop, Margery made her living running fishing trips and renting boats to tourists. From the looks of things, the bait shop was closed, and other than the small boat Margery used to get around, there wasn't a vessel worth chartering among the half dozen tied up at the pier.

He eased his craft closer to the houseboat. Margery had once told him that the day she buried her husband she had returned to the marina, boarded the houseboat, and stayed. After a year she had found the strength to return to the house they had shared and clear it out before putting it up for sale. All of this came back to him now as the boat she'd loaned him rocked gently and he tried to decide on his next move.

His heart was beating so hard it was as if he could hear each thud. It had been a very long time since he had reached out to anyone. It came back to him that Samuel had mentioned the fisherwoman was staying with Jeannie Messner. But there were definite sounds of occupancy coming from the houseboat.

"Margery?" He sniffed the air as he brought his boat closer to the side of the houseboat. Coffee. Bacon frying. If vandals had taken over the place, they were surely making themselves at home.

"Margery?" This time he shouted the name.

"What?" Margery barked, coming onto the deck, waving away an unseen bug with a spatula. Then she saw him, and her eyes widened, as did her smile. "Well, now, will you look at what the tide brought in! Praise God and pass the cranberry sauce—I never ever thought I would see this day."

He threw her the rope. "You gonna help me tie this thing up and invite me in for breakfast or stand there yapping all morning?" he grumbled.

True to form, Margery made no further comment about his unexpected visit. Instead, she guided him the rest of the way into her pier and looped the rope over a post. Then she gave him a hand as he made the short leap from boat to pier and led the way into the galley kitchen, where she turned on the gas under the skillet and cracked four large eggs into the bacon grease.

"Moved back here four days ago," she announced. "Jeannie's place was nice, too nice for the likes of me. Lots of pretties in that house, and you know me, clumsy as the day is long. I kept worrying I might break something. And with school starting they were all busy with that. Truth be told, I could not wait to get this old bucket in good enough shape so I could bunk here again."

John attacked the food as soon as she set the plate in front of him. He'd been eating little other than prepackaged meals or canned goods for days now, and he couldn't remember the last time that he'd had a hot meal. "Good," he muttered with his mouth full of scrambled eggs and biscuit. He glanced up when he realized Margery had stopped talking and was leaning against the sink, arms folded as she watched him eat.

"Didn't you forget something?"

John felt color rise to his cheeks and was grateful for the sun-scorched skin that he assumed hid his embarrassment. "Sorry," he muttered and put down his fork. He leaned back and waited for Margery to fill her plate and join him.

"I'm touched," she said as she set her plate down and took the chair across from him, "but I was talking about saying grace. I thought a good Amish man like you—"

"I. . ." John decided not to debate the point. Instead, he closed his eyes and bowed his head. After a moment he resumed eating.

"Arlen's sending me some help today," Margery said.

"MDS team?"

"Not officially. Just neighbors helping neighbors, as Arlen likes to put it."

He drank a full glass of orange juice before he found the nerve to make his next statement. "I have some time if you can use an extra hand."

John was pretty sure it was his unsolicited offer to help that had struck Margery speechless for once. But when he glanced at her, he saw that she was fighting the urge to burst into laughter. "What?"

"An extra hand and maybe one good leg," she managed, her laughter escaping as she pointed to his cast and wrapped ankle, "is about all you're in a position to offer."

John couldn't help himself. The situation was so ridiculous that laughter seemed the only response. And once he got his own good humor rolling, it seemed as if he had unleashed a wellspring that had for far too long been capped.

Hester and Arlen exchanged curious glances as they walked the length of Margery's pier and heard her hearty laughter rolling out the open windows of the houseboat. Then they heard the unmistakable raspy growl of John Steiner's voice. "All right already," he was saying, but he was laughing as well.

"Hello," Arlen called as he stepped onto the deck and then offered his hand to Hester.

Margery stuck her head out the missing door. She was wiping tears of merriment from her eyes with the hem of her oversized T-shirt. "Come on in and have some breakfast," she invited. "You are not going to believe who has offered to lend us a hand." This last seemed to set her off all over again, and when Arlen and Hester stepped into Margery's cramped living space, Hester was stunned to see John apparently still recovering from whatever joke Margery had told. The effect that his smile had on her was unsettling, and she looked away.

"Well, now, this is a nice surprise," Arlen boomed as he grasped John's shoulder and gave it a squeeze. "How are you faring over at Tucker's Point, John?"

All traces of humor disappeared. When Hester glanced his way, she saw that John's deep-set eyes had darkened like storm clouds over the Gulf. "Well enough. I should thank you for sending Samuel to check in on me from time to time. The loan of his camper has been a special blessing."

Hester and her father exchanged a look. Neither of them had had any idea that Samuel had continued to visit John after he had gone out there to leave his camper.

"Samuel makes his own choices," Arlen replied.

The tiny space was suddenly filled with silence until Margery came to the rescue. "Well, we'll get nothing done standing around here jabbering. Go on out there on the deck where there's more room. Find some shade and have something to eat. Whoo-ee! Guess this is what folks up north call Indian summer. Cool nights and scorching days. Welcome to autumn in Florida."

"We ate at home," Arlen told her, "but I always leave room for at least one of your biscuits, Margery."

"Let me help you," Hester offered, taking down two more

plates from the open shelving above the sink and holding them while Margery dished up bacon with one hand while scrambling more eggs with the other. Hester was glad to see John take his almost-empty plate and coffee mug and follow her father outside. "When did he get here?" she asked Margery in a near whisper.

"John?" She glanced at the clock and shrugged. "Half hour ago. You could've knocked me over with a feather when I saw him out there, steering that old piece of junk of mine with one hand." She chuckled. "I'll bet it took him near quarter of an hour just to get her fired up and backed away from his pier, but the man is stubborn."

"What does he want?"

"Want?" Margery looked at Hester as if she had suddenly started speaking in tongues. "He says he's come to help."

"After two years?"

"Oh, honey, it may seem like two years, but that storm blew here only just over a month ago." She topped off the plates Hester was holding with two hot biscuits each. "Oh, I get it. You mean why come now when he's never made the move before?"

Hester nodded and waited for Margery to pour coffee in two chipped, mismatched mugs.

"People change all the time," Margery said. "Admittedly some take longer than others, but he's here, and that's the main thing." She led the way out to the deck, where John and Arlen had found shelter in the shade. John was pointing to something above them, and Arlen was nodding.

"You want a refill?" Margery asked John. He held out his coffee mug.

"Get it yourself," Margery barked. "This cook's done her thing for the morning."

Hester watched as John got up and made his way back to the galley. He was limping.

"What happened to your ankle?" she asked.

"Stepped in a sinkhole and twisted it," he replied and disappeared inside.

"One good leg and one good arm?" Margery called after him.

"You're a real bargain, John Steiner." She turned her attention to her breakfast but gave Arlen a conspiratorial wink. "I think the boy might be coming around finally."

"He looks terrible," Hester whispered back.

"I expect he's not sleeping much. He was pretty bitten up before Samuel brought the camper and mosquito netting and such." Margery glanced up as John started back toward them, his plate loaded with the rest of the bacon and biscuits. "You're gonna eat me out of house and home," she growled.

"I figured we'd all save energy if I just brought out what was left."

"Yeah, everybody knows you're a real sweetheart," Margery said as she helped herself to another biscuit from the plate and plopped one onto Arlen's plate.

Hester was sure she wasn't seeing right. Had John Steiner almost smiled as he took his seat again? Somehow Margery had gotten to the man, won him over.

The crunch of car tires on packed sand and gravel followed by the slamming of car doors and voices told Hester that the rest of the crew had arrived. Arlen and Margery went to meet them and help with the unloading of supplies. Hester started to clear away the breakfast dishes.

"I can do this," John said. "You go on and help Arlen and the others."

She glanced at the cast that looked as if it had been through its own hurricane. "Let me look at that," she said, taking his arm before he could refuse. "What have you done to yourself?" she muttered as she examined the fiberglass cast that in places was worn down to his bare skin.

"I'm fine," he grumbled, pulling his arm away and ducking his head to clear the galley doorway.

"You are not fine, John. Your wrist probably needs resetting, and then there's the matter of that ankle. You're wearing a compression bandage?"

"I do what I need to do to get around."

"And you're wearing flip-flops? When you're working in

areas hard hit by a hurricane, that is just plain stupid. With all the debris, you could easily trip or step on a nail." She followed him inside and set down the stack of plates she was carrying. "As long as I'm here, you might as well let me take a look."

"Don't do me any favors, lady."

Hester released a weary sigh. "Could we call a truce here and agree that you might actually benefit from my examining you?"

He eyed her suspiciously.

"If you want to help Margery, then you're doing her no favors by not taking care of yourself." She took down Margery's first-aid kit from the shelf above the door.

She decided to maintain her professional demeanor in spite of the fact that what she really wanted to do was to lecture the man that his refusal to accept help when it was offered had endangered his health.

"Did you ice it?" she asked as she removed the filthy compression bandage and dropped it in the trash.

His answer was a snort of derision that she suspected just might be covering a grimace of pain as she probed the bruised skin. "Sure. I used the icemaker on my refrigerator. You know, the one that got thrown halfway to Siesta when the hurricane blew through?"

She glanced up at him. "A simple 'no' would suffice." She continued to examine him, her fingers working their way over the arch of his foot and up and around his ankle.

"You're going to bite the tip of your tongue off," he said.

From her kneeling position on the floor next to his chair, she looked up to find him studying her closely. His eyes roamed over her features, her hair, her prayer covering. "Why are you always so angry, Hester Detlef?" he asked when she quirked an eyebrow at him.

"If you take my seriousness about my work for anger, then maybe that's because you're the one who walks through your days with barely concealed hostility."

"Maybe I've got my reasons."

"I'm sure you believe that you do, but I would remind you that the people you have been fortunate enough to meet here have nothing but your best interests in mind. They—we—do not deserve to be treated with such—"

"Got it. And so we come back to you."

She decided to ignore him. "Point your toe," she instructed and was amazed when he complied. "Now trace the letters of the alphabet using your toe like a pencil."

"Why?" He eyed her with suspicion.

"Because my goal in life is to make you look as ridiculous as possible," she snapped. Then she forced herself to swallow her annoyance. "It's a rehabilitation exercise, one you can practice on your own while your ankle heals. Try the vowels."

He slowly traced the letter *a* and then an *e*.

"Good," she said. "Try that later with the entire alphabet and repeat it three to five times a day. It will help improve your range of motion."

"What else?"

She checked to see if he was baiting her, but he was continuing the exercise on his own. "Okay, here's one more. Put your foot flat on the floor. You need to be sitting in a chair for this one."

"I am sitting in a chair," he pointed out.

"I mean when you do it on your own. Foot flat on the floor. Now move your knee from side to side slowly while keeping your foot pressed flat."

He tried it.

"Slower," she instructed. "Good. Do both of those three to five times a day, and it should help." She took out a tube of ointment and started applying it to the insect bites on his good arm. Then she stood up and bent over him to treat the bites on his face. She paused. It was her turn to study his features. His skin was scorched a deep russet. The beginnings of a beard had sprouted on his chin, golden-red like his hair. His eyes were deep-set under a strong forehead accented by thick eyebrows that had been bleached almost white by the sun. His eyes, fixed on hers, were the verdant green of a tropical forest. And yet his overall appearance was that of a man who was deeply troubled, who had known great sadness in his life. Hester felt a twinge of empathy for him.

"We, my father and Samuel and the others included, do not wish to cause you further pain, John," she said as she continued to apply the salve to his cheekbones and temples. "I don't know why it seems important to say this to you, but you are safe here."

She stepped back, recapping the tube of ointment as she checked to be sure she hadn't missed any bites. "Better," she said more to herself than to him. "As for that wrist," she went on, "we'll have to go into town for that to be looked at. It may need to be reset."

"Now?"

"What's to be gained by waiting?"

"I came here to help Margery."

"There'll be plenty left to do once we go and come back." She took a fresh compression bandage from the first-aid kit and knelt to wrap his ankle.

"I thought you said this wasn't a good idea."

"I'm just covering it loosely. It will serve as a reminder to you to take care as you move around on it, at least until we can get you a proper pair of shoes."

She put away the first-aid kit and poured water over the dishes to let them soak while they were gone. "Coming?" She waited by the doorway.

"Coming," he said as he grudgingly got to his feet.

Hester took visual stock of the room until she spotted a walking stick leaning against the wall. "Use this," she said. "We'll stop by the distribution center as long as we're in town and find you some work boots and a hat that properly covers your ears, neck, and face."

"Don't push it," he muttered as he followed her onto the pier and walked on toward the car while she collected car keys from her father and explained why they were leaving. To her surprise, when she got to the car, he was holding the door open for her.

"Thank you," she said as she slid in and pushed the key into the ignition. She watched him walk around the front of the car and with some satisfaction noticed that he was not limping nearly as badly as he had before she'd treated him. She also couldn't seem to stop noticing that John Steiner was one good-looking man.

Chapter 13

Predictably the wait in the emergency room promised to be a long one, and they hadn't been there half an hour when John suddenly stood up.

"This is a waste of time."

"That depends on how you choose to look at the situation," Hester replied. "Your wrist needs a new cast. Without it you will likely do further damage and set back your efforts to restore your own property and help Margery."

He sat back down and Hester slid a bench closer to him. "You should keep that ankle elevated when you're sitting."

"Steiner," the attendant called.

"Do you want me to come with you?" Hester asked as John struggled to his feet.

"I'm not twelve, Hester," he grumbled and hobbled off.

Down the hall a cheery aide greeted him with, "And how are we doing today?"

John answered her with a nearly inaudible, "How do you think?"

Hester sighed. Whatever common ground John may have found with Margery earlier that morning, it certainly had not carried over to others.

But when John emerged from the examining room, he was wearing a smaller cast that left his fingers free to move, as well as what Hester had come to understand was for him a pleasant expression. He crossed the room wiggling his fingers, and that was when she noticed that the ER doctor had also outfitted him with a boot to support his ankle.

"Ready?" she asked, realizing instinctively that it would not do to make a fuss about this change in his attitude.

John nodded, his focus still on experimenting with how he might use his hand and fingers.

"That's quite an improvement," Hester ventured as she drove back to Pinecraft so John could get some sturdier shoes and perhaps some clothing.

"Yeah."

She turned onto Bahia Vista and followed a stream of traffic east. "You know, now that the cottages in Pinecraft have been restored, I'm sure Dad would be willing to send a team of workers out to help you, once they've finished with Margery's bait shop, of course."

"I'll be okay," he said.

"Yeah, we can all see that you're managing just fine," she said. And then on a whim she pulled her father's car into the parking lot of Big Olaf's Creamery. "I need ice cream," she announced as she cut the engine and got out of the car.

When John gave no sign of moving, she turned and called back to him. "Chocolate or vanilla?"

"Vanilla," he replied after a moment.

"Figures," Hester muttered to herself. As she waited in line to order their cones, she considered why she was prolonging her time with John Steiner. Didn't it make more sense to take him over to the distribution center and let Rosalyn help him find shoes and clothing there? But no, she had stopped for ice cream. Like they were on a date or something.

She shook off that thought and stepped up to order. The man behind the counter was a member of her father's congregation. By the time he had chatted with her about the storm, the cones he'd handed her were beginning to melt.

"Sorry about that," he said as he placed two plastic sundae dishes under the cones so she could invert them into the cups. "A new invention," he teased. "You've heard of upside-down cake? Well, these are upside-down cones."

Hester couldn't help laughing, and by the time she returned to the car, her mood had lightened considerably. "Let's sit out here in the shade," she invited, holding up the dishes and leading the way to a bench that was shaded by the eave of the building.

John joined her a moment later and accepted the dish she offered him.

"Earl is a talker," she offered by way of explanation. "These started out as regular cones, but then. . ."

"It's fine," John said, filling his spoon and then his mouth with the ice cream. "Thank you."

"I had an ulterior motive," Hester admitted.

John cocked one eyebrow but kept eating his ice cream.

"Look, we kind of got off on the wrong foot, you and me. It was my fault. I'd like to rectify that since it looks like we might be traveling in the same circles now and again." She saw a hint of mistrust flitter across his face and sighed. "Whatever happened to you back in Indiana, John, I assure you that my father and I and Samuel and Margery and anyone else you might meet around here are exactly who and what we appear to be."

"What you see is what you get?"

"Something like that."

He scraped a spoonful of ice cream from the dish and then picked up the cone and took a bite.

"So what did happen back there?" Hester asked, her gaze fixed on the passing parade of cars and bicycles. It was none of her business, and she wasn't sure why she should care. The question had just popped out as if it had been lodged there in her throat for days.

To her surprise John did not rebuff her. Instead, he leaned back on the bench, propping his injured foot on top of his good foot as he licked ice cream.

"Did you ever read the book *Walden* by Henry David Thoreau?"

"A long time ago. My mother had a copy, and then it was on the required reading list in college. Why?"

"Tucker's Point is—was—my Walden."

"It was your dream," Hester murmured. She understood all about dreams, all about wanting things you weren't supposed to want but believing that—for you—they were the only path.

John nodded and took the last bite of his ice cream. He savored the taste of it. Hester had already finished hers, including the cone.

"But why here? Why not back in Indiana?"

"It started there actually, a few years ago. That's when I first read the book. It was at a time in my life when things were changing, and I was looking for some direction. I had prayed on the matter for weeks, but nothing seemed right to me. Thoreau wrote about men living lives of 'quiet desperation.' That certainly was a fit way to describe how I was feeling at the time."

"You were a grown man."

John shrugged. "I had just turned thirty, but what's in an age? I had lived my whole life on that farm, in that community. Even when other teens went off to try their wings before being baptized, I stayed. My dad had died and Mom would have been alone. Maybe that's where the desire came from," he mused, more to himself than to her.

"So you decided to leave everything and come here?"

"That may be oversimplifying it, but yeah."

"You just picked up and left? Your family and friends? Your community? The woman you were to marry?"

He frowned at her, and his eyes narrowed as if what he was revealing about himself had just dawned on him. "I didn't desert anyone or anything, if that's what you think. If anything, that shoe was on the other foot."

"Meaning they deserted you."

"They weren't bad people," he said defensively.

"I didn't say they were." She waited until he had bitten into the last of the cone as if he were chomping down on something far tougher than a sugar cone.

"What about your family? Siblings?"

"I told you, my father died of a heart attack when I was thirteen. My parents never had other children."

"I'm sorry for your loss. Your mother has never remarried?"

He was quiet for such a long moment that Hester thought perhaps he hadn't heard her question. And then very quietly he said, "My mother died the year I decided to come here. That was. . ."

Hester watched as an expression of abject sadness crossed his features. She was so taken aback by the pain and fragility she saw in that expression that she felt compelled to change the subject and spoke aloud the first thought that popped into her mind.

"Grady Forrest told me you had left your community," she ventured, uncertain of what could possibly drive her to want to explore such a painful topic.

"I was banned," he said quietly, his eyes daring her to pursue the topic any further. When she said no more, he stood up and threw the empty dish into a nearby trash bin. "Are we getting those shoes today or not?" He limped to the car and got in, slamming the car door like an exclamation point to his silent announcement that this conversation was over.

Meddling little do-gooder, John thought as he waited for Hester to dispose of her ice cream dish and climb behind the wheel of the car. She had gotten to him, and he'd almost told her about his mother's tragic death, about his part in that tragedy. He'd almost trusted her.

"Sorry," she said finally. "Look, I. . ." She sat for a moment with both hands in her lap, working the car keys like worry beads.

"Let's just go," he said and fastened his gaze on a spot on the windshield where a small insect had met its end.

With a sigh, she turned the key and eased the sedan into traffic, pausing to let a three-wheeled bicycle pass and returning the rider's greeting with a prepackaged smile.

When they reached the thrift shop and donation center where clothing and other goods were stored, Hester led the way inside. A young woman looked up from her sorting work and smiled. In spite of a face marred with burn scars, she had the most strikingly beautiful smile, and her eyes were so guileless that John felt his annoyance with Hester ease slightly.

"Rosalyn, this is John Steiner," Hester said in a monotone. "He needs shoes and some clothing and a decent hat. I'll be in the office." Without another word she stepped inside a small office and closed the door.

"Well, John Steiner," Rosalyn said, sizing him up with a glance, "I would say you need some jeans for starters. Thirty-four waist, I'm guessing?"

"Right, but in this heat. . ."

"Aren't you the Amish guy living out there on Tucker's Point?"

"Right again, but. . ."

She took hold of his good arm and steered him toward a line of shelving. "Trust me, you want some long pants if you're tramping around out there among all those downed trees and weeds and such." She pulled out three pairs of jeans and handed them to him. "Okay, moving on. Shirts." She plucked three of those from the well-organized stock. "Oh, and how about these cargo shorts?"

"I thought you said. . ."

Rosalyn gave him an exasperated smile. "Well, not all the time. Now and again a pair of shorts comes in handy." Then her eyes widened in horror and she grabbed the Hawaiian print shirts she'd handed him back. "I almost forgot. I mean about you being plain like us. The jeans will work, but. . ."

Gently he relieved her of the shirts. "These are fine," he said. "Now how about those shoes?"

On their way down a second aisle, she tossed him an unopened package of tube socks and then nodded toward a second bin that held brand-new packages of underwear. "Help yourself," she said. "Target's finest, bless them." She gave the store's name a

French pronunciation that made John smile. By the time he had rummaged through the bin and found a package in his size and followed her to the back of the storeroom, Rosalyn had pulled out three pairs of work boots for him to try.

"Sit," she instructed as she worked the lace loose on one boot. "Socks?" she added, nodding toward the unopened package.

John took out a fresh pair and gathered one onto his good foot. Then Rosalyn handed him the boot. He pulled it on and tied the laces then stood up. "Feels fine," he said.

Rosalyn smiled and uttered a soft, "And the kid does it again." She boxed up the other shoe and then glanced around. "So, a hat—and then our work here is done." She held out a traditional Mennonite straw hat with a stiff wide brim and black band. When he hesitated, she grinned at him. "I thought you were Amish," she teased.

"He is. . .was," Hester said softly. She turned her attention to John. "It's a hat," she rationalized. "It's what we have in stock, and it will serve the purpose of protecting you from the sun while you work."

John took the hat from Rosalyn and put it on.

"And once again, folks, we have a perfect fit," Rosalyn said, her naturally vibrant spirit restored.

John couldn't help smiling, and when he glanced at Hester, he saw that the burn-scarred woman had disarmed not only him of his bad temper but Hester as well. "How do I look?" he asked, directing his question to both women.

"Ah, John Steiner, the sin of pride," Hester warned, shaking a finger at him, but she was smiling. She had the loveliest smile. It was a pity she didn't use it more often.

The door opened at the far end of the storeroom, and a Mennonite man stood for a moment silhouetted in the entrance.

"Samuel Brubaker from Pennsylvania," Rosalyn called out before either Hester or John recognized the carpenter.

Samuel hesitated. "*Guten tag*," he said when he finally met them halfway up the aisle. "Hester, I saw your father's car, and I thought perhaps. . . Ah, John."

"We went out to help Margery this morning," Hester explained, "and John was already there. He needed medical attention, so. . ."

"You do not need to explain," Samuel said gently. "Are you not well, John?"

"My ankle," John replied, pointing to the boot. "And the cast on my wrist had to be replaced."

Samuel examined the cast with interest. "I see they've given you more freedom for your fingers. *Das ist* gut."

John did not miss the fact that the vivacious Rosalyn had turned uncustomarily quiet and that Samuel had yet to look at the young woman. "Then Hester decided I needed clothes."

"You do," Samuel agreed. "You have worn your own clothing to tatters." He glanced up at John. "The hat is good."

"It'll get the job done," John replied.

The four of them fell into an uncomfortable silence.

"So, you were working, Samuel?" Hester said finally as she relieved John of the stack of clothing he'd collected and started up the aisle toward the front desk.

"Ja. In spite of the hurricane, your father had orders to fill. One cabinet needed to be stained and prepared for shipping by the end of the week."

"But you've finished that?"

"Ja. I could come with you and John to help Margery."

"Dad would appreciate that," Hester said as she bagged the clothing.

John reached for his wallet, far thinner these days than it had once been. "How much?"

Hester thrust the last of the clothing into the bag with unnecessary vigor. He was mystified by her sudden change in attitude until Rosalyn helped him understand his mistake. "Now, John Steiner, you know very well we won't take your money. Mennonite or Amish, we are alike in this. Neighbor tends to neighbor. Put your wallet away."

"Thank you," he said as he stuffed his wallet back into his pocket and accepted the bag Hester held out to him. "Thank you all for. . .everything," he added, taking Rosalyn and Samuel into the circle of his gratitude.

Samuel nodded. Rosalyn grinned. Hester looked down and then announced, "We should be getting back."

At the car, Hester handed Samuel the keys. "I'll sit in back," she said.

They rode along without a word passing between them for several minutes until John found he could not stand the silence a moment longer. Ironic, he knew, but it wasn't really lack of conversation that bothered him. It was more that the car was filled with things unspoken.

"How did Rosalyn receive those burns?" he asked, and saw Samuel glance in the rearview mirror, deferring to Hester.

"It was a house fire," she said. "The rest of her family died in the fire. She was the only one we were able to rescue."

John half turned in his seat to look back at her. "You were there?"

"Among others," she said softly. "It was my father who saved her."

"Not only Arlen," Samuel corrected her. "She says that while your father pulled her from the fire, you were the one who treated her and held her until the paramedics arrived."

"I'm a nurse," Hester replied with a slight shrug.

"And you have been her good friend," Samuel added. "She tells me that without your support she could not have endured the recovery she had to go through, and she would not have found her way past all the stares of pity."

It struck John that Samuel seemed to know quite a bit about Rosalyn. He thought about the way Samuel and Rosalyn had both seemed reticent in the other's company back in the thrift center. The way Samuel looked at Rosalyn, stealing glances when he thought she was otherwise occupied, was the look of a man who found that particular woman fascinating. It was the way his parents had looked at each other years into their marriage. It occurred to John that he could not recall a single time when Samuel had looked at Hester that way. For that matter, had John looked at Alice Yoder, the woman he'd been about to marry, that way?

He couldn't help wondering if Hester had noticed, or if she cared. She certainly seemed indifferent to Samuel, at least romantically speaking. On the few occasions when John had seen them together, she had interacted with Samuel more as a colleague, the way she was with Grady Forrest.

Well, it was hardly his concern. Why should he care if Hester's intended fell for another woman? Why should he care about her happiness at all? Not that she didn't deserve to be happy, he thought, as Samuel turned onto the cracked and broken asphalt road that led to the parking lot for the marina. She was clearly a good and caring person, a little too bossy for his taste, but her sincerity when it came to her concern for others could not be questioned.

The marina parking lot was filled with cars and trucks. John could see men shingling the roof of the bait shop as Arlen directed progress from the ground. The combination of the medical boot and closed shoe gave John more confidence in his movement, and he was out of the car and walking down to the pier before Samuel and Hester.

"You're looking more like a human being than a lagoon monster," Margery commented. "The hat's a nice touch."

John grimaced as he fingered the brim of the straw hat. "It does the job," he repeated. "And speaking of jobs, looks like you'll be back in business within a couple of days."

"Yep. Amazing what friends and neighbors can accomplish when they work together," she said. "And when you let them help," she added dryly. "You ought to try it sometime, Johnny." She didn't give him a chance to respond. Instead, she walked away, calling out encouragement to the roofing crew.

John stared up at the crew, watching as the men worked on the roof and a group of women scraped peeling paint from the exterior walls of the marina, chattering and laughing together as they worked. Suddenly he was a boy again back on the farm, working alongside his father as they rebuilt a neighbor's barn after a tornado had roared through their valley. In the laughter of the women, he heard his mother's laughter, deep and rich, and he remembered how his father would stop what he was doing just to look at her for a moment. It was as if he wanted to memorize every detail of her.

"John?"

Coming back to the situation at hand, John blinked and turned his attention to Hester. She was standing next to him, looking up at him with a puzzled frown. "Are you all right?"

"Ich bin gut," he said softly and realized it was the first time since leaving Indiana that he had used his German. "Fine," he added, clearing his throat. "I came here to help, and so far I've done nothing. Time to get to work." He picked up a hammer with his left hand and began pulling nails from the discarded boards that had been replaced by new wood.

A moment later, Hester was working alongside him. John sighed. The woman was as bad as Margery, always hovering around.

Chapter 14

Samuel had taken his place on the roof, helping the other men finish the shingling. When the last nail had been pounded in, the men stood for a moment checking their work. Then Samuel waited his turn to come down the ladder and saw Hester working alongside John. She was unaware that he was watching her, and so he took the time to study her, consider his feelings for her.

Hester was by anyone's measure an incredible woman. The care she had devoted to her mother for five long years was in and of itself an act of such astonishing selflessness, but she had not stopped there.

Rosalyn had told him that in the months that followed Sarah Detlef's death, Hester had thrown herself into her work. She had stayed nights with sick children, and with elderly people whose main affliction was loneliness. And then the fire had come, and when Rosalyn had regained consciousness, it was Hester who had broken the news that her family had not survived. It was Hester who had stayed with Rosalyn and worked with her day in and night out until she recovered.

And yet in all the conversations they had shared, Samuel had not once heard any of this from Hester herself. She was a plain woman in the larger sense of that word, taking none of the credit for the things she accomplished. And Samuel admired her greatly.

He simply did not love her.

He had come to Pinecraft in the spring. He had seen Hester every day, spent numerous hours sharing meals with her and her father and grandmother, attended services and other church and community functions with her. Yet when he examined his feelings for her over that time, he had to admit that they had not changed. He respected her enormously, and in the beginning he had told himself that was a good start. They could build on that.

He also understood that she liked him. He had seen it in the way she would run her palm over some furniture he had finished for a customer. He saw it in the way she smiled at him when he teamed with Arlen on the shuffleboard court in the evenings after they had closed the shop. And he had told himself that in time they would find their way.

And then he had met Rosalyn.

In the weeks since the hurricane had passed, he had tried hard to tell himself that Rosalyn was merely a good friend to him, as she was to Hester. But when he found himself looking for her and at the same time trying to avoid her, he knew that his feelings had already blossomed beyond the point of simple friendship.

The fact that Rosalyn seemed oblivious to his attraction only made matters worse. For because of her work for MCC and her close connection with Hester, Rosalyn was often with Hester, and whenever Samuel was with them, Rosalyn did not treat him any differently than she did anyone else. He knew that he should have found that reassuring, but the fact that she clearly did not see him as someone special was downright depressing.

He could hardly avoid Rosalyn without raising questions about why he was avoiding Hester. So he buried himself in the work at the carpentry shop, insisting to Arlen that he could fulfill the back orders while Arlen attended to his work with MDS. And as he worked on a china hutch or desk that would find its way north to some snowbird's home, he silently prayed for God's guidance.

For Samuel was deeply troubled by the state he found himself in—falling in love with a woman he'd barely exchanged more than four true conversations with while having in theory agreed to a union with the pastor's daughter. If he turned his back on Hester, then what right did he have to continue to work for Arlen? He loved his work and had found his true calling in the crowded shop where sawdust and wood shavings littered the floor throughout the day.

And his sense of loyalty was not just to Arlen. It extended to Hester as well, for it had been clear to Samuel from their first meeting that she had surrendered to the idea that one day they would marry and make a home and raise a family. She had accepted the life her father had planned for her in spite of the fact that Hester Detlef rarely acceded to the plans and wishes of others. And given her innate willfulness, Samuel could not help but wonder why Hester would acquiesce to her father's wish.

Samuel paused at the top of the ladder to watch Hester and John pull nails from discarded wood. It was true. In her way Hester was every bit as determined and stubborn when it came to doing things her way as—say—John Steiner was. More than once Arlen had alluded to the comparison. Arlen had always counseled patience, meaning Samuel's need to practice patience with Hester, of course. And perhaps that was why Samuel had taken to visiting John Steiner more often. Perhaps in getting to know the Amish man who was in many ways like Hester, he was hoping to come to a better understanding of the woman who seemed destined to become his wife.

<center>~~~≋~~~</center>

Once Margery's place had been restored and she was back in business, John was anxious to get his place to the point where he could move into the packinghouse and start planning how best to revive the groves of citrus trees that had been wiped out in the hurricane. During the three days it had taken Arlen's crew to repair the damage to the marina, John had faced the reality that even without his fractured wrist and badly sprained ankle, he might eventually have to accept more help than Zeke could provide.

"But no government people," he told Margery one night as the two of them sat on the deck of her houseboat sharing supper.

She rolled her eyes. "Did you see any so-called government people working here?" she asked. "No, you did not. If I had waited for them to show up, I'd be out of business 'til a month from next year."

"I'm just saying," he grumbled and turned his attention back to his food.

"I suppose it's too much to hope that your sudden epiphany or whatever it was that brought you over here to lend a hand might extend to accepting Arlen's help."

John frowned. He had neither the physical strength nor the cash to rebuild the second story of the house. In the meantime, he had continued to focus his efforts on what he could repair—the planting beds, the packinghouse, the chicken coop. And yet. . .

"Thought not," Margery said as she stood up to clear away their plates. "You want pie, or is that against your principles?"

"Got any ice cream to go with it?" he replied.

"No, but you'll never have a better-tasting pie than this one." She ducked inside and emerged a few minutes later with two large pieces of shoofly pie on paper plates. "Hester made it," she said, setting a piece in front of him.

John recalled the pies cooling on the counter in the Detlef kitchen the morning the creek flooded. "They're back home now?"

"Not quite. Drywall is up and the paint's drying in most of the properties from what Arlen told me. They'll wait to work on their place last, get everybody else home and settled before they take care of themselves. That's their way."

"What about the garden? Arlen's wife's garden?"

Margery shrugged. "I expect that'll be even further down the list, although I know it must be killing Hester not to be tending it. She planted it, you know. Called it therapy. Only question is who was it therapy for."

"I don't understand."

"She thought of it as therapy for her mother. Toward the end there when Sarah could no longer do anything but sit in that wheelchair and just blink her eyes to show yes or no, Hester got this idea of turning the front yard into a garden."

"You think the therapy was for her—Hester," John said. It wasn't a question.

"Well, of course it was for Sarah. But long after Sarah passed, you'd see Hester out there tending those orchids, ferns, and bromeliads like they were precious babies."

John took another bite of the pie. He had to admit that it was the most delicious thing he'd tasted in weeks. "She bakes. She raises orchids. She runs a charity. She's a nurse. What doesn't this woman do?"

Margery grinned. "Interested, are you?"

"Not the way you mean it. Besides, she and Samuel—"

"Are beyond wrong for each other." Margery sighed. "I don't know what Arlen was thinking. Sarah must be rolling over in her grave thinking that her spitfire daughter might end up with that mild-mannered man. Not that he's not a perfectly good man— kind and generous to a fault, but not for our Hester."

John fought to disguise his interest. "You think so?"

"You think so?" Margery mimicked in a high falsetto before taking a bite of her pie and washing it down with a long drink of iced tea. "You sound like some high school boy. Get to know the woman. Come to think of it, the two of you. . ."

She eyed John, sizing up the possibility. He raised both hands, palms out as if stopping traffic. "Get that idea out of your head, Margery." He was willing to tolerate Margery's attempts to get him involved in the larger community, but allowing the woman to get any idea of matchmaking would be disastrous.

She shrugged and turned her chair so that she could prop her feet up on the railing of the houseboat and look out toward the sunset. "Suit yourself, but methinks the man doth protest—"

"I have to get back," John interrupted. "Thanks for supper, and if you see Zeke, ask him to stop by, okay?"

"Yep." Margery sounded half asleep.

A Stranger's Gift

He made the short leap from the deck to the pier and then into the boat Margery had lent him, thankful that she had loaned him the boat when she probably could have rented it out. "And don't go spreading it around that I'm looking for help," he said.

"Got it, you stubborn blockhead."

The following morning Zeke was there, sitting on the stump of a cypress tree when John crawled out of bed. "Morning," he called. "Margery said you could use a hand."

John glanced around, saw no boat other than his own and no other visible means of transportation.

"Did Margery bring you?" he asked, hoping the fisherwoman hadn't talked about him in front of others.

"Nope. Caught a ride." Zeke nodded toward the lane. "Want some coffee?" He held up two large cups from one of several fancy coffee vendors John had noticed on Main Street.

"Thought you were broke and homeless," John commented as he gratefully accepted the hot liquid.

Zeke grinned. "Can still sing for my coffee," he said. "Had to give 'em two songs this morning, so you owe me." He glanced around and released a long, appreciative whistle. "You've made some real progress here."

"Getting there," John admitted.

"Got yourself a small generator, I see."

"Samuel Brubaker brought it out one afternoon."

"Good man."

"Yeah."

"So what's on tap for today, boss?" Zeke drained the last of his coffee and crushed the cup in one fist.

"I'd like to finish closing in the kitchen and get it covered."

"No worries," Zeke replied and set to work.

For the next several days he came every morning, bringing John coffee and then getting to work. After a week, though, John noticed that Zeke didn't look well, and he took frequent breaks either to relieve himself or simply to sit for a long moment, his head bent low to his knees.

"You feeling okay?"

163

"Picked up some kind of bug," Zeke replied. "It'll pass," he added and grinned. "Hotter today, though, so I'm knocking off. See you tomorrow?"

"Take a couple of days and rest up," John said. "We've made good progress here. Take care of yourself, okay?"

When Zeke did not return the following day or for two days after that, John figured he'd taken the advice to get some rest. But when he hadn't come back after a week, John began to worry. He was well aware that Zeke marched to his own drummer on his own unique time schedule, but he also knew that if Zeke had committed to doing something, he was there until the job was complete.

Something was wrong. He fired up Margery's boat and sped under the Stickney Point Bridge then past the mouth of the creek, leaving a wake that earned him a warning blast from the shore patrol.

How could he not have seen that Zeke was getting worse? The man had switched to tea the last day he arrived, telling John that he needed something to settle his stomach. And he was thinner than usual. He kept hitching up his pants, the same ones John had seen him wear every day for a week, and knotting the rope belt a little tighter.

But John's focus had been on the incredible progress they were making. The night before, he had slept in the packinghouse under an actual roof for the first time since the storm. He'd still slept on the sleeping bag that Samuel had provided and covered himself in the netting, but he had been inside, not in the cramped camper.

As he navigated, he scanned the shore for any sign of Zeke. He passed under the Siesta Bridge. Nothing. Zeke was the kind of person who stood out with his long hair and his guitar slung across his back. As John passed the botanical gardens, he spotted the abandoned boat Zeke had shown him. Slowly he circled it, calling Zeke's name but getting no answer. He pulled into a vacant slip at the far north end of the city's main marina. Remembering Zeke's description of where he had set up his "crib" as he called it, John ran down the sidewalk, dodging runners and dog walkers until he reached a small patch of exposed mud flats. He was very near the Ringling Bridge that carried traffic from the mainland over to Lido and Longboat Key and the fancy shopping area known as St. Armand's Circle.

Glancing around, he saw a cluster of mangroves and sea grape bushes where the seawall curved. He ran toward them, seeing a man lying there. "Zeke!" His heart hammering, he touched the inert shoulder of a body folded in on itself and was relieved when he heard a low moan. "Zeke? It's John."

"Oh, sorry, man. I. . ." Zeke sat up suddenly and wretched in dry heaves. "Pretty sick," he said with a weary smile, his voice husky.

"Let's get you to a doctor," John said.

"Hester," Zeke protested. "Get Hester. Hospital takes forever."

"All right. Hester, then. But I'm not leaving you here. Can you walk?"

"No worries, man." But when he tried to sit fully upright, a wave of dizziness overtook him.

In spite of the stench of his clothing and body, John scooped his friend into a fireman's carry and headed back toward the marina.

"Guitar," Zeke moaned.

"I'll come back for it," John promised.

"Tide coming in," Zeke managed.

"Then I'll buy you a new one if it gets ruined." He could barely afford groceries, much less a guitar, but the important thing was to get Zeke some medical attention—and fast.

~≈~

As Hester had predicted, once the sun came out and the floodwaters receded, the public's attention moved on to other matters. No longer did she turn around while restoring the houses along the creek to find a television reporter and cameraperson carefully picking their way across a soggy lawn, hoping for a story. And after it became clear that there had been massive property damage but little human loss, the media packed up and moved on for good. The National Guard, too, had moved on, as had other disaster-relief groups that had set up temporary headquarters in Sarasota.

Even the out-of-state volunteer teams from Mennonite and Amish congregations that had appeared in droves during the first seventy-two hours following the storm had headed back home after a few weeks. The difference there was that they sent replacements, crews of teenagers or college students who were eager to spend a few days rebuilding someone's house and rejoicing in the reward of seeing a family moved from one of the cramped FEMA trailers back into their own place.

It was a pattern that Hester was well used to and one that she saw as a natural part of the rhythm of life on Florida's Gulf Coast. When another storm struck their shores—and it would—if not this season then next, or the one after that, these wonderful caring people would be back, ready to once again help the residents of Pinecraft and the surrounding area rebuild.

She was putting the final touches on her father's house when the phone in Arlen's study rang. "Pastor Detlef's residence," she said as she cradled the phone on her shoulder and wiped her paint-stained hands on a rag.

"Hester?"

John Steiner sounded as if he'd run a marathon and called her straight from the finish line. "It's Zeke Shepherd," he said. "Can you come?"

"What's happened?" Hester asked, already setting the rag aside and reaching for her bag. "Where are you?"

"He's really sick. We're at the city marina, north end. I'm illegally parked."

"You drove?"

"I've got Margery's boat. I'm in one of the vacant slips. When Zeke didn't show up at my place for over a week, I went looking for him. I mean, it wasn't like him to disappear for over a week without at least stopping by."

Hester didn't see the need to tell John that it was exactly

like Zeke to disappear for long periods of time without letting anyone know where or how he was. Eventually he would show up, his impish smile all Jeannie needed to forgive him for giving her such a fright.

"I'm on my way."

She wrote a quick note to her father, grabbed the car keys, and prayed the traffic lights would be with her.

They were. She reached the marina in record time and saw John standing at the end of one of the piers near a pay phone. He was looking far healthier than he had the last time she'd seen him. In the days that had passed since they'd worked together on Margery's place, the ankle boot was gone, and his bruises and insect bites had healed. Only the wrist cast remained, and the way he was waving his hands around, it didn't look as if that was much of a concern.

She followed him out to the boat. Zeke was lying on the deck curled into a fetal position. He moaned and rolled onto his side, clutching his stomach. The stench from his clothing and lack of proper hygiene almost overpowered her, but she sucked in a deep breath and knelt next to him. "Tell me what's going on, Zeke," she said softly as she began taking his vitals—pulse, temperature, pupils.

"Hurts," he moaned.

"Where?"

"Head. Stomach. Everywhere."

"John, could you get Zeke some water?" For once John did as she asked without questioning her.

"No!" Zeke protested weakly but firmly. "Goes straight through me," he added as he pulled his knees up to his chest and rocked from side to side.

"You're dehydrated, Zeke. We have to get some fluids in you. How long has this been going on?"

"Couple of days like this, maybe a week in all. Seems like forever."

Hester was beginning to have her suspicions as to a diagnosis. "Anybody else sick?"

"He lives alone," John reminded her.

She ignored him. "Zeke?"

"Yeah. A couple of others that I know of."

"Okay, let's get you to the ER, and then I'll go check on the others." She turned her attention to John. "Can you carry Zeke?"

Once again he lifted Zeke in a fireman's carry. Hester held the door of her car open as John laid the man across the backseat. Then he got into the passenger seat while she took the wheel.

"What others, Zeke?" she asked as she navigated traffic between the marina and the hospital.

"Danny, for one." He paused. "I can't think."

"Okay, well then, let's get you to the emergency room, and then I'll go see what I can find out."

"I can stay with Zeke," John volunteered.

"No worries, man," Zeke mumbled. "Go help Hester."

It was clear that the ER staff was less than thrilled to see this disheveled man who reeked of sweat and the aftermath of severe diarrhea come through the door. But Hester ignored their displeasure and gave them her credentials as a registered nurse. "He's showing all the symptoms of crypto," she said curtly. "I suspect there are more cases among those of the homeless community that hang out around the library. We're going there to check on them. You got this?"

The admissions person and a burly aide who had brought a wheelchair out to the car to help Zeke inside both nodded.

"Good. We'll be back as soon as possible." She squeezed Zeke's hand and then headed back to the car.

"What's crypto?" John asked as she started the engine and eased into traffic.

"Cryptosporidium—a parasite. Causes a pretty awful gastro-intestinal illness called cryptosporidiosis. Mostly it comes from consuming contaminated food or water." She leaned forward as if willing the light they were stopped at to turn green. "People like Zeke are at risk because they tend to get their food and water from unorthodox sources—trash bins behind restaurants, and water from streams or other places."

She waited for a car to pull out of a parking space across from the library, a large white concrete structure surrounded by pineapple-shaped columns. "Uh-oh," she murmured.

"What?"

"Nobody around. Normally there would be clusters of two or three people sitting up there on the steps or over there in the park." She pointed.

"It's close to ninety degrees," John reminded her. "Maybe they went inside to take advantage of the air-conditioning."

"Maybe." She hoped John was right. She started across the street and was surprised when John took her arm to stop her from stepping out in front of a car speeding up the short side street.

"Careful," he said, releasing her arm before crossing.

She caught up to him. "You don't have to come," she said. "I mean, you can wait in the car or out here if you'd rather. I know this really isn't—"

"I'm here, aren't I?" For reasons Hester couldn't fathom, his characteristic gruffness gave her comfort. "That's better," she said as they climbed the steps together. "For a moment there I thought you'd gone all soft on me."

"Not a chance," he said, but he was smiling.

Inside she sent John upstairs to walk through the stacks and see if there were any likely candidates while she did the same on the first floor. She even checked out the children's library with its popular arched aquarium entrance as well as the used bookstore operated by the Friends of the Library.

"Bathrooms," she said when John came down the stairs, shaking his head. She led the way to the corridor where the public restrooms were located. Again nothing.

She was considering where else they might go to look when she spotted the library's security person. "Excuse me," she said.

She watched as the security guard took in her plain garb and John's traditional straw hat before smiling politely. "Yes, ma'am?"

"The men and women who are. . .*regulars* here," she said, and the guard's eyes narrowed.

"The homeless people?"

"Yes. Do you have any idea where they are?"

"Try Rainbow House," he said and prepared to turn away.

"It's closed down," Hester continued, fighting to maintain her patience. "The county never reopened it after the hurricane. Someone I know in the county government tells me it's unlikely it will ever reopen."

"Well, they aren't here," the man replied curtly.

"We can see that," John said, his terse tone forcing the guard to meet the intensity of his stare. "And since this is where they are normally, what happened?"

The guard sighed and looked at something beyond their heads. "Look. You didn't hear it from me, but there were complaints from our, you know, other patrons. Some of those people were coming in here and stinking up the place and throwing up in the restrooms and just in general making it—"

"*Those people* are ill," Hester said. "Some of them may be dangerously ill, and if we don't find them, one or more of them could die. At the very least they could spread a parasite that might infect a great many others. Including your other patrons. Now where did they go?"

"I really don't know. We called the cops, and they moved them away from here. That's all I know about it."

Hester dismissed the man with a look and turned her attention to John. "Any ideas?"

"We could try the bay front, near the public restrooms there."

Hester nodded, and she did not miss the fact that as she and John headed out the door, the security guard was already squirting disinfectant from the dispenser near the front doors onto his palms and rubbing them vigorously together.

Chapter 15

W hat made you think of the bay front?" Hester asked as she pulled into the parking lot near a popular tiki-style restaurant and found one of several open spaces.

"It's where Zeke lives, so I figured maybe. . ."

He was not about to admit to her that Zeke had taken him to these same restrooms one day and suggested he wash up.

"You stink, man," Zeke had told him in that 'no worries' tone he used to address every topic. "And until they get the water back on out your way, this may be your best bet."

"Do you think maybe that's where he got the infected food or water?" Hester asked.

"Could be. From what I've observed, Zeke is pretty resourceful and tends to take what he needs wherever it's available."

John recalled the day he and Zeke had first met. The way Zeke had drunk the bottled water and then refilled the plastic container with the runoff from the awning at the abandoned warehouse.

"They need a safe haven," Hester muttered as she headed for the women's restroom.

"Can I ask a question?" John said, stopping her before she could enter the open door.

"Okay."

"What are we going to do if we find half a dozen or more sick people in these restrooms?"

"Get them some help," she said and handed him a pair of latex gloves she'd pulled from her bag. "Wear these." She pulled on a pair of her own. "And this," she added, handing him a mask.

"And after you get them help, then what?" John wondered aloud as he took a deep breath and went in to check the men's room.

Moments later, he emerged supporting a rail-thin man who stumbled along beside him. Hester was sitting with two women—one who had to be in her sixties and the other a decade or so younger. They seemed to be in far better shape than either Zeke or the man John was supporting.

"Best diet I was ever on," the older woman crowed. "Look at this." She stood up and pulled out the waistband of her trousers to show how big they were on her. "Need a belt just to hold them up."

"Dangerous diet," Hester corrected her. "We need to get your friend there to the hospital. Will you two wait here until I can get back with some medicine?"

"Got nothing but time," the younger woman grumbled, fanning herself with an old magazine.

"You get Danny there the help he needs," the older woman urged. "He's been sicker than a dog for days now."

"Have you got any cash with you?" Hester asked John.

"Some."

"Could you get these ladies each a bottle of water from the stand there?"

"Sure." John headed off.

"Could we make that a nice cup of coffee?" the older woman shouted.

"Water," Hester said firmly. The woman grinned a wide, toothless grin and shrugged. "Anybody else sick?" she asked the women as she waited for John to return with the water. The one thing she knew was that the homeless community was almost as tight as her own Mennonite community was. They all knew each other, knew who was a newcomer and who had been on the streets long enough to know their way around. And as was true of any group, not everyone got along. There were petty jealousies, turf wars, and cliques. But if there was a threat from outside forces, these people would stand together. The two women exchanged a look but remained silent. "Okay. If anyone starts to show signs of running a fever or especially diarrhea or throwing up, make sure they drink lots of water, *clean* water. You have to boil it if you don't get it from a reliable source, okay?"

"Drink boiling water? In this heat?" The younger woman shuddered as John returned with two bottles of water and handed one to each woman.

"You let it cool down first," the older woman said. "Right, Doc?"

"She's a missionary, dope."

"Who you calling—?"

"I'm a nurse," Hester interrupted. "Yes, let the water cool to room temperature before drinking it, and stay away from anything with caffeine like soda or tea or coffee. That will just cause the dehydration to worsen."

"Yeah. Yeah. Got it. Any medicine to clear this thing up?"

"There are some over-the-counter anti-diarrheal medicines that I can bring you." She sighed in frustration. "Look, it just has to run its course. If anyone is really suffering, take them to one of the walk-in clinics or to the emergency room."

"Yeah, that'll work," the younger woman said sarcastically.

"Try it," Hester said, "and please spread the word." She took her place to one side of Danny while John supported him from the other and they led him toward the car. "I'll stop back later," she called, but both women were already gone.

With her help, John got the semi-conscious Danny into the backseat and they headed back to the hospital.

"After we pick Zeke up, I want you, Zeke, and Danny there— if he's not admitted—to come back to our house and take a long, hot shower. You've been exposed to this thing now, and you need to take precautions."

But when they reached the emergency room, Jeannie was there. "I was visiting a neighbor," she explained. "And on my way out, I saw an aide wheeling Zeke out from the ER. He looks terrible. Don't you think he should be admitted?"

"I'm okay, Jeannie," Zeke said weakly.

"Well, at the very least you're coming home with me and having yourself a nice hot shower and changing out of those clothes. You stink to high heaven."

Zeke managed a grin and put up no resistance as Jeannie led him across the driveway to her car, chattering all the way. Hester saw her open the trunk and remove an old quilt that she placed on the front seat before letting Zeke get in. Meanwhile, the aide had helped Danny into the wheelchair vacated by Zeke and taken him inside.

"Jeannie, wait," Hester called. "John needs a ride back to the marina."

Jeannie nodded. "Tell him to come on," she said.

Back inside, Hester saw John conferring with the doctor.

"Danny passed out while the admissions person was taking his information," John explained.

"Are you the family?" the doctor asked.

"Close enough," John said before Hester could go into an explanation of the situation.

The doctor studied the chart the desk clerk had handed him. "Looks like he's been here several times before in the last couple of months. Whether or not this is an outbreak of crypto, he is dangerously dehydrated, and we're going to have to admit him at least overnight."

"Surely he has family we could contact," John said.

"I'll stay with him," Hester said.

The doctor was clearly relieved. "Okay, then. We'll get him stabilized and then contact social services here in the hospital."

After he'd left, Hester turned to John. "You go on to our house and take that shower and change into clean clothes. Jeannie's waiting for you, and I'll call Rosalyn at the center and have her bring you some things so you don't have to take time to go home first. There are clean towels in the—"

"I'll find them," John told her. "I need to call Margery. I'm sure she knows somebody who can get the boat back or at least get the okay for it to stay there until I can come back for it."

"Good thinking."

He started for the exit and she walked with him. "You'll be all right?" he added.

"Yes. I just want to go and wash up, and then I'll stay with Danny—make sure he's settled."

"You don't even know this guy," John reminded her.

"I know that he's a child of God, as are you and everyone else on this planet. He's alone and probably a little scared. If I can ease that some, then I will."

She waited for more argument, but John just nodded. "I'll be back after I get cleaned up."

"That's okay. Go on back to the marina and take care of the boat. I can. . ."

"I'll be back," he repeated firmly. This time she saw from the look he gave her that arguing would be useless.

"Fine."

John asked Jeannie to drop him off at Arlen's shop instead of the Detlef house. He wanted to let Arlen know he would be there in case he came in and heard the shower running.

"You saved me a trip," Arlen replied jovially as he held up a stack of clothing. "Rosalyn just came by to leave these for you."

"Thanks." John accepted the clothing. "Must be a relief to be back in your house."

Arlen beamed. "Yes. We've been back in residence for a few days now. Others, like my mother's place, were a bit of a challenge, but with God's blessing everyone is back home safe and sound."

"That's good," John said.

"And you? Samuel tells me progress is slow."

John shrugged. "I do what I can." He nodded toward the cast on his wrist. "The ankle's much better, which helps a lot."

Arlen frowned. "It is not only your physical injuries that hinder your progress, my friend. I think you know that." He lightly tapped his own chest over his heart. "But this, the hurt that is here. . ."

John looked away. "I'd better get going," he said. "I told Hester I'd meet her back at the hospital."

"No need," Arlen told him. "Samuel and Rosalyn have gone to sit with her and bring her home. You go and get that shower and some rest. And don't forget to drink plenty of fluids," he added as John headed for the door.

The Detlef house smelled of fresh paint mingled with the faint odor of bleach and other cleaning substances. Everything was as pristine and organized as it had been on his first visit.

The first thing he did was call Margery, but there was no answer, and he decided not to leave a message. Knowing that Samuel and Rosalyn were going to the hospital to be with Hester, he decided he could handle things at the marina.

John took the clothes Arlen had handed him down the hall to the small bathroom and set them on the counter. He undressed and then let the shower run over him for several long minutes, relishing the coolness of the water after he had soaped and scrubbed himself with hot water. As he dried himself and dressed, it occurred to him that he felt physically lighter, as if pounds of dirt compacted by sweat over the last several days had flowed down the drain with the soapy water.

Once dressed, he made sure to leave the bathroom as clean as it had been when he entered it. He dropped the towel into the hamper and then bundled his soiled clothing. On his way out, he walked down the front path that had once guided visitors through the garden—Hester's garden. Her therapy while her mother moved daily closer to dying.

He stood on the porch and saw that the garden looked exactly the same as it had weeks earlier when he'd first stayed the night. There wasn't a shred of evidence that Hester had spent any time replanting. Even the orchids that she had told him had been taken inside to avoid being damaged by the hurricane had not been brought outside again. He didn't know much about growing orchids, but surely by now. . .

She's been a little busy, he reminded himself, thinking of all the different things that Hester was managing. The distribution center, getting the houses along the creek fit for occupancy again, working on Margery's place, cooking and cleaning and caring for her father, and presumably finding some time in there to spend with Samuel. It would be nice if someone might notice that maybe Hester could use a little help, that restoring the garden might be just the ticket to ease those lines of worry and exhaustion that so often marred her face. Maybe he should mention it to Samuel. It would be a way that Samuel could show his affection for her. It might even move things along for the two of them.

John frowned. Try as he might, he could not see Samuel and Hester together long term. Friends, yes. Married and facing a lifetime of evenings across the supper table from each other— nope. Still, from everything Margery had told him and everything he'd observed on his own, that was the plan. Hardly his business, he thought as he tucked the bundle of soiled clothing into the basket of Hester's bicycle and headed for the marina. The last thing Margery needed was to have her boat towed.

Later that evening after he'd retrieved Zeke's guitar and returned to his place, he built a fire and set a large kettle filled with water to boil. Then he walked his property and came across a patch of ferns growing wild near the packinghouse. He had no use for the things himself, but it occurred to him that they would make a nice lush addition to the garden. She could set the orchid pots on the ground and let the dark green lacy foliage of the ferns hide the pot and highlight the blossom. He'd point them out to Samuel when he stopped by to pick up Hester's bike and suggest he dig them and take them to Hester. Or maybe he would do it himself. After all, the plants were likely to get trampled over the next couple of days while he was working on rebuilding the damaged wall of the packinghouse. Besides, why was he troubling himself with matchmaking? Wasn't the match between Hester and Samuel already made?

Even a few days later when Jeannie assured her that Zeke was on the mend and eating like a horse, Hester couldn't seem to get Danny and the other homeless people out of her mind. Before the suspected crypto outbreak, her interactions with that sector of the local population had come either through Zeke or through her work distributing clothing and food for MCC. Zeke was homeless by choice mostly. He had family in the area, family he was in touch with from time to time, and, of course, he had Jeannie and her husband looking out for him.

Besides, Zeke was always well groomed, and his clothes were always clean, if ill-fitting. He made some money by playing his guitar at the city's downtown farmers' market during the high tourist season, and at other times of the year he could be found strumming his guitar on Main Street outside one of the vacant storefronts. He never actually panhandled. He simply left his guitar case open on the sidewalk next to him, and people dropped money in as they passed by.

But most of the others clearly had no such connections. Their hair was matted, and their clothes reeked of the need for a good washing. She recalled the two women at the bay front with their battered grocery cart, rusted and piled high with a variety of black plastic garbage bags filled with who-knew-what. Both the women and their cart had disappeared without a trace, and Hester couldn't help wondering what had happened to them. Without the safety net of Rainbow House—a place where homeless people could get a hot shower, a decent meal, and a cot—where would people like those two women go? She hadn't even gotten their names.

Something needed to be done about getting the shelter back in operation. She had no direct association with Rainbow House, but she knew people who did—Grady, for one. She would call him and let him know about the women.

"There are still some of those trailers FEMA sent down parked over near the park," her father told her when she raised her concerns for the homeless population that night at supper.

The house trailers had arrived after a story about the flooding in Pinecraft and other Sarasota neighborhoods that sat along the creek hit the national news. Grady had tried to assure the FEMA reps that the community was well prepared to care for their own, but those in charge of the agency in Washington had insisted. They had also insisted that Grady make sure the delivery was well documented by local media, and he had orchestrated the move of half a dozen families from the shelters to the trailers.

"It's a temporary fix at best," Hester said, "but they're not doing anybody else any good, and the homeless folks could sure use them."

After supper Hester and Samuel drove to Grady's house and explained the problem.

"I'd like to help. I really would," Grady told them. "But we've got a bunch of Homeland Security bigwigs on their way down here to tour the area. Some talk show host did a sensational piece focused on what hasn't been done, so the folks in DC are nervous. They sent those trailers for people wiped out by the hurricane, and if we use them to house folks who were homeless before the hurricane. . . Well, you know how these things go."

"But no one is using them, and until Rainbow House can be reopened—"

"Rainbow House is closed, Hester."

"I know, but maybe some local charity could—"

"There are dozens of local charities, and at times like this we definitely count on their support. But starting up something new?" Grady shook his head. "Money is tight, and I hate to say it, but that's not going to happen."

Hester sighed. "I understand. I just hoped that maybe there was something we could do."

Grady's wife, Amy, offered dessert, but both Hester and Samuel turned her down. "Thanks, but we should be getting back." Not wanting to leave her friends to think that she was upset with them, she smiled at Amy. "Hey, I'm a nurse, and you should be off your feet."

Amy patted her very pregnant midsection. "This little guy doesn't like sitting around. I think he's going to be a football player the way he kicks."

Grady wrapped his arm around her shoulders. "It won't be much longer now," he promised.

Amy laughed. "Then we probably won't get any sleep at all—either of us." But in spite of her complaints, Amy seemed so very happy and content that Hester found it hard not to envy her.

"If either of you get any ideas about helping these folks, let us know, okay?"

"Tell you what," Grady said as he and Amy walked them down the driveway, "I'll introduce you to our visitors from DC if I get a chance. I mean, it would be a long shot, but you never know."

"I'd appreciate that," Hester said as Samuel opened the car door for her. "And don't worry, Grady. We'll figure something out."

"You always do," Grady said.

Hester sighed heavily, and after Samuel pulled away from the curb, he glanced at Hester. "He's right, you know. You will find a solution for this."

"I wish I had your confidence."

Samuel laughed. It was a good laugh, hearty and filled with the pure joy of being alive. "Oh, Hester, the one thing you do not need is any more confidence. You are perhaps the most self-confident person I have ever known, man or woman." But then he sobered and focused on his driving. "You take on too much, Hester. You cannot save the world."

Why not? she thought. Not that she was so egotistical as to think she could, but wasn't the world, and more to the point the people in it, worth doing everything possible to save? Hadn't God entrusted His creation to their stewardship? Wasn't that the whole point of life on this planet? "I know, but if we don't do our best, then don't you think we'll regret not at least trying?"

"So we'll do our best," he said. "We just have to figure out what that might be."

Reassured, Hester leaned back and closed her eyes. There

was comfort in his words. She wasn't in this alone.

"There is one regret that I have," he said after several minutes.

His tone was so solemn that Hester's eyes flew open, and she turned in her seat to face him. "What?"

He grinned. "That we turned down Amy's offer of dessert. I find that I suddenly have a real craving for a chocolate sundae."

"With pecans?" Hester asked, falling so easily into the rhythm of his teasing that it might have been something they had shared for years. She couldn't help thinking how different this ice cream date with Samuel was from the one she had shared with John, not that the cone she'd shared with John had been a date. Far from it.

"And whipped cream?" Samuel was smiling at her, a twinkle in his eye. Nothing like the glowering John Steiner.

"Of course," she said. "And a cherry on top."

"Two," Samuel assured her.

———

Later that night as she lay awake and relived the hour that she and Samuel had spent sitting outside the ice cream shop, she realized that in many ways it had been their first real date. Always before whenever they were together, other people were there as well— at family meals, at church functions, even working together after the hurricane, they had always been in the company of others. Not tonight though. Tonight it had been just the two of them, and she had to admit that she had enjoyed herself immensely.

For one thing she had never fully appreciated Samuel's dry sense of humor before. But as they shared a huge sundae with all the trimmings and even one made with the chocolate ice cream that he knew she preferred, he had kept her laughing with his wry take on various people in the community.

"And then there's Olive Crowder," he said with an exaggerated sigh. "I owe her a huge debt of gratitude."

"Why?"

"She warned me."

"About me?"

"About Arlen."

"Dad? She's always spoken so highly of him."

Samuel grinned. "And nothing about that has changed. She told me he would treat me like a son, trying to replace your four brothers according to her. She indicated that I would have a great deal to live up to in that department. Olive seemed to think that might be a problem. She's been most vigilant in offering me advice."

"She means well," Hester said. "It's just that sometimes she. . ."

"Oversteps?"

"That's one way of looking at it."

Samuel scraped the last of the hot fudge from the side of the dish and offered it to her.

"No more," she protested with a laugh.

He shrugged and licked the spoon. But then he sobered. "I think you might want to watch yourself when she's around."

"Oh, she's harmless. She's been on my case practically my whole life. I fear I have been a bitter disappointment to her with a few exceptions."

"Such as?"

"She was surprised, I think, when I cared for my mother for the last five years of her life. In all that time I don't think she could find one single fault with me."

"Must have driven her crazy," Samuel said with a grin.

"She's making up for it these days."

"I kind of heard that the two of you had some words when you were working on the houses by the creek."

"Kind of heard? How do you kind of hear something?"

He actually blushed. "Rosalyn mentioned it. She wasn't gossiping," he added hastily. "She was concerned about you, and so am I. . . . I mean, what if Olive decides to find some concern about you to bring before the congregation?"

"Oh, it's nothing so dire. She's just determined to get me to quit MCC and go to work for CAM. Rosalyn worries about me," Hester said with a smile.

"So do I." Samuel stared at her for a long moment, his eyes

flitting across her features. "I want you to be happy."

"I am happy."

He gave her a skeptical look. "Really?"

"Well, I mean, lately there's been a lot for me to do, and—"

"And yet you keep adding to that pile—now you're trying to make the world better for homeless people. It's like you're always running from one project to the next. Where in all of that is there time for you?"

"That *is* me," she replied, hating the defensive edge that crept into her voice. She stood up and threw their trash into the container near the car. "We should get back. Dad will worry."

In the silence that cloaked their drive back to her father's house, Hester had thought about Samuel's comment about wanting her to be happy. And lying awake now, she thought about the lie she had told in declaring that she was.

Chapter 16

In the week after John rescued Zeke, a few other homeless men whom Zeke had brought with him from time to time showed up to help John get the first floor of the house back in good enough shape that he could move from the packinghouse to the main house. He could hardly believe that he was finally able to enjoy breakfast at his own table in his restored kitchen after his first night back in the main house. The first floor had been scoured of mold and silt, and the space was protected by one of the signature blue tarps that dotted the landscape where roofs had been ripped away all up and down the coast. Margery had given him a single bed complete with mattress and linens that she claimed to have no use for, and Rosalyn had sent him dishes and pots and pans from the thrift shop.

"Housewarming present," Samuel had told him when he protested.

For the first time in weeks he felt something like hope that things just might work out for him. And not wanting anything to disturb this idyllic moment, he decided to ignore the approach of a car, the slam of a door, and the muffled voices followed by the sound of the car leaving, and the rhythmic click of hard-soled shoes climbing the steps to his door.

There was a knock. A pause. A repeated knock. And then a pounding. "I know you're in there, John Steiner. Now open up."

The last person John thought he would see standing at his makeshift front door was his aunt. Congresswoman Elizabeth Carter-Thompson from the great state of Virginia was dressed in a hot pink designer suit and four-inch stiletto heels. She also wore a ridiculously floppy straw hat that matched her suit and completely hid her platinum hair except for the wisps of bangs.

"How did you get here?" John asked as soon as he recovered from the initial shock of seeing her. The real question he'd meant to ask was, "What are you doing here?"

"I came by covered wagon," she quipped as she glanced back at the cab already headed back to town. "Now please tell me you have air-conditioning, or failing that, a bucket of ice and a gallon of sweet tea."

"No air-conditioning," he said, stepping aside so she could enter what there was of the house. "No ice. But there is tea, and I have sugar."

She pulled off the hat and glanced at her surroundings. "Primitive," she said in the same polite tone she might have told someone else that their home was charming.

"We had this little storm pass through," John replied, falling easily into the banter that he had shared with her throughout their lives. "Perhaps you heard about it?"

"Thus my visit. I'm here on what we politicians laughingly call a fact-finding tour. Seems to me the facts are pretty straightforward and we could have read all about them in the reports sent by the FEMA reps." She fanned herself with his copy of *Walden*, then glanced at the cover. "Oh, please do not tell me you are still on this mission." She was almost pleading with him as she continued fanning herself. He set a glass of tea in front of her and pushed the sugar bowl across the scarred table.

"It's hardly a mission. It's an experiment. It was for Thoreau, and it is for me."

"How about a life?" She shoveled three heaping teaspoons of

sugar into the tea and stirred. "Ever consider going after one of those?"

He gestured to the space around them as if to say, *For the time being, this is my life.* Liz's answer was to laugh, snorting tea out her nose in the process. "I don't know who you think you're fooling, John, but this is me. I know you, and I know why you are doing this." She stood up and strolled around the kitchen. "This is your version of sackcloth and ashes. This is not a life. This is penance, and I am here to tell you that my dear sister, your beloved mother, would be downright horrified."

John opened his mouth to say something, anything, to forestall the lecture he knew she'd been working on through all the weeks that he had not been in contact. But she was not to be denied.

"You want to honor Rachel's memory? Good for you, but this is not the way to go about that. You know it and I know it. Holing up here like some hermit. . ." she muttered.

"My mother chose a plain life," he reminded her.

"In a community surrounded by dear friends and family, shared way too briefly with a husband who adored her and a son who gave her more joy than most of us know in a lifetime." She ticked off each item with her long manicured nails. "For you to abandon that community, those people, that life, to hide away here like some wounded puppy, borders on blasphemy."

All he needed to do was lift one eyebrow at her to remind her of the circumstances under which he had come to Florida.

"Oh, right. Rachel died and then you got yourself banned or shunned or excommunicated, whatever the term is. Well, so what? Life on this planet is tough, thus the promise of a better afterlife. The key is to make something of this life while you have time. My sister ran out of time to do all the good she set out to do, but I would be willing to bet my next election that she died thinking that you would carry on where she'd left off."

John had had enough. "She died because of me," he reminded her.

Liz placed her hand on his back and abandoned her soapbox

voice. "She died in your arms. You were the last person she saw, the last voice she heard, the last conscious thought she had."

The silence between them was punctuated by the slow, steady drip of the faucet. Liz took a long swallow of her tea, and John pushed himself onto a countertop.

"Why do you think she stayed?" he asked. "I mean after Dad died. She could have just walked away. After all, she wasn't born Amish. It would have been so much easier for her to return east to the life she had known as a child, the life she shared with you and your parents."

"But she fell in love with Jacob. She chose to live his life, and she was so very happy living that life, John. It suited her. That's why she stayed. Thinking back on it, she was never comfortable in the life of a politician's granddaughter. She used to ask Grandpa Tom, 'Why are those men taking our picture, Papa?' Me? I was always wondering why they *weren't* taking our picture more."

John smiled as a memory flashed through his mind like the midday sun. "She used to tease Dad that she'd only married him and become plain to avoid the camera."

Liz walked over to the door and then out into the yard. John followed her. He stood on the porch Zeke had helped him rebuild, watching her. Both of them were lost in the memory of a very special woman—her sister, his mother.

Then he heard the buzz of a motorboat approaching and prepared to introduce his aunt to Margery. It occurred to him that the two women would get along famously. Margery was something of a politician herself, not that she had ever seen her name on a ballot, but she certainly knew how to work the system when it suited her.

"Look who's back among the living," Margery shouted as she pointed to the back of the boat where Zeke stood, poised to help her dock the boat. "He insisted on coming out here to give you a hand. Do not ask me to understand why he would turn down a—" When she spotted Liz in her pink suit, her mouth remained open, but no sound came out.

Liz had removed her shoes and now walked barefoot along

the makeshift boardwalk that John had laid over the mud and silt down to the pier. "Hello," she called. "I'm John's aunt Liz. I'm sure he's been singing my praises." And as John had mentally predicted, Margery was immediately captivated. As apparently was Zeke. He gave her a mumbled greeting as he combed his hair back from his face with his fingers and then made his way toward the house, casting furtive glances back at her.

"You're looking better than you did the last time I saw you," John said. He could not hide the relief he felt at seeing Zeke doing so well.

"And you're still the same scruffy guy I've been having to look at for weeks now," Zeke replied as he perched on the edge of the porch and watched the two women. "That's your aunt, huh?"

"My mother's sister," John said.

"She's definitely not *plain*, is she?"

"She's a congresswoman."

"Well, I suppose that explains some of it," Zeke said. "She staying long?"

John caught the drift of Zeke's question and laughed. "She's not staying here at all. She and her so-called 'fact-finding committee' are probably booked at the Ritz-Carlton."

"The people's tax dollars at work," Zeke murmured.

"*Your* tax dollars maybe. Anyway, since my mom died, Liz has taken it upon herself to watch over me."

"She doesn't look old enough to be your mom."

"No, Liz is closer in age to a cousin or big sister. Big gap between my mother and her, in years, not to mention personality."

Zeke studied Liz for a long moment. "She's hot," he said finally in a tone that declared an assessment had been made and this was the final verdict. Then he took a deep breath and surveyed the property. "Well, I can see you've been able to make some progress without me." He glanced around. "So what's our plan?"

John had heard this question every time he'd been with Zeke. At first it had been "What's *your* plan?" But in the time they had worked together, it had become "What's *our* plan?"

"First we need to get my aunt back to town. Margery is already filling her head with her version of what I should and should not be doing." He nodded toward the pier where the two women were deep in conversation, or rather Margery was talking nonstop, and Liz was nodding as she listened intently. Liz kept flicking a glance over to where John was sitting with Zeke and giving him her tight campaign smile. This was not a good thing. It meant that she was agreeing with Margery's assessment of how he should be conducting his life, and the last thing John needed was two women trying to mother him.

"Dad? I'll see you later. Grady and Amy are here," Hester called out as she gathered her things and glanced out the window.

Her father lifted his bifocals to the top of his head and leaned back in his chair. "This meeting, Hester. What is it again?"

"It's not a meeting exactly," she hedged, unwilling to admit that she was about to attend a reception for the visiting congressional committee at Sarasota's fanciest hotel. "It's more of a gathering."

Arlen said nothing, just lifted one eyebrow skeptically.

"They just want to know how FEMA works with the various volunteer agencies, Dad. Since the oil spill and Katrina, they are looking at ways the agency might be more proactive."

"Will Emma Keller be there?"

"I don't know for sure."

Arlen caught her hand and held on. "Meaning you think probably not?"

She shrugged. "I'm doing this for Grady," she said as if that explained everything.

"I should not need to remind you that it is not our way to get involved in these outside politics, Hester."

"But it is our way to help a friend in need, and Grady can use our support to show those in authority that we respect the work he does here. With the baby coming and all, he really shouldn't have to worry unnecessarily about how others are judging his work."

"Still, you don't have to go to this event. You could write a letter to these government people praising Grady's work. In fact, we could all sign it."

"He's done a lot for Pinecraft, Dad. I think this is the least I can do," Hester told him as she heard Grady lightly toot the horn of his car a second time. She flicked the porch light switch off and on to signal that she had heard him. "Besides, this committee is interested in hearing ideas for how to improve the coordination of disaster relief efforts. The president himself appointed them to this commission."

"Impressive, but nevertheless, none of our business." He squeezed Hester's fingers, then released them.

"Are you asking me not to go?"

"I am asking you to remember who you are, who *we* are." He gently touched the ties of her prayer covering.

"I know all that, Dad."

"I am asking you to think about how this might raise questions among people in our community, our congregation."

"Olive Crowder?"

"*Liebchen*, surely you know that if Olive should ever become so concerned that she actually files a formal complaint against you, there is nothing I can do except to follow the protocol of our faith."

"I know," Hester admitted. "But I cannot let Grady down, Dad. He's been a good friend. I will go tonight to support Grady, and that will be the end of it. I give you my word that I will turn all of my efforts toward helping others through the church, starting first thing tomorrow. No more meetings with outsiders, no more—"

Her father stood and embraced her. "I am asking no such thing of you, Hester. I would never ask you to be other than the woman God has led you to be. The only thing I ask of you is that you be certain in your heart and mind that the choices you are making are those that God has led you to make and not those of your own choosing."

Hester hugged her father harder. "Even if those choices go against—?"

Arlen held her by her shoulders so that they were face-to-face, his blue eyes piercing as they held hers. "If you have prayed on these matters and listened for God's answer, then I will stand with you, and together we will see what plan God has in mind for you."

"Danke, Papa," she whispered as she kissed his cheek.

He chuckled. "You have not called me 'Papa' since you were seven or eight, and as I recall, you always did so when you had gotten your way." He gave her a little push toward the door. "Now go—before I change my mind."

At the reception, Hester was relieved to see that everyone attending was dressed in regular daytime attire. Only Jeannie and a woman whom Grady pointed out as a member of the committee as well as John Steiner's aunt arrived wearing something that could be called fancy. Jeannie was dressed in a flowing ankle-length caftan-style dress, and John's aunt was wearing a silk pantsuit in peacock blue.

Likewise the food was basic—cheese and crackers, vegetables and dip, and no alcohol. Instead, they served fresh-squeezed orange juice.

"Are we having fun yet?" Margery murmured as she came alongside Hester and bit down on a cracker. "Bunch of politicians trying to act like they might actually make something happen," she huffed. "Although that one there"—she pointed toward John's aunt—"she has potential." She chewed her cracker and continued her monologue as if Hester had raised the question of how she might know that. "I had a chance to spend some time with her this afternoon when she was out visiting Johnny. Oh, she knows how to push his buttons." She cackled with delight. "Got him so riled up that he actually agreed to show up here tonight."

In spite of herself, Hester made a quick scan of the crowded room.

"He's over there," Margery said with a nod toward a marble pillar at the far end of the room where, sure enough, John Steiner was leaning with arms crossed, his signature scowl firmly in place.

"So that's his aunt," Hester said, swinging her attention back to the woman in blue as John's eyes met hers. "She looks young enough to be his sister."

She nodded. "She gave me the whole family history. After Johnny's father died, his mom would have Liz come and spend summers on the farm with them. She told me she would have come here right after the storm passed, but duty had to take precedence. That's why she called the mayor here, who called Grady. . .who called you."

It was definitely hard to picture the anything-but-plain woman on a farm at all, much less one in the midst of an Amish community. Still, she had a way about her that made her seem downright approachable. Perhaps it was that she focused all of her attention on the person speaking to her at any given moment. Her eyes met theirs, and her features registered genuine concern and sympathy. Now and then she would place one manicured hand on the person's arm, give them a few words of what appeared to be reassurance or appreciation, and then move on to the next person.

Hester focused her attention on a man who Grady had told her was also on the Homeland Security Committee. In sharp contrast to John's aunt, the man appeared to be lecturing those gathered around him when he should have been listening.

"Hester?"

She turned to find Grady approaching her with the congress-woman close at his side.

"I'd like you to meet Congresswoman Elizabeth Carter-Thompson," he said. "This is Hester Detlef, the woman I was telling you about."

"It's a pleasure to meet you in person, Hester. May I call you Hester?" She had taken Hester's hand between both of hers and lasered her with eyes that were the same color as John's.

"Yes," Hester replied.

"And I am Liz. Margery Barker told me about the work you've been doing through your agency—MCC, is it? And your father as well with MDS, I believe. Both groups were so key to our efforts after Katrina. Walk the talk, we like to say, but so few of us really ever do."

Hester felt herself caught up in the whirlwind that she understood was Liz's way of drawing total strangers into her circle of supporters. Instinctively she pulled her hand free and took a small step away. She saw something pass across Liz's eyes that she would not have expected. She saw a hint of embarrassment.

"I'm sorry," Liz said in a tone that sounded far more sincere than the bright chatter she'd delivered before. "Give me a second to retire my politician hat." She pantomimed removing a hat and casting it to the wind; then she turned back to Hester. "I really want to hear any ideas you might have about how best to help those affected by this hurricane," she said. "Can we go sit somewhere that's a little quieter and have a real conversation?"

Realizing that Grady had moved on to another group after making the introductions, Hester hesitated.

"It's not a trap," Liz assured her. "I really want to talk."

"All right." She would take the congresswoman at her word, for now. But remembering the stories that Grady had told her about how government worked, she would also be cautious.

"Shall we ask my nephew to join us?"

But it was a moot question since Liz was already signaling to John. Hester glanced over at him, fully expecting him to ignore his aunt and walk away, but to her amazement, he started working his way through the crowd toward them.

"I know he can be a pill of major proportions," Liz confided, "but he does have a way of thinking outside the box. That's what got him in trouble in the first place." She sighed, then plastered on her brightest smile as John reached them. "John, I believe you and Hester know each other?"

He nodded and then focused his attention on his aunt. "You summoned?"

"Oh, stop being so contentious," Liz replied as she reached up and straightened his shirt collar. John let her without shrugging away. He was wearing jeans and one of the tropical print shirts Rosalyn had pulled for him from the supplies at the center. He was clean-shaven instead of sporting the stubble that she'd gotten used to seeing on him. It surprised her that this pleased her. She had always found the stubble slightly pretentious.

"Now, then," Liz said, pointing to a cluster of three upholstered chairs in the atrium outside the crowded ballroom. "Let's talk. Rather, you talk. I'll listen." She nodded to a young man who had trailed them from the ballroom. "This is Alan. He's a member of my staff. If you don't object, he'll sit quietly and take notes."

John shrugged and Hester nodded.

"Excellent," Liz said as Alan moved a straight chair behind and to her left and pulled out a notebook and pen. "Where shall we begin?" she asked. "Tell me about the efforts MCC and MDS have already made, Hester."

It got easier after that. Once Hester started to list the various projects coordinated by MCC and MDS and describe how the two groups worked together with the better-known secular agencies, she was in her element. Now and then John would interject a comment or Liz would ask a question that would lead them into the discussion of something else. They told her about the distribution center, the RV teams, and the work that had been done to get Margery back in business.

"Tell me about the flooding in Pinecraft," Liz asked.

"That wasn't Grady Forrest's fault," Hester said, and then she blushed at her uncensored remarks.

"Why would anyone think that it was?" Liz said quietly. "Are you saying there was a problem there?"

"They were busy with me," John told her. "It's what happens when people try to pull strings from a thousand miles away."

Hester watched as John and his aunt locked eyes. "I was concerned," she said through a tight smile even as she quietly placed one hand on Alan's to stop his moving pen.

"And with good reason." Hester could not help her instinct to try to smooth things over between them. Now their gazes shifted to her. "I mean, at times like that, it's hard to know where to put your resources first. The human tendency is to protect those you know and love. You don't think much about how it affects others."

"I was the one at fault," John said quietly. "If I had left when

Hester told me to, then. . ."

Liz's eyes widened with interest. "I wasn't aware that the two of you knew each other before the hurricane."

"We didn't," Hester said.

"Then why send. . ."

"Drop it, Lizzie," John growled. "It's over and done with. Let's move on." He did not look directly at Hester, but she understood that John had come as close as he would ever come to admitting that he had been wrong to stay.

"All right, then, let's talk about plans for the future and the resources available to help." Liz signaled Alan that his note-taking could resume.

"Whose?" John asked.

"Yours makes for an interesting case study. How are things coming out there at your version of *Walden*?"

Hester's heart went out to John as she watched his features collapse into an expression of such utter defeat that she had to stop herself from reaching over to comfort him. He had done as much as he could to repair the damage to his property. Did his aunt have any idea what it had been like that first day after the hurricane passed through?

"I have the first floor of the house fairly livable." He held up his left hand, cast removed. "I have the use of both hands for the first time in weeks." He hesitated as if searching for words.

"But?" Liz asked, her voice gentle.

"But the undeniable fact is that the orange trees that Tucker planted and I worked at reviving for the last two years are gone." His voice trailed off as if he had just realized this, when Hester knew that he must have known it all along. The rows of trees had for the most part been snapped off in the high winds, and those few trees not totally wiped out by the hurricane were half buried in the salty muck left behind when the waters of the bay finally receded. They were as good as dead.

"So how will you support yourself and your work on that place?" Liz pressed, her tone that of a mother nurturing a small child.

John blinked as if he were just awakening from a nightmare. "I have no idea," he admitted. "I put everything I had into that property."

"You still have the packinghouse," Hester reminded him.

"And exactly what would we pack there?" he asked her, but this time he was the one who had assumed a tone that one might use in speaking to an overly optimistic child. He turned his attention back to his aunt. "So there you have one of what must be hundreds of sad stories, Lizzie. What are you and your fact-finding team going to do about it?"

A commotion just inside the ballroom drew their attention away from the tension that radiated between John and his aunt.

"Somebody call 911," a voice yelled. "This lady's having her baby."

Hester was on her feet instantly. With John and Liz not far behind, she worked her way through the throng surrounding Amy and Grady. Amy was sitting on one of the small straight-backed and gilded chairs at a white-cloth-covered table, a pool of water at her feet. Grady was on his knees next to her.

"Hang in there, honey," he coached. "They've called for an ambulance."

Amy's response was a prolonged keening of pain that sent everyone into retreat as she gripped Grady's hand. "Can't." She gritted out the word. "Now."

"Get back," Hester heard John order the onlookers, and to her amazement everyone complied.

"People," Liz shouted, clapping her hands. "Please follow Alan here out into the atrium while we wait for the ambulance." The crowd shifted only a little. "That's the way," she said, encouraging them to keep moving. "Let's give these folks some privacy," she said as the others headed reluctantly toward the doors.

"When did the pains start?" Hester asked.

Amy was between contractions and breathing heavily. "This afternoon," she said.

"This afternoon?" Grady shouted. "And you didn't say anything? We should have—"

"You needed to be here," she replied, panting in preparation for the next round of pain. "Job," she managed, as the pain gripped her once more.

Grady glanced at Liz then back at his wife. "You don't worry about that. We're going to be fine," he murmured.

Liz waited for the contraction to pass and then knelt next to Grady, taking Amy's free hand. "Now you listen to me, both of you," she said. "There is nothing so precious—or important—in this world than the beginning of a new life. That child could change the world."

Amy's eyes brimmed with tears.

Hester saw John clasp Grady's shoulder. "Your job's not on the line," he said. "Right, Liz?"

"Oh, for goodness' sake," she grumbled as she got to her feet. "We aren't monsters. We didn't come down here to check up on or make anyone our scapegoat, Grady. We came here because. . .it's what we do when the media pushes our buttons and we don't know what else to do," she finished lamely. "I'll speak with your boss, okay?"

"Thank you." Grady squeezed Amy's hand. "See, honey? It's all going to be fine." In the quiet that followed, they could hear the siren of the arriving ambulance. In seconds the room was a beehive of activity as Amy was checked, then placed on a gurney and rolled away with Grady clinging to her hand and running alongside.

"You coming?" he shouted to Hester.

"Sure."

Grady dug into his pocket and tossed his car keys in the air. John caught them with one hand, then passed them to Hester.

"I could have caught them," she said.

"No doubt."

When he started walking with her toward the exit, Hester hesitated.

"Lead the way," he said, holding the door open for her. "It's not like I know what Grady's car looks like."

Chapter 17

It took Hester a minute to familiarize herself with the mechanics of Grady's hybrid car. John seemed to instinctively know that it would be best to remain silent and let her work things out for herself. Still, she could practically feel him wanting to offer his ideas about how to start the thing. Finally, she got it started, and they were on their way to the hospital.

"You don't have to do this," she repeated. "Come to the hospital, I mean."

"I'd do pretty much anything not to have to stay another minute at that party," he said and grinned.

"Reception," she corrected. "And I don't know why you were there, but I was there for Grady."

"Sure you were."

Was that a smile? Hester clamped her mouth shut and concentrated on driving. "I take it your sarcasm means you think I was there for other reasons?"

"I think you like being where the action is. I think you really struggle when it comes to being in the background."

"I. . ." She absolutely could not find the words to refute that, but he was wrong. Wasn't he? "And you know this because. . . ?"

"An observation. Nothing more. And it's not like it's a bad

thing." Out of the corner of her eye, she saw him study her for a long moment, but she refused to take her eyes from the road. "Anyway, let's talk about something else."

"Such as?"

"I don't know. We're on our way to the hospital, where in a few hours Grady and Amy will bring a new life into this world. Did you ever wonder what it might be like to be a parent?" he asked as they stopped for a light that was notorious for taking forever to change.

She felt herself relax as she thought about Amy and Grady and all the ways this night was going to change their lives forever. "Sure. I think everyone must wonder about that."

"Maybe you and Samuel—"

"What about you?" she interrupted before he could pursue that thought, a thought that she had not really wanted to consider in all the time she'd spent imagining a future with Samuel.

The light changed to green, and a car behind them honked impatiently. Hester eased the car forward much as she might have coaxed a horse and buggy into motion, deliberately taking her time. "You never married?"

"I came close, I guess," he said as the impatient driver passed them on the right, horn blasting.

"You guess? How do you guess at a thing like that?"

"Same way you think maybe you and Samuel might marry one day," he shot back. "It seemed like it was going to happen and it didn't, in my case."

"Fair enough," she murmured as she turned onto a side street.

"The sign says the entrance to the emergency room is that way." He pointed.

"But the parking lot is down this side street."

She pulled into the first available space and had barely turned off the engine before she was out of the car and walking quickly toward the hospital entrance. *It seemed like it was going to happen.* His words beat a cadence that matched her steps as together they hurried along long deserted corridors to the main lobby.

"Mrs. Forrest has been taken to our obstetrics unit," the

person at the desk told them. "Take these elevators to three, and the waiting room is on your left as you exit."

As soon as they stepped off the elevator, a nurse whom Hester knew assured them that Amy was doing fine and Grady was with her. "The contractions have stopped for now," she said. "It could be a while." She turned her attention to John. "Are you the family?"

"We're friends," John replied before Hester could.

"I'll let Mr. Forrest know you're out here. There's coffee and tea," she said, motioning toward a machine in the corner, "and our vintage selection of three- to five-year-old magazines." She offered an apologetic smile, and then continued on her way through a pair of swinging doors that whooshed shut behind her.

"You don't need to stay," Hester said.

"If you keep saying that every time we end up in the same place, I'm going to think you don't like my company," John said and sat down on a chair facing away from the television that was on but muted. He picked up a magazine and started flipping through it. The cover featured a colorful summer fruit salad and a bold headline about weight loss. The picture of the fruit salad reminded Hester of rainbows.

"Do you think there's any chance your aunt and her group will help get Rainbow House reopened?" she asked.

"I doubt it. It's not what they do."

"I've been checking up on some of the people who were so sick. They seem to be okay physically, but it's hard for them and the others. . .all the others. . . ." Her voice trailed off.

"How's the guy we left here that day? Dan?"

"Danny. His brother came and took him back to his home in Georgia. That's pretty much all I know about him, but at least he had family."

"Margery tells me that Zeke also has family, locally."

Hester nodded. "Zeke comes from a fairly prominent family in this area. They give him money regularly, but he just gives it away, takes care of the others, especially his fellow veterans. Some of them take advantage." She paced the room, ending up finally in front of the coffee machine. "Do you want something?"

John shook his head and continued paging through the magazine, stopping now and then to skim an article.

"If we could just find a place," Hester continued as if there had been no pause in the conversation. She pushed the button for tea and, once it was ready, cradled the Styrofoam cup between her palms instead of drinking from it.

"Isn't finding homes for homeless people a little out of your jurisdiction?"

"I don't have a jurisdiction. When people are in need, then it's our mission to try to help them."

"And what about the people devastated by the hurricane— property and job loss and such as you must have mentioned to me at least five hundred times. . . ."

"Don't exaggerate." She fought against a smile. "It wasn't more than two hundred tops. There are systems in place to help them."

"Systems that don't work much of the time," John reminded her.

"I know, but when we were helping Zeke and Dan and the others, it struck me that for these folks—people who live on the street and have to rely on public facilities for their basic needs and eat out of trash cans and—"

"Some would say they should get a job."

"How? Where? Everything's against them—their hygiene or lack thereof, their age in many cases, their mental health. They are invisible and lost, and no one really notices them until they interrupt the tourist season by hanging out down at the bay or get businesses all nervous or in some cases cross paths with the police and. . ." In spite of her determination not to, Hester started to cry. She'd been repressing her concerns and worries for so long that there seemed to be no place to put anything more. "Don't mind me. It's just been an emotional few weeks, and I'm worried about Grady and Amy and. . ."

John laid his magazine aside and moved to the chair next to hers. He put his hand on her back and leaned in closer. "Hey, you're doing the best you can, okay? You can't save the world, although Samuel tells me you are stubborn enough to try."

She glanced up, swiping at tears with the back of her hand. "Samuel said I was stubborn?"

"I said you were stubborn. Samuel seems to think you can do whatever you set your mind to."

"Takes one to know one—stubborn, I mean," she said, far too aware of John's face close to hers, his large palm resting on her back. His eyes with their fan of golden lashes held the promise of understanding and acceptance. And in that moment she fully comprehended that she and John Steiner had a lot more in common than she might ever have imagined. For, like her, he was a person who looked at the world and saw possibilities and challenges that required going beyond the norm to solve. She had never talked like this with Samuel, and even when she raised these issues with her father, more often than not he looked mystified and counseled her that there were many in her own community in need of her help.

John leaned in closer and wiped one tear from her cheek with his thumb. She thought for one incredible moment that he might kiss her, but instead he rested his forehead on hers. "Ah, Hester Detlef, we might be a formidable team if we stopped fighting each other," he said softly.

"You would help me?"

"I would help Zeke," he corrected. "You don't need help."

Yes, I do, she thought, and for the first time since her mother had died, she admitted to herself that she had been running on empty for months now, lost in her desperate need to find some way that she could save *someone*, because she couldn't save her mother.

~⚞≈≈⚟~

It was well past midnight when Samuel closed up the workshop and saw Rosalyn walking along Bahia Vista. He cut across a parking lot behind the cabinetry shop to catch up to her and was just about to call out to her when a convertible filled with teenagers roared past her going at least twenty miles over the posted speed limit. One of the occupants shouted at her, and then Samuel saw something fly out of the car and strike Rosalyn in the face. Glass shattered as the object hit the ground, and before he knew it, the car was making an illegal U-turn. Rosalyn was holding her hand to her forehead. As the driver and another young man got out of the car, he started to run toward Rosalyn.

From their unsteady gait, he was pretty sure that the two young men were drunk, and instinct told him they had not come back to help Rosalyn.

"Hey, honey," he heard one of them croon. "You shouldn't be out walking alone at this hour. How about a ride with me and my friends here?"

The second young man snickered as one of the two who had remained in the car called for his friends to come back so they could be on their way.

"Why, you're bleeding, sweetheart," the driver continued, a wide smirk of a smile contradicting his words of concern. "We'd better get you to a hospital and get that looked at right away." He took hold of Rosalyn's arm and started pulling her toward the car, while his friend stumbled back to open the passenger door for her.

"Let her go, man," the man in the backseat said. "Let's get out of here."

"Shut up," the driver growled. "What happened to your face, honey? It's all purple and stuff."

When he was within a couple of yards of the group, Samuel slowed to a walk and forced his breathing to calm. "Is there a problem?" he asked as he emerged from the shadows, deliberately startling the young man who was holding Rosalyn's arm.

"What do you want, Amish boy?" the guy holding the car door snarled.

Now that he was closer, Samuel saw that all of the men in the car were barely out of their teens, if that, and the car they were driving was an expensive one. Everything about them screamed money and entitlement. Samuel had encountered guys like these before when he was attending public school. They truly seemed to believe that their family money could buy them anything they wanted, or in the case of Rosalyn, anything they decided to take.

He took a few seconds to gauge the situation. He was pretty sure that at least the two guys in the backseat were not a threat. One was nearly passed out, and the other looked like he wished he were anywhere else but on this street corner.

Samuel memorized the license number of the car as he moved closer to the man holding Rosalyn's arm.

"We got this, man," the one standing by the open car door said.

"Let her go," Samuel said calmly.

The driver released Rosalyn's arm as he took a step toward Samuel. Rosalyn seized the moment and ran to Samuel's side. He wrapped his arm around her shoulder and faced the young man who was swaying unsteadily.

"There are four of us," he pointed out. "And I've heard that you Amish boys don't believe in fighting."

Samuel glanced at each of the other three, relieved that the two in the backseat had made no move to join their friend, and the one standing next to the open door of the car would do whatever this guy told him to do. The person he needed to deal with was standing not three feet in front of him, his eyes glazed and his smile cocky.

"Actually, we are Mennonites, but you are right," he said, and the driver's grin widened as he once again reached for Rosalyn.

Samuel pressed her closer to his side as he smiled at the man and at the same time looked him directly in the eye without blinking. "So here is my suggestion," he said quietly. "You and your friends leave now, and my friend and I will not report the matter."

"Yeah. Right. Do I look like a complete fool?"

Actually, yes, Samuel thought, but he forced an expression of contrition. "You seem to know something of our ways, and therefore you probably know that when a man of my faith gives his word then you can count on it."

From the corner of his eye he saw that one of the group who'd been sitting in the backseat had moved to the front, into the driver's seat. "Come on, Robbie," he called. "We got places to go and beer to drink. Time's not on our side."

Samuel stepped back, creating more distance between the drunken young man and Rosalyn. He nodded to the man behind the wheel. "You okay to drive?"

"Yes, sir," he said. "I've only had one. Sorry about that." He nodded toward Rosalyn. "Is she okay?"

"She'll be fine," Samuel assured him as he watched Rosalyn's attacker sway slightly as he made his decision. Finally, he climbed into the backseat and slumped down. Samuel felt his fist clench and wondered at the power of his instinct to rip the guy to shreds. He closed his eyes and silently prayed for the strength he needed to see this through. "Just go," he said quietly, and to his relief he heard the last car door slam and the car roared away.

Rosalyn slumped against him and broke down sobbing.

"Come on, now. It's all over," he said, gently leading her to a streetlamp so he could assess the extent of her injury. "It doesn't seem to be that bad."

"It's fine," she said, accepting the handkerchief he offered her and pressing it to her forehead. "It was just that I was so scared, and if you hadn't come along, and what if. . ."

"Shhh. . ."

Samuel pulled her into his arms and held her, rocking her gently from side to side as they stood together under the amber glow of the old-fashioned streetlamp. "I'm right here and I'm not going anywhere," he promised, and he knew in that moment that where Rosalyn was concerned—and Hester—he had made his decision.

━══━

By the time Amy had her baby, both her parents and Grady's had arrived to greet their first grandchild. The waiting room had become a beehive of activity as other family members were called with the good news. Amy had delivered a seven-pound boy at 4:12 in the morning. Both mother and child were doing fine.

"We're naming him Harley," Grady announced, his eyes sparkling with new-dad wonder in spite of his exhaustion.

Hester congratulated him as well as each set of grandparents and then realized that John was no longer in the room. While everyone else headed in to see Amy and Harley, Hester went into the hallway and found it empty. She checked at the nurses' station, and a weary night nurse pointed down a connecting hall. "I saw him head to the nursery," she said.

And there he was standing outside the nursery window, his hands twisting the rolled magazine as he stared at a row of newborns tucked into their bassinets.

Hester stood next to him, gazing at the new babies. She couldn't help wondering if she would ever know the special joy of motherhood. "John?"

"You have to wonder," he said without preamble, "how it will all turn out for them. I mean, I sure never thought. . ." He shook his head and turned to her. "Ready to go?"

"We came in Grady's car," she reminded him.

"Right. Well, let's give him the keys, and then if you're up to it we can walk back to Pinecraft."

"That's pretty far out of your way."

He shrugged and then smiled. "I thought you might be in the mood to celebrate."

Hester must have looked at him as if he had suddenly grown another head, because he explained, "The truth is, I'm famished, and breakfast at Yoder's sounds pretty good to me right now."

"But first a five-mile hike," she said, pointing out the obvious.

"Unless you've got another idea of how we might get there."

She was beyond tired but knew that the fresh air would do them both good, and at this hour of the morning it was unlikely to be as hot as it would become later in the day. "Okay. Just let me give Grady his keys and say good-bye."

John was waiting by the stairway when Hester left Amy's room. She was smiling, but he sensed it was a private smile, not meant for him. He expected it had to do with the baby. It occurred to him that she would make a good mother, and he tried to imagine the kids she and Samuel Brubaker might have someday. It surprised him that not only could he not imagine such a thing, but he also really didn't like imagining her having a family with Samuel.

Whoa! he thought as she came toward him, her eyes still with that dreamy dazed look women tended to get after being exposed to babies. *You barely know this woman.* But he wanted to know her. He didn't know when his attitude toward her had changed, but it had. He wanted to know everything about her.

He held the door for her, and she started down the stairs ahead of him, never once questioning why they hadn't used the elevator. Outside, they walked along without speaking, the noisy traffic whizzing past them on the busy four-lane road, until they crossed onto Bahia Vista and started walking toward Pinecraft.

"You were an only child, right?" she asked.

"Yeah."

She didn't seem inclined to pursue the matter, and John was relieved to let the subject drop.

"You're still carrying that magazine," she said when they'd walked half a block in silence.

He hesitated and glanced back toward the main street. "I forgot. I should return it. . . ."

"I can do it when I go to visit Amy and the baby later today."

"You're going back? Today?" *Do you ever sleep?*

"Well, she'll probably go home tomorrow, and they live some distance away, so, yes, today would be best. I made a crib quilt for the baby." She held out her hand for the magazine, and he gave it to her.

"Thanks. I expect it won't be missed, but still. . ."

"As Zeke would say, 'No worries.' " They passed the local branch of the YMCA, where childlike chalk pictures decorated the running track that surrounded the main building. "You know what you said before about wondering how they'll all turn out? Those newborns?"

"Yeah."

"I think about that sometimes myself. I mean, how did I get this far in life without really having a plan?"

"You? Seems to me you've always had a plan. You went to nursing school. You took care of your mother while she was so ill. You take care of others now." He avoided mentioning the possibility that within the coming year she would probably marry Samuel. *Would not saying it aloud help to keep it from happening?* he wondered. And more to the point, why shouldn't it happen? She deserved to be happy, after all. "I'd say you not only found your calling, but you've followed it to the letter."

"I certainly didn't plan to spend five years caring for a terminally ill parent," she said in a tone that was so filled with sadness that John felt guilty for having brought up the subject at all.

"I expect that Grady and his wife will make good parents," he said, trying to find some other path for their conversation. It worked. When he looked over at her, she was smiling.

"They are so excited and the baby is beautiful. Harley Forrest is one fortunate child."

They waited for a light to change even though there was no traffic on the cross street. The green seemed to signal yet another shift in conversation.

"I like your aunt," Hester said. "She's not at all what I would have expected a politician to be like, or anyone related to you," she added with a teasing smile.

"Meaning?"

"I don't know. You strike me as someone who is constantly carrying around a heavy burden, one that you refuse to allow others to help you lighten."

Her guess was closer to the truth than John would have expected, and he was tempted to confide in her. He was so tired of the exhausting weight of his past. But would a woman who had tenderly nursed her mother for five long years and fought every day to bring joy and beauty to a life that was surely slipping away understand a son who had been the cause of his mother's death?

Hester waited for some response, but John said nothing. They had reached the restaurant, and he held the door for her without comment.

The restaurant was already busy with locals who made a habit of starting their day there. The counter was completely occupied. The patrons there barely glanced up as the hostess led John and Hester to a booth and placed menus in front of them. "Coffee?"

"Please," they chorused as each of them opened the menu—one Hester practically knew by heart—and studied the list of breakfast items.

"How's the garden coming?" John asked, setting his menu aside and adding cream to the coffee the waitress had brought.

So they were going back to safer topics of conversation. "I haven't had much time to work on it," she said.

"I have some ferns you can have. They might work in the shady spots under the arbor."

"That would be nice. Thank you."

He shrugged. "They'll just end up trampled now that I'm ready to paint the packinghouse."

Hester sighed. "Why do you do that?"

"What?"

"Turn a nice gesture into something else—like I'd be the one doing you a favor."

"Well, you would and it's our way, yours as well."

She shook her head. "No. This is different. It's like you don't think you deserve the gratitude of others. I noticed it last night when Grady tried to thank you for coming to the hospital."

"I—"

"And then there was that day we went searching for Zeke's friends. You didn't have to do that, and yet you were as concerned for them as I was, but when they tried to thank you—especially Danny—"

The waitress appeared at their booth and hesitated. "Should I come back?"

"No. Two eggs over easy on whole wheat toast with a side of fruit," Hester said.

"Pancakes—triple stack," John muttered.

"Well?" Hester said when the waitress had left them alone again. "I mean, what is it with you, John Steiner?" She knew that her exhaustion only added to her exasperation with the man. "Ignore that," she added before he could respond. "I'm just tired. I'll come out and dig the ferns next week if that's all right."

"Fine."

If Hester had learned one thing about John, it was that he was anything but fine. She rearranged the condiments on the table and refrained from starting any further conversation.

A few minutes later, the waitress set their plates in front of them, steam rising from both, as Hester folded her hands in her lap and bowed her head.

And it came to her that the burden John was carrying had something to do with his mother's death and that the birth of Grady's child had somehow brought all of that back to him.

"You don't have to answer this, of course—after all, it's certainly none of my business."

He continued pouring syrup on his pancakes, but she saw his hand twitch slightly.

"How did you mother die?"

With more care than necessary he set the syrup pitcher down. "I killed her."

Part Three

And a man shall be as an hiding place
from the wind, and a covert from the tempest;
as rivers of water in a dry place,
as the shadow of a great rock in a weary land.
ISAIAH 32:2

There is more day to dawn. . . . The sun is but a morning star.
HENRY DAVID THOREAU, *Walden: Life in the Woods*

Chapter 18

Hester was searching for words to respond to John's astounding admission when they were interrupted.

"Hester? Is that you?" Olive Crowder brushed past the hostess with Agnes trailing behind her. "What on earth are you doing out at this hour?"

A question that Hester understood wasn't complete without the unspoken "with a strange man." Olive focused all of her attention on John.

"I might ask you the same thing," Hester said, fighting to keep her tone light. "It's early even for the two of you. Olive and Agnes Crowder, this is John Steiner." Hester's mind raced with how she might quickly get rid of the spinster sisters and get back to addressing the astounding confession John had just made to her.

But Olive's eyes flickered with interest when she heard John's name, even as she bristled at the idea that he was having breakfast with Hester.

"Hello," Agnes said with a smile.

Olive stepped between her sister and John as if she needed to protect Agnes. "You're that man—the one who bought land at Tucker's Point. The one who got wiped out by the storm. The Amish man."

"Guilty on all counts," John said. He had stood up when Hester made the introductions, and he now met Olive Crowder eye-to-eye. "And you are. . ."

He glanced at Hester, who was holding her breath, silently praying that he would not say something to set Olive off.

"You are the lady of whom Hester speaks so often," he said.

Olive looked past John to Hester. "What are you doing here?" she demanded again.

"We're having breakfast," John replied as if she had addressed her question to him. "Perhaps you know Grady Forrest and his wife, Amy?"

"Oh, they are the loveliest couple," Agnes chirped.

"They had their baby last night," John explained. "Hester and I happened to be with them, so we went to the hospital to be sure everything was all right."

"And stayed the night?"

"Yes, Olive, we were at the hospital," Hester said quietly. "The child was born a little after four this morning. Now if you'll excuse us, our breakfast is getting cold, and both Mr. Steiner and I have a busy day ahead."

"Well," Olive huffed and turned on her heel. "Come, Agnes. Let's find another place to have our meal. We know when we're not welcome."

"But, Olive," Agnes said, pointing to a row of empty tables. Then, seeing the futility of arguing, she smiled apologetically. "It was so nice to meet you," she said in a near whisper as she scurried after her sister, who was already out the door and striding toward the larger restaurant across the street.

"Well, that can't be good," John said. "Will you be all right?"

The question confused her. "Oh, you mean Olive? That's just her way. No doubt she will stop by the house later to have a word with my father. He'll assure her that he'll look into the matter, and that will be the end of it." He was still standing next to the booth. "Let's just finish our breakfast." *And our conversation.* "You were about to tell—"

"I should go." He folded his napkin and left it next to his

half-eaten pancakes; then he reached into his pocket and pulled out a slim fold of money. "Think this will cover it?" he asked, placing a five and four singles on the table.

Hester saw that this left him with a single bill, a twenty. She wondered how long that had to last him. "It's fine, but, John. . ." She didn't want to make a scene, but surely he was aware that he'd made an incredible admission to her, and she could hardly just let him walk away without an explanation.

"I didn't murder her," he said, "but I was responsible for her death." He took a long swallow of his water and then left. Outside he ran to a bus stop, where a westbound bus was just pulling away. He flagged it down and jumped on board.

"Anything else, miss?" The waitress hovered uncertainly, holding a carafe of coffee in one hand and their check in the other. She was new at working here, and that comforted Hester some. At least whatever she might have witnessed, she wouldn't be telling it to others who knew she was the preacher's daughter having breakfast with a man who was not her father—and not Samuel Brubaker. But why worry about a gossiping waitress when Olive already had a head start?

"No, thank you. I have to. . ." She picked up the money and handed it to the waitress, then practically ran from the restaurant as if she might be able to flag the bus and stop John from leaving. He was the most exasperating man.

"Miss?" The waitress had followed her out to the parking lot. "You forgot your magazine."

Hester turned back to meet her halfway. "Thanks." She rolled the magazine and looked up and down the street. Pinecraft was already bustling with business owners out sweeping their entrances or unloading stock for their shops. Her days had begun to run into one another, but she might as well head for the MCC office—the haven she had gone to every day since her mother's funeral. It was where her mother had done so much good, and the constant work made the hours fly by.

She was surprised to find the door locked. Rosalyn almost always arrived ahead of her, her bright smile something Hester had been especially looking forward to seeing today. Of course it was early yet, just past seven.

But Rosalyn still had not come by nine. . .or eleven. By that time, Hester was seriously worried. She had called several friends and neighbors. No one had seen her. She'd even stopped by Rosalyn's house. Out of ideas of where she might be and beginning to worry, Hester decided to stop at her father's shop. He would know what to do.

"She's with Samuel," Arlen told her as he concentrated on sanding the double doors that would attach to a large china cabinet that had already been stained and polished. "There was a bit of trouble last night. Fortunately, Samuel was nearby when the bottle hit Rosalyn—"

"What bottle, Dad? Is Rosalyn all right? Who—"

"Some rowdies had been drinking. They were driving in the area and spotted Rosalyn on her way home. According to Samuel, one of them threw away his beer bottle, and it hit Rosalyn in the forehead. She has quite a nasty cut. You weren't here, so Samuel took her to the walk-in clinic, and they stitched it up fine."

"She had to have stitches?" Hester was appalled at the calmness with which her father was relating this news. "Where is she now?"

"You just missed her. This morning Samuel stopped to check on her and was worried that she seemed to have a fever, so he brought her to the house for you to have a look. When you weren't there, he took her back to the doctor just to be sure she was all right. Samuel stopped by to let me know he was taking her home so she can rest. The doctor says she should be fine in a couple of days but that she's had not only a physical trauma but an emotional one as well."

"I would say so." Hester decided to ignore her father's inference that it was odd she wouldn't be at home first thing in the morning. Instead, she perched on a stool and watched him work. "What about the men who did this?"

"Samuel said they were barely men, more like boys trying to play at being grown up. He spoke with them and they left."

"I should go see if she's all right."

"Yes, perhaps later." He put down his paintbrush and pulled a stool next to hers. "Olive Crowder brought cookies," he said, nodding toward a tin on his workbench. "Oatmeal with chocolate chips."

"No thanks."

Olive Crowder had been bringing her father baked goods and sometimes huge casseroles since the day after Sarah died. The casseroles always came with the implied message that Hester was far too busy with her nursing and volunteer activities to take proper care of her father.

Come to think of it, she had been bringing him baked goods for most of Hester's life. Her mother had marveled at what a gifted baker Olive was, which only encouraged her. As girls, Olive and Hester's mother had been the best of friends and rivals for Arlen's affection. And while there had been some distance between the two women once Sarah and Arlen married, Hester could not deny that Olive had been a devoted friend to both her parents all through the long years of Sarah's illness. She had often suspected that once Sarah died, Olive had permitted herself to think that maybe in time Arlen would turn to her, that one day they might even marry. Of course, her father seemed oblivious to any underlying motive that might accompany Olive's baked gifts.

"Olive has a concern," her father said as he bit down on a cookie and took his time chewing.

"Dad, I know that she has become more and more upset about my work with MCC. She believes that CAM is—"

"Her concern is about you being seen walking with John Steiner before dawn and then having breakfast with him. Her concern is that there was no reason you needed to stay the night once Grady and Amy arrived at the hospital, and I have to say that I agree."

"Papa. . ."

He held up a finger and continued speaking. "I began to think more about this after our conversation last evening, liebchen. Since your mother died, you have run from one project to the next, and in between you have taken on the running of our household, something you had been doing more and more as Sarah's health failed. I have to admit that I allowed this, even encouraged it once your brothers moved away and your mother was gone—"

"Oh, Papa." Hester stood and wrapped her arms around her father's shoulders.

His eyes filled with tears, but he pulled a handkerchief from his pocket and wiped them away. "You have fallen into the habit of caring for everyone but yourself. Olive has made me see that I have been selfish, Hester, and that the time has come for us to consider your future and happiness, not mine."

"She said that?"

"No, I am saying that. Olive chastised me for allowing you too much freedom."

"I am a grown woman," Hester protested.

"And a good Mennonite woman. But Olive has a point. You know my concerns. You have become so involved in matters of the world outside Pinecraft. Not that the people you have befriended aren't perfectly wonderful, and in most cases God-loving people, but you cannot find happiness out there, Hester."

"I'm happy. I'm busy with so many things because that is the work God has called me to do." She hesitated, wondering where this was all coming from. It wasn't like her father to become so emotionally invested when a member of his congregation came to him with a concern. Of course, this concern did involve her, but still. . . "What exactly did Olive say?" she asked, taking her seat across from him so that they were knee to knee.

"Oh, you know Olive. She was quite upset seeing you this morning. She said that you and John seemed to be having quite a serious conversation. I told her that you had been trying to help that young man get back on his feet, but she was adamant that this conversation appeared to be of a more personal nature and, given the circumstances, was totally inappropriate. She raised the question of whether or not she should report her observations to Samuel."

"She can report her observations to anyone she pleases, and she no doubt will. John Steiner and I were indeed having a serious and personal conversation. The man had just told me that he killed his mother when Olive interrupted. I really can't imagine things could get much more serious or personal than that." She clasped her fingers over her mouth, horrified that she had revealed such incriminating information when she had no idea what it meant.

"He killed his own mother?" Arlen closed his eyes for a moment, and Hester knew that he was sending up a prayer for John.

"He didn't murder her," she hastened to assure him. "He was just somehow involved in her death."

"In what way?"

Hester blinked. "I don't know," she admitted. "Olive started in, and then once she left John left without elaborating. I think he regretted saying anything at all."

"I knew the man was deeply troubled, but this. . ." Arlen began to pace, wringing his hands as he considered this news. "I think it best if you stay away from him."

"You would judge him?"

"The man has admitted a crime to you, Hester."

"And what if his only crime is guilt, Dad? I would stake everything on that being the case. It explains so much about the way he is, his lack of trust, his running away from the only home and community he's ever known. His determination not to make connections here." The more she talked, the more she saw parallels between John's actions and her own.

"You can't know that until we know the whole story."

"But that was what I felt, what I have felt every day since Mom died. I am a trained nurse, and still. . ."

"There's no cure for ALS, Hester. You know that. You did everything you possibly could have done to see that her last days and months were the best they could be, and it took its toll on you. I should have seen what it was doing to you. I should have recognized it when you spent so many hours in the garden after her death—the garden you had created for her. I thought once Samuel came to work here and became our friend. . .I hoped. . ."

She took his hand between both of hers. "I know. I know."

Father and daughter sat that way for a long moment.

"I will go and speak with John," Arlen said, finally getting down from his stool and turning to his workbench.

"No, Dad. Let me go. He almost told me this morning, and if Olive hadn't interrupted, I'm certain that he would have told me the entire story."

"I think it best if you keep your distance for now. Give Olive a few days to calm herself."

Hester glanced down at the tin of cookies. "She's in love with you, you know."

Arlen shrugged. "I know. Your mother even suggested that if I remarried, Olive would be a good match."

This was news that Hester had never imagined. "Mom said that?"

"Yep. Badgered me for a promise that I would do just that almost right up to the end. Even when she could no longer speak, it was there in her eyes every time Olive stopped by."

"But you didn't. Why?"

"Because Olive may love me or think she does, but I don't love her."

"But if you promised. . ."

"I promised only that I would find peace in God's will for Sarah and that I would move forward with my life. I have done that," he said, gesturing to the shop, where partially completed pieces of hand-crafted furniture lined the walls.

"But if you didn't like it that Mom chose Olive as the most likely candidate, why would you do the same by bringing Samuel. . ."

"I know that you and Samuel have not yet found your way, but I am convinced that his coming here was God's will. You and Samuel are young, Hester, and with time all things are possible, even falling in love. Just give him a chance, all right?"

She wrestled with the double standard that lay behind his

words. There was some truth to the idea that two young people just starting out might find love after years of companionship, but something about the idea did not seem right to Hester. "And what about John Steiner? I truly believe that he has begun to trust me, to reach out for help."

Arlen sighed. "Ja. The man is in danger of becoming a lost soul. I can't order you to stay away from him, but I would prefer that you give me time to speak with him before you get involved with him any further."

"And if he won't talk to you?"

"Then you must let this go, Hester. Clearly his community and church have dealt with the matter in their own way. It is out of our hands, and I am asking you to stay away from the man."

"Are we to shun him as well, then?"

"Hester, can you not understand that my concern must be first for you? John Steiner—whatever his sins may or may not be—has made it clear that he does not seek or want our help. You said it yourself when Grady first asked you to go see the man—there are others in greater need who need you."

"But he seems so lost."

"Only God can find him and lead him back into the fold, child. You can do much good, but only God can truly rescue a soul in peril."

Hester reluctantly agreed, but the saga of John Steiner still troubled her after she had stopped by to take Rosalyn some lunch. And then later as she pedaled her way across town to deliver the crib quilt she'd made to Amy and Grady, she silently prayed for guidance, for some sign that she was to either let the matter rest or pursue it. She believed God had given His answer when she entered Amy's hospital room and found John's aunt Liz cooing over the baby. Here was the one person who might tell her the whole story without her having to disrespect her father's wish that she stay away from John.

Samuel was deeply troubled. He had always thought of himself as an honorable man, and he was well aware that in coming to work for Arlen Detlef, he had not only agreed to apply his skills as a carpenter and furniture maker; he had also agreed to consider asking Hester to be his wife. Arlen had made little secret of his wish for that.

"I know that you can only do what God leads you to do," Arlen had told him. "Only God can guide your heart, and Hester's, but I do pray that a union between you two will be His will."

It couldn't get any plainer than that. Now that he'd gotten to know Hester and watched the interaction between her and her father, he had decided that Arlen probably had not been quite so direct with his only daughter. Hester had a strong will and a streak of independence. It was those two characteristics that made her the community leader whom she had become. It was also those two traits that had made Samuel question whether or not he could ever make her truly happy. And in the meantime, he had fallen deeply in love with Rosalyn.

After taking Rosalyn back to the doctor and then seeing her home to the small cottage he'd helped restore following the hurricane and flooding, he had gone to the park and walked along the banks of the creek, sorting through his feelings and trying to decide what to do. After an hour and with no real answers, he headed back to work. Arlen was bent over his workbench, carving the molding for a china cabinet.

"Is Rosalyn all right?" Arlen asked.

"She will be once she has a few days to rest and heal," Samuel said as he hung his wide-brimmed straw hat on a hook near the door and put on a carpenter's apron.

"Hester stopped by."

"Ah," Samuel replied and gathered the tools he would need to attach the hinges for the cabinet doors that Arlen had finished staining.

"She was at the hospital overnight with the Forrest couple. They had a baby boy."

"That's good news." Samuel barely heard Arlen's conversation, his mind was so troubled.

"John Steiner was there as well."

"Ah," Samuel murmured as he measured once and then again and thought about the fact that he loved working here with Arlen.

"You may expect a visit from Olive Crowder," Arlen added. "Apparently she saw Hester and John having breakfast after they'd stayed all night at the hospital with Grady and his wife. It upset her." When Samuel said nothing, Arlen asked, "Does it not upset you?"

Samuel looked up from his work and saw that the older man had turned away from his workbench and was watching him closely. "Rosalyn says that Olive is often upset with Hester," he replied evenly.

The shop was silent for a long moment. Samuel laid down his screwdriver and the hinge and turned to face Arlen. "I have something to discuss with you."

Arlen folded his hands in front of him and waited.

"I do not think that Hester and I . . . I am in love with another woman." There, it was said. Samuel pictured himself packing up his camper and heading back to Pennsylvania. Rosalyn would be loyal to Hester, he knew that—loyalty would win every time.

"I see. And this other woman returns your feelings for her?"

"I believe she does, but I also believe that she would deny her feelings as I have—until now."

"Have you spoken to Hester of this matter?"

"Not yet."

Arlen closed his eyes, a habit that Samuel had noticed whenever the minister was faced with a dilemma. "How do you think my daughter will take this news?"

"I believe that she will be relieved," Samuel replied without a moment's hesitation, and because he hadn't so much as considered the possibilities, he was certain that he had spoken the truth.

Arlen nodded. Then he opened his eyes and smiled. "You are probably right," he said and turned back to his workbench and resumed carving a piece of trim for the cabinet.

"I will stay until the end of the week, if that's all right. We can finish the orders by then—"

The carving knife that Arlen was holding clattered into a pile of wood shavings that littered the floor around him. "You are leaving?" He clutched the now-ruined piece of wood.

"I thought that you would. . . I cannot marry your daughter, Arlen."

"One thing has nothing to do with the other. We work well together, and. . ." Arlen fumbled for words. It was the closest that Samuel had ever seen his employer and friend come to being concerned for himself instead of others. "I am asking you to reconsider and stay on here with me as my partner. I'm hoping that one day this business will be yours."

Samuel felt his heart swell with the possibilities Arlen had just offered. If Rosalyn would agree to marry him, they would have a secure future.

"I would like that," he said, "but I cannot give you my answer until I've spoken with Hester. She has a right to be part of any decision I might make to stay on here."

"Of course," Arlen said. "She's gone to the hospital to visit the Forrests and their new baby. Perhaps this evening? Come for supper."

"I'll stop by," Samuel promised, and as he took the damaged molding from Arlen and went to find a matching piece, he couldn't seem to stop smiling.

Chapter 19

W ell, Johnny," Margery said as she leaned the kitchen chair she'd carried out to John's porch back on two legs and braced her feet against the porch railing, "what are you going to do with this place? I mean, you've got the main floor here and the packinghouse pretty well back in shape, at least until the next storm comes by. But the grove there?" She shook her head. "That'll take years, if you can get anything to grow."

John knew she was right. In fact, he'd been thinking the same thing before she'd stopped by with a cooler filled with her southern fried chicken, potato salad, and fresh sliced tomatoes. She'd been stopping by a couple of times a week ever since he'd helped out with the refurbishing of the marina. Sometimes she read his mood and simply left him the food and headed back to her place. Other times, like tonight, she seemed to instinctively understand that he would welcome her company. On those occasions, she did not hold back, but said whatever was on her mind.

"Maybe the experiment has run its course," he said.

Margery snorted. "This is life, Johnny, not some lab research. Are you saying you're giving up after everything you've put into this place?"

"I'm open to suggestions."

"Well, there's a first," Margery muttered.

John ignored her sarcasm. "I don't want to give up, but what choice do I have?"

"What choice did you have when you packed up and left Indiana? What choice did I have when I walked down to the marina and found it in ruins? What choice did those folks over in Pinecraft have when the creek washed through their homes? Start over or give up. You've got your quirks, but I never figured you for a quitter, Johnny."

"I could sell the place, I suppose."

"And then what? What are you going to do with your life? You're neither here nor there—not Amish but not one of my world either. Who are you, John Steiner, and what are you planning to do—not just with this place but with the rest of your life?"

"I don't know—on either count," he admitted.

Margery pushed herself to her feet and slapped at a mosquito on her arm. "Well, the clock's ticking, son."

She could have been saying that it was getting late and time for her to head home, but he understood that she was issuing a warning. John walked with her down to her boat and helped her in.

"Careful there," she said with a teasing grin. "You're coming mighty close to becoming a real gentleman. Next thing I know you'll be out courting the ladies." She gave the pull cord on the motor a brisk yank and it fired to life. "Hester Detlef might be a good start since you two seem to be getting along so well these days," she called out as she putt-putted her way back toward the mouth of Philippi Creek.

Instantly he regretted telling Margery about the previous night's reception and the trip to the hospital. He groaned. How many times over the course of the evening had he uttered the words "Hester and I," or "Hester thinks," or just plain "Hester." Margery was a romantic and would take such things as a sign. But he could not deny that his opinion of Hester Detlef had changed. He stood on the shore where he had stood weeks earlier and watched her wade through the murky waters with her father and Samuel. He remembered how her manner had been brittle, but her touch when she tended to his cuts and other injuries was gentle, even tender. He also remembered how she had tried to reassure him. He wished she were here now. There was something about her, a unique combination of practicality mixed with just a pinch of the whimsical. Somehow it made him think that she would see possibilities for this place that he no longer could.

He started back toward his house, although he wasn't ready to settle in for the night. He was restless, his mind racing with the details of the work yet to be done and the costs still ahead of him. Costs he could not afford.

True, he wasn't homeless, and he was a far sight better off now than he had been right after the hurricane. Despite the dire predictions of others, he had been able to move back into his house and so far no one from the government had come around to ask if he'd filed the required paperwork. He hadn't and had no intention of doing so. This was his land, his home. He did his cooking—what little he did—over a camp stove that Zeke had rescued from a Dumpster; the two of them had managed to rig the stove to the propane gas line that ran to the house. He had water and a bathroom, although no shower or tub. Those were in the full bath on the second floor, or at least they had been. All in all he had what he needed. But he lived under a makeshift roof, and the second floor of the house was still a disaster.

He wandered between what had been a grove of orange trees—several dozen of them that he had salvaged from the grove Tucker had originally planted. There had also been a grove of lemon and key lime trees that he had planted and nursed as if they were his children. They weren't his children, but they had been his future—the source of income he would need if he hoped to keep this place running. That ship had sailed, as his aunt Liz was fond of saying. The soil was completely ruined by the salt water. Even if he could afford to replant, there was no way anything would grow.

He considered the ruined beds of celery, tomatoes, beans,

and other vegetables he had planted. In spite of the fact that the salvaged cypress beams he'd used as borders had been ripped free and scattered across the property during the hurricane, Zeke had worked for days gathering them and putting them back into place. The problem was that the rich, fertile soil that had filled them, along with the plants themselves, had washed away. It would take several truckloads of soil to refill them, and that would cost a lot of money. On the positive side, the toolshed and chicken coop were restored and ready for use. The problem was use for what?

Depressed and defeated, John walked back to the house. The sun had set, and the last rays of light were waning. Wearily he climbed the porch steps, picked up his and Margery's glasses, and went inside. He lit the battery-powered lantern and pulled a chair up to the kitchen table that was littered with drawings he had created when he first bought the Tucker place and kept stored in a metal box. Dreams he had allowed himself to entertain as if they were fact.

He swept them off the table with his forearm, in the process uncovering the two books he'd managed to salvage after the hurricane. *Walden* lay next to his Bible. He picked up the paperback volume and paged through it; then he tossed it onto the pile of papers littering the floor. He had walked with Thoreau for two long years, and where had it gotten him?

He pulled his Bible closer, cradling it with his folded arms as he rested his forehead on its crackled leather cover and prayed. From this night forward, he would walk with God, listening for His still, small voice and opening himself to the kinds of messages delivered by couriers like Margery and Zeke—and perhaps even Hester. No, not Hester. He thought of how he had left her sitting there in the restaurant earlier that morning. He had told her the truth that his mother's death had been his fault. And then true to form, he had run away, hopped a city bus without explaining the details. He had assumed that she would judge him, as others had and as he had judged himself. And who would blame her?

And yet he missed her, missed talking to her, missed her

no-nonsense ways, her wisdom. He realized that for most of the day he'd been watching for her, listening for the crunch of her bicycle or Arlen's car tires coming up his lane. But she hadn't come.

"She's to marry Samuel," he reminded himself. Samuel was a good man, a far better man than he was—and besides, the carpenter could offer Hester a secure future. What did he have to offer her? He was broke and living in a half-finished house on land that would not yield even so much as a kitchen garden for some time to come. Perhaps once she and Samuel had married, the three of them could be friends.

"Perhaps you ought to stop daydreaming and face reality," he growled. He had few choices. He could stubbornly refuse to change and end up like some of the people whom Zeke had introduced him to at the bay front. Or he could face facts, sell the property, and use the money to start over once more. He thought about the farm he'd sold in Indiana, the land where his father had worked such long hours. The place where for so many years he and his mother had lived. The place he had planned to bring his bride and raise his family. Could he go back there and start again, asking forgiveness, admitting the error of his prideful ways to the congregation in which he'd been raised?

He closed his eyes and silently prayed for guidance. When he opened them minutes later, he knew that he had made his plan. Tomorrow he would go to Arlen and ask for help getting the rest of this place restored, and then he would put it up for sale.

———

Hester stayed at the hospital longer than she'd meant to. But when she'd seen Liz Carter-Thompson handing Amy and Grady a huge gift basket that was filled to overflowing with items for baby and mother, she had seen her opportunity to find out once and for all how John had been involved in his mother's death. It took close to half an hour for the new parents to properly exclaim over each item and hold it up for Hester as well as Harley's two sets of grandparents to admire. But Hester was determined to stay, hoping that she and Liz might take their leave at the same time and that she could perhaps suggest they share a cup of coffee before the congresswoman hurried off to pack for her flight home.

After the grand finale of the gift basket was unveiled, a cashmere shawl for Amy to wrap herself in while she nursed, Hester waited for Grady to place all the items back in the basket and set it on a side table already filled with vases of flowers. Then she handed him her package.

"Congratulations," she said.

"Oh, Hester, you made this yourself, didn't you?" Amy exclaimed as Grady spread the crib quilt over Amy's bed. "It's lovely. His room is blue and it will be just perfect. Thank you."

Hester fought against a swell of pride. "You're welcome. Nelly helped with the actual quilting," she added.

"Hester's grandmother," Amy explained to the others as she lifted a corner of the quilt to show her mother the tiny stitches.

Hester saw that Liz was watching her closely as if trying to figure her out. "You are a most remarkable young woman," Liz said with such genuine admiration that Hester felt herself blush. "The reports about the work you and your community have been doing in helping others to get back to normal are impressive."

"My father and the Mennonite Disaster Relief teams have done most of the work," Hester said.

"You know, ever since I joined the Homeland Security committee, I've been hearing more and more about the work people from the Mennonite community do whenever there's a natural disaster. You certainly don't get the credit you deserve, and I think it might be high time we did something about that. Why, you and your volunteers are every bit as much of a national treasure as any federal or state agency. They just have better marketing."

Hester glanced pleadingly at Grady, hoping that he would intervene. To her relief, he nodded.

"The Mennonites don't really believe in blowing their own horn," he said. "They prefer to perform their good deeds without fanfare."

"I'm not suggesting they hire a public relations firm," Liz said. "But. . ."

"Our reward comes in having served others," Hester said quietly. She could see that this was in many ways a foreign concept to the congresswoman, as it was to others in the outside world, where award ceremonies were common and highly anticipated.

"You remind me a great deal of my sister," Liz said. "Rachel was always doing things for others, and never once did she receive the recognition she deserved."

"Your sister lived in an Amish community. It was not their way to offer or accept praise either."

"Tell me about it," Liz said, and then she smiled. "I'm afraid my big sister struggled mightily with our family's lack of understanding when it came to the lifestyle she chose. And yet," she said almost wistfully, "I don't think I have ever known a person more at peace with herself and her life."

"Then she had her reward," Hester said, fairly itching to pursue the topic of John's mother now that Liz had brought it up. But this was neither the time nor the place.

"Oh my, if you're not careful, I'll sit here babbling on all afternoon—occupational habit." Liz gathered her oversized leather purse and swung it onto her shoulder, then glanced at her watch. "I have a flight to catch in two hours. Can I give you a lift back to Pinecraft, Hester?"

"I have my bike, but I'll walk out with you."

They said their good-byes, cooed over the sleeping baby, and tiptoed from the room.

"Ah, babies," Liz sighed as soon as the door closed behind them. "If ever I need a refresher on why I put up with all the political mumbo-jumbo it takes to get anything done in this job, I go visit a hospital nursery and right there is my answer. Harley's generation will someday inherit the work I do now. Makes a person think."

"You have no children of your own?" Hester asked as they stepped onto the elevator together.

"Nope. My sister, Rachel, was the earth mother in our family.

231

She should have had a dozen kids."

"But John has no siblings."

"Unfortunately, no. Maybe if Rachel had remarried. . . She certainly had offers."

The elevator doors slid open, and Hester found that her heart was hammering. It seemed as if God might be giving her the opening she needed to find out what John had meant in saying he had killed his mother.

"I'm over here in the parking structure," Liz said as they exited the building.

"The bike rack is there as well," Hester replied, and the two women continued walking together. "John told me his mother died shortly before he moved here. Was she ill?"

"Not a day in her life," Liz said. "One January evening at dusk, she'd set out in the buggy for some church meeting. Something spooked the horse and it took off. Rachel was a fighter, and she was not about to let that horse have the upper hand, but she didn't count on a patch of black ice. The horse slid, and she was thrown from the buggy, hit her head on a field rock, and died before the ambulance could get there."

Okay, so now she had the circumstances, but for the life of her, Hester could not find anything in any of it that would even hint that John had had anything to do with his mother's unfortunate accident.

Liz looked both ways and jaywalked across the street as Hester hurried to keep up with her. "Was John with her?"

Liz paused by the bike rack. "He found her, and that's part of his grief. I don't think he's ever forgiven himself for not being the one driving that night." She got the kind of faraway look a person had when lost in memories. Then she shook it off and offered Hester a handshake. "It's been a real pleasure to meet you, Hester. I know you and your people don't take to compliments, but know that on behalf of a government that is deeply overextended, you have our deepest gratitude."

"You're welcome," Hester replied, still trying to reconcile what Liz had just told her with the conversation she'd had with

John. John had lost his mother just a short time before her own mother had finally succumbed to her illness. In her case she had known death was coming. John had had no such warning.

"Be patient with that nephew of mine, Hester. Rachel's death hit him pretty hard."

"I can understand that. My mother died of Lou Gehrig's disease a couple of years ago."

Liz pressed Hester's hand. "Then you know all too well. I'm so sorry for your loss. Still, it's a blessing that John has landed here, where he can hopefully find the kind of peace and contentment Rachel would have wanted for him. Rachel would say it was no mistake, his being here. It's God's will." Impulsively she bent and kissed Hester's cheek. "Have to run. Stay in touch," she added as she waved and headed off past a row of cars, her stiletto heels clicking on the pavement long after she was out of sight.

Hester unlocked her bike. She thought about going to Tucker's Point. It wasn't that much farther, but then, it was also close to suppertime, and her father would be wondering where she was. Besides, she had agreed not to seek John out. Mentally she checked the contents of the refrigerator and decided on a cold supper of chicken salad, fresh fruit, and whole grain bread. After all, it might be late September and the humidity had noticeably lessened, but it was still Florida, and it was still hot.

She pedaled fast, enjoying the wind cooling her face and whipping at the hem of her dress. The hurricane and its aftermath seemed light-years away, and yet each day they faced more work to be done. At the center they were still seeing a steady stream of people in need of clothing, bedding, and household goods. Food goods were still pouring in, although not nearly as strongly as they had right after the storm hit.

She thought about Rainbow House. Grady had told her that there was no way the agency would be able to start over. They'd need a building, a couple of them. Before the hurricane, the agency had offered shelter for the homeless, a food and clothing bank, and an educational center. There, people with no other options could come to learn job skills and hopefully find their way out of the ranks of the nameless, faceless men and women who gathered outside the library or along the bay front. Bundled all together, Rainbow House had offered hope to the hopeless. Without those services, where would these men and women—more and more of them in these hard times—go?

You're a nurse and Mennonite, Hester. These outsiders have their government to care for them. That is their way, not ours, she could practically hear her father reminding her. But hurt was hurt, and these people were in pain. It sure didn't seem like their government would come to their rescue anytime soon, so where better to focus her skills? Maybe she could organize a walk-in clinic to serve the homeless population. She would speak to Grady about it as soon as he came back to earth and got through his first week of sleepless nights. Maybe there were federal funds available. Maybe John could talk to Liz. Maybe. . .

Maybe her Dad was right. Her habit of running from one project to the next had escalated in the years since her mother's death. Surely her grief should have begun to abate in all that time. But it hadn't. Her work had become her life, her way of escaping things that confused her, like falling in love and marriage and raising a family. Like managing a household instead of a community center. Perhaps in her zeal to save others she was really avoiding the obvious—the need to save herself.

"I was beginning to worry," her father said when she wheeled her bike to a stop just outside the front gate. The fence had been repaired along with the house. Only the garden still showed signs of the flooding and wind damage that had accompanied the hurricane.

Arlen was sitting on the front porch, his wire-rimmed glasses pushed onto his forehead, a book in his lap. "How's the Forrest family?"

"Still a bit dazed but fine. Amy has both her mother and Grady's mom just chomping at the bit to help, and who can blame them? That baby is so precious." She tucked a piece of hair that had worked its way free back under her prayer covering, and then cleared her throat. "I spoke with John's aunt. She was there visiting as well, and we walked out together. She told me the circumstances of his mother's death."

"How did that subject come up?"

"We were talking about babies, and she mentioned that John's mother, Rachel, should have had more than just John."

"I see."

"It was an accident, Dad. John was nowhere near her when it happened." She repeated the details that Liz had told her. "So I think I was right about John feeling guilty that he wasn't there and couldn't save her."

Arlen took several minutes to consider this. "Still, he is a troubled soul, Hester. Perhaps we need to respect his need to work this all out himself."

"Are you still asking me to stay away from him?"

"I think it best if we let John come to us when he's ready. Samuel tells me that he is a man of strong faith, and we have to trust that God will guide him through this dark period in his life, as He did you." Arlen stroked her cheek. "As I recall, after Sarah died you needed your solitude."

Solomon himself could not have found a more effective way to frame his decision. Arlen had found the one argument for letting John determine who he saw and when that Hester could not debate. For it was true that it had been months after her mother's death before Hester had opened herself to others. "You're right," she said as she began taking ingredients for their meal out of the refrigerator. "I'll have supper ready in just a few minutes. I thought we'd have cold chicken and—"

"I'm having supper at your grandmother's," Arlen said as he followed her into the kitchen. "But you go ahead and fix two plates. I invited Samuel to come by."

Hester stopped.

"And you won't be here?"

"No, I told you—"

"Why not have Grandma come here?"

"Because you and Samuel need some time."

"Dad, I really don't need you orchestrating my social life."

"That's a matter of opinion, liebchen," he said and tweaked her cheek. "But Samuel's purpose in coming here this evening is not. . ." He faltered, clearly trying to find the right words without giving too much away.

"Is not what?"

"Just keep an open mind, Hester." He took his hat down from the hook next to the door and walked down the front walk. "You know where I'll be should you need to talk," he said.

Samuel is going to propose. Hester had never been more sure of anything in her life, nor had she ever been less prepared. She had thought she would have more time. But here it was. The moment of truth, as Jeannie would say. And why not? Perhaps this was the first step on the path to finding her true place in this community. She would still be able to volunteer. Samuel would never ask her to sacrifice that. And she had always dreamed of having children. Yes, perhaps the time had come.

Hester closed her eyes and tried to imagine herself standing next to Samuel as her father pronounced them man and wife. But the man she saw in her imagination was not Samuel Brubaker. It was John Steiner.

She shook off the image. Of course she would think of John. She'd been focused on him ever since he'd made his shocking confession to her that morning. Even the conversation she'd had with his aunt had done little to clear up the mystery, so naturally he would be the man on her mind, she reasoned. It meant nothing.

She set the table and prepared the food, then returned the serving dishes to the refrigerator as she waited for Samuel. The clock her grandfather had built chimed six. Maybe Samuel had gotten cold feet. *Please, God, let him get cold feet.*

The telephone jangled, startling her.

"Oh, Hester, hi," Samuel said, his voice unsteady.

"Hi. Dad said you were coming for supper, but maybe he. . ."

"I'll be there. I just. . . Six thirty, okay? We can go out if you'd rather."

"No. It's just cold chicken and such. It'll keep. Samuel, are you all right?"

There was a pause. "I am. I'm out at John Steiner's place. We got to talking, and I lost track of time. I'm really sorry, Hester."

"It's fine," she assured him.

"John's sending you some ferns for the garden," he added. "See you soon."

"Sure." As she hung up the phone, she spotted the magazine she'd meant to return to the hospital waiting room. Now she'd have to make a special trip. It was lying on the table next to the phone where she'd placed it so she would remember to take it with her. She picked it up and went out to the porch to wait for Samuel.

Chapter 20

When Samuel stopped by, John was surprised that he was inordinately glad to see the man. He had come to a decision, and he respected Samuel as someone with a level head and as someone who was good at listening before he jumped in with an opinion of his own.

"I've decided to sell this place and go home to Indiana," he said. When Samuel made no comment, he went on, laying out the facts that he'd already gone over dozens of times in the last hour. "The trees won't come back, and the vegetable beds need to be completely rebuilt. It'll take several truckloads of good dirt to fill them, and who knows what that'll cost. I'm pretty close to being broke, and I'm going to need to find work. So even if I could afford to keep working on the place, when would I do it?"

Samuel tipped his hat back with his thumb and looked around. "You truly think of Indiana—the life you left behind—as your home?"

In his calm, quiet way Samuel had identified the one sticking point of John's plan. For he did not think of Indiana as home. This was his home. This was the place where he had invested everything, where he had formed friendships that he hadn't even recognized as such until now.

"In time," he said, "I will. I grew up there, after all." Wanting to change the direction of the conversation, he looked around. "Of course, before this place can be put on the market, I've got a lot of work to do."

"You could let us help," Samuel said. "Arlen and me and the others. Zeke and some of his friends. With so many hands, you would have things back together in no time, and you could stay here. . .if your mind isn't made up, that is."

"I was thinking about that. . . ." John conceded. "Still, there's the matter of money."

"Ja. There is that."

"And even if I get the place back in shape, it'll still take time before any new crops start to come in."

"Ja."

"Selling solves my problem."

Samuel frowned and set his hat back on his head as he looked directly at John. "Selling will be hard in this economy. Besides, I think you know as well as I do that your lack of income is not the source of your poverty, my friend."

"I can't eat or keep a roof over my head without money, Samuel."

"True. But if you leave this place, give it up as you did your farm and the life you once knew, how will you feed your soul, John? Your spirit?" He climbed into the cab of his camper. "I'll speak with Arlen about organizing a crew to help you."

John had never before accepted charity on such a scale. It still went against all he'd set out to do. "No. Let me take care of it," he said, his throat closing around the words.

"Das ist gut." Samuel turned the key. "I'm late for an appointment, but I'll come back tomorrow, and we can speak about this some more if you'd like."

John nodded. "I'd appreciate that."

"Do you mind if I bring Rosalyn with me?"

The question surprised John. "Why?"

"Because she is someone like you who has been terribly wounded both physically and spiritually, and yet she has found

239

her way through it. I just thought that perhaps she might be someone who could listen and understand."

John moved away, stepping back from the camper, putting distance between himself and Samuel. "I'd really rather just. . . Could we just keep this between us for now?"

"Of course." Samuel shifted the camper into gear.

"Wait," John called as he ran to get a bucket filled with ferns. "Could you drop these off at Hester's? For her mother's garden."

Samuel reached across and opened the passenger side door so John could set the bucket on the floor. "I'm on my way there now," Samuel said. "We're having supper together." He waved and drove the camper down the rutted lane.

John stood watching him go and thinking that it was odd the way he'd spoken of being late for an appointment when clearly he had a date with Hester. And then he thought how unusual it was that he had suggested bringing Rosalyn out to Tucker's Point when surely Hester had suffered the aftermath of nursing her mother through all those years, watching her grow more frail and dependent day by day, unable to do anything to stop the downward spiral. It seemed to John that in many ways his situation had far more in common with what Hester had experienced than what Rosalyn had gone through. And why would Samuel suggest allowing Arlen to help, and Zeke, and even Rosalyn—but not Hester?

~⚒~

After stopping at a gas station to call Hester, Samuel used the rest of the drive to practice how to tell her that he had fallen in love with Rosalyn. Perhaps he shouldn't mention Rosalyn at all. Perhaps he should just state the obvious, that he and Hester did not love each other and were unlikely ever to share such feelings. Perhaps he could phrase things in such a way that she would be the one to break off with him.

But that would be dishonest and manipulative. The gossips in Pinecraft would forever lay the blame for their failed relationship at her door. No, he was the one who wanted to end things, and he should be the one to say so.

"Dear God, may the words of my mouth and the meditations of my heart be acceptable in Thy sight," he murmured as he turned down Hester's street. "And hers," he added when he saw her sitting on the porch.

He parked his camper and got out. "Good evening, Hester. I'm sorry to be so late."

She was engrossed in reading a magazine. When she looked up at him, he understood that as usual something in that magazine had caught her attention so completely that she'd been unaware of his arrival until he spoke to her.

He thought about the way Rosalyn had looked at him after the doctor had stitched her forehead and she'd returned to the waiting room to find him standing there. Her eyes had widened with pure joy as she moved toward him, as if the distance was too great and she couldn't wait to be closer. There was the essential difference between the two women. One of them now openly looked forward to seeing him, having him near, sharing her day with him. The other gave him a distracted smile and waved her hand in dismissal at his apology for being late.

"It's okay," Hester said. "Come on inside. It will only take me a moment to put everything on the table." She walked ahead of him into the kitchen and started pulling dishes from the refrigerator. "How was John?" She pointed to the place he normally took whenever he shared meals with her and Arlen.

"He has decided to sell his place and return to Indiana for a fresh start." He watched her scurry around the large kitchen, slicing bread and placing a plate of it on the table, then hurrying back to the refrigerator for butter and applesauce. She seemed distracted, and he wondered if she had heard him. She stood in front of the open refrigerator door for a moment, a jar of orange marmalade in her hand. "The applesauce is fine," he said, "unless *you* prefer the marmalade."

Again she gave him a distracted smile. "No. I was just. . ." She removed a pitcher of lemonade and then shut the refrigerator with her foot. "John's giving up?"

"That's one way of looking at it, I suppose. But he seems genuinely relieved to have made the decision. I think he has some unfinished business in Indiana that he needs to address, but he seems prepared to do that."

"I see. He's leaving soon?"

"Not so soon. He can't put his place up for sale until the house is finished and everything is in order." He stood up and pulled out a chair for her. "Come and sit, Hester," he said. "We have everything we need."

She glanced at her father's empty chair and then sat down at her usual place. When she poured lemonade into the two tall glasses on the table, her hand shook, and Samuel realized that she was nervous. "Dad said you wanted to talk to me," she said, offering him the chicken salad first and then helping herself. "I think I know what this is about, and before—"

Samuel relieved her of the pitcher and set it on the table. She did not protest. Instead, she kept her gaze focused on her plate. "I just—"

"Shhh," he whispered when she glanced up, looking ready to speak. "Pray with me, Hester."

She nodded and closed her eyes, and they prayed in silence. After a moment Samuel murmured, "Amen."

She looked directly at him for the first time since he had arrived. Samuel drew in a long, resolute breath and uttered the words he'd come to say. "I can't marry you, Hester."

He didn't know what he had expected. Perhaps tears, anger, those fathomless blue eyes filled with hurt. He had even prepared himself for her eyes to widen in surprise, perhaps even shock. What he had never considered for one moment was the reaction he got.

"Really?" she said. "That's what you came to say?" She leaned toward him, her expression one not of hurt but of hope.

He nodded, half afraid to utter any sound until he could be sure of her reaction. She sank back in her chair, a half-smile twitching the corners of her mouth. She pressed her fist to her lips as her eyes filled with tears, and then she burst out laughing.

Soundless, shoulder-shaking laughter that she seemed incapable of controlling.

It was worse than anything he could have imagined. The woman who had always seemed stronger than any person—male or female—he had ever known was now clearly hysterical. "In time," he began, but the words only seemed to set her off again. "Hester, please," he pleaded, wishing Arlen were there.

She shook her head and used her napkin to blot away the tears. "Oh, Samuel, I thought. . ." A fresh wave of laughter threatened, but she controlled it and continued, "I thought you were coming here tonight to propose, and I was trying to find a way to tell you that I couldn't marry you."

It was Samuel's turn to feel the flood of relief that led to a smile that matched hers and then shared laughter as the two of them rocked back in their chairs. It was the closest he'd ever felt to Hester, and whatever the future might bring for each of them, they had found tonight something even more precious than they could have imagined, given that they both had understood that theirs most likely would have been a marriage of companionship. They had each found a friend for life.

＝≈～

When Arlen came home an hour later, Hester and Samuel were still sitting at the kitchen table, their heads close together, the dishes still on the table along with a legal pad, pens, and the magazine Hester had meant to return to the hospital.

"Dad, read this," Hester said, tapping her forefinger on the magazine. She waited while her father scanned the article that she had practically committed to memory. A decade earlier a woman in California working with a group of teenagers had come up with the idea of collecting the unwanted fruit from her neighbors' backyard orchards and turning it into jam to donate to food banks.

"I don't understand," Arlen said, handing her back the magazine. "Now you are thinking of working with young people to collect fruit? I thought we had discussed this, daughter. I thought you had agreed that you need to concentrate on your volunteer work here in Pinecraft."

"But this is about our people, Dad. Our young people will be an enormous part of this. I'm counting on the women of Pinecraft to make the marmalade and jam that the young people will sell at the markets."

"But you also plan to include others from outside. . . ."

"Yes, homeless people and maybe senior citizens looking for something to do, some way to make a contribution. But, Papa, that is what we do. Think of the auctions we held these last several years to raise money for the people of Haiti. Are we saying that those funds can be used only for Haitians who are Mennonite? No."

Arlen pulled out the remaining kitchen chair and sat down. "I'm listening."

But Hester knew from the furrowing of his brow and the way he glanced at Samuel that he remained unconvinced.

"The process that they used in California might not work exactly for us here, but there's a similar program in Tampa that we could follow. The point is that we can make this work, Dad, and we can use it to rebuild Rainbow House, and after that. . ."

Arlen folded his hands over his stomach and waited.

Hester took a deep breath. "This woman in California got the word out that these teenagers were willing to clean up unwanted fruit in private yards for free as long as they could take the usable fruit for their jam-making project."

"That was the start of it," Samuel explained. "But then they received so many requests, and there was so much fruit, that it was impossible to keep up with making it all into jam."

"So they went to the local food banks," Hester said, taking up the story, "and offered to give them the best of the whole fruit. Dad, they collected as much as twelve hundred pounds of citrus, all of it from private residences each with just a few trees."

Samuel searched the article and then showed Arlen a passage. "Right here it says that just two years ago they collected nearly one hundred and seventy-five *thousand* pounds of fruit from just five hundred homes, and they now have nearly a thousand volunteers of all ages."

"I still don't see—"

"Dad, think about it. Grandma has at least half a dozen citrus trees in her yard, and Jeannie Messner? She must have six lemon trees and another four key lime trees."

"Slow down and help me to understand this. I can see where you might gather the fruit. I don't see how this raises funds for Rainbow House."

"We make marmalade and jam and sell it at the local farmers' markets. Perhaps even some of the specialty stores would stock it, as well as the shops right here in Pinecraft." She made another note on the legal pad. "We need to speak with Grandma," she said to Samuel. "She has a wonderful recipe for marmalade."

"And I've tasted some jam made by the Crowder sisters that was quite tasty as well," Samuel said. "It might be good to get them involved."

"I suppose," Hester said reluctantly; then she brightened and made an addition to her list. "And Emma. I must speak with Emma first thing tomorrow. She always has such wonderful ideas when it comes to organizing these kinds of projects, and it will be great to work with her on something like this." She sat back and looked across the table to her father. "Wouldn't Mom just love the whole idea?"

"She would indeed," Arlen murmured thoughtfully, and Hester could see that he was beginning to warm to the concept. He pushed back his chair and began gathering the dirty dishes and taking them to the sink. "So the two of you have been planning this. . .all evening," he asked.

Hester shot Samuel a smile and then went to her father. She placed her hands on Arlen's shoulders. "Not all evening," she admitted. "There was a little matter of deciding we were not right for marrying each other that came first." She felt the tension drain from his shoulders as easily as the soapy water circled the sink and disappeared. He rinsed a plate and set it in the dish rack.

"And you are all right?" he asked, turning so that he could

read Hester's expression.

"It seems that Samuel and I were thinking along the same lines," she told him. "He came to say he wouldn't be proposing, while I had sat here since you left trying to figure out how to turn him down if he did. Grady always talks about that as a win-win situation."

Arlen was not completely convinced. "But you must be. . ."

"Hurt?" Hester asked. "Oh, Dad, how could I be when I had been agonizing for days now over how best not to hurt Samuel?" She smiled. "Now all we have to do is figure out how best to get Samuel and Rosalyn together."

She heard Samuel suck in a surprised breath. She turned to face him. "Oh, come on now. I'm not blind, you know. Half of Pinecraft knows the two of you are perfect for each other."

"You might try telling her how you feel," Arlen suggested. "In my limited experience that always seems to work best."

"Ja, Samuel, look how much time we wasted not speaking our true feelings."

Instead of relieved, Samuel looked worried. "Rosalyn is very loyal, especially when it comes to you, Hester. She would set her feelings aside if she thought being with me might hurt you."

Hester sighed. "All right, I'll talk to her for you. Coward," she teased, and Samuel grinned. "In the meantime, Dad, what do you think of our idea? We could have a shelter, a food bank, even a free clinic."

"You could certainly do all of that," Arlen agreed as he dried his hands on a dish towel. "The question, of course, becomes where you would do all of this plus set up a kitchen to make the jam with a space for collecting and packaging the fruit for delivery to the food banks."

"Okay. I know we have some things we have to work out, but the idea is a sound one, don't you think? I mean, it worked for this group in California."

"It has merit," Arlen admitted.

"And if anyone can make it a reality," Samuel added, "it's you, Hester."

"But it is a huge undertaking," her father warned her, his expression leaving no doubt that he was concerned that this was yet another of her grand projects that would distract her from the need to focus on herself and her future.

"I don't know how I know this, Papa, but I feel in my heart that God is leading me to do this. I have never felt anything so strongly in my life."

"Then His will be done." Arlen held out his arms to embrace her.

But in spite of her relief, Hester could not repress a feeling of panic. When she had thought she would marry Samuel, there had been a certain security in that. She could clearly see her future laid out in front of her. Now that was gone. She found herself thinking about the Crowder sisters. Neither had ever married. Hester couldn't help wondering if either of them had ever come close. Would her future be like theirs, caring for others through her volunteer work? And as the years passed, would she reflect the giving, joyful spirit of Agnes or the bitter, controlling personality of Olive?

She shuddered at the thought and firmly reminded herself that her calling had always been that of service to others. Tomorrow she would begin the process of devoting all of her energy to the new project. She would turn her work for MCC over to Rosalyn and focus all of her waking hours on making sure that the faceless, nameless, and homeless souls she had seen on the streets of Sarasota would have a chance to start fresh, to make a life, to find their purpose. And if some people in her father's congregation took exception to that calling, then too bad.

She fingered the magazine that had followed her for days now—from the hospital to the restaurant to her father's house. The article had caught her attention at the very moment when she knew that her life was about to reach a crossroads. If God was not showing her His plan for her life, then what was all that about?

No, Samuel would marry Rosalyn; Rosalyn would take over Hester's position as the local MCC representative; Hester would join forces with Emma and Jeannie and others and create a new, bigger, and better Rainbow House. And John would go back to Indiana and, God willing, find happiness and peace.

The following morning as she sat with her father having breakfast, Hester studied her to-do list.

Get Grandma's recipe for marmalade
Have coffee with Emma
Talk to Rosalyn
Set up meetings with:
Grady
Emma
Jeannie
Samuel
Olive and Agnes
Zeke
John (???)

She was not at all sure why she had added John's name to the list, but there it was. She had hesitated far less time over including the Crowder sisters than she had adding his name to the list. In the end she crossed it off.

But when Samuel had mentioned that John had decided to put his place up for sale, she had felt a jolt go through her that she could only equate with panic. *What was that about?* she wondered. Why should it matter to her one way or another if John Steiner sold his place, moved back to Indiana, and she never saw him again?

And there it was. What if she never saw him again? It wasn't so much that she might never know what he'd meant by saying he had killed his mother—in terms of the facts, Liz had cleared that up. It was more that she would never know if he found what he'd come to Florida searching for.

She went to sleep and awakened the next morning thinking

about him. It had come to her that she and John shared many of the same personality quirks. They were both stubborn and determined. They both looked at difficult situations as challenges to be overcome. They both wanted something more than the normal that seemed to satisfy others. And in the predawn as she finally gave up on getting any more sleep, she realized that the reason she and John Steiner had so often knocked heads was because they were missing the obvious. Working together instead of alone or against one another, they could accomplish a great deal. The problem, of course, was going to be convincing John of that.

Chapter 21

S amuel might have a point," Zeke said as he stood up from repairing a gutter at one end of the packinghouse and stretched the muscles of his back. "We're going to finish this up by the weekend, and then the only thing not restored is the top floor of the house. You know, if you had a whole crew working on the place. . ."

John continued to roll paint onto the cinder block wall without comment. It had been ten days since Samuel had suggested the same thing. It had been only yesterday that John's aunt Liz had gone home to Washington after she'd stopped by his place one last time.

"John," she'd said, "I'm only going to say this once, and then I am off to the airport and out of your hair, for a while anyway."

John had steeled himself for the lecture he knew was coming, but instead Liz had cupped his cheek, forcing him to meet her gaze. "I know that you loved your parents deeply, John, but is this suppressed rage at the world any way for you to honor their memory?"

"This has nothing to do with them."

"It has everything to do with them. Look, I have tried and tried to understand this crusade you seem to be on, this life of absolute isolation. But then ask yourself why you chose this place? Why would you buy property near the heart of a bustling community where avoiding others is next to impossible? Why would you tolerate Margery Barker and that homeless man and, for that matter, Hester Detlef and her father and Samuel?"

He started to answer, but she just squeezed his jaw a little tighter the way his mother had when he was a boy. "Wake up," she whispered. "Life is short, and even if you think life on this planet is only a stopping-off place, God expects you to make the best of it, and so would my sister." She released him. "You have allowed your pride to get the better of you, John. Rachel would be disappointed. Frankly, I am disappointed. You are better than this." She waved her hand around the room with its tarp roof and a stairway that led nowhere.

Outside, a car horn honked.

"That's my ride to the airport." She held out her arms to him, and he accepted her embrace. "I just want you to be happy."

"I know."

The horn sounded again, and together they walked out to where the sleek steel-gray town car was waiting. The driver took Liz's suitcase and put it in the trunk while John opened the back door for her.

"Get a life," she advised John from the backseat as the driver got behind the wheel. "I'm serious," she shouted as the car moved slowly back down the lane.

John had stood watching it go, his hand raised in a wave until the car was out of sight, and then he had walked slowly back up the steps to his unfinished house, knowing that his aunt was right.

"Hey"—Zeke called him back from his revelry—"did you hear what I said?"

"Sorry." John shook off the memory of his aunt's farewell words.

"I said that October will bring the snowbirds. Some retiree who is looking for a place to call home just might be interested. Or barring that, some developer. It's prime land, and you know what they say in the real estate business."

John glanced over at him and waited for the answer.

"Location, location, location."

"How do you know that?"

Zeke shrugged and went back to work. "I hear things. I read. It's a sound byte like pretty much everything else people say that makes the world turn these days."

A west wind carried the sound of reconstruction at the south end of Siesta Key across the bay. That area had been even more devastated than John's property had been when Hurricane Hester roared through, but property owners and developers over there had insurance to rebuild without having to rely on Zeke scrounging for materials.

Or on the charity of others.

"You could repay Arlen's crew out of the money you make selling the place," Zeke said as if John had spoken aloud.

"They wouldn't accept payment," John said. "It's not their way."

"Then you make a donation to one of those committees Hester and the others are on—MDS or MCC or whatever the alphabet soup of the hour might be."

"With the economy the way it is, it could take years to sell this place," John said.

"Or it might sell in a week."

John fought the grin that threatened to ruin his foul mood. Zeke was a glass-half-full guy. Hester was like that, too, he thought, and then he wondered for maybe the hundredth time why he hadn't seen or heard from her.

"Margery tells me that Samuel and Hester are no longer. . .together," he said, unable to keep himself from probing to see what Zeke might know. "Do you think that Samuel will go back to Pennsylvania?"

"Not likely, unless he can persuade Rosalyn to go along with him. Why would he leave a partnership that could secure his future?"

"You're saying that Samuel and Rosalyn. . ."

". . .are an item, and it's about time, from what Jeannie tells me. According to her, the two of them have been making moon eyes at each other practically since the day they met." He tipped a bucket of water up and over his face and neck. Then he shook himself off like a dog coming out of the surf and grinned. "Arlen took him into his furniture business as a full partner. My guess is that there will be wedding bells before Christmas."

"Arlen made him a partner?"

Zeke sighed. "You really need to get out more, my friend. This is week-old news."

John ignored that. "How's Hester taking all of this?"

"Haven't talked to her personally, but from what Jeannie tells me, she's taking it with a huge sigh of relief. She never loved Samuel, not that you need love to make a good marriage, but it helps. Besides, that whole arranged marriage thing. . . That ship sailed a long time ago, especially for someone as independent as Hester. Don't know what Arlen was thinking."

"He's okay with all of this? Arlen?"

"Yeah. I expect he just wants Hester to be happy, and he finally figured out that he couldn't make that happen. She'll find her way—a survivor, that one. Of course, I expect she's a little surprised." He shrugged. "She might be relieved, but her future just got a little murky, if you ask me."

"How so?"

"Think about it. You have this life all laid out for you; marry this guy, start a family, set up a household. Then—*poof*—all of that's gone."

"Samuel's not the only man available."

Zeke glanced at him and grinned. "You offering to step up?"

"Don't be ridiculous," John growled.

Undaunted, Zeke continued to talk. "On the other hand, Samuel sure came out of it all right. He's in love with Rosalyn, and now he's got a solid future with Arlen's business."

Still, John couldn't help feeling sympathy for Hester. After all, she might not have wanted to marry Samuel, but now she was back at square one—starting over—and he knew how that felt.

"She's working on some new project," Zeke continued as he climbed back up the ladder to paint the trim. "Got most of

Pinecraft all excited about it, from what I hear."

"What's the project?"

"She's set up a meeting with a bunch of us to work out the details. She's pretty determined to get a program like Rainbow House back up and running."

"But that's not part of a Mennonite agency, is it?"

"Nope. The county ran it and then, once it was destroyed in the hurricane, decided to shut it down. Hester has this idea about getting it going again as some kind of nonprofit community thing."

John frowned. It seemed to him that Hester was moving way too fast in reacting to her breakup with Samuel. She was casting off pieces of her life like the years of work she'd devoted to MCC, as if they were of no importance. He'd done that once. Back in Indiana when the elders of his community had opposed his ideas, he'd been so determined to prove them wrong, to show them that he could make a life for himself without them. That had been a mistake, and he couldn't help but think that Hester was making a similar mistake now. "A nonprofit still needs funding," he muttered.

"Yep. That's one stumbling block. If she does raise the cash, the trick is going to be to find a place to do all that work, and trust me, there are very few people who want a bunch of homeless people hanging out anywhere near them or their businesses, so good luck to her on that one."

They worked for another hour before Zeke put away his tools in the restored shed and left, promising to return the following day. "Weather permitting and the creek don't rise," he called as he gunned the motor of Margery's boat and took off. John had finally understood that the translation of that last statement was really "If nothing comes up that's higher priority." He had learned never to directly ask anything of Zeke, and for accepting the man the way he was, John had been repaid a hundred times over in friendship and free labor.

Under threat of showing up to watch over him herself, Margery had gotten John to promise that unless either Zeke or

Samuel were around, he would not try any work that involved climbing or hauling or lifting. "I don't want to be responsible for coming out here one day to find you lying flat on your back after falling off a ladder," she'd groused.

"I wouldn't hold you responsible," he said.

"Well, I would, so don't do it."

Having gotten used to Margery's unique style of mothering, he'd stuck to her rule. Once Zeke left, he used up the rest of the paint in the tray, then cleaned up the roller and brushes and left them ready to start again the following day, assuming Zeke returned. With at least three hours of daylight left, he turned his attention to working on the planting beds. He'd found a stretch of his property that ran along the main road where the soil had been left undamaged by the surge that came with the hurricane. It was decent growing soil probably hauled in years earlier by Tucker, and having been left to its own devices for a decade or more, it was rich enough to form a solid base for planting vegetables once he separated it from the grass and wildflowers that had taken root. Every day since he'd made the discovery, John had taken a shovel, pickax, and wheelbarrow out there and worked at gathering the usable soil and hauling it back to fill in the planting beds.

The discovery had been a double blessing, because in digging out the soil, he had begun to create a drainage ditch where the water would run away from the house and outbuildings instead of turning the yard into a swamp. On top of that he now had enough of a soil base to fill the beds without having to spend a fortune on topsoil from a nursery. Now that the weather had started to cool off some, he could try planting some seeds. Surely the place would have a better chance of selling if he could show that the land was viable for growing things. Besides, it might be months before he could find a buyer for the place. If he could raise a few vegetables, he could save himself some money and not have to rely so much on Margery stopping by with food.

As he worked, he thought about the news Zeke had told him. So Hester and Samuel would not marry. The idea gave him unexpected pleasure. Most of all he was happy for Samuel. The man had talked a lot about Rosalyn whenever he stopped by, and it had been pretty clear that he was falling for her. He liked thinking that Samuel and Rosalyn would end up together.

He thought about Alice, the woman he'd come so close to marrying, and tried to imagine what their life might have been like had she stood by him instead of siding with the rest of the community. He'd been drawn to her physical beauty. She was seven years younger than he was, and maybe that had accounted for her reaction when he'd begun talking to her about his fascination with the Walden experiment. Alice had listened politely but shown no enthusiasm for the idea. Indeed, she had seemed mystified by his interest in the book. Why, she had asked, would he even bother to think of trying anything other than what others in their community had done for generations?

His mother had counseled patience, but he'd seen in the reserve with which she treated Alice that she thought he was making a mistake. "Just because you've waited this long before settling down doesn't mean you can't take some time to find the perfect partner. It's for life, you know," she'd told him once.

Instinctively, he knew that she would not have reacted that way to Hester. No, something told him that she would have loved Hester's independent streak and her can-do personality. Like his mother, Hester was a person who looked for ways to help others, whether they wanted her assistance or not, he thought wryly and smiled at the thought. Between Zeke and thoughts of Hester, his earlier bad mood had completely disappeared.

He leaned on his shovel after spreading the last load of dirt for the day and looked out toward the bay. The waters were calm and clear. They had long since receded to normal levels. Nothing like that day when she and her father and Samuel had come wading ashore. And certainly nothing like they must have been the night before the hurricane hit when she and Margery had come to get him to leave.

"She gave up pretty easy," he muttered aloud. But he could not ignore the fact that she had come back the following day.

And over the weeks that had passed since that day, she had stayed in touch in some way or another—or he had. In spite of his best efforts to annoy her into leaving him alone in those early days, not to mention that she clearly wanted nothing to do with him, the two of them had found themselves cast together time and again. He missed her, even her sometimes-irascible personality.

Was it possible that having some kind of relationship with Hester Detlef was part of God's plan for him? Perhaps he should take some time to examine that more closely. Why would God bring this feisty, my-way-or-the-highway woman into his life and keep bringing her back even when John was certain that they were on two very different paths and there was no reason for them to see each other again?

And yet, it was to Hester that he had spoken the single thing that he had carried with him all the way from Indiana to Florida. The guilt that he had buried so deep under long days of work and endless nights of loneliness and isolation that he had thought he finally had overcome it. It was to her that he had spoken the words he had never said aloud. *"I killed her."*

Hester could not seem to stop thinking about John. She was so sure that he was going to regret selling his place, and she couldn't see such a proud and independent man going back to Indiana and begging forgiveness from the very elders he had opposed. She itched to talk to him, but she had promised her father that she would not initiate contact, and she had never gone back on a promise. Still, it certainly seemed as if God was guiding her down a new path, given the way the silliest thing seemed to bring John to mind.

For instance, she was having ice cream with Emma one day, and it struck her that every time she had ice cream she thought about the time she and John had sat in that same spot. It occurred to her that sitting outside Big Olaf's that day, they had formed a kind of truce, fragile as it was. Of course, it hadn't been anything so formal as all that, but looking back on it now, she realized that on that day she and John had changed from being natural adversaries to. . .what?

"Okay, you are a thousand miles away," Emma said.

"I was just thinking about another time I was here recently."

"With Samuel?" Emma guessed and gave Hester a sympathetic smile.

The date she'd shared with Samuel had not even entered her mind. "Okay, stop looking at me as if you think I might burst into tears at any moment. I am fine, really. And so is Samuel."

Emma raised a skeptical eyebrow. "Still. . ."

"It's the best for everyone. Samuel and Rosalyn were meant for each other, and Dad still gets a gifted partner for his furniture business."

"Everyone just wants you to be happy," Emma told her.

"I am happy. The Rainbow House project—"

"Not with work or projects, Hester."

"My work and new projects give me a great deal of pleasure."

"Not the same thing as having that special person to share it all with. You deserve that kind of happiness, Hester. Don't surrender yourself to a life of service to the exclusion of everything else." Emma stood up. "I'm not finished with probing what this all means for you and your future, Hester, but I really have to go. Jeannie and her family are coming over for supper."

"Tell Jeannie I have some more names for her, people who will have fruit ready beginning in October." Emma waved and headed across the street. But as she watched her friend leave, Hester could not deny that Emma's words had rung true. Her decision to place all of her energies in the Rainbow House project had been made at least partly because she did not want to face the fact that she was unlikely ever to marry now that Samuel was out of the picture. Who was she kidding? If her father hadn't brought Samuel to Pinecraft, her chances of ever marrying had already been slim to none.

Hester and Rosalyn spent the rest of the afternoon sorting through donated goods, and all the while Hester kept trying to figure out the best way to break the tension between them. Ever since her breakup with Samuel, things with Rosalyn had been uncomfortable, despite her talk with the younger woman.

"Samuel told me that you've made good progress recruiting neighbors to donate fruit for the Rainbow House project," Rosalyn ventured. As had become her habit, she did not look directly at Hester when she mentioned Samuel's name. But at the same time she couldn't seem to hide the shy smile that lit up her face. Hester recalled the day that Jeannie had talked about not seeing such a glow on her face, at least not when Samuel's name came up.

"Have you and Samuel decided on a wedding date yet?" Hester asked. At least Rosalyn wasn't trying to pretend there was no courtship going on.

"Oh no, it's much too soon," Rosalyn protested.

"For what? You're in love. You're of age."

"Past age," Rosalyn murmured.

"Aren't we all? Which is exactly my point. Why wait?"

Rosalyn fingered a donated blouse that was embroidered with tiny blue flowers. Carefully she clipped a couple of loose threads before placing the blouse on a hanger. "I just have to be sure," she said.

"About Samuel?"

Rosalyn turned and looked directly at Hester. "About you." When Hester started to protest, Rosalyn held up her hands. "I know what you say, Hester, but are you sure?"

"Sure that I admire Samuel enormously? Yes. Sure that there are moments when I wish he might have been the one? Yes. Sure that I don't love him and that we would have bored each other to tears? Absolutely."

Rosalyn's eyes flickered with hope but also caution. So Hester put her hands on Rosalyn's shoulders and leaned in close. "He loves you. You love him. Marry him already. I may not be ready to be a bride, but I am hoping to be a godmother before this time next year."

"Hester!" Rosalyn's cheeks darkened with embarrassment.

"Oh, don't sound so shocked. You get married. You have

kids—at least that's the way it's supposed to work."

"So if your father were to include our names among the list of couples to be married next month. . . ?"

"Let me put it this way: if he doesn't include your names on that list, the gossips of Pinecraft are going to be buzzing like you've never heard before. And knowing Olive Crowder, I will get the blame. Frankly, I don't have time for that. So do everyone a huge favor and get on that list, okay?"

Rosalyn hugged Hester hard. "You are the kindest person I know, Hester Detlef," she exclaimed. "I am so glad that God sent you to care for me after the fire. I don't know what I would have done without you."

Hester couldn't help but think that it was Rosalyn who had been *her* salvation. With her positive attitude and determination to go on with her life in spite of her injuries and the loss of her entire family, she had brought Hester through her own period of grief. Hester's mother could not recover, but Rosalyn could—and did. With Hester working beside her every day, she had grown physically stronger, not weaker, and in the process, Hester had found at least some peace with her mother's passing.

"Well, I'm glad that's settled," Hester said as she returned Rosalyn's hug. "Now let's get this stuff put away and go shopping for fabric for your wedding dress."

"Oh, I have that already," Rosalyn said and then blushed again. "I mean. . ."

"I am shocked," Hester announced, and then she grinned. "Pretty confident that I was going to give you my blessing, weren't you?"

"Hope is a powerful thing," Rosalyn admitted.

The two of them went back to sorting through the boxes of clothing, working in easy silence for several minutes until Rosalyn said, "How are things going with John Steiner?"

Hester swallowed as she considered her answer. "Samuel would know more about that than I do."

"And why is that?"

"Well, I haven't seen much of—"

"So Samuel has mentioned. And why is that?" she repeated.

"It seemed for a time there that the two of you were getting closer. I mean, at least you weren't coming in here all irritated and such after being with him."

"Are you trying to play matchmaker?" Hester said, keeping her tone light and teasing.

"I am trying to figure out why the woman I admire probably more than anyone I know and the man that Samuel thinks very highly of have suddenly gone their separate ways. Samuel thinks that John has come to some kind of spiritual crossroads. You could help him, you know. You *should* help him."

Hester could hardly tell Rosalyn about her promise to her father, mostly because Rosalyn would want to know what had made her promise such a thing, and she certainly wasn't about to say, *Well, John told me that he killed his mother, and Dad thought. . .*

"And how do you suggest I go about helping a man who has repeatedly made it crystal clear that he doesn't want or need help, from me or anyone else?"

"Well, what if you asked him to be part of the planning committee for Rainbow House?"

Hester opened her mouth to refute that ridiculous suggestion, but Rosalyn rushed in. "I mean, the man is a farmer. He knows stuff."

"He has enough to do right now," Hester said in a tone intended to end this thread of conversation once and for all. "Samuel tells me that he plans to sell and move back to Indiana."

But Rosalyn was not on that particular wavelength. "That could take months. I mean, I know the two of you are like oil and water sometimes, but that's the very reason he would be good for the project. He looks at things from a different perspective."

"He does at that." Hester pictured John's expression whenever he was mulling over a new idea.

"So you'll think about asking him to help?"

"I'll think about it," Hester agreed. It looked like agreeing with Rosalyn was going to be the only way to get her off the subject of John Steiner.

"Good. Now I have to run. I promised Samuel that I would

meet him at the park. He's playing shuffleboard with your father. Come join us."

"Maybe later," Hester said. "I have some things to do first."

"Why doesn't that surprise me?" Rosalyn asked with a wry smile as she hurried off.

John helping on the Rainbow House project. John serving with her—and Emma, Jeannie, Grady, and the others—on the planning committee. It might work on a number of different levels, she thought.

But how to convince her father of that?

On Saturday evening as Hester and Arlen shared the task of washing and wiping the supper dishes, she decided the time had come to address the matter of John Steiner. "Dad?"

Obviously distracted, Arlen said, "Samuel brought me a letter from John today."

"A letter?" She tried to contain her excitement at news that John had been in contact. Perhaps this was a good sign. She had certainly prayed long and hard for God to show them the way. And she couldn't deny that underlying every prayer was her hope that God's will would include the opportunity for her to see John again. The more she thought about the pain he must have suffered after his mother's tragic and sudden death, the more she felt that they shared something in common and could possibly provide the understanding and comfort that others could not. After all, each of them understood at least some of what the other had been through. She could help him.

"Hester?"

She'd been so lost in thought that she'd failed to pay attention as her father talked on. Now Arlen was holding a sheet of yellow paper ripped from a pad and folded several times.

"Read it, and see what you think. You know John as well as any of us."

She dried her hands and unfolded the paper.

Dear Pastor Detlef,

    This is my formal request for you and your disaster committee to consider whether or not your offer to help in restoring the second story of my home is still valid. If so, I would be grateful for a meeting to discuss terms.

Yours in the Lord,

John Steiner

Hester felt a smile tug at her mouth. This was so like him. Blunt and to the point and yet leaving the reader somewhat mystified. She could almost see him struggling over the choice of each word.

"What do you think it means?" Arlen asked.

"Well, it seems pretty clear that John is finally ready to accept the help you've offered," she said as she carefully folded the letter and handed it back to him. "On the other hand, he's determined to maintain control of the process."

"But why now?" Arlen scratched his head. "We have made numerous offers and all have been rejected. Samuel tells me that Grady also made attempts to provide assistance and was turned away. And just what does he mean about 'discussing terms'? What terms?"

Hester shrugged. "Samuel did mention that John was thinking of selling the place. Perhaps he's come to accept that he'll have more success with that if the property is fully repaired, especially the house."

"It's certainly prime real estate," Arlen agreed. "And now that the hurricane has ruined the soil for growing anything, I suppose the most likely buyer might be some developer. But a developer wouldn't care about the house, and with the economy still uncertain. . ."

"Will you help him?"

Arlen was clearly surprised by her question. "Of course we'll help him. We judge not, Hester. You know that."

And yet in a way he had judged John, she thought. When he had asked her to promise to stay away at a time when the man clearly needed every friend he could turn to, wasn't that the same as judging him?

"I don't think you can just show up there with a crew, Dad," she said as she dried and put away the last pot. "He asked for a meeting."

Arlen unfolded the letter and read through it again. "I could send word by Samuel on Monday. In the meantime, after church tomorrow, I'll speak with some of our volunteers and see when they might be available."

"You could drive out there after church," Hester suggested. "That would give you time to see exactly what the work might be before you put a crew together."

"That's a good idea," Arlen said, kissing her lightly on her temple. He headed for his study, where he would spend the rest of the evening going over his sermon for the following day. "And, Hester? If you have no other plans, perhaps you could ride along? It occurs to me that you, as well as John, have had some major changes in your life's journey these last days. Perhaps it would help him to talk to you, and vice versa."

She tried without success to quell the sudden leap of pleasure she felt at his invitation. "That would be fine," she said, turning away so that he would not see that she was smiling.

Chapter 22

Sunday morning held all of the promise of a day that would yield many blessings. A blue sky sprinkled with marshmallow clouds greeted those arriving for services at the Palm Bay Mennonite Church. There was an aura of excitement. In the Mennonite tradition, this was the day Arlen would announce the planned nuptials for four happy couples, among them Samuel and Rosalyn. Even Olive Crowder was smiling, at least until she spotted Hester outside the church.

"I understand that you have abandoned your duties as our representative to MCC," she said.

"I would hardly say abandoned," Hester replied, trying to smile through gritted teeth. "I have asked Rosalyn to assume those responsibilities while I—"

Olive sighed and raised her eyes to the blue skies above as if praying for patience. "Ja. Ja. We have heard of your new *project*. And I would ask you how the gathering of fruit from the yards of outsiders can possibly measure up to the work you have performed for MCC since your dear mother's death. Work that you took on in order to honor Sarah."

"My mother," Hester began and then found she had to gulp in a deep breath of fresh air before continuing. "I believe that my

265

mother would be proud of all the work I do for others. She made no distinction between helping those outside the community and those within."

Olive pursed her lips, and Hester could see that she was considering her next words very carefully. Just then her sister Agnes came rushing over. "Oh, Hester, so glad to catch you before the service. I wanted to tell you that yesterday at our quilting session, everyone was just buzzing about your plan to collect fruit and rebuild the shelter. Oh, there are a few who cannot yet see the brilliance of your idea. . . ." She paused for a breath and cast a sidelong glance at Olive, who huffed and left to find her seat. Then Agnes squeezed Hester's arm. "May God bless this wonderful work you are undertaking to help those less fortunate, Hester."

"Danke, Agnes."

"Whatever I can do to help, you just let me know," she pledged and hurried off after her sister.

Inside the small frame church building, the women sat apart from the men on wooden pews. Several ladies fanned themselves with cardboard fans mounted on sticks. The building was not air conditioned, and although the weather outside was mild, inside the packed church, the air was close. Hester slid in next to her grandmother, Nelly, and a minute later, Emma and her daughter, Sadie, squeezed in next to them as Rosalyn took the seat on the aisle.

"Exciting day," Emma whispered to Rosalyn.

"Ja," Rosalyn replied as she cast an adoring glance at Samuel, who had just entered the building. "Ja," she repeated, folding her hands and closing her eyes tightly as she bowed her head in what Hester guessed was a prayer of thanksgiving.

As everyone settled in and grew still, Emma Keller's husband, Lars, stepped to the front of the crowded room to deliver the call to worship.

For I was an hungred, and ye gave me meat: I was thirsty, and ye gave me drink: I was a stranger, and ye took me in.

"Matthew, chapter 25, verse 35," Lars said and then took his seat as everyone found the first hymn and stood as one to sing.

Their voices rose in the a cappella harmony that in their faith left no room for the organ or piano accompaniment common in churches of other faiths.

It always made Hester smile that those members of the congregation who seemed the most reserved outside the church were the very ones who sang out with the greatest enthusiasm and gusto. Agnes Crowder's powerful alto, for example, could be heard above all the rest of the women combined.

At the close of the hymn, her father stepped forward to lead them in prayer. Several years earlier he had persuaded the congregation that this opening prayer should be a silent one with each member of the congregation setting aside whatever joys and sorrows he or she might have carried to church with them that morning. "It is a time to open our hearts and minds to consider God's concerns and how you might best serve Him in addressing those concerns."

From outside the open windows came the sounds of traffic, the occasional distant siren, voices of those on the street. But inside the crowded sanctuary, everything and everyone was absolutely still.

Next to Hester, Nelly put down her fan and took in a deep breath then silently moved her lips in prayer. On the other side of her, Emma folded her hands in her lap and closed her eyes. But Hester's mind was clogged with everything she had to do in the coming week. Even now, nearly two months after the hurricane, the work went on. And on top of everything else, the Rainbow House project was moving forward almost with a will of its own.

Jeannie had called a reporter she knew at the local Sarasota newspaper and provided him with information about the project. Since that article had appeared, Jeannie's telephone had been ringing constantly with people across the entire city offering to donate fruit that would be ready to pick in just a matter of weeks. Jeannie's daughter, Tessa, had come up with the idea of recruiting her friends and their grandmothers to prepare the jars and labels they would need for making the marmalade they would sell. Emma's daughter, Sadie, who was far more outgoing than her cousin, had gone from store to store on both Main Street and around St. Armand's Circle collecting cash donations. And Jeannie had persuaded the manager of the city's largest farmers' market to give them a space for the coming season at no charge. So whether Hester was ready or not, the Rainbow House project was on the march.

The problem was that they had no place to store and sort the fruit or make the marmalade. No means to distribute their goods. They had no viable building that they could say was the future location for the shelter. The homeless population was still out there, wandering the bay front and downtown, being harassed by local police if they stayed too long in any one place, eating their meals in the dwindling number of open shelters. Those shelters had been set up to provide a haven for victims of the hurricane. But with school in session and most of those affected by the storm having found other accommodations or moved back home, the need for such community resources had ended.

Be still and listen, Hester could almost hear her father counseling her. Instead, Arlen began reciting the Lord's Prayer, the signal that the time for silent prayer had ended, and everyone joined in. Hester squeezed her eyes closed, knitted her fingers together, and prayed the familiar words, pleading with God to show her the way.

". . .is the kingdom and the power and the glory forever and ever. Amen."

She opened her eyes and blinked against the light that followed the darkness. She glanced toward an open window. Just outside the church she saw John Steiner pacing back and forth, his hands clenched behind his back, his head bowed.

~⟨≡⟩~

John had come into Pinecraft for two purposes. He was fairly certain that Arlen would take his change of heart about letting the MDS volunteers come out and help him rebuild the second story of the house as good news. He was not nearly so certain that Hester would be willing to listen as he explained his part in his mother's tragic death. For he had been the one to sever the fragile thread of friendship they had begun to forge all through the long night when they had waited together at the hospital.

The truth was that he felt a unique connection to Hester. He had seen a side of her that made him want to confide in her. On the other hand, he owed her an apology. As had become his habit, he'd run off that morning and holed up at his place, licking his wounds like an injured animal, waiting for her to come and find him. But she had made no effort to contact him, and why should she?

As a peace offering, he had brought her a wild orchid that he'd found growing along his lane. He had gone to the Detlef house and only realized that it was Sunday and she would be in church when he saw a cluster of bicycles gathered around a house across the street. Several Amish boys were standing around in the yard. John well remembered how he and his friends had lingered outside, always the last to go inside whatever home the service was being held in that week. The Amish held services in private homes, while the Mennonites had a separate church building— in Sarasota, John had learned, there were several of them.

He set the plant down among the ferns he had sent earlier, ferns that were still sitting in the bucket of water they'd arrived in, although they had clearly been tended with fresh water and kept out of direct sunlight. For reasons he didn't examine too closely, it was disturbing to him that she had not found the time to plant them in the garden that had been her solace after her mother died.

Unsure of his next move, he had wandered over to the restaurant where they had shared breakfast and then noticed the church on the opposite corner. Its plain white exterior gleamed in the morning sun, and through the open windows he heard voices raised in song. He moved closer and heard Arlen's familiar voice as he invited those in attendance to pray with him.

After a few minutes of silence, Arlen began reciting the Lord's Prayer and everyone joined in. Even John found himself mouthing the familiar words around the lump that had formed in his throat.

Although he was dedicated in his routine of morning devotions and evening prayer and often read the Bible—especially these days when his future was so uncertain—he missed the ritual of the worship. He missed hearing scripture read by others and silent meditation shared and feeling the press of a neighbor's shoulder against his own. He missed what Margery had been telling him he needed for over two years now—he missed community, the comfort and commiseration that were part of living with others, sharing happy as well as sad times.

He'd been thinking a lot about those newborns he'd seen in the hospital nursery. He'd thought about Grady Forrest being a father, about his own father, who in their too-short time together had taught John so much, and he thought about Samuel Brubaker, who was clearly looking forward to the day when he and Rosalyn would have a family of their own. He'd envied Samuel and Grady. He had thought that he would be the one raising a family by now.

The congregation had finished singing another hymn, and Arlen had opened the part of the service where any member of the congregation could stand up and share with the others. He heard a man announce that he and his wife would be leaving Florida to move back north where they could be closer to their children and grandchildren. He heard another man request prayers for the diagnosis he had received of diabetes. He heard a woman thanking the members who had been so kind in taking her in and bringing food and clothing after her home had flooded. And when the woman seemed inclined to ramble on, naming every person and how he or she had supported the family, John tuned her out.

Instead, he thought about the passage he'd stumbled across in Thoreau's book the night before. Once he was able to at least occupy the first floor of the house, he'd decided to build a bookcase in the living room and celebrate the addition to his meager furnishings by giving *Walden* a shelf all its own, at least until he could afford more books. Then as he'd positioned the book on the shelf, he'd noticed a piece of loose paper sticking up from the top. He'd turned to the page and read a passage he must have marked the first time he read the book.

"...*things do not change; we change.*"

"John?" Samuel Brubaker stood at the door of the church with an elderly man who had apparently been overcome by the closeness inside. Two women followed him and took charge of getting the man a drink of water and finding him a chair so that he could sit in the shade of the church vestibule and take advantage of the light breeze.

"Hello, Samuel."

"Are you. . . ? Would you like to come inside?"

And without hesitation John nodded and followed Samuel into the crowded church, removing his hat and clutching its stiff, sturdy brim like a lifeline. Samuel indicated the seat that he had vacated on the end of one pew and then went back outside to attend to the man. John was aware of a gentle flutter of whispered comments and the rustle of bodies shifting as people turned to look at him.

Arlen had begun his sermon and paused only a second to glance John's way before continuing. "We have made a covenant with God to love Him with all our hearts, minds, and beings. That is the first commandment. But how are we to do that? Ah, it's right there in the second commandment—we are to love our neighbor. But that raises a new question. What is the manifestation of such love?"

Arlen went on to mention four couples, including Samuel and Rosalyn, whose betrothals had been made known to the congregation during the period of announcements. He talked about other couples in the church who had been long married. He talked about parents loving children and sisters loving brothers and neighbors caring for neighbors. Then he broadened the scope to make it citywide and then statewide and national and international. He talked about love for the land and the sea and the heavens. He spoke of love for other creatures, animals domesticated and wild, and of love for all things growing on this planet that God had created. "And so we see that our love for God is made visible in our love for all humankind and all of God's creation."

He was on a roll, and still he had not provided the answer to the question he had originally raised, a question that John had wrestled with in so many ways.

"Which brings us back to our original question: What is the manifestation of this love in all its forms?" Arlen repeated. "It is sacrifice. It is putting aside our personal comfort and wants and desires anytime we know that there is someone out there who is in need, even strangers we have never met. For they are our neighbors as much as the person who lives next door."

John examined this under the light of his actions over the last several months. When had he put aside his needs for the greater good? Certainly not when he had foolishly insisted on remaining at Tucker's Point instead of going to a shelter. Not even that time when he had gone to help Margery, for he had not had to sacrifice anything for that. And most definitely not anywhere near the number of times that Hester had risked censure by others or put aside her own needs to tend to him or others.

"Brothers and sisters," Arlen said, "I close with the words of the prophet Isaiah, chapter 58, verse 12: 'And they that shall be of thee shall build the old waste places: thou shalt raise up the foundations of many generations; and thou shalt be called, The repairer of the breach, The restorer of paths to dwell in.'

"Shall we pray?"

Every head bowed as Arlen beseeched God to hear those prayers, silent and spoken, that had come from this gathering. And as John prayed with him, he felt more certain than ever that God was leading him to take a new path and change his ways. His experiment had failed because he had thought only of himself. He had spent more than two long years feeling sorry for himself, wallowing in grief and guilt. And while he had opened himself to the friendship of Margery and Samuel and Zeke, he had continued to keep anyone else, including Hester and her father, who had tried to help him at arm's length.

"*. . .things do not change; we change.*"

~~≋~~

Once the service ended, there was the usual crush of people at the door, some wanting to talk to Arlen at length and others just wanting to have their presence acknowledged before leaving. Hester deliberately hung back, visiting with Emma and Sadie for longer than usual until Emma caught Lars's eye. "My husband is ready to go," she said. "I'll see you tomorrow for coffee?"

"Yes," Hester said. Lately she and Emma had gotten into the habit of meeting for coffee every Monday morning. It was a good way to begin the week, and it had done wonders for reaffirming their friendship. "Bye, Sadie," she said, but the girl was already halfway to the door, waving to a friend and chatting with two others.

"Hester, do you have a minute?"

She turned to find John standing in the row of pews behind her. He was dressed in the clothes he'd gotten from the distribution center weeks earlier and holding the Amish straw hat that Rosalyn had found for him. He was clutching it actually, and it surprised her to realize that he was nervous. "Hello, John," she said. "How are you doing?" She kept her tone impersonal and just the slightest bit suspicious.

"Do you have time to take a walk with me? Maybe to the park?"

Hester was well aware that setting off after church with any man for a walk in the park would set tongues to wagging. Taking that walk with John would likely draw curiosity even from those who usually avoided gossip. "Why?"

He smiled. She had forgotten what that smile of his did to her. The way his eyes crinkled. The way his entire face seemed to soften. The way her heart suddenly beat in staccato rhythms.

"Direct and to the point as usual, I see," he said. "Well, because the last time we talked I was rude, and I'd like to apologize. Would that be all right?"

"Apology accepted," she said as she picked up her grand-mother's forgotten fan and prepared to leave.

He stopped her by gently touching her arm. "And," he added, his expression completely serious now, "I'd like to explain."

"You've apologized," she said breezily. "No explanations

necessary. It was good to see you in church today, John. And I understand that you and my father—"

"Stop it," he grumbled. "You know what I mean. Will you let me explain or not?"

She sighed. "Come home with Dad and me for Sunday dinner and you can tell both of us."

John frowned. "I prefer—"

"Final offer, John. Take it or leave it."

His frown deepened, but she stood her ground, cocking one eyebrow as she waited for his answer. And then he did the one thing she never would have expected. He fingered a dangling tie of her prayer kapp. "You drive a hard bargain, Hester."

For one incredible moment Hester lost herself in the depths of his eyes. For one incredible moment she felt the kind of shared attraction she had only imagined as she watched her parents or Emma and Lars. And then she heard someone clearing her throat, reminding her that she and John were not alone, and looked over John's shoulder to find Olive Crowder scowling at them. The older woman turned on her heel and headed up the aisle to the exit.

John cleared his throat as well. "What's for dinner?"

"Chicken, potato salad, tomatoes, and my grandmother's chocolate cake."

From the look on his face, Hester suspected that John was about as close to having his mouth water as anyone could come without actually drooling. She couldn't help herself—she laughed. "If you could see your face," she said, pointing with one hand while she used the other to cover her laughter. "Come on. Dad looks like he's about ready to leave. Maybe the two of you can talk about how MDS can help you while we walk."

It was unusual for Arlen and Hester to eat their Sunday dinner at home. Usually Arlen was invited to dine with one of the families that attended the church, and since her mother's death Hester was usually included in the invitation. If they did eat at home, her grandmother joined them. But on this Sunday, Arlen had made sure that Nelly had an invitation to eat with friends and that he had turned down any invitations he and Hester might receive.

"We'll have our dinner and then drive out to Tucker's Point," he'd told her that morning at breakfast. "Or we could make it a picnic and include John." He had seemed so pleased with the idea that Hester had fried several pieces of chicken and put potatoes on to boil for potato salad while her father was eating his breakfast. All she had left to do was to mix the potato salad and slice the tomatoes.

"Dad? John has agreed to join us for our dinner," she said when her father had sent the last church member on his way.

"Excellent. We had planned to bring a picnic out to your place, John, so that you and I could talk about how MDS might be of service to you."

"Now we can eat at home," Hester said.

"No picnic? On a glorious day like this one?" Arlen faked a frown.

"A picnic would be nice," John said politely. "I understand that it means more work for you, Hester, but I'd be glad to help."

Her mouth dropped open and then closed again without a sound. Had this man—this Amish man of the women-have-their-place variety—just offered to help out in the kitchen?

"No. A picnic is fine. Besides, Dad, you wanted to see what progress John has already made before deciding how best to help, right?" She had carefully avoided eye contact with John since they'd joined her father for the walk home.

"So a picnic it is," Arlen announced.

The phone was ringing when they reached the house, and Hester hurried ahead of the men to answer it. There was only one reason someone would disturb their Sunday, and that was if there had been some misfortune that required Arlen's help. Mentally Hester took stock of who had not been in church that morning as well as who in the community had recently been ill.

"Pastor Detlef's home," she said.

"Oh good, Hester, it's you." Jeannie Messner's normal voice was always so filled with excitement that it was hard to know why she might be calling, especially because Arlen was not her pastor.

"Is it Emma?" Hester asked, her mind racing with possibilities. Emma had mentioned that she and Lars and the children were having Sunday dinner at Jeannie's house. "Zeke Shepherd's brother, Malcolm, and his family will be there as well," Emma had said and then smiled. "You know Jeannie. It has to be a party." Of that guest list only Emma and her family were members of Arlen's church.

"Emma? She's fine." Jeanne seemed momentarily mystified at the question. "Oh, you thought. . . I guess I shouldn't be calling on a Sunday, but this is such wonderful news that it can't wait."

But Hester did have to wait while Jeannie turned from the phone. "Go ask your parents," she said, her hand apparently muffling the sound. "I'll do it if they say it's okay." There was a teenage moan, and then Jeannie's voice was clear once again. "Sorry about that. Sadie wants to get her learner's permit, and you know how Emma and Lars are."

Arlen was standing in the doorway, obviously expecting the call to be for him.

"It's Jeannie Messner," Hester mouthed. "Jeannie? Dad and I were just on our way to—"

"Okay, I'll make this quick," Jeannie said. "Zeke's brother, Malcolm? He might be interested in setting up a foundation for the Rainbow House project."

"Why are you whispering?" was all Hester could come up with as a response to such startling and admittedly thrilling news.

"Well, it's not a done deal yet. I mean, he said that giving the money to Zeke is like trying to bail out a sinking boat with chopsticks. You know how Zeke does things, just gives everything away to this one or that, no questions asked."

"Jeannie, what exactly did Malcolm offer?" She hated to dampen Jeannie's excitement with a strong dose of reality, but in this case it was important.

"I told you. He said giving Zeke the money was a waste and that he really liked what I was telling him about the project and. . ."

. . .from there you just naturally assumed the rest, Hester thought, disappointment taming her initial excitement. "Jeannie, did he actually mention setting up a foundation?"

"No, that was my Geoff, but Malcolm certainly agreed that it was a way to go. I mean, there would be conditions, I'm sure, before he'd be ready to fully commit. He is a businessman, after all, and you know how they are—bottom line and measures of success and all—but I'll just assure him that you and Emma could get that all figured out."

"What does Emma think?"

There was the slightest pause. "Well, I could tell that she was thinking about it. She probably plans to talk to you about it at your coffee tomorrow. Oh shoot, I'll bet she wanted to tell you the good news herself. Well, just pretend I didn't say anything, okay? Gotta run." And the line went dead.

"Is everyone all right at the Messner home?" Arlen asked when Hester came into the kitchen. He and John were seated at the kitchen table drinking iced tea.

"Yes, fine," she replied as she started pulling containers from the refrigerator to pack their picnic. "You know Jeannie. She gets something on her mind and can't wait to share it."

Arlen smiled. "Yes. She's a delightfully positive person, always has been."

John took the knife and the tomato that Hester was slicing and nodded toward the bowl of cold potatoes. "I can do this while you mix the potato salad."

She tried to concentrate on listening to her father singing the praises of Jeannie and her husband, Geoff, but it was hard to do with John working alongside of her as if this was something they did all the time. Before long, images of the two of them working together became visions of them laughing together and then sharing meals and. . .

Stop it.

She finished mixing the salad, then wrapped the chicken and packed the picnic basket. She was about to close the lid after John handed her the plastic bag filled with more sliced tomatoes than three people could possibly eat when he stopped her by holding the basket lid.

"I thought you said something about chocolate cake, but I don't see any sign of it in here. Frankly, I was really looking forward to that."

Arlen laughed. "So am I," he agreed as he retrieved the dessert from the counter and handed it to John. "Hester, your mind is too much on other things today."

She could not argue the point, for between John Steiner's sudden reentry into her life and Jeannie's idea that Zeke's brother might actually help fund the Rainbow House project, she was definitely having trouble concentrating on anything.

"Okay, are we ready to go?" she asked and knew by the look that John and Arlen exchanged that she had sounded anything but cheerful. The truth was that Jeannie's news had been unsettling, even threatening.

Chapter 23

Neither Hester nor her father was prepared for how much work John had actually been able to accomplish. "If you did most of this work with a broken wrist, it would be quite interesting to see what you could do with two good hands," Arlen said.

Uncomfortable with compliments—even subtle ones—John directed their attention to the packinghouse. "Zeke was able to finish the trim and gutters when he was here yesterday. This building is in better shape than it was before the hurricane hit, thanks to Zeke and Samuel."

"And so we can concentrate on the house," Arlen said as the three of them sat on a blanket that Hester had spread on the ground and shared the picnic dinner. Arlen poured lemonade from the thermos and passed the cups around. John laid a two-by-four across the center of the blanket to keep it from blowing in the cooling breeze.

"Instant table," he said, setting his cup of lemonade on it. Arlen followed suit, and then John picked up Hester's cup from its unsteady resting place on the ground and added it to the lineup.

For reasons she didn't want to explore, Hester found herself studying John's hand. It was large with long fingers. His nails were clipped short, and calluses had hardened the skin on his palms. The backs of his hands were sunburnt to a permanent russet, and the coarse hair that covered his forearm glinted golden in the afternoon sun. His hands, like the rest of him, were strong and solid. And yet she felt certain that his touch would be gentle, even tender.

Now where did that thought come from? "Another piece of chicken, Dad?" She forced her thoughts away from the man who was suddenly sitting far too close to her and who seemed to be watching her every move.

"Not for me." Arlen patted his stomach and grinned. "I need to save some room for that cake."

"John?" she offered without meeting his gaze.

"No, thank you." The words came out as if she'd startled him, as if he hadn't really been following the conversation at all. He got to his feet and offered a helping hand to Arlen. "How about we take a walk through the house, and then maybe we can discuss those terms I mentioned in my letter," he said.

"MDS does not place restrictions on our work, John. We give of our talents freely to those in need."

"I'm afraid I can't accept that," John said. "I insist on paying."

The two men stood at an impasse for one long tense moment, and then Arlen smiled. "Why don't you give us the tour and then we can talk more over a piece of Nelly's chocolate cake."

Hester could not help but be impressed with the tidiness of the downstairs rooms where John was currently living. The kitchen was sparsely furnished with a single chair and the heavy oak table that Hester remembered from the night she'd come to get him to leave. An assortment of mismatched dishes lined the shelves on each side of the porcelain sink. The countertops were bare of the usual assortment of small appliances and such that cluttered the counters in Jeannie's large kitchen. Hester suspected that if she opened any of the three drawers, she would find the utensils lined up perfectly inside.

In one narrow room that they passed on their way from the kitchen to the living and dining rooms, he had placed a single bed and small dresser. Hooks on the wall across from the window held the clothes that he wasn't currently wearing. The single window was unadorned. The bed was made up with spotless white sheets, a single flat pillow, and a blanket folded across the foot. It was the bedroom of a plain man, an Amish man. It was the room of a man who was no longer fighting against his roots.

Hester forced her attention to the living and dining rooms. The dining room was bare of any furnishings at all save an ornate chandelier that hung from the center of the ceiling and seemed incredibly out of place. Across the hall, the living room was almost as devoid of furnishings. A bookcase next to the old woodstove caught her eye because the wood was new and there was only one book on the otherwise-empty shelves. She moved closer, unable to suppress her curiosity.

Walden: Life in the Woods.

John and her father were still standing in the front hallway while John pointed out the carving on the banister that led up to the second floor. There was another far less ornate stairway in the kitchen, John was telling Arlen, or there had been until it had collapsed under John's feet the night of the storm.

Hester picked up the book. As she had told John, she had read it when she attended college, but for her it had been little more than another assignment to be completed. Clearly for John it held a great deal more significance. There was a small yellow paper marking a page. She let the book fall open and moved the bookmark in order to scan the two facing pages, trying to guess which passage had resonated with him. And the words that caught her attention just before her father called out to her and she closed the book and replaced it on the shelf were "we change."

"Hester, did you ever see such fine workmanship?" her father was saying as he examined the front door. "Even warped as it is," he added as he ran his fingers over the wood. Her dad had always admired the talent of other carpenters, especially those who had lived well before his time.

"It is beautiful," she agreed.

"Was," John corrected.

"And will be again," Arlen added. He turned his attention back to the stairway. "Is it safe to go up?"

For an answer John led the way. The treads of the stairs were bare wood, and his heavy work boots echoed on each step. When they reached the top, Hester understood why the sound had been so pronounced. An entire wall of the second story was gone, exposing what had been a large bedroom and bathroom to the elements. Wallpaper hung in tatters from the walls that remained intact, and they would need to be stripped, then scrubbed down and whitewashed. The wood floor was gouged and scarred in places.

John entered the first bedroom and pointed to the large banyan tree outside. "A third of the tree broke off and landed inside here. It took Zeke and me an entire day to get it cut up, but it left its mark on the floor, I'm afraid."

Arlen examined the damage and said nothing.

"There are two other small bedrooms on this floor. They suffered water damage, and the storm blew out the doors and windows, but at least the walls are there."

"Excellent," Arlen said, more to himself than to either of them. Hester knew that he was already making a mental list of what would be needed, muttering to himself as he moved around the space, "Electric, water, plaster, paint. First the exterior wall. . . Is there an attic?"

"There was." John pointed to the opening where the roof had been ripped free of the rafters.

"Das ist gut," Arlen said as he removed a small notepad and the stub of a pencil from his pocket and made some entries. "This is the extent of it?" he asked, looking up at John.

"Pretty much."

Arlen smiled and touched the sleeve of John's shirt. "Then you are blessed." He started back down the stairs while Hester and John exchanged a look that shouted, *Blessed? Is he kidding?*

"Let's have some cake, and you and Dad can talk," Hester suggested as she followed her father back to the first floor.

John offered Arlen the only kitchen chair, then brought in

two folding chairs from the porch. Hester cut slices of the cake and placed them on the three plates that she found on John's kitchen shelf. He took forks from a drawer, and she saw that she was right in thinking the utensils would be lined up precisely inside.

Then over large pieces of that chocolate cake washed down with the last of the lemonade, the two men talked over the details of what would be needed to renovate the house. Hester had sat in on dozens of such conversations with her father over the last several weeks, and knowing she would have little to add to the discussion, she finished her smaller slice of cake and then wandered back outside.

We change, she thought as she walked along the property, remembering how it had looked the first time she had come here after the hurricane. All around her was evidence of how that fierce storm had changed the landscape, open spaces where before there had been lush tropical plantings, barren land where there were now stubs of the grove of fruit trees that had flourished there. The pier that had been indefinable that morning had been replaced, using reclaimed materials that she assumed either Samuel or Zeke had provided.

The sun was high, so she sought the cooler shade of the old packinghouse. Outside, the walls had been painted a deep forest green and the flat roof was marked by three ventilation fans housed in metal cupolas. She walked up a short ramp to see the inside where the original conveyer belt made up of a series of rusted metal rollers had remained intact, along with the rough-hewn work counters where once Tucker's employees had sorted fruit for distribution throughout the region.

She walked the length of the long building, her fingers skimming along the equipment as an idea began to take shape. A major piece of the puzzle that was the Rainbow House project that no one had yet solved was that of where to sort and wash the fruit once it was collected. It would need to be packaged or processed, and the resulting products would need to be stored until they could be distributed.

As she walked through the packinghouse, she was barely aware that along the way she was mentally designating the very spots where each step in the sequence could take place. And when she stood in the doorway at the far end of the building and closed her eyes, she could see it all—volunteers working at various stations, their chatter and laughter echoing as they worked. Crates of fruit stacked up and sorted and ready to be turned into marmalade or delivered whole to food banks around the city. Over there a large cookstove and the supplies necessary to make and bottle the marmalade.

"It's perfect," she murmured aloud as she rummaged in her pocket for a piece of paper and pencil. "We'd have to replace the conveyer belt, but otherwise it's exactly what's needed." Now all she had to do was to convince John of that and stop him from selling the place.

John wasn't really listening to Arlen. He was thinking about Hester and how he might find some time to be alone with her. He was as surprised as she would no doubt be to realize that his intentions were romantic. But then he had seen her wandering around his property as he stood at the sink washing the plates and glasses that she'd used to serve the dessert. She walked slowly with her hands clasped behind her back, her head shifting to take in everything around her. He saw her pause near one of the garden beds long enough to pick up a handful of soil and let it sift through her fingers. Moving on, she had touched the shattered trunk of an orange tree destroyed by the hurricane winds and then glanced around as if realizing that something was missing. Finally she had patted the trunk of the tree and then slowly walked past the repaired toolshed and empty chicken coop to the packinghouse. Shielding her eyes from the sun, she had stood looking up at the roof and finally disappeared inside.

". . .like to get Samuel out here to have a look," Arlen was saying. "Maybe tomorrow if that works for you?"

"Sure," John replied, wondering what Hester was finding so

fascinating in the empty packinghouse.

"You know, John, if you're planning on selling the place. . ."

"I am," John said, giving Arlen his full attention. *I don't really have a choice.*

Arlen nodded. "Well then, we'll figure that into the work we do. We can keep things pretty simple. After all, your most likely buyer for such a prime piece of property would be a developer who will no doubt tear everything down anyway."

It wasn't that John hadn't thought of that himself. It just hurt to hear the words spoken aloud. "As long as the developer can pay the price," he said. "I won't be able to repay MDS until the place sells. You understand that, right?"

Arlen took a moment. "And you understand that, as I've already told you, we do not accept payment." He actually sounded insulted and seemed dangerously close to losing what little temper he had.

"But. . ."

"No." Arlen pushed himself away from the table and stood up. "But since it seems so important to you to keep a balance sheet on this project, I have a suggestion."

"I'm listening."

"Open your eyes and your heart, son. God has blessed you in many ways, but He also expects those He has blessed to be a blessing to others."

The concept that he had been blessed was debatable, given his complete failure, but the old man meant well and so he nodded. "I'll give that some consideration," he said.

"Excellent. Now where do you think that daughter of mine has gotten to?" He glanced around as if just realizing that Hester had left them alone.

"She's outside."

"Well, we're going to need some measurements. Do you have a carpenter's tape?"

John opened a drawer and handed him the measuring device. "What else?"

Arlen took paper and the pencil from his pocket. "Nothing I

285

can think of. Do you mind if I. . ." He nodded toward the front hallway.

"Not at all. I'll help," John said.

"No. If it's all right, I like to do this part alone. I seem to think better in silence and solitude. Go find Hester. Do you have some more of those ferns you gave her for Sarah's garden?"

"I do," John said.

"Good. Go help her dig them. Perhaps it will inspire her. The garden has been sadly neglected for weeks now."

John got a pitchfork and shovel and large bucket from the toolshed and then headed for the packinghouse. Inside, he found Hester perched on one of the long sorting tables that had gone through the hurricane untouched. She was writing furiously on a small pad of paper and muttering to herself.

"Arlen thought you could use some more ferns for the garden," he said. He leaned the gardening tools against the worktable. "What are you working on there?"

"Nothing, a sketch. . .idea."

"May I see it?" She handed him the rough sketch, and he saw at once that it was the packinghouse. "And may I ask why?"

"Remember that magazine you picked up at the hospital and asked me to return for you?"

John nodded.

"Well, there was this article about people around the country— ordinary people—who have put together programs to help others. A woman in California who had gotten the idea to have teenagers collect unwanted fruit from private yards was featured."

"And you thought why not here in Sarasota?"

"Well, yeah. Since then we've discovered that there's a similar program in Tampa and they've been very helpful." She took the sketch from him and put it in her apron pocket. "It just helps to see the layout of a building that was once used for similar work." She motioned around the large, cavernous building, then shrugged. "Ready to dig those ferns?"

"You sure you've got time to get them back in the ground?" he teased.

"Guilty. How did you know I hadn't gotten around to that yet?"

"I found a wild orchid growing along my lane that I thought you might be able to save. So this morning, before I figured out that everyone would be at services, I stopped by your house and saw the ferns still sitting in the bucket." He held up the empty bucket he was carrying. "At this rate I'm going to run out of buckets pretty soon."

Her smile was both beautiful and sad. "I never seem to get around to the things that really matter."

"Right. Like saving an entire homeless population or making sure the survivors of the hurricane get the clothing and household goods they need to start over, like—"

"Honoring my mother's memory," she said quietly. She had not moved from her perch on the sorting table, and her gaze met his directly. "How do you honor the memory of your parents, John?"

So here it is, he thought. She had given him the opening he'd been looking for earlier, but it had come so unexpectedly that he suddenly found that he did not have the words. "I know I owe you an explanation," he said as he put down the garden tools and pushed himself up onto the table beside her.

"You don't owe me anything, but if you're inclined to finish the conversation you started that morning at breakfast, I'm listening."

He glanced at her, expecting to see judgment or at the very least skepticism in her eyes, but instead he lost himself in their sapphire depths. "It's hard to know. . ."

"Start with how she died."

He stared down for a minute, gathering his thoughts, or maybe he was just fighting the memories, reluctant to go back to that horrible time.

"It was winter. There was snow, a lot of it, and it was bitterly cold. Worst winter in a decade, the weather people kept saying. But she insisted on going out."

"Why?"

"It was my fault." He felt tears well and willed himself to contain them. "I had started on this Walden thing that fall, and at first everyone seemed to think the idea might have merit. It's not unheard of even for an Amish community to find itself caught up in more worldly ways."

"So when you read Thoreau's book, you thought that here was a guide for getting back to the old ways?"

John nodded and cleared his throat. "But the more I talked about how the community might apply certain elements of Thoreau's experiment to our lifestyle, the more people seemed to be alarmed by it, and by me."

"Your mother was concerned?"

"Not *with* me, for me. She had heard from a friend that things were getting out of hand. What had begun as trivial was quickly escalating into something much more serious, but I was too stubborn to see that. Mom insisted that we needed to make sure the leadership of the congregation had my side of the story. She hated gossip in any form." He paused and shut his eyes to block out the memory. "She had learned that the bishop would be meeting with the elders that night, and she was determined that I be there."

"So you and she. . . ?"

"No. I refused to go. We had had this really terrible argument, and I had stormed off to take care of the evening milking. Mom and I could knock heads now and then. I come by my stubbornness honestly." He stared up at the light filtering in around the roof vents. "Next thing I know she's got our horse hitched up to the buggy and is climbing into the driver's seat. She hadn't driven that buggy once since my father had died. Either I drove or we didn't go anywhere."

He sucked in a breath and let it out with a shudder. Hester placed the flat of her palm against his back and remained perfectly still, waiting for him to continue.

"But that was Mom. In some ways she had always felt like the outsider in the community, especially after Dad died. She was determined to make my case to the powers that be, even if

I wasn't. I started after her, yelling at her to stop, but she was so strong-willed, nothing was going to stop her from going."

A bird flew through the open door and settled on a crossbeam in the ceiling.

"What happened, John?"

"The driveway was covered in ice. I could see that the horse was nervous. I kept yelling for her to stop, but then a passing car backfired and. . ."

"The horse bolted?"

John nodded and tried to swallow around the lump that filled his throat. "He slipped and the buggy turned over, and Mom. . ." He swiped at the tears he could no longer hold back.

"But you weren't in the buggy with her," Hester said softly. "There was nothing you could have done to prevent this, so why did you say that you killed her?"

"Because afterward I knew what others were saying. I knew full well that I was on the brink of being called before the congregation. I mean, any fool understands that once the bishop gets involved, things have gone to a whole new level. And I should have known that when I stubbornly refused to back down, she would take matters into her own hands. She was fierce that way."

"The old saying applies—hindsight is twenty-twenty. But John, if this is the whole story—"

"It is. . ."

"Then the fact remains that you had nothing to do with her death. It was her choice to go out that night, John. You did everything you could to stop her."

He continued the story as if she hadn't spoken. "A passing car saw the overturned buggy and stopped. The woman had a cell phone and called for help, then stayed with us until the ambulance arrived. But it was already too late."

"She died in your arms?"

John nodded. "She put her hand on my cheek and said three words: 'Find the balance.' "

"I don't understand."

"It was an old joke that we shared. Whenever things got

overwhelming and she had trouble adapting to the Amish life, Dad would always tell her to find the balance. After he died, and I would come home after getting into some argument with another kid or in a bad mood, she would remind me that if Dad were there, he would tell me to 'find the balance.' And as she got older and became frustrated with knees that hurt and eyes that needed glasses for fine needlework, I would throw it back to her: 'Find the balance, Ma.' " He savored this sweeter memory for a long moment, and then looked around. "Haven't exactly done that, have I?"

"I suppose that depends on how you define *balance*," Hester said. "But I do know that for you to go around saying you killed your mother is just one more tactic you've developed to keep people at arm's length."

"It's not something I go around saying to folks," he protested.

"You said it to me," she challenged. "And you don't even like me."

"What gives you that idea?"

"Oh, I don't know. Could be the way we're always on guard around each other. Could be—"

Without taking time to consider what the possible consequences might be, John pulled her against him and kissed her. "I like you, okay?" he whispered, and when she did not fight him, he kissed her again. Then he released her and hopped down from the table. "Are you going to help me dig these ferns or not?"

~⟶~

Hester could not move, much less find the energy to dig ferns. Her body felt like water, and her mind was racing like a speedboat. And she wasn't sure she could handle thinking about the somersaults her heart seemed to be attempting.

John Steiner had kissed her. Twice. Without any warning at all. Without for one second stopping to consider what *her* feelings might be. *Typical.* The man was so. . . She realized she was running her forefinger over her lips. "Oh, get over yourself," she muttered and picked up the shovel he'd left for her.

Outside, John was stabbing the pitchfork into the hard soil.

For all the rain they had had earlier in the season, it had been dry for weeks now.

"Be careful," she said. "You'll break them off without getting the roots."

"We do grow ferns up north," he said, and she could hear frustration in his voice. It didn't help that he refused to look at her.

They dug in silence for several minutes, nothing passing between them other than the sound of metal hitting hard-packed earth. "Maybe if we soak the soil," John said, but it was evident that he wasn't asking for her opinion.

Hester leaned on her shovel. "Look, we cannot just ignore what you did back there."

"You don't have to make it sound like—"

"I'm not trying to make it sound like anything. I just think we need to talk about it."

"Look, it was a kiss, all right? Okay, two kisses."

"Yes, I know. The question is, why?"

"Why? You want me to analyze something that was completely—"

She straightened to her full height, which was still several inches shorter than he was. "I am going to assume that it was a spontaneous reaction."

"Do you always have to make more of a situation than it really is?" Without giving her a chance to respond, he jammed his pitchfork into the suddenly yielding soil and headed back to the house. "I'll tell Arlen you're ready to go," he called over his shoulder.

"Fine," she snapped. "I'll be in the car."

Chapter 24

It took the MDS team only ten days to complete the work on John's house, and by the first week in October, the property was ready to be listed on the market. Hester couldn't help but marvel at the crew her father had put together—a small army of experienced carpenters along with an electrician and a plumber. At her father's subtle insistence and with his promise that he would make sure that John was busy elsewhere, she had asked Emma and Jeannie and their daughters as well as Rosalyn to help her paint the restored rooms and clean the entire house after the workers were finished. Margery had shown up to help as well.

"It's a beautiful house," Jeannie exclaimed. "Wouldn't it make a perfect Rainbow House?"

"Not really," Emma said. "It's too far from town. How are the homeless men and women supposed to get here? Besides, there's only one bathroom."

As usual, Jeannie was undaunted by her sister's practical streak. "Well, it would make a great something. I hate seeing it torn down and yet another multistoried monstrosity going up in its place."

"The packinghouse would be a good place to sort the donated fruit once we start collecting it, and we could even make the marmalade there if we got the right equipment." Hester had been thinking about how perfect the space was for their project practically nonstop since she'd gotten the idea, but she only grasped that she'd spoken aloud when Jeannie squealed.

"It *is* perfect, and we have to find a place soon. I'm already getting calls from people wanting to schedule a date to have the volunteers come get their fruit."

"Same problem," Emma said as she stood back to check her daughter, Sadie's, work on the trim. "I thought we decided that because of people's discomfort with having homeless people in their homes, we were going to have them do the sorting and distribution and we were going to recruit young people to do the collecting. Again, how will people without any means of transportation get here?"

"I know, but. . ." Jeannie got no further.

"Emma's right," Hester admitted. "Even if the place were available—and it isn't—how are we going to transport the volunteers out here to sort and pack?"

Margery snorted. "Well, now, it's going to be a while before John can sell this place. I don't care what that fast-talking realtor says. In the meantime, how about I run a little ferry service? Collect folks down at the marina in town and bring them here by boat on the days you need them to work?"

"Samuel could bring people in his camper," Rosalyn volunteered.

Hester felt a prickle of excitement, but then she looked out the window and saw the realtor's FOR SALE sign prominently posted near the water. There was a mate to the sign posted by the road and another pointing the way from Highway 41. Besides, John would never agree to let them use the packinghouse even on a short-term basis now that the property was on the market. *Would he?*

"Hester could ask him," Rosalyn suggested.

"Ask who what?"

"Ask John if we can use the packinghouse until he sells. It would buy us some time before we had to put the whole project on hold for lack of a proper space to handle the sorting and such," Jeannie explained.

"He might just agree," Margery mused. "He's changed some these last weeks, actually shown some indication that he's begun to realize this going-it-alone thing may not be his best move."

"Do you want me to ask him?" Emma said softly. Emma was the only person who knew that John had kissed her. Her reaction had not been the shock that Hester had been expecting. Instead, she had asked, "Did you kiss him back?" And Hester had nodded.

"Thought so," Emma had said with a smug little smile. But when there had been no further contact with John, Emma had adopted the pitying look that was now on her face whenever his name came up.

"I can ask him," Hester said as she put the finishing touches on the wall she'd been painting. "But be prepared for him to say no."

"Where is he, anyway?" Margery asked. "I haven't seen him all day."

"I asked Dad to—"

"He went off with that realtor," Jeannie said. "I don't like that guy. He's so. . .slick."

"He's just doing his job," Emma said. "And speaking of jobs, it looks like we have finished here." She wet her finger with spit and scrubbed a speck of paint off Sadie's cheek.

"Ah, Mom," Sadie protested, and all the women laughed. Then they heard male voices downstairs.

"Looks like here's your chance, Hester," Emma said. "John's back."

"Hey, John, come see what a woman's touch can do for this place," Jeannie called.

John looked up the restored stairway, its carved wooden banister now gleaming with fresh polish, and saw the women gathered at the top. *All but her,* he thought. And then Hester stepped out of the large bedroom and joined the others. She was not smiling, but she met his eyes for the first time since the day he'd kissed her. On the other hand, she was wearing that expression that he'd come to know so well, the one she seemed to reserve just for him.

The one that shouted, *Let's get one thing straight, mister.*

He forced a smile and climbed the stairs. "Looks great," he said, glancing around. "Thank you. I—"

"Oh, you can't see anything from there," Jeannie said, taking his arm and leading him into the bedroom that had been his sleeping quarters before the hurricane. "Check this out."

The walls had been painted a pale blue, a softer version of the color of Hester's eyes, he thought, and he glanced at her. The woodwork and ceiling were white, and the wood floor that Samuel and Zeke had sanded and restored was a soft blond. The whole effect was one of "Come on in and rest for a while."

"This room alone would sell the place," Margery said. "Some young couple looking to start life together." She nudged his arm with hers. "Wait 'til you see the nursery down the hall." Subtlety had never been Margery's strong point.

"We should find you one of those old-fashioned white iron beds," Jeannie said. "And a wicker rocking chair over there to look out over the garden and—"

"He's selling the place," Emma reminded her. "He doesn't need to spend extra money on furnishings."

"Well, I've always heard that a house shows better when it's staged properly with furniture and all."

"Let's see the rest," John said, heading down the hall to the other two bedrooms. The larger one had been painted a melon color with the same accents on woodwork and floor. "Nice," he murmured and moved on to the smallest bedroom—a cramped, dark space that Tucker had used for storage and John had done little to change in the time he had lived on the property.

He stopped at the door, speechless. The women had transformed the space into a bright and welcoming oasis. Sunny yellow walls made the room look larger than he'd remembered. Simple lace curtains hung on either side of the single open window. It would indeed make a perfect nursery. The house that he had thought of only as a place to eat and sleep now had the feeling of *home.*

"I don't know what to say," he murmured. "I can't thank you

enough or think of how I will ever repay you for your kindness."

"Oh, we'll think of something," Jeannie said. He noticed how she directed this not at him but at Hester.

"Is anyone else starving?" Sadie moaned, and the women all agreed it was time to eat and headed back down the hall.

On the way they passed the tiled bathroom, where every inch had been scrubbed to a high sheen. A stairway led up to the attic, a cavernous space that could be converted to more living space, John thought. But as he followed the women downstairs and into the kitchen, he shook off any ideas he'd started to have about a real family buying the place. As the realtor had pointed out to him, vacant land on water was rare, and that rarity made it valuable, if he was willing to sell to a developer. He wondered if he could insist that the buyer name the development Walden. Or maybe a better name would be Steiner's Folly.

The women set to work preparing sandwiches for themselves and Arlen's team of workers, who were completing the landscaping outside. John had eaten his lunch in town with the realtor. He wandered outside and down to the packinghouse, where he knew he could have a moment to himself.

But he'd barely been there five minutes when he heard the side door open and turned to see Hester standing there in a shaft of sunlight. "John? Do you have a minute?"

"Returning to the scene of my crime, Hester? Could be dangerous."

She stepped inside the building and let the door swing closed behind her. "I don't think kissing a person has yet risen to the level of criminal activity," she said primly. But he couldn't help noticing that she kept her distance. Indeed, she moved away from him along the long worktable that ran the length of the opposite wall. He stayed where he was until she had circled the room and come back to stand near him. "I. . .we, that is, the planning committee for Rainbow House—"

He let out a relieved but disappointed breath. "It's always business first with you, isn't it, Hester?"

Her eyes flickered with irritation. "That's not. . .This is. . ."

"Just spit it out," he said wearily. "I'll do what I can."

Her eyes widened with what he could only describe as hope. "We would like your permission to use this space until you sell the property. The calls for our volunteers to go out and gather fruit are starting to come in, and we have no place to store and sort it, or make up the marmalade that we plan to sell—"

"Breathe," he said, placing his hands lightly on her shoulders as she sucked in air. "Okay, now start from the beginning."

Over the next hour Hester laid out the entire plan for how the program would work and how the packinghouse figured into the equation. As always, they debated various points and even argued over some of her ideas, but in the end he saw how it could work. Specifically he saw how it would benefit Zeke and the other homeless men and women he had met. But more than that, he began to see it as the perfect way to repay everyone who had given so freely of their time and talent to get his property restored and on the market.

"Okay," he said.

But Hester thought he was only giving in, so she continued making her case. "Look, I know this can't be a permanent solution, but. . ."

"I said okay, Hester. You can use the packinghouse."

It was such a delight to see the woman speechless for once that he couldn't help grinning at her. "Anything else?"

She turned to face him, studying his features for a long moment. She placed her hand on his cheek. "Thank you," she whispered. And then she did the one thing he was totally unprepared for—she wrapped her arms around him and rested her cheek against his chest. "Oh, thank you so much."

Tentatively he completed the circle of their embrace and rested his chin on the top of her head where her prayer covering met the center part of her hair. "My pleasure," he said.

The realtor was anything but pleased to arrive the following week for a showing of the property to find it buzzing with activity. John was in the kitchen watching Nelly and Agnes instruct a crew of homeless women in the process of turning baskets of whole fruit into jars of homemade marmalade. He'd suggested they set up this part of the program in the house since the kitchen easily provided everything they needed.

He'd heard the approach of what sounded like an entire motorcade and glanced out the window. The realtor had practically leapt from the lead car before it came to a full stop, ran back to say something to the occupants of the cars behind him, and then headed up to the house.

"John, I thought we had an appointment," Peter York said, his smile revealing overly white teeth and not quite reaching the hard glints of his steel-gray eyes. "What's going on?"

John ignored the question by asking one of his own. "Developers?" He nodded toward the two other cars, where men in suits had gotten out and were beginning to look around in the proprietary way that John hated, as if they already owned the place.

"From Tampa," York replied. "I told you that they were driving down today and that we would be here at eleven and that after they—"

"Okay. Show them around. I'll open the front door so you can come in that way to show the house, although I doubt they care what it's like. I'll be in the kitchen if you need me." He started back inside and heard York following him.

"Look, you cannot have these people around when I'm trying to show the property," he seethed.

"*These people* happen to be friends of mine, and as long as I own the place, I'll have anyone I like around, okay?"

"But John. . ."

Suddenly John remembered how the young man's eyes had fairly danced with excitement the day that John had chosen him to represent the property. At the price he had suggested, the young realtor stood to make a hefty commission. Clearly, at the moment he saw that commission going up in smoke.

"Look," John said, feeling a little sorry for him, "you said this place would sell itself, so why should it matter who is here or what they are doing?" He sniffed the air, catching the aroma of fruit mixed with spices cooking, and smiled. "Take your time, Pete, and there might be a jar of homemade marmalade as a bonus."

York winced, and then he noticed Zeke sauntering across the yard toward his clients and he took off to intercept him. John saw Hester standing outside the packinghouse, watching the scene unfold. He caught her eye and signaled that everything was all right. She smiled and headed back inside.

John stood for a moment staring at the spot where she had been. Ever since he'd agreed to let her use his place for the project, they had worked together in a kind of easy camaraderie. There had been no repeat of the embrace they'd shared, an embrace that had been interrupted by the sound of workers seeking the shade outside the building to enjoy their lunch. Shyly she had pushed away from him and thanked him again before running to the house to tell the others the news.

After that, she had come every day bringing others with her as they worked to set up the packinghouse. With nothing else to do, John had fallen into the habit of working alongside them and become part of the group that bantered back and forth in easy friendship as they worked together to install a new conveyor belt and build more counter space for the sorting and packing processes. More and more Hester would turn to him with some new idea and seek his opinion. More and more when she left at the end of the day, she would take a moment to find him and thank him again for loaning them the space. And more and more as he watched her pedal off, he felt the need to call her back, keep her close.

"You're not making this easy on the kid," Margery observed when John came back inside. She had taken to calling Peter York "the kid," and the way she said it John understood that it was not a compliment.

"He stands to make a boatload of money," John replied. "Making that kind of money shouldn't come easy." He picked up a dish towel and started to dry some of the marmalade jars that she'd been washing.

Margery grinned. "Some would say you're starting to have second thoughts about selling this place."

"And some would be wrong."

"You planning to stay around here after the sale?"

"I'll probably head back to Indiana."

To his surprise Margery burst out laughing. "And do what? Go back with your tail between your legs to those folks that shunned you? That's not you, John. Amish or not, that is not who you are, and that place is no longer your home."

"If I stayed I'd have to find work." He hadn't allowed himself to think about staying. It was what he wanted, but he hadn't seen any option other than to go back to Indiana.

"I'll hire you," she said.

John laughed. "Yeah, that'll work. I know so much about boats and running fishing charters, and I'm such a people person."

"You're improving on that last score, and the rest can be learned, but you've got a point." She put her wrinkled hand on his. "It's a serious offer, John. Give it some thought, and if not, then something's bound to turn up." And then she turned her attention to one of the homeless women standing just inside the door smoking a cigarette. "Get that poison out of this kitchen," she barked and shooed the woman out the door and followed her down the porch steps, passing Hester along the way.

"Hi," she said, wiping her brow with the back of her hand. "How are things going in here?"

"Coming along," John said.

"Do you have time for a walk?" she asked.

"Sure." He folded the towel and followed her outside.

Down near the pier they could see Peter York gesturing and pointing out something that had the businessmen looking anywhere but up to the house and yard, where John had to admit the scene was not exactly enticing to a prospective buyer. Zeke lounged under a tree, strumming his guitar, his long hair falling over his face. Nearby two men dressed in cast-off and out-of-season clothing unloaded baskets filled with oranges and set them on the conveyer belt that carried them into the packinghouse. Rosalyn in her traditional Mennonite garb and the toothless woman and her friend carried empty baskets out of the packinghouse and stacked them in the back of Samuel's beat-up camper.

"Not exactly good advertising for this place," Hester said.

John shrugged. "They aren't buying the people, or the buildings for that matter. What those guys want is the land and the location."

"Still, we're not doing you any favors here. Maybe if you know someone is coming to look at the place, we could shut down for that time period."

"And what? Hide in the attic?"

She smiled and ducked her head. "I was thinking more that we simply wouldn't come out to work that day. I mean, you know in advance, right?"

John shrugged. "Most of the time, not always. It's going to be fine, Hester." He cast about for a change in topic. "Did you get those ferns planted?"

"Not yet," she admitted. "I actually don't think there's much hope for them. I'm really sorry."

He shrugged. "As long as you kept them in water and shade, they should be fine. Besides, I have plenty more. How about I come over tonight after we close things down here and we get them in the ground?"

"Come for supper," she said. "I'll invite Rosalyn and Samuel."

He took her hand. "Does it always have to be a group, Hester?"

She looked up at him but did not pull away. "No, but if you are asking for a date, John Steiner, then ask."

"Okay. I'd like to come by and help you plant those ferns, and after that I thought maybe we could go for ice cream, chocolate."

She ducked her head, surprised that he had called her bluff. "Now you're talking my language," she murmured.

Hester felt like a silly teenager the way she was worrying over her hair and touching her cheeks and lips and wondering if John might kiss her again. *Grow up,* she silently chastised herself. She should be grateful that God had seen fit to let them become friends. Who would have thought that might ever happen given the way they had met?

But when she'd challenged him to call the evening a date, he hadn't backed down. Of course, he never backed down when challenged. She sighed. That was his way, and his way was going to make it impossible for him to sell his property if she didn't do something. After all, using his packinghouse had always been intended as a temporary fix so that they could get the project up and running. But it had worked out so well and John had been so accommodating that little thought had been given to finding a more permanent solution.

"Well, that will stop right here and now," she murmured as she gave her hair a final pat and went to her father's study to use the telephone.

"Jeannie?" she said when her friend answered. "Sorry to bother you, but I was thinking that we really need to be looking for another place to sort and store the fruit. I remembered that you had said Zeke's brother, Malcolm, showed an interest in the project. Do you think he might know of a space we could use?"

"But John's place is so perfect," Jeannie protested. "The season is upon us, and we have to act or wait until next year."

Hester told her about the realtor's visit that day. "When those men got back in their cars, it was clear that they had lost interest. They looked like they couldn't wait to get away. Like it or not, Jeannie, we are hurting John's chances."

Jeannie sighed. "I know. Okay, here's the number for Malcolm's office."

"Thanks," Hester said, jotting down the information. As she hung up the phone, she heard John coming up the front path. He was whistling and sounded like he didn't have a care in the world. Somehow that made Hester think that things might just work out after all—for everyone—and she closed her eyes in a silent prayer of thanksgiving before going out to meet him.

To her surprise he had arrived on a bicycle. He leaned it against the fence and made his way to her. "Ever tasted gelato?" he asked.

"No."

"Me neither, but I hear it's something pretty special, and I thought we might celebrate the restoration of the garden by taking a ride to town. There are a couple of places on Main Street that sell it."

"Where did you get the bike?"

"Zeke brought it by this afternoon." He picked up one of the buckets of ferns. "So where do you want these?"

They worked together in an easy silence until all the ferns had been planted and watered and he had helped her place the orchids so that they received the proper light and showed off their beauty to perfection. "My mom used to say she had a black thumb," John told her. "Couldn't grow a thing."

"But you lived on a farm. Surely she had a kitchen garden."

"She did. My dad planted it for her and tended it until he died; then I took over."

"My mom could get anything to flourish," Hester said. "She used to have a little herb garden out back and her orchids, of course. We'd hear her out there in the yard talking to them." She took on the singsong cadence of her mother's voice. "Now, look at you hiding there. Come on out here where you can get some sunshine, baby." She chuckled at the memory.

"You do know that you were doing the same thing when you were placing that last orchid," he said.

"I wasn't," she protested, but she saw in his smile that she had been talking to the plant.

"You like to keep that soft side of yourself hidden, don't you? Why is that?"

"I don't know what you mean." She felt a familiar defensiveness tighten her throat.

"Yes, you do," he said, stopping to lean on the shovel and meet her eyes directly. "When you think no one's looking, you let go a little. Like that day when the creek flooded and we got everybody to the church. I saw you with the children and your grandmother's neighbors. And out at my place when you're working with the volunteers from the homeless community, there's a kind of tenderness to you that doesn't always come out."

She stiffened. "Well, I'm sorry to disappoint you."

John sighed and set the shovel aside. "I'm trying to pay you a compliment, Hester. I guess I've been living like a hermit for too long, but I'm trying to tell you that when I see you in situations like that, like this, I realize why I can't seem to stay away from you." He held out his arms to her.

Silenced by the feeling of joy that seemed sure to overwhelm her, she walked into his open arms and rested her cheek against his chest. And for the first time in a very long time, she felt as if she had found the safe harbor that she had always thought she would find only in her work. "Thank you, John," she whispered. His answer was to tighten his hold on her. Then as she lifted her face to his, she heard Agnes Crowder calling her name.

"Hester, come quick. Sister has taken a terrible fall."

Chapter 25

Together Hester and John followed Agnes back to the Crowder house at the end of the cul-de-sac. They found Olive lying in the middle of the kitchen floor surrounded by shards of broken glass and an overturned stepstool. Her arm and hand were covered in blood, and her coloring was almost ghostly.

"Olive," Hester said as she grabbed two kitchen towels and folded them into a compress then knelt next to the injured woman.

"Stupid," Olive murmured, her eyes rolling back until only the whites were visible.

"Stay with us now, Olive." She was relieved to see that John was already on the phone, giving the ambulance directions. Agnes stood in the far corner of the kitchen, twisting her apron into a knot as tears streamed down her cheeks. "Agnes, do you have a first-aid kit?"

Agnes looked to Olive as she always did.

"Under the bathroom sink," Olive instructed, and Agnes scurried off to fetch it.

John hung up the phone and found a broom. He was sweeping

the pieces of glass away from Olive when they heard the distant wail of sirens. Olive struggled to sit up.

"Stay where you are, Olive. We need to get this bleeding stopped and make sure you have no other injuries."

"Bossy as always," Olive snapped, but she did as Hester ordered.

By the time the EMTs rushed into the house, Agnes had brought the first-aid kit and Hester had the bleeding under control. She moved away and let the medics do their work, hiding a smile when they started shouting questions at Olive.

"Please lower your voices," Olive demanded. "We are not at a sporting event, and I do have neighbors that I do not wish to know my business."

The fact that there was an ambulance outside her house with its red lights whirling like a lighthouse beacon did not seem to enter her mind. But when the paramedics tried to help her to her feet and into a chair, it was Olive who cried out in pain. In the end it was decided that Olive should be taken to the hospital for X-rays to determine whether or not she might have fractured her hip.

"I'll come with you," Hester said.

"Don't be ridiculous," Olive said. "These young people are perfectly capable of handling the situation, Hester. Agnes, bring my purse and come along." But just as the medics were preparing to load the gurney into the ambulance, Olive grabbed Hester's hand. "Thank you for coming," she whispered. "Agnes was so very frightened."

Hester saw the fear that she had chosen to attribute to Agnes in Olive's eyes and knew that this was as close as she might ever get to receiving Olive's approval. She squeezed her hand. "I'm just glad I was able to help."

As they watched the ambulance drive away, John put his arm around Hester's shoulders. "You okay?" he asked.

She stepped away, suddenly aware that anyone observing them might take his comforting gesture for a sign of courtship, and in their society, that was not the way things were done. "I'm fine, but do you mind, though, if we skip the gelato tonight?"

"Not at all. I'll walk you home."

"Actually, I thought I would stay here and clean up the mess so they don't have to come home to it later." In spite of her concerns about the prying eyes of neighbors, she stood on tiptoe and kissed his cheek. "Thanks for helping with the garden," she said, "and this." She waved a hand to indicate the Crowder house, its back door still wide open and every light blazing.

"How about I help?" John said as he followed her back inside.

John was falling in love with Hester Detlef. The admission hit him like a thunderbolt as he peddled back to Tucker's Point later that evening. "Great timing," he muttered. "You finally find the perfect woman, and you have nothing to offer her. No visible means of support. No home, or at least not for long. No prospects for the future."

Of course once he sold the property, his prospects for a financial future would be decidedly better, but he had never stopped to look beyond the day when Peter York would present him with a buyer. If he and Hester were to marry, where would they live? What would he do to earn a living? He could work for Margery, but what did he know about fixing boats or running fishing charters? He knew how to work the land and make things grow, but this wasn't exactly farm country, and the idea that Hester might be willing to leave her father and the community of friends she had built in Pinecraft was ludicrous.

Marry? Talk about a ridiculous idea. Where did he get the arrogance to believe that she would even consider such a thing? That she returned his feelings at all? A couple of kisses? Some tender moments in her garden and later tonight when they'd gone to help the Crowder sisters?

"You are seriously losing it, dude," he said, quoting one of Zeke's favorite lines as he trudged up the steps to his house and went inside. He drank a glass of cold water and then headed for the small room off the kitchen that he had set up as his bedroom until the second floor could be restored. His Bible now rested on the small nightstand next to his single bed. He picked it up, but instead of opening it, he held it to his chest and closed his eyes.

"Lord, I have come to a crossroads and don't know which way to turn. In my life I have turned away from others so many times—and maybe in doing that I was also turning away from You in spite of my daily prayers and devotions. I am asking now that You show me the way." He found himself thinking of a joke that Margery had told him one evening as they sat together after sharing one of her suppers.

"There's a hurricane and this guy's house is totally flooded out," she'd said. "He's on the roof, and the water is still rising. A neighbor comes by in a rowboat and urges him to get in. 'No, God will rescue me,' he assures the neighbor. Then a FEMA crew comes by in a pontoon. Same thing. Finally a helicopter hovers overhead, and he sends that away as well."

"Not funny so far," John had muttered.

"So the guy drowns and gets to heaven. When he goes before God, he's really upset. 'Why didn't you save me?' he demands. And God says, 'I sent you a rowboat, a pontoon, and a helicopter— what were you waiting for?' "

He could still hear Margery's laughter as she slapped her knee and announced, "That one cracks me up every time."

John opened his eyes and thought about how God had sent him Margery and then Hester and her father and then Zeke. Each of them had changed his life over the last several weeks. He thought about Samuel showing up that day and leaving him the camper. He thought about Grady Forrest and his aunt Liz. "What were you waiting for?" he wondered aloud, truly getting Margery's message for the first time.

That night he slept better than he had in weeks. He had no solutions to his problems, just a new confidence that things would work out if he was wise enough to heed God's signs. He was up with the sun and had coffee brewing by the time Margery brought the workers to start their shift in the packinghouse and the Mennonite women began arriving to take over his kitchen to stir up more jars of marmalade.

But Hester was not with them.

"She had a meeting, and then she was going to the hospital to check on Olive," Rosalyn told him. "Her hip was broken after all. She's going to need surgery and then a lot of rehab therapy. She is not a happy person, and Hester is trying to do some damage control."

John was on his way to the packinghouse to see if he could be of help there when he saw a car coming up the lane. He waited for the vehicle to come to a stop and for the driver to emerge, a man who looked to be in his late forties and whose car and clothes left no doubt that he was a man of means. But when he saw John, he smiled and moved toward him with an outstretched hand. "Mr. Steiner? Malcolm Shepherd—Zeke's brother."

The resemblance was startling. This man embodied what Zeke would look like if he cut his hair and put on twenty pounds. "Hello." John accepted the handshake. "I'm not sure if Zeke's here yet."

"I didn't come to see my brother, John. May I call you John?"

John nodded and waited.

"I understand your property is for sale."

"That's right."

"How about showing me around?"

"You're interested?"

Malcolm laughed. "I'm a businessman, John. I hear about a prime piece of land on water and I'm curious."

"You called Peter York, the listing agent?"

"Nope. Thought I'd deal with you directly. If you and I work something out, then we can get York involved." All the time he was talking, he was looking around. "So do I get that tour or not?"

Over the next hour John walked his property with Zeke's brother. Malcolm asked a lot of questions and showed little interest in the house itself. But instead of being turned off by the presence of homeless people sorting fruit in the packing-house or a bunch of Mennonite women cooking up marmalade in the kitchen, he seemed to find both processes fascinating.

"What's the marketing plan?" he asked Rosalyn as he watched her funnel warm marmalade into jars and then set them aside to cool.

"We've got orders from several businesses in Pinecraft, and we've secured a space at the farmers' market, just in time for the snowbird migration," she said with a smile.

"You might want to think about mail order—a website," he said, more to himself than to Rosalyn. Then he smiled and nodded toward the coffeepot. "John, could I trouble you for a cup of that coffee—black?"

"Sure." By the time John had poured the coffee, Malcolm was sitting out on the porch.

"You do know that you're sitting on a gold mine here in terms of land values," he said as he sipped the hot coffee.

"That's what Peter York tells me."

"So if you find a buyer, and you will—it's only a matter of price—what happens to all of this?" He gestured toward the packinghouse and then back toward the kitchen.

"They understand it's temporary," John said.

Malcolm was quiet for a long moment. And then he said the words that John knew could change everything. "What if it didn't have to be?"

"I don't understand."

"I don't know what my brother has told you about our family, John, but we've done all right for ourselves over the last several generations. Of course, you wouldn't know that looking at Zeke. Believe me, I've tried to help him out, but he takes the money and just gives it away."

"Zeke's a good man," John said and couldn't help the note of warning that crept into his voice as he defended his friend.

"He's salt of the earth," Malcolm agreed. "I wish. . ." He stared off toward the water for a long moment. Then he set the coffee cup on the porch railing and gave John his full attention. "Hester Detlef came to see me this morning. She can be quite persuasive, not to mention single-minded when it comes to something she's passionate about."

"Yes, that's true," John agreed. "She means well."

Malcolm stood up suddenly and walked to the edge of the porch, looking over the land. "Here's what I'd like to do. I'd like to buy your place and set up a foundation for Rainbow House right here. The house could function as the headquarters for the organization, and in time we can find a decent place in town for a shelter and soup kitchen, maybe a clinic. What do you think?"

It was Hester's dream come true, so what did it matter what he thought? If he could help make this happen for Hester—for Zeke. . .

"I think you've got a deal," he said, and this time he was the one offering his hand to Malcolm to seal the bargain.

"Okay then, I'll get in touch with this York fella so he can draw up the paperwork," Malcolm said as he shook John's hand firmly.

"Don't you want to know the price first?"

Malcolm grinned. "Already checked all that out on the Internet. Nice meeting you, John. Zeke's told me a lot about you. I want to thank you for watching out for him."

"He's done far more for me than I ever could have done for him," John said. He was thinking more about the hours of conversation and companionship that Zeke had provided than any physical labor his friend had contributed to restoring the place.

"We're going to need a director to oversee the whole project," Malcolm said. "Somebody with experience in running things, managing budgets and such."

Hester, John thought.

"Ms. Detlef suggested that you might want to apply for the job," Malcolm added as he walked to his car. He glanced back at the house. "No reason you couldn't turn that upstairs into living quarters and have the foundation offices and kitchen and such on the first floor." He got in and took one more look around and then grinned at John. "Thanks, John. I'll be in touch."

John watched the convertible drive back down the lane and disappear. Had he imagined what had just happened?

"What was my brother doing here?" Zeke asked, coming up beside him.

"You were here all the time?" John asked.

Zeke shrugged. "Sometimes Malcolm can be a little much to take," he said. "I like to keep a low profile until I know what's on his mind."

"He just bought this place."

Zeke's expression reflected disappointment, anger, and sadness in rapid order. "Sorry, man," he said softly as he clutched John's shoulder. "I know it's what you need, but I always felt it wasn't what you wanted."

"He's buying it for you, and the others. He's going to set up a foundation for Rainbow House. Hester talked him into it."

"You mean, he's not going to shut us down and rip the place apart?" Zeke was incredulous.

"It's all staying just the way it is," John told him. Almost before the last word was out of his mouth, Zeke had taken off, running toward the packinghouse. A moment later, John heard shouts of joy echoing across the yard.

He thought about going back up to the house to tell Rosalyn and the others the good news, but he knew that Zeke would take care of that. There was only one other person who deserved to know what had happened as soon as possible. John mounted his bike and headed for the hospital.

～≋

Hester had finally succeeded in persuading Agnes to leave her sister's bedside and go home to get some much-needed rest by promising that she would stay with Olive until Agnes returned. Since Olive was dozing, she busied herself searching the classifieds for possible alternate locations for Rainbow House. Malcolm Shepherd had finally agreed to drive out and look at John's place, but that was as much of a commitment as he was willing to make. And as her father had reminded her, he was an outsider and a businessman. What was in this for him?

She circled one property on the north end of the city, but then saw the asking price per square foot and knew that the rent alone would eat up any profits they might acquire. She sighed and refolded the paper to show the next column.

"What are you doing?" Olive demanded, although her voice was little more than a croak.

"We need to find a new space for the Rainbow House project, someplace we can sort and store the collected fruit at the very least."

"I thought John Steiner was letting you use his place."

"He is, but he's trying to sell his property, and, well, not everyone is as accepting of. . .some people as others are."

Olive received this news with a snort. When she fell silent, Hester assumed she had dozed off again.

"You've been spending quite a bit of time with that young man," Olive said after a moment.

"I—"

"Has he kissed you yet?"

Hester was so surprised at the question coming from this woman that she automatically gave the answer. "Yes."

Another snort. "Thought as much. I saw the two of you out there in the garden the night I fell. So where is this going?"

"Going?"

A long, dramatic sigh. "Are you in love with the man or not?"

"Really, Olive. . ."

"I thought as much." Her lips thinned into the familiar judgmental line Hester knew so well. "Do not let this opportunity pass you by, Hester Detlef. You are not a young woman anymore. Your prospects are limited. Trust me, I know. If you love the man and there's any possibility at all that he has feelings for you, then you must take the initiative."

Okay. This has to be the anesthetic from the surgery talking. "Olive, would you like a little water to—"

"Oh, don't patronize me, Hester. I promised Sarah that I would make sure that you didn't give your entire life over to caring for others to the detriment of your own happiness. Well, I have failed miserably at that vow until now. But seeing you with John the other night, I accepted that God had sent this young man to you and that it was my responsibility to see that you didn't miss the only opportunity you may have to marry and have a family of your own."

"I'm not quite that desperate," Hester said tightly. "I mean, I do have male friends, and I do go out now and again."

"For work, always for some project you've dreamed up," Olive said with a dismissive wave of her hand. "We are speaking of love here, and either you speak up now or forever hold your peace, as the saying goes."

Hester had the sudden thought that they were not really talking about her but perhaps about Olive's unrequited love for Arlen. "Olive, once John sells his property, there's no telling what he will do. He might even decide to go back to Indiana."

"Then it is up to you to see that he doesn't. If you love him, and he returns that love—"

"And that is the question, isn't it?" Hester said.

Olive's mouth worked to find a retort and came up empty. She closed her eyes and feigned sleep.

Hester smiled and got up to stretch her back. She walked out into the hallway and heard the ding of the elevator bell and then the whisper of the sliding doors and looked up to see John coming her way. Without hesitation she went to meet him, not caring whether he returned her feelings or not but wanting only to bask a moment in the warmth of his smile.

"What are you doing here?" she asked.

"I came to find you. I have some news."

"You sold the property," she guessed. He nodded and her heart fell. "That's—"

"To Zeke's brother, Malcolm."

"Malcolm Shepherd bought Tucker's Point."

"Not to develop. He's going to fund Rainbow House."

"But when I met with him, he seemed so underwhelmed with the whole idea. He asked me a lot of questions, and not once did he show the slightest enthusiasm for the project."

"Well, you must have said something right. He's going to establish the Rainbow House Foundation and use the house as the headquarters. You can stay, Hester. Everything can go on just as it is now."

She could hardly believe what he was telling her. She had prayed so hard for God to find a way for them to make the project a success, and now her prayers had been heard and answered. With no regard for the bustling throngs of medical personnel and patients and visitors moving up and down the corridor, she let out a squeal and leapt up to wrap her arms around John's neck. He spun her around.

"Stop that," Olive ordered.

But as soon as John set her back on her feet, Hester grabbed his hand and pulled him into Olive's room. She just had to share the news. Then Agnes appeared at the door, so they had to repeat the story again. "And John's been asked to be the director of the foundation. You can have an office right there in the house and live upstairs," she told him. "And maybe there would even be room for me to set up a free clinic," she said. "And in time—"

"So that inappropriate display of affection just now was because of the sale of your land, John Steiner?" Olive demanded. "Not because you proposed to this young woman?"

Hester's face felt as if it might melt under the sudden heat of her embarrassment.

"I was getting to that, Miss Crowder," John said. "Although I had thought to make the occasion something a little more inviting than a hospital room."

Olive snorted derisively while Agnes clapped her hands together and beamed.

"On the other hand, there's no time like the present, right?" John dropped to one knee as he held both of Hester's hands in his own. "Marry me, Hester Detlef."

"Oh, for goodness' sake," Olive groaned.

John ignored her. "I love you, Hester," he continued. "And with God's blessing, perhaps someday you will come to care for me in that way as well. But for now. . ."

Hester pulled one hand free and stroked his hair away from his forehead. "Get up, John," she said softly.

"First answer the question. Will you marry me?" he asked again.

She felt tears leak down her cheeks. "No," she whispered and fled the room.

***

Outside the hospital, Hester stopped, uncertain of where to go or what to do or how to think of the incredible string of events she'd just experienced. Her elation over the eleventh-hour rescue of the Rainbow House had been short-lived when John had suddenly announced his intention to propose marriage and then had actually done so. Was he making fun of her?

Of course, he had no idea what her feelings were—but still. Surely in his giddiness over the sale and the possibility that he might be offered a position that would support him, he had only thought to make Olive and Agnes laugh with his silly antics. His social skills had never been fine-tuned, especially after he'd spent over two years living as a near hermit. Maybe he'd thought she would join in the joke. But it was a cruel joke, and she had never thought him to be a cruel man. Stubborn, immovable on certain issues, but never intentionally cruel.

For she knew—had known but not admitted—that she loved him. She fled through the hospital lobby and out to the street. In minutes she found herself at the corner of Highway 41 and Bahia Vista. To her right was Pinecraft. She considered going home and letting her father console her, but her unhappiness would only make him feel bad as well. So she turned left and walked to Orange Avenue and then past the parking entrance to the botanical gardens and around the corner to the little beach that led into the bay.

Without bothering to remove her shoes, she waded into the calm shallow waters, uncaring of the way her skirt was getting soaked with salt water and would show the stains once it dried. Far more important was the fact that it was low tide and the exposed mud flats stretched out all around her. She could walk all the way out to the clam beds in water that never rose higher than her ankles. And she had the place to herself. There were a few boats anchored offshore, but the only sounds she heard once she moved downshore from the beach were the clinking of metal riggings against masts and the call of shorebirds as they strutted about collecting their afternoon meal.

"How can you possibly love him, Hester Detlef? You have known this man for a matter of maybe three months, and for much of that time you thought he was the most. . ."

And yet, presented with even the suggestion that they might make a life together, she had begun to think that it might actually become a reality. When she had seen him coming down the hospital corridor, his smile meant only for her, how her heart had sung with joy at the sight of him. She had practically run to him.

"Fool." She bit off the word and splashed on toward the clam beds, hoping that at least one of her favorite horse conches would be feeding there. Their sunset-colored bodies always made her smile, and right now she needed anything that might take away the bitterness she was feeling toward men in general and John Steiner in particular. At least here she didn't have to encounter the man, didn't have to think about what she might say to him the next time they—

"Hester!"

She turned long enough to see John leaning the bicycle that Zeke had brought him against a stretch of wire fencing and kicking off his shoes before he splashed into the bay and tried to cover the distance between them.

"Go away," she shouted and pressed on toward the clam beds.

"We need to talk," he replied and then grunted as he almost lost his balance and then righted himself and kept coming.

"You're going to cut your feet, and I am not in the mood to patch you up. Just go away, please."

"No."

"You are without a doubt the single most obstinate human being I have ever known," she grumbled.

"Well, at last we have something in common, Hester, because that goes double for you." He had come even with her now and dogged her steps as she moved on. "Why won't you marry me?"

"Because you don't really want to marry me. It was sweet

of you to want to entertain Olive and Agnes, but I get it that you proposed on a whim. Olive embarrassed you into it, and I certainly won't hold you to it."

"And maybe—just maybe—I meant it when I told you I love you." His tone was gentle so that the words came at her not as another jab of their argument but as more of a caress.

"How do you know?" She fought against the flutter of fresh hope that stirred within and bent to pick up a small, perfectly striped banded tulip shell.

"Because when I look to the future, I can't imagine meeting the challenges ahead without you there with me. Because, other than my mother, you are the only woman I've known who is strong enough to admit that she had dreams of her own."

"I'm not your mother."

"I'm not looking for a mother. I had the best. I'm looking for a wife, Hester, a partner I can share life with."

"Sounds like starting up a business," she grumbled, but inside she was holding his words close to her heart.

"It's a marriage, Hester, a sacred union."

They waded through the water side by side for another ten yards until they reached the clam beds. "Careful here. The edges of the shells are sharp."

He stayed where he was as she picked her way to an open spot and bent to pick up a large shell. "Hi there," she said softly as she turned the blackened shell over and was surprised when the coiled resident of the shell did not snake back inside and close its aperture to keep danger out. Instead, the creature stretched its sunrise-orange body outward, as if welcoming her. "Look," she murmured, holding the shell up so that John could share in this rare display of God's wondrous creation.

"It's beautiful," he said, and then as she bent to replace the shell on its feeding ground, he added, "But not half as beautiful as you are, Hester."

It was not the way of her people or his to offer such compliments. They came from plain stock, simple people who found beauty in serving God. And yet she could not help but rejoice that this man whom she had come to love found her pretty.

"We should get back," she said softly as she picked her way around the sharp edges of the clams until she was standing with him on a sandbar. "By now no doubt Olive has spread the word of the debacle she witnessed."

She turned to go, but he stopped her by taking her hand and weaving his fingers between hers. Then he lifted both their hands to his lips and kissed hers. "Hester, I believe that everything that has happened for me these last two years has been leading me to this moment, to you. I believe that God has brought us to each other. I know that separately we can each do good, but together just think what we might accomplish." He touched her cheek. "I love you."

She looked up at him and saw in his gaze what she knew she could not hide in her own. She loved him, and in that moment she saw as clearly as if she were gazing into a mirror that he did indeed return that love. "Marry me," he whispered.

"Yes," she answered.

And when he kissed her, she knew that he had been right, that this was right and that God had indeed led two strangers to find each other so that they might travel the rest of the way together.

ANNA SCHMIDT is the author of more than twenty works of fiction. Among her many honors, Anna is the recipient of the *Romantic Times'* Reviewer's Choice Award and a finalist for the RITA award for romantic fiction. She enjoys gardening and collecting seashells at her winter home in Florida. To contact Anna, visit her website at www.booksbyanna.com.

Return to Pinecraft in May 2012

for the story of sisters Emma and Jeannie in

A Sister's Forgiveness

a story of family, forgiveness, and redemption.